Twenty Tales
Murder from T
Ambassadors of Suspense

—_m—

P. M. Carlson

Richard Timothy Conroy

Sarah Booth Conroy

Peter Crowther

Barbara D'Amato

Janet Dawson

Carole Nelson Douglas and Jennifer Waddell

Pamela J. Fesler

Linda Grant

Jan Grape

Judith Kelman

John Lutz

T. J. MacGregor

Barbara Paul

Anne Perry

Nancy Pickard

Gillian Roberts

Kristine Kathryn Rusch

Sarah Shankman

Carolyn Wheat

THE FIRST LADY MURDERS

EDITED BY

NANCY PICKARD

POCKET STAR BOOKS

New York London Toronto Sydney Tokyo Singapore

This book is a work of fiction. Names, characters, places and incidents are products of the author's imagination or are used fictitiously. Any resemblance to actual events or locales or persons, living or dead, is entirely coincidental.

An *Original* Publication of POCKET BOOKS

A Pocket Star Book published by
POCKET BOOKS, a division of Simon & Schuster Inc.
1230 Avenue of the Americas, New York, NY 10020

ISBN: 0-671-01444-7

First Pocket Books printing February 1999

10 9 8 7 6 5 4 3 2 1

POCKET STAR BOOKS and colophon are registered trademarks of Simon & Schuster Inc.

Cover art by Earl Keleny

Printed in the U.S.A.

Copyright Notices

CONTENTS

Contents

INTRODUCTION

<hr style="width:20%">

NANCY PICKARD

Think of the top secrets they knew; imagine the scandalous confidences they kept. Privy to the innermost circles of power on earth, our First Ladies could tell many tales, if they would. Of course, most of them haven't, and most of them won't. There are history and reputations to consider, not to mention morals and ethics and honor. But writers can say almost anything they want, take history and twist it a bit, give it a dramatic or a humorous turn, and spin it out as a story that feels as if it could have happened just that way, even if it didn't, really.

For this collection, we invited nineteen of the most talented mystery and suspense writers of our time to select a First Lady from another day and age, and to concoct a story about her. Interestingly, several writers felt drawn to the same First Ladies — there are multiple stories about Edith Wilson, Dolley Madison, and Mary Todd Lincoln. Some writers interpreted "First Lady" very loosely, to say the least: One chose a daughter who served as hostess for her presidential daddy, and another invented a First Lady for a bachelor president. In other words, this is a collection where imagination rules, and where history doesn't necessarily create an unpassable boundary.

The writers themselves reported that they loved researching and writing about "their" First Ladies. I have been thrilled and honored to be the first to get to read their audacious and wonderful stories. And now it's your turn to sit back and have a wonderful time with some of the most amazing, brilliant, and daring women of the past two hundred years of American history.

THE SECRET PRESIDENT

~~~

BARBARA PAUL

*T*HE PENALTY FOR *murdering a United States senator is probably quite high,* Edith Wilson thought and pasted a smile back on her face. "Perhaps you don't understand, Senator. The president is ill and can see no one. *No one.*"

Henry Cabot Lodge turned on the charm, smiling and taking a step toward her. "Not even me, Mrs. Wilson?"

Especially not you. "Not even you, I'm afraid." *You myopic backstabbing rubble-rouser.* "When he has recovered, I'm sure the president will want to meet with you." *Wearing a full suit of armor.*

"But how ill is he?" Lodge asked. "All we hear on the Hill are rumors. One rumor says he's become a drooling infant reciting nursery rhymes."

A rumor you yourself started. "What nonsense."

"Of course it is. But if I could see the president for

just one moment, then I could reassure my colleagues that the rumors have no foundation." He smiled winningly and came another step closer.

Edith held her ground. "Senator Lodge, surely you would not ask me to disobey the physicians' instructions just to satisfy your curiosity, would you? Dr. Grayson and his consultants have all made it quite clear that the president's recovery *depends* upon his not being disturbed. You must be patient, as we all must."

The charming mask slipped. "This is unconscionable. You are deliberately keeping everyone in government away from the president."

"In every way I know how," she agreed cheerfully.

Lodge didn't bother with the amenities but turned and strode angrily away. With a sigh of relief, Edith returned to her office and to the work the importunate senator had interrupted.

The pile of papers on her desk had grown during her brief absence. Nothing went to the president that didn't go through Edith first. Most of the business seeking presidential attention could be delegated to various members of the cabinet; and Edith delegated ruthlessly, penciling notes in the margins. A piece of proposed legislation that Woodrow wanted contained several passages of ambiguous language; Edith sent it back for revision. Very little for the State Department, fortunately; the secretary of state had sided with Henry Cabot Lodge in opposing the League of Nations and was no longer to be trusted. But that's what undersecretaries were for, and executive assistants, and section chiefs—*somebody*; Edith wasn't going to bother Woodrow with anything that someone else could handle.

But here was a bill that needed his signature, one Edith knew had his full approval. She gathered up the papers and headed toward her husband's sickroom.

When he saw her come in, he smiled, using the half of his face that still worked. He might not remember the events of last week, and sometimes he might not recognize his longtime coworkers, but he always knew Edith.

She was smiling too, as usual: *Never show anything but a cheerful face.* "Woodrow, I've brought some papers for you to sign." Without prompting, the nurse moved a small table to the chair by the window where he was sitting; the president was allowed out of bed one hour a day now.

"Tell me," he slurred.

Edith explained the bill and the accompanying legislative memos until he remembered; it was one of his lucid days. But when he tried to sign, his whole arm was shaking so badly he could scarcely hold the pen. Edith steadied his hand with her own; between the two of them they got a barely legible signature on the papers. Not elegant, but it would do.

It was times like this that the muscles in her face ached from holding her smile. "That's all for today," she said lightly, gathering up the papers. "It's quiet on the Hill, for a change. Everyone at the House is in a meeting, and the Senate is having a nice nap. And you'll be delighted to hear that no one declared war on us this morning, although some Canadians were observed throwing rocks at Senator Lodge."

Woodrow made the sound that she recognized as a laugh. "Serrsim righ." *Serves him right.* Then, quickly, his laugh turned into a frown.

She'd made a mistake, mentioning Lodge. Before Woodrow could get too deeply into thought about the League of Nations, she diverted him with some Washington gossip about the pecadillos of a junior senator from the Midwest. Woodrow mustn't be allowed to brood, to build up anxieties.

Edith chatted away, drawing a few more grunting laughs until her invalid husband began to tire. How on earth had he been able to keep his sense of humor after what had happened? Woodrow had been a giant before the stroke hit him. And now . . .

When the nurse had the president settled in his bed, Edith quietly left the room, smile still fixed firmly in place. At the bottom of the stairway a long-faced young man was waiting for her, a White House aide who was the nephew of a New England political ally. "Yes, Mr. Danby?"

"Mr. Arnold Griffin is here. From the *Post?*" His horsey young face looked worried. "He requests an interview with the president."

Edith closed her eyes, opened them again. "I assume you told him that was out of the question?"

"Yes, ma'am, I did. But he says he's coming back every day until he sees the president for himself. He says the White House press releases aren't telling the whole truth." The young man looked scandalized.

"I'll speak to Mr. Griffin. Where is he?"

"In the Oval Office, ma'am."

Edith didn't lose her smile as she said, "Mr. Danby, in the future you will *never* show a member

4

of the press corps to the Oval Office. If the smaller reception rooms are all in use, offer him a seat in the hall. But not the Oval Office."

The young man turned pink. "I . . . I'm sorry, ma'am. Shall I go get Mr. Griffin and—?"

"That won't be necessary. But do please tell Mr. Griffin I'll be with him in ten minutes. Thank you."

Danby hurried away to do her bidding. Edith stepped quickly to her private quarters and shut the door behind her. She dropped negligently onto a chair—not slumping; she never slumped—but, for a moment, no longer on guard. Just a few minutes to pull herself together, that's all she needed.

Edith couldn't let anyone see how unnerving her visits with Woodrow were. It was a second marriage for both of them; they'd planned to grow old together after a full life of public service. But now . . . It was that long nightmare of a trip west building up support for the League of Nations that had undone him.

He'd been ill when they started, unable to sleep and suffering from blinding headaches. And then on the train heading into Wichita, he'd collapsed. The rest of the tour was canceled, and back in Washington he'd seemed to recover a little—except that the headaches were even more severe than before. And then came the morning she'd found him lying on the bathroom floor. *Cerebral thrombosis*, Dr. Grayson had said. *His entire left side is paralyzed.*

Through the panic that followed, Edith had somehow managed to keep her composure, knowing what needed to be done and doing it. Dr. Grayson summoned consultants—a nerve specialist from Philadelphia, another specialist from Johns Hopkins, the head of the Mayo Clinic, still another specialist, someone else, another. One of the consultants had arrived fully prepared to treat Edith for hysteria and was surprised to find his services were not needed.

She simply *would* not allow her fear to take hold, although she'd been sorely tested when the consultants were mapping out a plan of action. She'd hidden her stress, but more than anything she'd wanted to shut out the yammer of male voices around her; she'd wanted the room to stop reeling, objects to come back into focus, the ringing in her ears to go away. She'd wanted the men to go away. But she'd needed to hear what those yammering voices were saying, and held her head a little higher.

Complete rest, they had all agreed. And it must be *complete* rest; the president had to be shielded against the demands of his office.

Then began a long and worried discussion as to which of the presidential staff could be trusted to keep the world away. This one was not always reliable, that one was willing but not very able, so-and-so could be intimidated, and so on down the line until every possibility had been eliminated.

And then, in that room full of physicians, every eye had turned toward Edith Wilson.

Mr. Arnold Griffin of the Washington *Post* would not be put off, so Edith resigned herself to the inevitable with as much grace as she could muster. She invited him to ride with her to a ceremony where she was substituting for the president, her secretary and two White House aides following in another car.

A Secret Service agent was their driver; another agent sat beside him.

"Why this cloak of secrecy, Mrs. Wilson?" Griffin insisted, once they were seated in the limousine. "The press releases only say the president is suffering from exhaustion."

"I do not write the press releases, Mr. Griffin," Edith answered easily.

"If it's just exhaustion, why is the entire White House staff being kept off the second floor? Why can't his aides get in to see him?"

So, we have a tattletale in our midst. "I'm afraid your sources have misinformed you," she replied neutrally. "There are two people with him right this minute." *His doctor and his nurse.*

"Is it true the president has a venereal disease?"

Edith flared, but quickly suppressed her anger. "That is nonsense, Mr. Griffin, as even you must realize. Why is it so difficult to understand? The president needs an undisturbed period of time in which to recuperate. Once he's back on his feet, he'll grant you your interview, I'm certain. He just can't see anyone *now*." How many times a day must she hold this conversation?

He raised an eyebrow. "You know, don't you, that the secretary of state is trying to invoke the Constitution on the disability of the chief executive?" he asked gently.

Of course she knew. And was outraged anew every time she thought of it. How quick the man had been to try to wrest Woodrow's power from him! But Arnold Griffin must know she knew; it was no secret. The man spoke softly, but the words he pronounced were chosen to hurt.

She considered the journalist sharing the backseat with her. A nice-looking man, light-brown hair, green eyes. A pleasant personable manner—but he wielded a venomous pen. The *Post* had opposed Woodrow in nearly everything he had tried to accomplish since the day he took the oath of office; Griffin didn't make the newspaper's policy, but he seemed to have no qualms about following it. And he was eloquent in his denunciations of the League of Nations. Between the *Post* and Senator Lodge, they could set the country back fifty years.

"Mr. Griffin, do you like your work?" Edith asked without preamble.

He was surprised by the question. "It's a living," he said cautiously. "And on the whole, yes, I enjoy it."

"On the whole. But there are aspects of your work you do not enjoy?"

"That's true of any job, isn't it?"

Aha, evasiveness. "You know I can't agree with your politics, but I do admire your way with language. I wonder why you stay at a newspaper when you could be writing books."

"A steady paycheck has certain charms. But as a matter of fact, I am writing a book."

"A confessional?" she asked lightly.

He shot her a look. "Observations on the Washington scene."

"Which I'm sure will be pointed and elegantly expressed." Well, she'd learned something: He was not satisfied, and nourished ambitions for greater things.

The public ceremony in which Edith was substituting for her husband was the opening of a new orphanage on Q Street, the construction of which had been suspended during the war and was only recently completed; Woodrow had wanted to make the orphanage a symbol of America rebuilding itself. When they arrived, Griffin tried to remain with the First Lady's party; the Secret Service agents politely but firmly edged him away.

The October day was pleasantly crisp; the sun was shining and the ceremony had drawn a good crowd. Edith was slightly dismayed to see that Senator Lodge was one of the other dignitaries in attendance; twice in one day was too much. But he spoke civilly if not warmly and did not bring up the subject of the president's health. He was there to be heard, as all the dignitaries were; so Edith assumed her most regal pose as she sat on the speakers' platform listening to all who went before her. When her time came, she told the audience how much the president regretted not being able to attend the opening but that he had sent along the remarks he'd intended to make on this auspicious occasion. Edith then proceeded to read the speech she had written herself.

When all the speechifying was done, the First Lady was offered a tour of the new orphanage. Edith handed the copy of her speech to her secretary and followed the orphanage director inside. There she was delighted to see bright, cheerful colors and children who didn't look as if they were being starved to death. She promised the director a donation; her secretary made a note.

Upstairs in one of the big dormitories, Edith was looking out a window at the children's playground and saw Senator Lodge and Arnold Griffin come into view. Edith couldn't make out what they were saying, but the two men were clearly arguing. Griffin seemed to be trying to persuade the senator of something, but Lodge clearly wanted no part of it. Finally the senator raised his arm and pointed in a theatrical *Begone!* gesture. Griffin seethed a moment but then turned and left. Lodge strode off in the opposite direction, radiating anger.

Interesting.

It turned out the orphanage wasn't quite finished after all. One wing still needed a roof and Edith was suddenly aware of the pounding of hammers; work had been suspended during the opening ceremony. At her request, the director escorted her and her party to the unfinished section. This last wing was to be a small infirmary, something new for orphanages.

They stepped outside for a brief stroll around the grounds, which covered no more than one small city lot. But near the infirmary Edith caught sight of a man sitting in a pushcart. Something about his posture . . . she turned toward him.

Another man ran up and grabbed the pushcart handle. "Sorry, Missus, I'll get him out of your way."

"No, don't move him." Edith tried not to stare at the man in the pushcart, but she could have been looking at a younger version of Woodrow. The right side of the young man's face was animated while the left was slack and soft. His left arm hung loosely by his side. He was sitting at the open rear end of the cart; his right foot tapped to some unheard rhythm while his left leg dangled uselessly.

"He ain't pretty," the other man said apologetically.

"Who is he?"

"He's me brother Jimmy. Jimmy Murphy. Murphy's our name. Jimmy, he used to do carpenter work, like me, and he missed seeing all the building goin' on. So I bring him along to watch. He don't bother nobody."

Edith's heart ached. "So young to have a stroke!"

"Stroke?" Murphy said. "It weren't no stroke, Missus. Jimmy got coshed."

Edith looked at him. "He got what?"

"Coshed. Couple of hooligans jumped him for the four dollars he had in his pocket." When the First Lady looked blank, he went on: "A cosh—it's a sock filled with sand. Nasty weapon. It don't draw no blood but it can ruin ya inside where it don't show. Jimmy there, we thought he was gonna be all right afterwards, but then one mornin' he woke up like that."

Edith felt her stomach turning over. "How long . . . how long between the time he was coshed and, and this?"

Murphy thought back. "Weren't more'n a coupla weeks. He had these real bad headaches, but that was all. Then . . ." He shrugged. "Now he can't even walk. That left leg's dead. But I s'pose he's lucky in a way. A good coshin' can kill ya."

Ohhhhh . . . Edith concentrated on not weaving on her feet. Then she said: "Mr. Murphy, you are a good brother. You're doing exactly the right thing, bringing him to work with you."

His face lit up. "Thankee, Missus!"

Edith told her secretary to get the Murphy brothers' address and arrange for a wheelchair to be delivered. She said goodbye to the orphanage director and waited anxiously for the limousine to be brought to her.

Alone in the backseat, she began to shake. Is that what had happened to Woodrow? Someone had tried to *kill* him? There'd been an attempted assassination right under their noses and no one *knew*? A sock filled with sand . . . hitting him from behind: Edith could see it in her mind and shuddered. But against that she had to put the combined expertise of the best medical minds in the country—all of whom said *stroke.*

Yet the symptoms were identical; that young man who'd been coshed was in exactly the same condition as Woodrow. Young Murphy had gone two weeks after being assaulted before degenerating into his present condition; for Woodrow, an older man, it had been one week. It was possible—*oh, dear Lord*—it was possible!

Edith reached for the speaking tube and told the Secret Service man driving the car that from now on she wanted agents on the second floor of the White House, guarding her husband's sickroom around the clock.

If someone *had* tried to kill Woodrow, it had to have happened on the train as they were nearing Wichita; that's where he first collapsed. But who could have done it? That train was packed with people—Dr. Grayson, Woodrow's secretary, other staff, the Secret Service, local politicians adding themselves to the entourage, the press. Oh yes, the press; there'd been an entire car of the train given over to members of the press . . .

Of whom Arnold Griffin had been one.

Edith stared unseeing out the back window the rest of the way home.

The young man's long face wore its usual worried look. "You wanted to see me, Mrs. Wilson?"

"Please sit down, Mr. Danby." When he'd perched on the edge of a chair facing her, Edith said, "I hope you'll forgive my asking a personal question, but are you still keeping company with the young lady who works as a secretary in Senator Lodge's offices?"

"Yes, ma'am, I am." Then he added hastily: "But we don't ever talk about our work. We made a pact. She doesn't tell me about the Republicans, and I don't tell her about the Democrats."

"Very commendable." Edith sighed. "But I'm afraid I'm about to ask you to break that pact."

"Ma'am?"

"Mr. Danby, please understand that you are perfectly free to refuse the request I am about to make. I have no right to make it, but it would be an enormous help to me if you would ask your young lady a question for me."

"Of course I'll ask her, Mrs. Wilson. What is it you want to know?"

"I'd like to know why Senator Lodge is so angry with Arnold Griffin. They've been political allies for years, but they've had a falling out. I need to know why."

Danby nodded. "I'll see if she knows. We're meeting for lunch tomorrow—"

"Could you ask her before then?"

His eyebrows rose as he realized the urgency of the strange request. "I'll call her right now." He stood up but then hesitated. "Perhaps it would be better to ask her in person?"

"Perhaps it would," Edith agreed.

There'd been no time for lunch, so Edith asked the kitchen to send a bowl of soup to her office. By five o'clock she'd worked her way through the pile of papers on the desk; there was nothing that the president need attend to except an ambassadorial appointment, and that could wait.

That done, she sent for the president's secretary and asked to see the appointment log he'd kept during the train trip west. Quickly she scanned the entries, looking for Arnold Griffin's name. And there it was: a 3:00 P.M. interview, on September 25, 1919.

The day Woodrow had collapsed.

Up on the second floor, two Secret Service agents guarded the president's door. It was what they'd wanted right from the beginning and were pleased the First Lady had changed her mind. Inside the sickroom, Woodrow was in bed, but awake.

Edith sat beside his bed and held his right hand, the one that still had feeling in it. He took a while to focus—the stroke had affected his vision as well—but he seemed in fairly good spirits. She told him about the opening ceremony for the orphanage and how pleased she was with the orphanage itself. America rebuilding itself. She did not mention the young man in the pushcart.

She worked her way up to the tricky part: how to

probe Woodrow's poor damaged memory without upsetting him. "You remember Arnold Griffin, don't you?" she began. "From the *Post*? You gave him an interview on the train."

" 'Member. Soft voice."

"Well, I think he stole something," she said in slightly scandalized tones. "The duplicate appointments log hasn't been seen since that interview. I only now found out about it." There was not, so far as she was aware, any such thing as a duplicate appointments log; but she was counting on Woodrow's not knowing that.

"Thief?"

"He appears to be. The log was lying on that little table we used to stack unanswered mail on, right at the end of the train car. Do you remember that table?"

"Yes, yes."

"He probably just picked up the log on his way out. Do you recall if he went out that end of the car?"

The mobile half of Woodrow's face frowned. "Came in other end. Don't 'member leaving."

Her heart went out to him. *No, of course you don't remember his leaving. Not if you'd just been struck on the head.* "Well, I suppose it doesn't matter," she said briskly. "It was only a duplicate log, and your appointments were pretty much a matter of public record then anyway. But it's always good to know when we have a light-fingered journalist in our midst, don't you think?"

"Agree. Watch him."

Oh, I will indeed watch him. She stayed a little

longer, doing her best to cheer him up, until a tray with his dinner arrived.

It was after seven before Danby returned. He had with him a pretty strawberry blond who looked as if she wasn't yet out of her teens. "I'm sorry we took so long, Mrs. Wilson," Danby apologized, "but Amy needed to go back to her office to get something." He introduced Amy Vernon, who was clearly nervous at being presented to the First Lady of the land.

When they were all seated, Amy screwed up her courage and blurted out, "Mrs. Wilson, I'm not a Republican, I'm not anything, really, but, but I do work for Senator Lodge and, I, uh, ah . . ." She trailed off.

"I understand," Edith said in her most reassuring manner. "And I don't expect you to tell me anything that would compromise the senator. It's Arnold Griffin I'm interested in. What can you tell me about him?"

Amy got an encouraging nod from Danby. "Senator Lodge has broken all ties with Mr. Griffin," she said. "And the reason is that he learned Mr. Griffin is a member of U.S. for Us."

Edith felt her mouth drop open and closed it again. "U.S. for Us? Is he certain?"

"Yes, ma'am. There's no question."

"Well." This was startling news. A number of anarchist groups had sprung into being at the close of the war, but U.S. for Us was at the opposite extreme of the political spectrum. At first the newspapers had tended to treat U.S. for Us as a sort of bad joke, a social club for malcontents, if only because of the flippant name they'd chosen. But when U.S. for Us declared its intent of clearing the country of "the foreign element" and began bombing the meeting halls of anyone who disagreed with them, then it was clear this group must be taken more seriously. And of course the very idea of a League of Nations meeting together in harmony was anathema to them: U.S. for Us wanted no truck with "foreign trash."

"Let me make sure I understand," she said to the girl. "You're telling me Arnold Griffin is a member of a reactionary group that advocates the use of *violence* to enforce its views?"

Amy nodded. "Senator Lodge doesn't want to have anything to do with them."

Well, that's something, Edith thought. The Republicans had officially disavowed the extremist U.S. for Us, but sometimes Edith suspected the GOP of secretly cheering them on. "How did the senator find out?"

"Mr. Griffin told him. He was trying to recruit the senator as a member."

In spite of the seriousness of the situation, Edith laughed. "What a mistake in judgment *that* was. Senator Lodge is an isolationist to the core, but to think he'd risk his position in government by allying himself with an outlaw group—how foolish of Mr. Griffin. But it's all very strange. Mr. Griffin himself doesn't have the manner of a violent man."

"Oh, he's violent, all right," Amy said in a rush. "He threatened the senator's life."

Edith was so astounded she couldn't speak.

"I'm not too sure about this part," Amy went on, "but I think Senator Lodge threatened to expose him. But *something* caused Mr. Griffin to make his death threat."

Danby said, "Show her what we went back to the office for."

Amy opened her purse and removed a piece of crumpled paper that she tried to smooth out on her lap. "The senator wadded this up and threw it away, but I, um—"

"But you retrieved it. Good for you." Edith took the paper, which was covered with thin, jagged writing in brown ink.

You have a choice to make. You can either speak of what you know of me and what I have attempted to do, or you can maintain a discreet silence. If you speak, it is you yourself who will be silenced forever. The question then becomes one of how highly you value your own life. Keep silent, and you will be safe.

Edith was appalled. "Didn't Senator Lodge inform the police? Or the FBI?"

Amy said not that she knew of.

Danby spoke up. "It sounds as if they both just decided to back off."

Edith nodded. "But he should have informed the FBI." Was Lodge afraid of Griffin?

"He probably doesn't want the adverse publicity," Danby said.

Edith looked at the note again. There were no names mentioned at all. "It's not signed."

Amy smiled crookedly. "It doesn't have to be. That spider handwriting—everyone who's seen it, knows it. And Mr. Griffin always uses that same brown ink. The FBI would have no trouble proving who wrote it."

"Well, it looks as if the senator and Mr. Griffin have arranged their own sort of truce. May I keep this?" Edith asked Amy. She nodded. "You've told me exactly what

I wanted to know, and I am deeply indebted to you. And for the first time in my life, I approve of Henry Cabot Lodge's political stance. U.S. for Us indeed!"

When the two young people had left, Edith once again climbed the stairway to the second floor and her husband's sickroom. Woodrow was asleep, but the Secret Service agents were wide awake.

That's what she'd come to check on.

The next morning she awoke knowing she was going to have to confront Arnold Griffin.

She was ninety-nine percent convinced that Griffin had tried to murder her husband, but all she had were indications, not proof. He advocated violence as a solution to problems—U.S. for Us, the threat against Lodge. But that was not evidence that he'd already committed violence. He'd been in the train car Woodrow had used as an office, and he'd been there on the crucial day—but so had several dozen other people. Edith needed to remove that one percent of remaining doubt before she took action.

She asked the Secret Service to station two agents outside her office door. Alarmed, they wanted to know why she'd asked. She'd put them off with vague excuses and they uneasily acceded to her wishes. The truth was, she wanted Griffin to see two burly guards within call before he entered her office.

He even remarked on it when he came in. "Expecting trouble?"

"That depends on you, Mr. Griffin." She ignored his surprised look and indicated a chair, keeping her desk between them. "I asked you to come here because I want you to tell me something truthfully. Do you honestly believe that this country will be better off if the president is dead?"

"W-what?" he sputtered. "What kind of question is that?"

"What did you hit him with? A sock full of sand? Or do you use a more elegant weapon for assassinating presidents?"

He stared at her. "Mrs. Wilson, I don't know what you think you're—"

"My husband did not suffer a stroke. His present condition is the result of a blow on the head, or more likely several blows, that caused extreme neurological damage. And you are the one who inflicted those blows. You assaulted him on the train, as we were approaching Wichita. On September twenty-fifth." When he continued to stare, she added, "Shortly after three in the afternoon."

He sank back in his chair, his arms falling loosely over the sides. "It's the strain. It's gotten to you."

Edith smiled sadly and shook her head. "I know you're a member of U.S. for Us, Mr. Griffin. From its inception your group has stood in violent opposition to the League of Nations. When you saw the president making some headway in convincing the country to abandon its isolationist ways, you decided to put a stop to it. But you must be new at murdering people. You botched the job."

His face grew dark. "You're out of your mind."

A silence grew between them. Edith broke it by saying, "I would like an answer to my question. Do you truly believe the country would be better off with my husband dead?"

"Let me ask you a question instead," Griffin replied. "Do you think you can accuse me with impunity? I have the power of the press at my back!"

"And I have the power of the presidency at mine!" she shot back. "Do you think the *Post* will support you once the possibility that you're an assassin arises? Why, they'll abandon you so fast—"

"Then the possibility had better not arise, had it?" he cut in softly. "Be careful what you say, lady. You try slandering me and—"

"And what? Are you threatening me, Mr. Griffin? The way you threatened Senator Lodge?" That struck home, so she pressed her advantage. "You see, I've learned a great deal about you. So don't go on pretending. There's no point."

"You've got no evidence," he muttered.

"I won't need evidence if you confess."

Griffin barked a laugh. "Now why should I do that?"

"To put an end to it. To keep yourself from becoming a real killer."

He leaned toward her, and when he spoke his voice was even softer than usual. "Lady, there's a revolution coming. American citizens are sick and tired of seeing their country traded away by powermongers like your husband. To answer your question, yes—I think we'd all be better off with Woodrow Wilson in his grave. And you know what? There are thousands of others just like me who think the same thing. Think of it, lady. *Thousands of people want your husband dead.* How does that feel?"

Edith didn't permit herself to wince. Instead, she stood and pulled herself up to her full height. "It makes me think that you are a very frightened man. Frightened and desperate and hitting out at the most visible target in your range. One last time, Mr. Griffin. Admit what you did. Face the consequences of your acts."

"What consequences?" he scoffed. "What are *you* going to do? You're just a woman leeching power from the man you married. Who's going to listen to you? You may be holding the reins right now, but that won't last. I don't have to threaten you. You can't do anything." He got up with a show of casualness and ambled toward the door. "You can't do *anything*," he repeated, and left.

Edith sank back down into her chair, her heart pounding. She'd known the interview would be upsetting, but it was uglier than she'd expected. When she'd calmed down a little, she tried to think. Griffin had never admitted to attacking Woodrow; she hadn't really expected him to. But that niggling little one percent of doubt—that was gone. Now she was one-hundred percent sure: Arnold Griffin had attempted an assassination.

All the decisions she'd had to make up to that moment now seemed like child's play. There was no one to advise her; she was on her own. She longed for Woodrow's learning and wisdom; when a difficult decision was called for, he used to shut himself away to think and then come back knowing what to do.

Edith didn't have even a high school education. There'd not been enough money in her family to educate all the children, so the boys had gone to school while the girls stayed home and learned to sew and cook. Yet here she was, running the United States government, and not doing a bad job of it. She knew what their enemies were calling her—the Iron Queen, the Secret President, the Presidentress. Petticoat government. The name-calling hurt, but there was nothing to be done about it.

It was the second time in her life she'd found herself in such a position. When her first husband died, she became the untutored owner of his jewelry business. She knew nothing about business. But she'd learned; she learned so well that the business prospered more under her guidance than it had under her late husband's.

She'd been delighted to find this unexpected competence in herself; she enjoyed running the business, and she enjoyed her life as a well-to-do, independent woman with real work to do. And she'd thought very little of politics until she found herself being courted by the widower president of the United States.

And now it had happened again: Woodrow was a broken man, and it was up to her to step in and take his place. She had to hold the pieces together until he'd recovered enough to finish out his term; if the vice-president was sworn in, Woodrow could never reclaim his office. She saw herself as a caretaker, guarding the presidency for the man to whom it belonged. And once again she had proved herself capable; she, Edith Bolling Galt Wilson, was running the country.

A muted cry of anguish escaped her lips. Oh, why did the man have to die or be disabled before the woman could come into her own? The price was too high, it was just too much to pay! Surely there was some better way!

But be that as it may, right then, at that moment in history, she held the power of the presidency in her hands.

So use it.

She called in the two Secret Service agents and told them that Arnold Griffin, the journalist who had just left, had attempted to assassinate the president and could well try again. Further, when she'd found out about it, Griffin had threatened her own life as well.

As proof of the threat against her life, she handed the agents a crumpled piece of paper covered with spidery writing in brown ink.

"Griffin?" Woodrow said, incredulous.

Edith nodded. "He certainly doesn't look like my idea of a wild-eyed fanatic, but there you are. He's been taken into custody."

"What'd do? Can't jail man for plitcal blees." *Political beliefs.*

"I don't know the details yet," Edith said untruthfully, "but I imagine it will all come clear in time." Woodrow must be told everything that had happened, but not just yet. When he was stronger.

He was mumbling something about reactionaries. "FBI?"

"They've been notified. Now, you mustn't worry, Woodrow. It's being taken care of."

"Must hurry. Get well."

"You must take your time. There's no hurry."

"Yes. Big hurry."

"But why?"

He grinned at her with half a face. "You migh' not le' me ha' my job back. You like it too much."

Edith smiled, and hid her hurt.

BARBARA PAUL

—〜◦〜—

BARBARA PAUL writes mysteries, science fiction, and e-mail by the truckload. Currently she is WebSister for the Internet Chapter of Sisters in Crime (**http: www.lit-arts.com/sinc_chap1/**), a chapter she founded and for which she served as president in 1998. Barbara's web page can be found at **http:// www.lit-arts.com/bpaul/**, and she invites readers to drop by her message board.

"I chose to write about the twenty-eighth First Lady," Barbara says, "because twice in Edith Wilson's life she was forced to step in and take over a man's work for him—when her first husband, a businessman, died and when second husband Woodrow Wilson was felled by a stroke. She had to assume those responsibilities with no experience and with no training. And both times, she brought it off splendidly. Who wouldn't want to write about a woman like that?"

POLITICAL DECISION

———— ❧ ————

JOHN LUTZ

THE THING WAS, hardly anyone recognized her without her famous bangs.

At a glance, anyway.

Which was why Mamie was at ease in the back of the plain black Ford sedan as it traveled at precisely the speed limit along rain-slick K Street in Washington, D.C. Her dark hair was combed back off her forehead, which made her appear serenely attractive rather than pert. This wasn't the much-imitated "Mamie Look" that adorned the glossy covers of most of the nation's fashion magazines.

Driving the unobtrusive car was Secret Service Agent Albert Drevel, who during the past several years had become Mamie's trusted and devoted ally in the White House.

Drevel was a large man, not well built, and rather unkempt for a Secret Service agent. But the watery brown eyes in his hound-dog face were alert and intelligent, and Dwight had told Mamie over breakfast one morning that he considered Drevel the most loyal and fearless of the agents assigned to the White House. Dwight knew men, and she was sure he was right about Drevel.

What he didn't know was that Drevel was loyal primarily to her. Agent Drevel would never tell anyone how she found relief from the pressures of being First Lady by sometimes secretly leaving the White House grounds at odd hours, hairdo altered, to have him drive her through the city or out into the countryside.

Sometimes they would stop at one of the drive-in hamburger stands for a quick meal. Mamie seemed never to have been recognized during these late outings, though a teenage waitress had stared at her oddly at one drive-in, stopped chewing her gum for a moment, then asked for their order. Mamie had at times considered a drive-in movie, something starring Clark Gable or Richard Widmark, but she knew that would be overstepping the boundaries of propriety.

What had brought her out late this warm evening was the sealed note she'd received through her secretary. Apparently someone *had* recognized her during her outings and was now requesting a meeting. She would have ignored the typed note, only it said the matter concerned her girlhood friend from Denver, Adelle Mallory.

Adelle and Mamie had gotten along well together while attending Miss Wolcott's private finishing school, almost flunking the table manners course because of their compulsive giggling. They'd been severely reprimanded. A few days later, Adelle had stolen some of her father's expensive scotch whiskey and used it as fortification in her attempt to pretend the table manners instructor's big Cadillac had struck her in front of the school's driveway. The play for attention and sympathy, which would also cast the instructor as a villain, didn't work. The police officers who came to the "accident scene" smelled liquor on Adelle's breath, and under their skilled questioning the frightened and uninjured girl had told the truth.

Which was when Adelle was suspended from the school. She and Mamie exchanged several letters during the following months, then lost touch with each other.

Mamie hadn't thought about Adelle in years and wondered what had become of the petite redhead with the shrill, infectious laugh and the penchant for mischief.

The man who'd sent the note and signed himself "Hollis" suggested that Mamie was the only one who might help Adelle concerning a private and highly sensitive matter. Mamie couldn't imagine how that might be true, but she saw no harm in meeting with this Hollis where he suggested, and no danger as long as Drevel was nearby. Life, though tremendously busy, could be repetitious and dull these days. A touch of adventure was needed now and then, like pepper in a recipe. And it would be wonderful if she might see Adelle again.

Drevel parked the Ford across the street from the Capital Royal Diner. The diner was brightly lit inside and reminded Mamie of that spare and strangely beautiful Hopper painting *Nighthawks*. There was a white-uniformed man working behind the counter, and the diner's only customer was seated in one of the booths. The customer was a blond man wearing a dark suit and tie. From this distance he appeared to be well-groomed and respectable, hardly the sort to become unexpectedly violent.

"I don't like this, ma'am," Drevel said, leaving the almost-silent engine idling.

"He looks harmless enough," Mamie said. "Like Richard Widmark."

"I've seen Widmark's movies, ma'am. That's why I don't like this."

Mamie never knew for sure if Drevel was joking—or for that matter if he had a sense of humor.

"I should go in with you," he said.

Mamie smiled at his reflection in the rearview mirror. "No, the streets of Washington are quite safe, Agent Drevel." She always referred to him as "agent," and to him she was "ma'am," maintaining in their relationship the acknowledgment of position and professionalism. They both wanted it that way. "Besides, there's a man behind the counter inside the diner."

"I'll be watching closely just the same, ma'am," Drevel said, as she opened the car door and stepped out onto the deserted street.

"He might not even be who we think," Mamie said, leaning down before closing the car door. "Maybe the note was a prank and Hollis didn't show up at all."

But Mamie was somehow sure it was Hollis whom Drevel watched as she crossed the street and entered the diner.

The pungent scent of grilled beef and onions struck her immediately. It was pleasantly warm in the diner. The skinny, elderly counterman glanced at her, then looked again with mild curiosity. He obviously decided she looked familiar, and just as obviously decided that her identity could remain entirely her own business. It was that sort of place, which was probably why Hollis had selected it as the site of their meeting.

He stood halfway up in the booth and let his napkin slide from his lap to the floor. The glazed expression on his face suggested that he was flustered, not quite believing she'd responded and was actually here at his request. He certainly did resemble Widmark—the same broad forehead and pale blue eyes, the slightly crooked, half-smirking smile. He wasn't movie-star attractive, however. His face was too fleshy and there was a bland, Everyman air about him. He would be hardly noticeable in crowds.

"I'm Hollis," he said, still smiling. He had good teeth like Widmark.

"Glad to meet you, Mr. Hollis."

He waited patiently until she was seated before sitting down again on his side of the table. A gentleman. She hoped Drevel was watching and had made note of that.

"Can I buy you a cup of coffee?" Hollis asked.

"Yes, thank you."

Hollis pointed with a manicured finger to Mamie, then to his own mug of coffee. The counterman immediately came over with another white steaming mug in one hand, a glass coffee pot in the other. He topped off Hollis's coffee, then poured a full cup for

Mamie. Though he did a slight doubletake again, he retreated behind the counter and tended to business, still obviously not knowing why she looked familiar. Maybe she was a previous customer, or some TV actress, he seemed to be thinking as he industriously wiped down the stainless steel counter.

"Your note mentioned Adelle Mallory," Mamie said, adding cream to her mug and stirring. "Is she in some sort of trouble?"

"I'm afraid so," Hollis said, his pale eyes fixed firmly on Mamie in a way that made her uneasy. "It concerns this." He drew a pearl-handled letter opener with a long silver blade from his pocket and handed it to her.

She examined it and gave it back. "It looks ordinary enough." She took a sip of coffee that was almost hot enough to burn her tongue.

Hollis slid the letter opener back into his pocket. "It isn't, though. It's a murder weapon."

Mamie sat forward, alarmed. "Adelle's killed someone?"

"No," Hollis said, "I killed her. Only a little while ago. In her apartment, right around the corner."

Mamie stared at him. It seemed that Drevel had been right. She thought about standing up and stalking out, but something kept her from moving. "This is a sick joke, I hope."

"Not at all," Hollis said. He glanced out the window toward the parked Ford and Drevel. "I know that's your man out there, and it doesn't matter. I've thought this out. The murder weapon with your fingerprints will be with the body. The counterman will remember you meeting a man in this diner at the approximate time of Adelle's death. Your driver will swear under oath that you were never out of his sight, but who'll believe him? Of course, none of this will happen if I don't make an anonymous call and reveal to the police where Adelle's body is hidden."

Mamie struggled for words. She knew that if she weren't so astonished she'd be more frightened. "This is astounding! And absurd!"

"Nope. I told you, I've thought it out. And it's the sort of thing I'm very clever about."

"I would never be found guilty," Mamie said.

"Of course not. That's not what my employers have in mind. If you're even remotely connected to Adelle's murder, think what it will do to your husband's administration, and to the chances of his designated heir being elected president. Think what it will do to your marriage, your family. No one will ever know for sure about you; they'll always suspect that you actually *did* kill Adelle and that your position made it possible for you to escape the consequences."

"Your *employers?*" Mamie said.

"Sure," Hollis said. "I wouldn't do this on my own. I fought in the Battle of the Bulge. Your husband was my commanding general. I voted for him."

"That's not very reassuring."

"It shouldn't be. Think on this, Mamie—if I may call you that. It would at the least do some political damage to your husband if it were made known you were driven around on these secret late-night jaunts. That's conduct hardly becoming a First Lady, especially if there might be murder involved. The press and his political opponents wouldn't be kind, either to you, to him, or to his party."

Mamie knew he was right. That was what political life was rapidly becoming, a matter of mud-slinging and intensely personal attacks. Of course, Hollis's employers might be underestimating Dick Nixon.

But maybe not.

"You should see this as a political decision rather than a personal one," Hollis told her with his toothy smirk.

"But I'm not a politician."

"Oh, sometimes we all are."

"What is it you want from me?" Mamie asked.

"I'll contact you soon and let you know. It's wonderful that you and your husband have such a close relationship, how he values and relies on your opinion, how you could influence him and shape *his* opinion on close issues."

Mamie understood now and was truly horrified. "Your employers are Communists! Do you really expect me to spy, to commit treason?"

Hollis smiled even wider, though not very warmly. "Nothing like that."

"I don't believe you."

"Well, I suppose you can't. Not for sure, anyway." Hollis stood up and laid a dollar bill on the table for the coffees and tip. "I'll be in touch, Mamie. Remember, you visited your old friend Adelle tonight, had coffee with her, got in an argument, and killed her." Now his smile did take on an odd warmth. "It's okay, though. Your secret's safe with me—the mysterious unknown man you were observed meeting the night of the murder."

He left by a side door Mamie hadn't noticed. When she looked down, she saw that her spoon was missing. Now he could plant two objects with her fingerprints on them, one of them an instrument of death. The murder weapon used in the slaying of a woman she knew.

If he'd been telling the truth. If he *had* actually murdered Adelle.

When the counterman's back was turned, Mamie stood up quickly and hurried from the diner. She kept her head low as she crossed the street and got into the car, this time up front next to Drevel. He'd smoked a cigarette while she was gone; the car's interior was stuffy and close with the acrid scent of burned tobacco.

"What's wrong?" he asked, glancing in the direction Hollis had gone.

"Quite a lot, I'm afraid," Mamie said. She held a white object out toward him, below the level of the dashboard. "Handle this gingerly," she said.

"What is it?"

"A coffee mug," she said. "I stole it."

"A woman named Adelle Flanders—maiden name Mallory—was reported by her neighbor as missing yesterday," Drevel told Mamie three days later.

Mamie found she'd been holding her breath. "Good Lord, Hollis was serious then."

"Looks that way, ma'am," Drevel said, without changing expression.

"Poor Adelle—"

"I made discreet inquiries like you told me," Drevel said. "Your old friend Adelle fell on bad times after she left Denver. The man she married beat her regularly, then died in a car accident five years ago that also killed their two children. The drinking problem Adelle had developed became more serious after that."

"I can imagine," Mamie said.

"She got mixed up with the wrong people. Hollis was among them."

Mamie sat down and placed the fingertips of both hands to her temples. She had a meeting in an hour with the Monument Beautification people and she didn't feel at all like facing them or anyone else. "Hollis must have killed her just so he could have something to hold over me."

"Yes, ma'am. Only his name isn't Hollis. It's Wallace Oakmont."

She lowered her hands and stared up at him. "You got that from the coffee mug already?"

Drevel nodded. "It had lots of good fingerprints on it. I managed to work it through the lab without involving you. Oakmont was with the OSS during the war. He became a field agent in 1947 when it became the CIA. He was fired four years ago when his loyalty came into question. There are those in the CIA who are sure he sold secrets to the Russians, including names of fellow operatives, but no one can prove it." He gave Mamie a level look. "Usually the CIA neutralizes people like that."

Mamie knew what he meant. It was a hard world. Sometimes the people in charge had to choose one life over another—or many others. There was the civilian population, the specter of atomic attack. And even if it never came to that, the devious work of a double-agent like Oakmont could result in the exposure and deaths of dozens of other agents. "Why haven't they—"

"He's managed to avoid them for the past four years," Drevel said. "He even faked his own death in Iran. It took several years before our operatives there discovered he'd killed someone else and planted his identification on the man. The CIA kept it a secret from him that they knew he wasn't dead, so he'd get careless. But they couldn't find him even if he was still alive. Then he surfaced recently, working his trade again."

"For the Russians?"

"No."

"What other country would hire him?" Mamie asked.

"No country, ma'am, a consortium of some of the largest defense contractors in this country."

"My God! You mean they put him up to using me so they could influence my husband's political decisions?"

"More or less. I doubt that they know his methods. On the other hand, I doubt that they care." He stood with his hands in his pockets, looking his usual somber, saggy self. They might have been discussing the latest harmless Washington gossip. "It was smart of you to come away from your meeting with his coffee mug, ma'am. And lucky for the rest of us."

Mamie wasn't sure what he meant. "What are we going to do now?"

"You should go ahead and make another appointment to meet with him, ma'am."

She stood up and stared at Drevel.

"These are difficult times, ma'am. For everyone. All of a sudden you find yourself in your husband's game."

"A man's game," Mamie said.

"You and I will be the only ones who know."

"It can't be that way," she said.

He shrugged. "No, I suppose not. The president will have to know, but afterward." He looked at her with his soft brown eyes full of sympathy, knowing the pain of her alternatives. "Can you do this?"

"I'll let you know, Agent Drevel."

"Yes, ma'am."

Two days later, Adelle Mallory's body was discovered in a drainage canal. She'd been stabbed to death, but no weapon was found.

Neither was Wallace Oakmont found. The CIA would presume he was still alive, though officially he'd died years ago in Iran.

That Saturday Mamie sat in the Oval Office before her husband's desk. Behind him were open drapes, a sunny garden view. The capital was basking in fair weather.

"I have something to tell you," she said, watching him continue to bend over the massive desk and write occasionally on the paper he was studying.

"Sounds like a confession's coming," he said with his wonderful smile, still not looking at her.

"It concerns Agent Drevel."

"I know about you and Drevel and your late-night jaunts through the city and surrounding countryside," he said. "It's all right, Mamie. I understand how a woman would have to get away from the pressure of being First Lady. There are the Monument Beautification people, then representatives of Women for School Dress Codes, then your speech to the DAR, your tour of that children's hospital. It's not an easy schedule for any woman."

"How did you find out about my nighttime drives?"

"I *am* the president. I have ways of learning things and still keeping them secret, Mamie."

"You too?"

He stopped writing and looked up at her sharply. Then he relaxed and smiled again. "So what do you have to tell me?" he asked.

She sat back in her chair. "It has to do with things military and industrial. It's complex, dear."

Hollis-Oakmont had been right about one thing. She *could* influence her husband.

When they were finished talking, she rose from her chair to go meet with the Monument Beautification people.

JOHN LUTZ

—✦—

JOHN LUTZ is the author of more than thirty novels and two-hundred short stories, and is a past president of both the Mystery Writers of America and Private Eye Writers of America. His novel, *SWF Seeks Same* was made into the hit movie *Single White Female*, and he coauthored the screenplay for the movie *The Ex*, adapted from his novel of the same title. He is the recipient of the Edgar Award, Shamus Award, and the Trophee 813 Award for best mystery short-story collection translated into the French language.

"Other's might like Ike, but I liked Mamie," admits John. "She is the reason countless beautiful women of the fifties wore bangs, and it always struck me that without hers, few people would have recognized her even though she was one of the most famous and admired women in the country."

"A" IS FOR ADAMS

—◦◦◦—

CAROLYN WHEAT

November 26, 1800
New York City

THE LITTLE MAN with the big voice spoke as if to the small circle of men around him, but his words were intended for a larger audience than that assembled in the courtyard of Fraunces Tavern, the chief watering place of New York's political class.

"As a true Federalist," he declaimed in a tone more suited to the meeting-hall, "I could wish for nothing more ardently than the reelection of a president of my own philosophy." He paused and clasped his hands behind his waist, thrusting one stockingclad leg before the other in a belligerent stance.

The orator's voice dropped a full octave as he finished in a low, thrilling tone, as if confiding a terrible secret, "But as a patriot, there is nothing on this earth I desire less than the reelection of that usurper. He shall have no support from this quarter, sir, not even if my worst enemy should win the prize instead."

Shrewd smiles and knowing nods said that every-one present recalled the last election, when Aaron Burr's support contrived to exalt that same enemy, Republican Thomas Jefferson, to the post of Vice President under the Federalist Adams.

"Aye," an old man with the piercing blue eyes and ruddy face of a seaman said, "We didn't topple King George from his throne only to exalt King John in his place, sir."

A tall man wearing the new fashion of trousers instead of knee-breeches, spoke up. "Ah, but will the prize fall to Mr. Jefferson, sir, or will it go to another who even now intrigues for a greater place than the voters intend him to have?"

"That remark can have but one meaning, sir," Hamilton said, his tone dangerously calm. "What in-trigue is Burr up to now?"

The red-faced seaman answered with a coarse laugh. "Hadn't you heard? He's going to marry his way into the presidency."

"What the gentleman means," the tall man said, with only the tiniest emphasis on the word *gentleman*, "is that Burr's daughter is engaged to marry South Carolina in return for its votes supporting him as president and relegating Jefferson to vice president."

"Aye, the prospective son-in-law is on his way to Monticello even as we speak," a small man in a large hat explained, "bearing a letter which conveys Burr's absolute and total loyalty. And you know, sir," he added with a snigger, "what that portends."

Hamilton's answering smile was not a pleasant sight. "Yes, Mr. Burr is always at his most treacher-ous when he is swearing fidelity, is he not? What, after all, can be expected of a man who served under Benedict Arnold in the late war?"

This sally, while shopworn with age and overuse, never failed to produce a murmur of approval from veterans of the War for Independence.

"What would happen if this letter failed to reach its intended recipient, I wonder," Hamilton ruminated. "What, indeed, would happen if the writer's true intention were to be made plain?"

The tall man in trousers gave a single nod. He and Hamilton stepped away from the crowd and sat together in a dim corner of the tavern. By the time the innkeeper shut for the night, they had their plan.

A substitute letter. A letter revealing Burr's true mind. A letter which would be found on the person of young Mr. Alston—for that was the South Carolina bridegroom's name. A letter to be "discovered" by accident and circulated intentionally in the circles where it would do the most harm to Burr—and the most good to Hamilton.

What Fraunces Tavern was to the Federalist party, the newly formed Tammany Hall was to the Republicans. There Aaron Burr, de facto leader of the party, held court at the table nearest the fireplace. He sat at his ease, a long clay pipe in one hand and a glass of Madeira in the other.

"Adams is finished," he proclaimed. "The Federalists' day is over, and the Republicans' day is dawning."

"All the same, Mr. Burr," a large man in a dirty waistcoat said, "do you not fear the Virginia junto as much as the Massachusetts faction?"

"Mr. Adams has no faction, sir," Burr replied with

a laugh. "Mr. Adams is far too contentious a man to attract sufficient following to constitute a faction. What he does have—" and here the speaker paused, with the sure instinct of a born orator, waiting for the curiosity of his listeners to mount, "what he does have, that our late, lamented first president lacked, is a son. A son worthy of a dynasty."

Brows knit. Throats rumbled. "Adams made his own son envoy to Prussia," one man said with a firm shake of the head. "General Washington never would have done that. Never."

All agreed that General Washington, who had just been laid to rest at his beloved Mount Vernon, was the one and only model of a president, and that the present incumbent was a poor substitute.

But what of the son? What of John Quincy Adams, that limb of Satan, that Prince Hal with a Harvard education?

"I tell you, sir," Burr declaimed, "it is plain as day that young Mr. Adams has his sights firmly set upon the same house his father now occupies with such a notable lack of distinction. It will do our cause little good," he went on, letting his dark eyes roam the circle, bringing the men under his spell, "to rid the country of Mr. John Adams so long as Mr. Quincy Adams is permitted to run free."

More nods and murmurs of agreement. Men who had never given one second's thought to the existence of John Quincy Adams were now determined to prevent his rise to the presidency.

"No," Burr continued, raising his voice once again, "the Federal City must be cleansed of Adamses, purged of the New England diocese, scoured from top to bottom like a milk-jug permitted to sour. Not a cat belonging to that family shall remain in the capital when I've finished."

This pronouncement was greeted with loud laughter, some applause, and many offers to buy Mr. Burr a small beer. He sat back in his chair with a self-satisfied smile on his saturnine face. He would do it, too: he would scotch the budding political career of the Adams brat, who was even now basking in the glow of a successful treaty with the Prussian king.

But how? That was the question.

Letters, he decided over a friendly pipe with one of his sycophants, an actor from Crumley's Theatre on Maiden Lane. Letters were the lifeblood of the Adams family. How ironically pleasant, how poetically just, it would be if a letter were to be the downfall of Adams the Younger.

November 30, 1800
Washington City

My dearest John Quincy,

I have but lately arrived in the place everyone calls the Federal City, but it is a city in Name only. Such mud I have not seen since that Spring in London, when the sewers overflowed and their contents spilled into every drawing-room in Mayfair. I only hope that if there is ever a City named for your Father it will boast finished streets instead of rutted lanes stinking of horse droppings.

Of the President's mansion, the less said the better. It is a castle of a house and will doubtless be a fine dwelling once it is staffed by the twenty or so servants it requires. As I have but five, you will draw your own conclusions as to our Style of living. The rear yard is a sea of mud; I have therefore chosen the East Room as the perfect place in which to dry the laundry. It will someday serve as an assembly hall, but at the moment it is hung with bed linens and table cloths, which even a constant fire in the grate cannot render dry enough to use.

Your father has chosen a rather odd egg-shap'd room as his office. The room above it is designated the Elliptical Saloon, and would be a charming location for my Tuesday afternoon levees, but for the fact that the plaster on the walls refuses to dry. There is also the trifling matter of the absence of a staircase between the first and second floors, but no doubt the guests could shinny up a pole if need be.

I need not tell you, dear Quincy, that these private jests are not to be repeated. We are well aware that this is a House built for the Ages and not for the convenience of the Adams family. Whenever anyone here asks how I like the house, I smile and reply—and quite truthfully, too!—that the situation is remarkably fine. It has become such a habit with me that when your father and I both ran across the muddy yard to the outdoor privy—oh, how I miss my modern water closet in Philadelphia, dear John Quincy!—he said, "Oh, but Abby, think of the situation. Consider the situation, my dear." And so we both commenced to laugh, which is the only sensible thing to do when living in a completely intolerable state.

All is not well with your brother Charles. Indeed, I brought little Susan with me—she is four years old and knows all her Goody Goose by heart. I cannot help but fear I shall never again see my Bonny Prince Charlie, and that the dear child will never again see her father.

I shall close for now, but will always remain,

Your loving mother, Abigail Adams

Another letter writer, an actor, sat at the writing-desk in the common room of Tunnicliff's Hotel, the only habitable hostelry in the raw, unfinished capital. He regarded his own handiwork with a smile of satisfaction.

His forgery was complete. It resembled to an uncanny degree the one Burr had given him to use as a model. The language was that of a scholar, flavored at intervals with a foreign phrase. He shook his head as he sprinkled sand over the parchment to dry the ink. These Adamses were just as bad as Mr. Burr had said; true Americans didn't use fancy French and German to express their honest sentiments.

He read the lines over again, holding the candle so close it was like to light the parchment and render it to ashes. Yes, he decided, the letter would do. It would convince anyone who read it that young Mr. Adams had made a lucrative financial gain from the treaty with Prussia.

There was but one more touch which would confirm the authenticity of the letter and seal Prince John's fate.

The actor smiled at his pun. For what he needed was John Quincy Adams's personal seal for the wax.

One look at that seal and anyone would believe the
letter genuine, for how could you sit in a hotel in
Washington City and forge a letter using the seal of
a man in Berlin?

You could do it if you had a duplicate seal.

And by tomorrow night, a duplicate seal was exactly what he would have.

December 1, 1800
Washington City

Dear John Quincy,

We have this Evening entertained a Visitor
from your part of the World. Count Rupert von
Hohensteiner presented his compliments at the
Tuesday levee and was most Effusive in his Praise
of your excellent Conduct of affairs in Berlin. We
were most gratified to hear news of you, dear
Quincy, and so we invited Count Rupert to a private supper.

My residence in this City has not served to en-
dear the world to me. I am sick, sick, sick of Publick Life and desire nothing more ardently than a
return to my beloved Braintree. This happy event
will not be long in coming, for your Father is certain that he will not be re-elected. For my own
Part, I am content, though I think it a Shame that
a man who has given so much to his country
should be thrown on the Ash-heap when that
country has finished with him.

You will say, no doubt, that as a Woman I have
no right to meddle in Publick affairs. If a woman
does not hold the Reins of Government, I see no

reason for her not judging how they are conducted. You will recall that when we lived in Philadelphia, I often visited the Senate to watch your Father preside over that contentious body. If I do not do so here in Washington City, you must attribute my absence to the immense amount of work to be done in the house, and not to a Want of Interest.

I remain, ever your loving,
Mother

It was the best trick of all, pretending to be a Prussian aristocrat, praising John Quincy Adams to his doting parents even as he contrived to slip away and secure the twin tokens of their ambitious son's downfall. The actor whistled as he walked to his hotel, and his fingers caressed the signet ring he had taken from the president's desk drawer.

Back at the hotel, he ordered a glass of the best port and settled himself at the writing desk in the common room. He would have preferred privacy, but the sleeping chambers in the hotel were so sparse, so barren of even the most rudimentary furnishings, that he had no room to complete his business there. Besides, who would take notice of a man at a writing desk putting the finishing touches on a letter?

He reached toward the candle atop the secretary, and used its flame to light a stick of wax in the exact shade of green favored by young Mr. Adams. He dripped several drops of wax on the folded halves of the parchment forgery, then carefully set the signet ring atop the melted circle. Quickly, he lifted the ring and placed the thimble on top of the still-soft initials. It was delicate and careful work; the resulting mark must look as if it had been made by a single seal.

The two impressions—the initials JQA from the signet ring, and the laurel wreath embossed on the thimble—together constituted the insignia on the seal used by John Quincy Adams.

The actor waited for the wax to dry, then stuffed the letter into his coat pocket and set out again into the raw November night.

A tall man in trousers leaned forward from his wing chair in the rear of the common room. He leaned forward just far enough to catch a glimpse of the signet ring and the resulting impression in the wax. The letter *A* stood out like a beacon, calling to him from across the room.

He was to wait for a man named Alston, who would stop at Tunnicliff's Hotel in Washington City on his way to Monticello. A man who carried a letter that must be replaced with another letter of far different import.

And here was the man, bold as brass, sitting in the publick room at his hotel, writing that very letter he was to obtain at all costs. Rising from his seat and setting forth into the deserted city at this ungodly hour when no one with a lawful purpose was to be seen abroad.

The trouser-clad man rose with a fluid motion and followed his quarry into the chill night air. He quickened his step and soon fell in behind the man with the letter.

He lifted his arm and, with the help of a stocking

filled with sand, delivered a crushing blow. The man bent forward and fell with a heavy thud.

As he reached toward the man's coat to remove the letter, he realized his victim had struck his head on a rock and lay very, very still. He touched the man's neck and felt no pulse. He placed a hand over the man's mouth; no air went in or out.

He was dead. Alston was dead.

Hamilton hadn't wanted the man dead. He had only wanted the letter replaced.

And replaced it would be. The letter Hamilton had forged would be found on Alston's body, and the world would believe he had been set upon by highwaymen.

The trousered man reached into the dead man's coat pocket and pulled out a parchment rectangle.

He gave it a cursory glance, expecting to see the seal of the Alston family.

Instead, he recoiled in horror.

The initials on the seal contained the *JA* that one would expect for Joseph Alston, but there was an additional *Q* in the center.

Q for Quincy. *JQA* for John Quincy Adams.

He had killed the wrong man.

December 2, 1800
The President's House

It was bright and shiny. Susan loved things that were bright and shiny. She loved her little locket that Aunt Nabby gave her for her birthday. But Cousin Louisa wouldn't let her wear it now. Cousin Louisa said she had to wear a horrid black necklace instead, just as she had taken Susan's nice blue dress away and made her wear a heavy, starchy black frock that caught under her slippers when she ran.

Cousin Louisa said she wasn't to run, either. Little girls whose fathers were dying weren't supposed to run.

She was sorry Papa was sick, but she didn't see how running would make him feel any worse.

The sun glinted off a bright little thing, which peeked out at her from underneath a leaf next to the outdoor privy. Susan knelt down and picked up the shiny object.

It was a thimble. A thimble Susan recognized as Gran's because it had a circle of leaves on its top.

She ought to take it to Gran at once. Gran would want to have it back.

But it was so pretty, and it shone like fire in the sunlight.

Gran wouldn't want her to prick her finger when she did her sewing lesson. Gran would want her to have the thimble. She was sure of it.

Susan slipped the bright object into the pocket of the huge black skirt, but then remembered that Cousin Louisa had a nasty habit of asking her to turn out her pockets. She'd hide the thimble in her special place, under the little pile of firewood, where no one would find it. She'd put it next to the other treasure she'd found that morning, the gold ring with an *A* on it.

"*A*," she chanted aloud as she skipped to the woodpile, "is for apple. *A* is for ant, and *A* is for Adams." She slipped the thimble under the log, setting it beside the *A is for Adams* ring. Then she went inside to ask Cook for a slice of bread and treacle.

December 3, 1800
Washington City

My dear John Quincy,

We have had a Most Disturbing Turn of Events at the President's house, but one that you shall not read about in the Publick Press. I thank God for the Sedition Act; if it were not in place, I shudder to think what the newsliars would make of it. They are as false as Hell—or as false as the English, which is worse.

I shall endeavor to set forth the Facts as they Occurred. First, Mr. Ingleby, our butler—he is a Virginian to the core and shows open Disdain for our New England ways—announced that there was a dead body in the privy. Your father insisted upon being shown the corpse, and was dismayed to recognize it as Count Rupert von Hohensteiner.

Such is the State of Disarray in the Federal City that even President Adams had no earthly idea as to whether there were Local Authorities who ought to be summoned. The City has no mayor, and even the lowly office of Town Watchman has yet to be filled. Mr. Ingleby mentioned that the only place in town with a sufficiently large Icehouse to keep the body fresh was Tunnicliff's Hotel. A servant was dispatched and Mr. Tunnicliff himself attended upon us within the hour.

Imagine our Surprize and Consternation when

he identified the corpse as that of Jeremiah Hazlitt, late of New York City—an Actor!

Why an Actor should impose himself upon the President and his Wife by impersonating a foreigner is unknown at present, but Mark this Well, John Quincy: the man did not pretend to be a Frenchman or a Hindoo. He acted the part of a Prussian aristocrat and he claimed a connexion with you.

Your Father believes the mischief to be the Work of Aaron Burr, who is a constant schemer and will stop at nothing to insure high office for himself. I have no Opinion on the Matter, although the Venality of a Man as Licentious as Mr. Burr is not to be underestimated.

My chiefest fear, dear Quincy, is that this affair will somehow recoil upon you and your work in Berlin.

I remain your Devoted and Ever-Vigilant
Mother

December 4, 1800
Alexandria

Dear Mr. Hamilton:

It is with mixed emotions that I greet you and render an Account of recent Events of Interest to us Both. Due to a circumstance entirely beyond my Control, I found myself staring into the Eyes of a Dead Man and realizing I had dispatched the wrong man to his Maker.

I could not leave the body in the Street, for it was too near the hotel, and I might be remembered there. No, I reasoned, the body must be moved. But where?

A cunning, wicked, low thought struck me at that moment. I bent down and lifted the body, then hefted it over my shoulder and carried it to the president's house, where I propped it up in the privy behind the mansion.

Let King John make what he can of that, sir, I said to myself as I sauntered away.

I have no doubt that you will thank me for a good night's work in spite of my little mistake. I am even now on my way to Monticello to meet the real Mr. Alston.

Your Devoted Servant,

Brutus

Post scriptum:

The dead man carried a letter on his person, along with a note saying the letter contained proof that John Quincy Adams is a corrupt betrayer of the publick trust. I considered that this Letter might serve as a Benefit to you, sir, and so I placed it into Hands that would disseminate it as widely as possible. I slipped it under the door for Mr. Adams's butler to find. He is no friend to the Federalist cause, and will use the letter to make much Mischief, if I am any judge.

December 6, 1800

My dear Sister,

I write this letter in a state of Perplexity and Confusion. I know you will have reason to understand my Situation, as your son William was once embroiled in a financial scandal that was not of his making.

Of all my children, John Quincy worried me least. He was always a helpmate to his father and me, and never gave Trouble in any way. You more than anyone know how Charles grieved me with his drinking and Thomas with his want of steadiness and Nabby with her marriage. Only John Quincy seemed above any possible danger.

Now that danger has come upon him, it is a bitter pill indeed. I do not know whether he is aware of it, but Washington City talks of little else. I journeyed to George Town today—which is the very dirtyest hole I ever saw for a place of any trade—and overheard a fishmonger remarking that "some people's sons were born to disappoint them." He said the words just loud enough for me to hear, and when I stared him down, he blushed and turned away.

That my son, my successful and brilliant son, should be spoken of in a derogatory manner by a fishmonger raises a gust of anger such as I have not felt since John was in Philadelphia at the Continental Congress and I feared we should capitulate to England! My very Soul rebels at the thought that John Quincy could act in a manner unbefitting to his station and his Name.

A letter has been shown round Washington City, passed from hand to hand like a scurrilous ballad. It purports to prove that John Quincy's treaty with Prussia was negotiated for his own financial benefit and not the Good of the Nation.

I contrived to procure a copy of the letter. The writing and phrasing are similar to John Quincy's, which signifies only that it was made by a competent forger. This alone would be damning, but the truly incriminating fact is that the letter was sealed with an insignia containing the letters *J, Q,* and *A* intertwined within a border of laurel leaves.

There may be many such seals, I do not know, although these are far from common initials. What I do know is that I ordered a seal of this exact description to be made for my son on the occasion of his appointment to the Berlin post.

There is not a single particle of my being that believes John Quincy capable of writing such a letter. Yet I cannot explain the presence of his seal on the forgery. Surely the writer did not travel to Berlin for the purpose of sealing a faked letter.

This has something to do, I am certain, with the dead actor in the privy.

Though vexed and concerned, I remain,

Ever your loving Sister,

Abby

Susan dashed across the yard, now hard and dry after the first frost, to her cubbyhole under the woodpile. She scrabbled under the log and pulled out her locket. She might not be able to wear it, but she could open it with her tiny fingers and gaze upon the miniatures of her mother and father. She wasn't sure what dying meant, but she knew she would never see her Papa again, and Mama was far away.

Perhaps Cousin Louisa would let her carry the locket with her, if she asked nicely.

She reached back inside the hole and fished around for the thimble. She knew she ought to take it back to Gran. But her hand touched something hard, something that hadn't been there before. She pulled it out; it was a buckeye. A plain brown buckeye. She hadn't put it there. She wouldn't have put it there.

She frowned and thrust her hand inside the hiding place, determined to make sure all her treasures were accounted for.

But they weren't. The ring was gone. The ring with the letter A for Adams was gone, and this ugly little thing left in its place.

She remembered a story her mother had told her, about the fairies carrying away a child. She'd thought for a moment that she'd like to be taken by fairies; their lives sounded so much more interesting than her own. And the fairies, Mama said, always left something behind in place of the baby. A cabbage or a rabbit or a magic lamp.

The fairies must have taken the A for Adams ring and left her this buckeye instead.

Susan sighed as she put her things back into their hiding place. Next time, she thought, I hope the fairies leave me something.

December 8, 1800

My dearest Betsy,

I know, my much-loved Sister, that you will Weep with me over the Grave of a poor unhappy Child who cannot now add another pang to those which have pierced my Heart for several years past.

Poor Charlie's tormented life ended last Week. He was the gayest of my children, and the one who was quickest to win hearts. John Quincy is the match of any man in the Republic for honor and depth of understanding, and Thomas is a shrewd lawyer, but Charlie was a man at whom everyone smiled. I do not know if it is Charlie the man I shall miss, or the child, for memories of his golden boyhood fill my mind more completely at this moment. I only know that a light has gone out of my life.

It is both Pleasure and Pain to have little Susan with us at this time. Pleasure, because her childish laughter warms this great Barn of a house, and Pain, because the sight of her playing Horsie with her Grand-papa brings back memories of Charlie as a little lad, and also calls to mind my own little Susanna, dead these many years.

At least two of our mysteries have been Cleared Up. The dead man in the privy seems to have been murdered by highwaymen; this Federal City is in the midst of wilderness and so such Occurrences, while Deplorable, are only to be expected.

As to the letter supposedly written by John Quincy, I have divined how the seal was counterfeited. You may recall that it was formed of his initials, which I copied from a signet ring he used to wear, and a wreath of laurel leaves like the one on the silver thimble Grandmother Quincy left me.

What could be more simple than to obtain these

two items, and so create a wax impression the spit and image of the seal? And what better way to gain entrance to the president's house than to pretend Acquaintance with his son?

I hastened at once to search for the ring and the thimble, and I am both dismayed and pleased to have had no results. Pleased, because this means my Theory is Sound; the ring and thimble must have been stolen by this very Actor whose Body we discovered in the privy. And dismayed, because without the ring and thimble to show how the trick was done, my protests will sound Hollow indeed.

John takes the View that we should be above politicks, which after all is a mere catch-penny, but I cannot be so Sanguine, as it is my son's Character which is at stake.

Your truly affectionate but afflicted Sister,

A. Adams

"Where *is* that thimble?" Gran poked her hands into the sewing basket and rummaged until the threads and ribbons lay on the floor in a colorful heap. It was the fifth time she had turned out the entire basket, but she refused to accept the notion that the thimble would never be found.

Susan stared into the fire, hoping no one would notice her. But then Cousin Louisa said, her voice as sharp as Gran's scissors, "Child, do you know where your grandmother's thimble is?"

"I didn't steal it, Gran," Susan protested. "I found it in the yard and I kept it because it was so pretty and shiny, but the fairies came and changed it into a buckeye."

"That child and her stories!" Cousin Louisa looked as though she wanted to slap Susan, who began to cry in anticipation.

"It's true, Gran," she protested, throwing herself upon the mercy of the older woman. "I put it in my secret place, only the next time I went there, it was gone and there was a buckeye instead. It was the fairies, Gran, truly it was."

Louisa murmured something about the path to perdition, but Gran said, "Let us go see this remarkable buckeye."

Susan led the way, her heart sinking. What if the buckeye was gone? What if the fairies changed it back into a thimble? She smoothed her black skirt behind her, as if anticipating the sting of a switch on her tiny rear end.

Under the wobbly log in the woodpile, they found one child's locket, a spray of dead flowers, a broken fan, a doll's hat, a comb with no teeth, a round pebble, and a fat, shiny buckeye.

Susan sighed with relief and said, "You see? That's where I put the thimble."

"Stuff and nonsense," Louisa said. "I daresay we shall find the thimble in the child's room."

Susan picked up the buckeye. "It used to be the *A* is for Adams ring, but then the fairies came and took it and left this in its place."

Gran frowned.

Susan blanched. Was there going to be a spanking in her future after all?

"What do you mean, child, *A* is for Adams?"

"I found it," Susan protested. "I didn't steal it out of Grand-papa's desk drawer. I didn't."

"How did you know it was in your grandfather's desk drawer if you didn't—"

"Hush, Louisa. Are you talking about a ring with the letter *A* on it, Susan?"

"*A* is for Apple, *A* is for ant, and *A* is for Adams," Susan chanted. "That's what Papa used to say."

A look of sadness came over her grandmother's face. It seemed as if everyone who talked about her papa did so with sadness now.

Louisa looked at her aunt as if she had lost her celebrated mind. "Aunt Abigail, all we need do is search this child's room, and you shall find your thimble. And, I daresay, a great many other things that have gone missing."

"I may be the President's Lady, Louisa," Abigail Adams replied, "but I am a farmer's wife at heart. And I think we will have better luck finding what we seek if we look in that hollow tree behind the privy."

December 12, 1800

Dearest Johnny,

I hope this form of Address does not Offend, but sometimes a Mother must surely be permitted to remember her Son as he was before he Attained his Exalted Position in the World. Perhaps it is Charlie's passing that makes me sentimental. Or perhaps the sight of little Susan sitting on her grandfather's knee and blowing soap-bubbles through his favorite pipe brings me in mind of my children when you were Young.

You will no doubt Remark that if you or Nabby had ever done such a thing, your Father would not have chuckled indulgently, but the World has long known that Grandfathers are far more lenient than Fathers when it comes to the little ones.

I write to set your Mind at rest concerning the Late Excitement regarding a counterfeit count. The matter has been most satisfactorily resolved, thanks to a small gray mammal known as the trade rat.

I had already divined that the seal purporting to be yours was contrived by the use of a signet ring and Grandmother Quincy's thimble. Both, however, were missing—and little Susan proclaimed that they had been stolen by Fairies. Something she said convinced me that in essence she was correct: The items had been removed and something else left in their place.

You will doubtless recall the Incident of the Missing Salt Cellar. I was overly Severe to a young maid, whom I believed had displaced our silver Salt Cellar that came down to us from the Boylstons. I cannot now recall whether it was Charles or Thomas who discovered the Salt Cellar in a hollow tree, along with other Interesting Objects hoarded by a trade rat, so called because he seldom takes one object without leaving another.

A thorough search of the trees in the yard behind the President's House uncovered the rat's nest, in which we found both thimble and signet ring. I quickly used them to make an impression in wax, which proved identical to the one on the fraudulent letter.

The end of it all is that while your Father will surely be sent packing by an Ungrateful Electorate, your reputation remains unstained by any Hint of Scandal. As you make your way in Publick Life, you shall have the satisfaction of knowing that you were spared by the efforts of your loving mother and a rat. My only uncertainty is as to which of us performed the greater service, but since he lost both home and treasure, I must own that the rat made the greater sacrifice and is therefore entitled to a larger measure of gratitude than

Your Loving
Mama

CAROLYN WHEAT

—⁓—

CAROLYN WHEAT is a triple threat, being not only an author, but also an attorney and a writing teacher. She is the author of the Edgar-nominated *Mean Streak*, and she is hard at work on the seventh book in her series about Brooklyn criminal lawyer Cass Jameson. Her short story, "Accidents Will Happen," won the Agatha award for Best Short Story of 1996.

"Abigail Adams hung her laundry in the unfinished East Room," notes Carolyn. "She wrote rafts of letters in which she spoke frankly and sometimes scathingly on the issues of the day. She supported her husband's political career by running the farm upon which their real income depended and by investing in the stock market. She was a remarkable woman, married to a remarkable man, and together they raised a son who would someday live in the White House and plant a garden in the muddy yard where the presidential privy once stood. She was like women everywhere: While the men debated and went to war and negotiated the peace, she stayed at home and kept it all together. She firmly believed that in her own sphere, Woman was the equal to her husband, a partner and not a subordinate."

YOU RUN

———∿∿∿———

SARAH SHANKMAN

San Clemente, California, June 1976

THIRTY YEARS SINCE Richard Milhous Nixon's first campaign for Congress, bankrolled by Pat Nixon's selling her interest in her family farm.

Twenty-four years since the 1952 presidential election when Richard Nixon's campaign funding was called into question and Pat sat by her husband's side as he made his "Checkers" speech, telling the nation about their dog, Pat's "Republican" cloth coat, and laying out the details of every cent they owned and owed.

Sixteen years since Nixon lost his presidential bid to John F. Kennedy by two-tenths of one percent of the popular vote and promised Pat that he would never again run for public office.

Fourteen years since Nixon's defeat in the 1962 California gubernatorial election.

Eight years since Nixon's decision, made without consulting his wife, to run for president once again.

Four years since the break-ins at the Watergate offices of the Democratic National Committee in Washington, D.C.

Almost two years since Richard Milhous Nixon, the only president ever drummed out of office, retreated with Thelma Catherine "Pat" Ryan Nixon to San Clemente and their vacation house, La Casa Pacifica.

Two months since the publication of Bernstein and Woodward's *The Final Days*, a minute-by-minute account of the death throes of the Nixon presidency.

One month before Pat Nixon would suffer her first debilitating stroke.

Perched above the sea, the long white-stuccoed house with the red tile roof was within earshot of Camp Pendleton, and sometimes, at night, if you listened hard, even over the waves, you could hear shelling and rifle fire from the ghosts of young Marines, killed in Vietnam, who'd trained there.

The house was light and bright inside, but eerily still. As the visitor entered, it struck him that La Casa Pacifica felt as if no one had ever laughed within its walls.

Pat Nixon, wearing a white blouse, a lightweight navy cardigan, navy trousers, and a smile, received her guest in a sitting room on the north side of the house. From there they could see her gardens: eucalyptus and beach palms, gardenias, purple ganzias, and pink and white geraniums. A man in grubby workclothes bent over an azalea border.

Mrs. Nixon and her visitor settled in chairs cater-cornered from one another. It was the cocktail hour, five P.M. Manolo Sanchez, who'd been with the Nixons for years, brought in a silver tray holding decanters of bourbon and scotch, glasses, and ice. "I work with the gardeners," Pat Nixon said, sipping her drink. "Sometimes I'm out there six, seven hours a day. Gardening has *almost* kept me sane." She laughed a small laugh. "The first year I went through four pairs of canvas gloves. All that ground cover there," she gestured, "that's where the rose garden used to be."

The visitor blinked, remembering that Pat Nixon, for all her love of gardening, hadn't spent much time in the Rose Garden at the White House. Those grounds had not been a pleasant place what with the war protesters raging just outside the fence, surveillance helicopters whirring above their heads. He could still hear the chanting: *One, two, three, four, we don't want your fuckin' war.*

"How's the president?" he asked.

"He's . . ." Pat Nixon paused, then began again. "He's fine. He's working on his memoirs, you know. Trying to sort it all out." She stopped once more and stared out the window for a bit. Then she brightened. "His health's much better. It was good to hear from you during the phlebitis, the surgery—"

"Yes, well," the visitor murmured.

"We heard from thousands of people, you know. Ordinary people."

"That's good. I'm glad. People *cared,* you know."

Pat Nixon shook her head as if she hadn't heard him. "Dick's illness came so quickly on the heels of our leaving Washington, that the jackals jumped on that too. They said he wasn't really ill, that he was faking so he wouldn't have to appear at the trial.

Haldeman, Erlichman, Mitchell. He almost died, you know. A year and a half ago, and he's only now really recuperated."

"Difficult times," the visitor said. "But I'm glad to hear he's well."

Pat smoothed the fabric of her trousers. "He is *not* well. He will never be well. They will never *let* him be well. They will never let him *be*."

The visitor nodded. What Pat Nixon said was true. Richard Nixon had always been a lightning rod for hatred. (Or was it his self-hatred that attracted even more ill will?) A wag he had once read said that while JFK represented America's dreams, its aspirations, who Everyman wanted to be, Nixon represented what the average American was: sweaty, ill-at-ease, plagued by paranoia and self-doubt.

Pat Nixon said, "Judge Sirica sent a team of three doctors from Washington to examine him to make sure he was too ill to testify."

"I remember. That was inexcusable."

From somewhere down a far hall, a clock sounded the quarter hour. When its tolling was done, silence crept through the house once more like a cold fog.

Silence was the thing that had struck him most about the Nixons over the years. He'd flown with them several times in the helicopter up to Camp David and watched them sit side-by-side the entire trip without saying a single word. No one else had dared to speak: the doctor, the Secret Service guys, the military aide. They'd been very awkward journeys.

It had been like that in the White House too. The Nixons had led almost completely separate lives. The president rarely ate dinner with his wife. He didn't consult her about matters which should have fallen into her purview—menus, entertainment for state affairs—and certainly not policy matters.

The visitor had asked her once, "Does the president try out speeches on you?" Pat Nixon had answered, "He never tries anything out on me."

It was ironic, he thought. For while Nixon was a whiz at speaking extemporaneously, he *looked* so miserable and so *phony*, that no matter how well-informed he was, his public appearances were always a disaster. Whereas Pat, who detested public speaking, was fabulous at it. She conveyed warmth and sincerity, the generosity of spirit that was truly hers, without turning a hair. When she went to South America on her own, after the Lima quake, they'd loved her. Just as they'd applauded her in Africa, as a *person*, as an ambassador of her country's and her own goodwill.

Perhaps, he thought, there was the crux of it. Pat Nixon loved people, loved helping people, but she *hated* politics, politicians, and the whole political process. Whereas, while Nixon was *interested* in people, *fascinated* by them, in fact, his interest was cool and detached, as if he were a Martian, *studying* humans. Socially inept and horrible at small talk, he *adored* the political arena.

"You know," Pat said now, her voice soft, with the sound of the faraway in it, "that very first election, when Dick ran for Congress in 1946, I sold my part of our family farm in Artesia to my brother Tom for three thousand dollars. We spent most of the money printing pamphlets to introduce Dick to the voters."

The visitor remembered. She'd told him this story before. But he nodded, Go on.

"And I was so naive, that was before I learned how *vicious* politics can be, that I was thrilled when a labor leader requested fifty pamphlets. I didn't realize that he was the opposition, that he'd use the pamphlets against us, or at best, throw them in the trash. But Dick was already wiser than I to the way these things worked, and he said I had to suspect everyone. So the next time there was a large request, I questioned the caller and got him to fess up that he was a Democrat.

"And you know, it wasn't long after that our campaign office was broken into. They took *all* the pamphlets that my money had paid for, every last one of them we hadn't yet distributed. We had such a slim chance of winning that election. No one knew Dick. We desperately needed those pamphlets. But did anyone care about *our* break-in?" She shook her blond head. "No, of course not. No one knew how devastating the loss of those pamphlets was to us. No wonder I couldn't understand the fuss over Watergate. By that time, I knew all too well the way the game was played. How could *anyone* think that this wasn't business as usual?" She paused, then added. "No, people have no idea."

Her visitor said, "I just read an article the other day about a young congressman who came to Washington thinking it was all about limos and parties and making *momentous* decisions."

Pat's laughter was not a pretty sound. "Thought

he was going to make a *difference*, did he? Well, you know," she said, settling again into her chair, "that's what Dick and I thought, back at the beginning. That first term, he threw himself into the work. There was the Alger Hiss case, and, of course, the Committee on Un-American Activities, and Dick was trying so hard to drum up support for the Marshall Plan, to help the Europeans who were starving after the war, we didn't even *discuss* whether or not he would run for office in '48. It was never a question. It was simply a given. You run. You run until you can't run anymore."

She paused. "Of course, while Dick was routing out Communists and taking care of the world, and working for the Dewey candidacy of '48, I was home in California, pregnant with Julie, taking care of Tricia, who was a baby, and looking after Dick's parents, both of whom were in failing health. Plus they were going through a terrible patch with that little farm of theirs. It was a hard time. I finally told Dick how hard it was. I said that I needed him to be around a little more." She ran her right thumb over the fingers of her left hand, glancing off her wedding band. "You know what he did? He wrote me a letter. In it he said that he'd try to spend more time at home."

Then Pat Nixon stood and turned and looked out past the gardener, out to sea, out at the horizon. "He was so caught up in it all. He was going to do such great things. Though I think I saw from that first election, back in '46, how hard it would be to actually accomplish good. I saw that politics were more complicated than that. That they'd never let us . . ." She paused. "Let *him* accomplish much of anything, or if they did, it would be at a terrible price. But it wasn't *us* anymore, you know. Not what *we* wanted. Dick stopped listening to me in that very first race. He thought his political consultant knew more than I did."

She strode back and forth before the window now. The visitor was struck by how thin she was—and how tightly wound. "Those people, those *consultants*. There are thousands of them, of *you*, a never-ending army of advisors and handlers and counselors. All with your own agendas. With your lists. All wanting to *play*. You wanted to play, didn't you? To play at politics?"

"Yes, I did," the visitor said. "I did."

"Why?" She'd wheeled and thrown the word at him.

He found himself startled. *Why?* Why had he wanted to participate in the Big Game? No one had ever asked him that before. No one, in all those years . . .

Pat was smiling at him, her head canted to one side. "Don't try to answer," she said. "I know you can't, because the answer is a part of who you are. That kind of lust is in your blood. You *have* to play. You start out saying, telling yourself, that it's about honor or nobility or governance or justice or the will of the people. Like Dick, you may start out believing that. But before long, you *have* to see the truth. You have to recognize that politics is nothing more than one long powerplay. An exercise in ego." She held up her hands. Empty. Then she plopped back in her chair. "You know what I think? That you ought to play at politics in an arena. Strip down, then use your fangs and claws and bludgeons, your skill at dirty tricks, your fists, your feet. Just go ahead and get filthy, knee-deep in blood and sweat. Stomp on your opponent's throat, then listen for the crowd's roar. Do it out in the fresh air, where everyone can see. Stand proud and show your hands, covered in shit and blood. All of you, Republicans, Democrats, whatever you call yourselves, what difference does it make? You are *politicians*." Pat Nixon spat the last word off her tongue as if it were a bug which had crept into her drink.

Her visitor sat. He had no response.

Now Pat Nixon was on her feet again, her posture as ramrod straight as it had always been. He'd forgotten how pretty she was. Even now, at sixty-four, she was still quite lovely, with young flashing eyes, the eyes of a girl whose father, Will, a goldminer, had nicknamed Babe. Her pale gold hair would be as close as Will Ryan ever got to the real thing.

"Pat Buchanan," she said. "Pat told them at the hearings that *everyone* was knee-deep in muck. Those high-and-mighty Democrats, sitting there in judgment as if *their* souls were saved, asked him what he'd do in the way of political tactics, and he said, 'Anything that is not immoral, unethical, illegal, or unprecedented in previous Democratic campaigns.'" Pat Nixon clapped her hands together. "Oh, I *loved* that. But no one wanted to hear it. They were out for Dick's blood, and they didn't want to hear that *everyone* was guilty. The FBI operations under Kennedy and Johnson were *much* more serious. They didn't want to know how Kennedy *stole* the 1960 election from us. *Stole* it. He did." Pat Nixon's voice rose as she warmed to her subject like a revival minister under the big tent, the hot lights. "That LBJ bugged the 1968 campaign plane. That Bobby Kennedy used *everything* he could put his hands on to get Jimmy Hoffa. That Adlai Stevenson's workers bugged JFK at the '56 convention. That JFK *in peacetime* tapped well over a hundred individuals, *way* more than the wartime Nixon administration. Did they want to hear that LBJ had wiretaps on Bobby Kennedy and Martin Luther King at the Democratic Convention? That Bobby in turn tapped King? That FDR's son John once said to a columnist, 'Hell, my father just about invented bugging. He had them spread all over, and thought nothing of it.' That Roosevelt had taps on Charles Lindbergh? No, of course not." She slowed now, and her voice dropped, almost to a whisper. "It all depends on which side you're on, doesn't it? The *Washington Post* adored publishing papers stolen from the senatorial committee investigating Watergate. It all depends on *which* office you're burglarizing, doesn't it?"

Yes, he agreed. It does. It did. It will.

"The *Post*," Pat Nixon repeated. "The goddamned *Washington Post*." Then she said, "Have you read it?"

He nodded. *The Final Days.* He knew that's what she meant. *Post* reporters Bob Woodward and Carl Bernstein's new book about Nixon's last days in the White House. The same reporters who had so doggedly pursued the story of the Watergate break-in. Who had broken story after incriminating story about the president and the president's men.

"They're all over the TV," she said. "The two of

them, gloating about that piece of trash. We can't even watch 'Bonanza' without running into them."

Pat turned then and fixed her eyes upon her visitor. "If you read the book carefully, you can see it. You know that, don't you?"

He shook his head. "No, that's not true. I really don't think so. Well, maybe, if you knew what to look for. But like I told you, back then, and I'm telling you now, no one's ever going to know."

Pat Nixon's hand trembled slightly as she lowered her glass of bourbon to the tabletop. "Not that it made any earthly difference what we did, of course. Nothing could have turned things around, not once they smelled blood."

"Absolutely. But you should never regret any of it. You did what you could, and that's what's important."

"What I *could*?" Her laughter spiraled high. "What could I *ever* do? Once I made the decision to stick it out, not to divorce him, back in 1962, I'd made my bed, hadn't I? Then, after he lost California. After that . . . well, it was over, really. We didn't talk. We didn't have *any* kind of real relationship." She lifted her drink again and took a long pull. "I was just along for the ride. For the girls. For appearances. And I did a little good for a few people."

"A little! You did wonders."

"No, no," she waved him off. "Even if I had, if I did help a few, nobody wanted to know about it. Even that business about trying to fix up the White House, that most *ladylike* of tasks. It was worn, you know. Filthy with those millions of visitors and hundreds of parties, but Lady Bird was smart, knew better than to try to touch a thing. And when I set to it, they *screamed*. I had *dared* to touch Jackie's handiwork."

"Yes, but in the end, you did so much more than she did in the White House. All those wonderful antiques. Twice as many as she acquired."

Pat shook her head. "It doesn't matter. *I* enjoyed it. And I was glad to do it. And Jackie herself was so sweet, *she* could see what I'd done with the house, when I arranged for her and the children to come and visit that time, to see her portrait. The children hardly remembered the place. She was quite lovely, you know."

He nodded. "She knew how hard it was for you. And she could have told you, even when you didn't see it, that people loved you. They did. All those children you visited and helped . . ."

Pat raised a hand. "Do not," she said, her voice clipped and low and dangerous, with long spaces between each word. "Do not patronize me. They hated me. I was attached to Dick, and no matter what I did, they'd hate me for that. They presumed . . ." Her voice broke. She stopped. Then she said, the words like shards of glass, "They called me Plastic Pat."

"I'm sorry," he said. "The last thing on earth I'd want to do is bring all that . . ."

Her head jerked up. That carefully coifed head. The only time she'd ever appeared in public with her hair undone was the day Nixon resigned. She said, "But that's why you're here, isn't it? To talk about our feeble plan. Our attempt . . . To remind me how stupid I was, thinking that I could save us some shred of dignity by siccing Woodward and Bernstein on some of those horrible little men. Those *insects.* Those bottom feeders." Her lip curled with disgust. "Why did we think that if we fed them bits of the story, of what *we* knew, or at least *I* knew, that they would stay away from Dick?" She waved her hand in front of her chest, above her heart. "That they would leave us alone? That they would go off on another track? That they would *desist?* All it did was unlock doors and open closets I didn't even know existed."

"It was a good plan," he said. "It was. It was solid." As he said the words, he was back in a dark parking garage in the middle of the night reliving the subterfuge, the fright, the cloak and dagger silliness of it all. And the sweat. Jesus, how long had he lived in his own stink? "It just didn't work."

"Because of those damned tapes," she hissed. "My God! Those tapes!"

"They were bad," he agreed. "Very bad."

She closed her eyes. "They killed us. Dick was so stupid. Those goddamn tapes. After that, well . . ." She shook her head. "There was nothing we could do, was there? Didn't matter how many times you met with Woodward, that son of a bitch, what you told him, who you sacrificed. *Deep Throat!*" She hooted suddenly, her face merry with laughter. "Dick was *offended* by that, you know. As much as by the leak, he was offended by the image. For all of his language, he's such a prude." She laughed again, and he could see, just for a moment, the fun-loving girl she'd once been. But he had to correct her on one point.

"We weren't a leak," he said. "We were a counter-offensive."

"Oh," she sighed, "we thought so. *I* did, anyway. I thought for the longest time the mess was all their fault. The plumbers, the Cubans, Haldeman, all of them out of control, acting on their own. I thought Dick was above all that, that he didn't know." She knocked back the last of her drink and reached for the crystal decanter of bourbon which Manolo had left on the silver tray. "What was I thinking? How *could* Dick not have known where every single body was buried?" She poured herself two fingers, three. "And to think that he did *nothing* to protect us. That he *recorded* it all. Was he *mad?*"

The visitor shook his head silently. He had no answers. He never had.

"No," Pat Nixon said. "Dick wasn't crazy. At least, not in the way you think. He made those tapes to prove to himself that he was president."

"I beg your pardon?"

"You heard me. So he could listen to them in the privacy of his study and know that he was *really* the president of the United States."

"Surely—" he began, but Pat Nixon cut him off.

"You don't think I'm going to let you get away with this, do you?" She was suddenly standing again, turning toward the huge plate glass window with her drink.

On the other side of the glass, the gardener in the scruffy clothes unbent from the white geraniums he'd been tending. In his arms he held a very ugly automatic weapon.

From behind him, three other men—tall, broad-

shouldered, with the short haircuts of the Secret Service—appeared, all armed. They stood still as statues,
their weaponry shining in the late afternoon California sun. It was much too pretty a day to die, the
visitor thought.

"I always knew," Pat said, "that this day would
come. That one afternoon I'd be sitting here reading,
minding what little business of my own I have left,
and you would call and ask to come visiting. With
your hand out."

"My hand is not out," he said. "You've misread
me."

She leaned forward. "Do not screw with me. Don't
even try. I've been screwed over by much bigger men
than you." She may have been a schoolteacher back
in Whittier, but this day, she spoke like a general.

"I assure you—"

"Do not assure me. Do not lie to me. And most of
all, do not threaten me."

He nodded, very slightly, not wanting to alarm the
armed men on the other side of the glass. "It seems
to me that *you're* the one doing the threatening."

"No. I am simply telling you the way things are.
These men are loyal to me. I have told them a story
about you which they believe because they *want* to
believe it. Because they want to think that they are
on the right side. That there *is* a right side. And that
their lives make sense. These years. Watergate. The
whole thing has been *such* a goddamned mess. It
would be good for them, a catharsis, don't you see,
if they could *kill* someone. To take slow and deliber-
ate aim and *kill* someone. Do you know what I
mean?"

He nodded slowly. Yes, he did. He knew exactly what she meant. He had often thought the same thing. How satisfying it would be to string someone up. The Roman arena idea she had, that was precisely the ticket. A public execution, a bloodletting in the open air, that's what they needed so they could begin to forget about the waste and the ruin and the stupidity. *Then* they could begin to see a little daylight. To feel better about themselves.

But, in the absence of that, he'd thought, a little money might be nice. After all, things had gotten rough. A little silver in his palm . . .

He could see now that he'd been wrong.

Pat Nixon watched him nod and said, "Good. That's good. Now, here's what you do. You will pick yourself up and you will go away and you will never *ever* again in your lifetime bother any of us again. For if you do, do not misunderstand or underestimate what I'm saying to you, they," she turned and smiled through the glass at the men, still at ready-alert, "will track you down and eat you. Do you understand what I'm saying? *Eat you.*"

"I understand," he said. And then, very slowly, very carefully, his hands out from his sides to show that he was unarmed, that he meant no harm, no, not really, he was innocent as a babe, the visitor backed out of the room. Then he turned and ran as hard as he could.

Pat Nixon offered the Secret Service men a small smile and a nod which, in lieu of blood, they accepted. Then they saluted sharply and withdrew.

Whereupon Pat Nixon returned to her chair, freshened her drink, and picked up her book, a Taylor

Caldwell novel of international intrigue, of plots and counterplots and conspiracies. Once more the silence enveloped the many rooms of the rambling house. Deep deep inside somewhere, in a dim quarter, Richard Milhous Nixon pored over his papers, hashed and rehashed, twisted and turned, and stewed. Pat Nixon had never visited that room, nor would she ever. Back in her bright, flowered perch above the sea, Pat Nixon found the page where she'd left off reading and resumed the story of imaginary people running, running, running. She settled into her chair and reached for her glass, secure in the knowledge that, at long last, her own running was done.

SARAH SHANKMAN

***

SARAH SHANKMAN is the author of the comic Samantha Adams crime series as well as other novels, including *I Still Miss My Man But My Aim Is Getting Better*. President of the international organization "Women Who Move Too Much," she is at home in the Bay Area or Manhattan or Santa Fe.

Sarah says: "It was perversity, I think, which attracted me to writing about Pat Nixon. As a child of the sixties and a lifelong Democrat, I naturally considered Richard Nixon to be the Enemy. But I felt sorry for Pat and have wondered about her life with Nixon, especially her years in exile. Also, I recently saw Carl Bernstein, a longtime acquaintance, who, of course, along with Bob Woodward, broke the Watergate story for the *Post*. And I thought, Watergate. Now, what if . . ."

THE BACHELOR'S WIFE

~~~

JUDITH KELMAN

December 4, 1856

My dear son Edgar,

With the holidays close upon us, I find myself mired in a deepening state of melancholy. Dr. Pettigrew has been most attentive, visiting daily to assess my condition and administer revivifying tonics, but I fear that he shall soon become discouraged by the resolute nature of my malaise.

I have searched my heart for the root of my intractable distress, and I can only conclude that it stems from the agonizing concerns you have caused me with your appalling change of occupation. As you are no doubt aware, Edgar, your father and I have endeavored to provide you with every advantage. We have made extraordinary sacrifices on your behalf, despite your striking lack of ability or achievement in any area of enterprise, whatsoever.

One would have hoped that, by now, you would

have come to accept your obvious limitations and seek guidance from those of superior means. But for some inexplicable reason, you insist on exercising your own highly questionable judgment. To surrender a position with Mr. Allan Pinkerton's National Detective Agency for a station so impermanent and demeaning is simply beyond my powers to comprehend. What can you be thinking, Edgar? Have you no regard for your family's wishes? Have you no consideration for the wife and issue you shall someday certainly choose to have?

Speaking of which, I must remark (though, as you know, it is not in my nature to burden you with my woes) that my suffering has been sorely intensified by the knowledge that you have offered yourself in service to a person of such dubious merit. As if being a Democrat and an attorney were not sufficient cause for dismay, I am given to understand that your Mr. James Buchanan is of that unspeakable persuasion that defies the natural laws of God: a Presbyterian. Tell me this is not so, Edgar. Spare me this crushing indignity at the very least.

Further, there is the matter of your employer's personal life. Surely you recognize the unfortunate example Mr. Buchanan sets with his refusal to conform to basic standards of acceptable comportment. Suppose the impressionable youth of our nation took his blatant embrace of bachelorhood as a suggestion that they, too, forego the rectitude and comforts of holy matrimony. Suppose the upcoming generation chose to emulate his unthinkable avoidance of the boundless joys and blessed obligations of parenthood (insofar as the offspring are not without redeeming virtue as is sometimes, tragically, the case). No doubt even you can *envision the cataclysmic consequences that would ensue if Mr. Buchanan's unconscionable preferences were embraced by polite society at large.*

I am in receipt of your recent letter in which you indicate that professional duties may preclude you from joining us in celebration this Christmas. Fortunately, my neighbor, Mrs. Worthington, was visiting when the note arrived and chanced to break my sudden fall. Dr. Pettigrew has warned that I must be hospitalized at once should such an episode recur, but you must not concern yourself. Such are the expected vicissitudes of aging, enfeebled parents. We must endeavor to bear our children's ingratitude bravely.

I cling to the comforting realization that my suffering, and that of your father, will soon come to a natural, final end. I trust that knowledge brings you some small measure of comfort as well, Edgar. Soon, very soon, you shall be free to enjoy the fruits of our lifelong toil and self-abnegation without any bothersome familial obligations.

As ever holding your interests and happiness above my own meager, failing reserves, I remain your selfless, adoring,

Mother

P.S. Your darling sister sends her regards. Needless to say, Dorothea is, as always, a pleasure and a joy. Her divine husband and beautiful, talented children provide us with such a source of pride. In them, praise the Lord, we are blessed.

Edgar Granby clipped the offending letter to the line and fed it to the distant end of the practice range. He leveled his brand new breech-load Smith &

Wesson revolver and, sighting with extraordinary care, emptied all seven chambers in rapid succession. Retrieving the page, he noted with considerable satisfaction that three of the bullets had pierced the *o* in "Mother" and one had torn away the *M*.

His aim was dead on, unassailable. Normally, Mother's carping reduced him to a quivering mass of insecurities. But this time, he was armored against her barbs. Soon, Mother would be forced to revise her opinion of the president-elect and of Edgar himself. Soon, very soon, she would come to recognize that his new position had been a most fortunate choice after all.

Not that the choice had been precisely Granby's to make. Though Mother was unaware of the facts, Edgar had been dismissed by the pompous Mr. Allan Pinkerton. The charge was cowardice, of all things, an entirely unreasonable contention.

Granby had been assigned to attend the security of a wealthy client's daughter. One day, the girl's former beau, an apelike man with a venomous temper—and a knife—paid an unwanted call. Granby might have shot the bounder, which would have been the easy way out, but total disengagement seemed the far wiser course. To that end, he'd hidden behind the latrine until the boorish man wearied of his ignoble enterprise and left the premises. Mr. Pinkerton had fired him forthwith, refusing to hear Granby's explanation. No serious injuries had been sustained, after all. The girl's hair would grow back in due course. Edgar felt confident that his actions had been entirely beyond reproach. And so they were now.

Granby could barely wait to hear Mother's fawning apologies, though wait he must. As a member of Mr. Buchanan's personal staff at the country estate known as Wheatland, he was entrusted with highly sensitive information and honor-bound to respect the confidence. Edgar had been among the first to learn that Old Buck (as he was known to privileged insiders) was planning a surprise guaranteed to elevate the nation's sagging spirits and divert attention from the mounting tensions between North and South.

The news would spark joy and celebration. Pro- and antislavery forces would be moved to set aside their differences and unite to fete the country's new leader. Hopefully, the truce would prove a permanent end to secessionary rumblings. At the very least, the lull in hostilities would offer an opportunity for constructive discourse toward an effective compromise on the vexing slavery issue.

Granby drew a bracing breath and smiled. Romance in the Rose Garden. Betrothal in the Blue Room. A wedding in the White House: sheer brilliance.

The plan had required considerable risk and sacrifice on Mr. Buchanan's part. The president-elect had met Constance Latham three years ago, while serving as Minister to the Court of Saint James. The ginger-haired young beauty had been touring the Continent after graduation from an Eastern normal school. She was an orphan, reared by a maiden aunt. Otherwise, little was known of her. Perhaps, it was her air of mystery that captivated the elusive bachelor. For years, countless young ladies had pursued Mr. Buchanan to no avail, but he had proved powerless against the fetching Constance Latham.

Through his close acquaintance with Queen Victoria, Old Buck had arranged for Miss Latham's attendance at various court functions. Smitten though he was, he had held himself at decorous arm's length. Few even suspected the powerful bond of affection growing between the pair.

Had he returned to his native Pennsylvania with a lovely bride in tow, Mr. Buchanan would have silenced those, like Edgar's mother, who found his unmarried status abhorrent and argued against his suitability to hold high office. As a married man, his popular mandate would have grown exponentially. But Old Buck had placed the good of the nation above his personal ambitions. Like Granby, Mr. Buchanan was never one to take the easy way out.

Over the next four months, Miss Latham would be introduced with all due deliberation, first to Mr. Buchanan's closest friends and advisors and then to the public at large. During that time, she would be prepared for the countless duties, rights, and strictures of her future station as First Lady of the land.

The nuptials would take place shortly after the inauguration on the fourth of March. With her beauty and reputed charms, Constance Latham was bound to achieve instant, unparalleled popularity. The wedding and the bride would be Mr. Buchanan's gifts to the nation he held so dear.

Those gifts held special significance for Edgar. This very morning, he had been summoned to the library where Old Buck was encamped, working on the transition and his inaugural address. There, the president-elect, dressed to the jowls in stiffly formal attire as usual, had humbly requested that Edgar assume the position of chief personal assistant to the future First Lady, charged with her comfort and security. Granby would have oversight and intimate knowledge of Miss Latham's every move. He would be privy to her conversations, able to observe her daily routines, exposed to her particular quirks and mannerisms.

Edgar could well imagine how the tenor of Mother's regard and correspondence would change once she learned of his new responsibilities.

How proud you've made us, Darling Edgar. To think that a son of mine has daily access to the lovely Constance Buchanan. Who but my wonderful boy could be more deserving of such trust?

Do tell, Edgar darling. What does the First Lady plan to wear next month when the French minister comes to call? How does she get on with Mr. Buchanan's niece, Harriet Lane? Are the rumors of rivalry between the women true? And most crucial: Are her vivid red tresses natural or dyed?

I do hope that you are able to set time aside from your demanding schedule to see to yourself, Edgar. Your father and I love and adore you completely and pray daily for your continued happiness, health, and success.

With deep and abiding love and affection,
Mother

P.S. Your sister Dorothea is muddling through as best she can with her modest family and mundane existence, poor dear.

An insistent tap on the shoulder shattered Edgar's reverie. Turning, he faced the florid, rotund Percy Maxwell, Mr. Buchanan's valet.

The servant was huffing hard, sweating despite the chill. "I've been dispatched to bring you to Wheatland at once, Mr. Granby."

"What's wrong?"

"Something to do with Miss Latham. Please, Sir. Follow me."

Granby's heart stammered as he trailed the plump, little man toward the waiting carriage. He could not bear the thought that some misfortune might have befallen Mr. Buchanan's fiancée. The young woman had arrived at Wheatland less than a week ago with countless trunks and a retinue of three cloaked servants and had taken immediately to her rooms. Since then, there had been barely a sign of her save the odd flurry of activity from the guest wing and her maid's regular appearance in the kitchen at mealtime to fetch Miss Latham's tray. The others on Miss Latham's staff prepared and took their meals in the small kitchen abutting the guest suite, and so remained largely invisible as well. Mr. Buchanan visited Miss Latham's quarters each evening after work, and she had been spied by Farraday, the gatekeeper, taking solitary late night strolls through the gardens. Otherwise, the young woman and those in her employ remained a tantalizing mystery.

"What is it, Maxwell? Is Miss Latham ill?" Granby asked.

"All I was told was it's urgent, Sir. Hurry please." With a grunt, the valet hefted his puffy form into the waiting carriage. Granby leaped in beside him, and the driver sped off toward the Buchanan estate.

Granby's mind spun like the large spoked wheels. He considered the direst possibilities: illness, an unfortunate accident, a sudden change of heart about the betrothal.

Or worse, perhaps Miss Latham was with child. From the trays prepared for her consumption, Granby had observed that the young woman was partial to exorbitant portions of the rarest roasts and elaborate sweets in grand quantities. Given the barren plates returned by her maid to the kitchen, one could see that she was of robust appetite, indeed.

His heart squirmed like a beached fish. *Lord, no.* Mother's torments would know no bounds if his employer were beset by such a scandal. Anything but that, Granby thought. He could imagine no circumstance more devastating.

The ride to Wheatland seemed an eternity, though the property was a mere mile and a half from the target range in Lancaster. Granby's anxieties rose by degrees, reaching feverish heights as the driver turned in at the gatehouse and crossed the field toward the sprawling Federal-style mansion.

Mrs. O'Flannagan, the cook, clad in a black frock, white lace apron, and muffin-shaped hat, greeted them in the foyer. "Thanks be, you're here, Mr. Granby," she trilled in her dense Kerry brogue. "Sure, and only one who's dealt with dangerous louts and deadly murderers might be up to the likes of this."

"What's the problem?"

"*Problem* doesn't begin to cover the question, Mr.

Granby. You'd best go see for yourself." She called for the parlor maid, "Grace-Marie!"

In seconds, a slight, obsequious girl appeared. She was a homely thing with a wall eye and a limp. "Yes, Mrs. O'Flannagan. How might this humble waif be of service to you, Ma'am?"

"You can stop your bootlicking and show the gentleman upstairs. I've got supper to tend."

"Sure, and I'll be delighted to, Ma'am. A pleasure, really. Please, follow me, Mr. Granby, Sir. Right this way, Sir. Mind your footing."

From overhead came a jarring thud. There followed a shriek, then a series of sharp reports like gunfire. The cacophony intensified as Granby trailed the maid down the mazelike second-story corridor toward the guest suite at the rear. Soon, distinct sounds emerged. The clatter of breaking glass. A feline hiss. The shrill of a predatory bird. Had Granby been asked to guess the source, he would have opined that a wild beast had somehow gained access to the house.

And he would have been correct.

As they approached the suite, the door burst open, and a shoe of cerulean *peau de soie* shot forth. Granby ducked in reflex, and the pointed heel of the shoe barely missed his astonished eye.

Slowly, he rose, arms caged protectively about his head. "Get back, Grace-Marie," he ordered. "I'll see to this."

The parlor maid limped out of harm's way down the corridor. Granby drew his revolver and crouched in the shadows outside the suite. "Hands up in there. No sudden moves."

A porcelain vase whizzed past his ear and shattered against the wall. Rose petals rained on the antique Aubusson rug, and a stain, shaped like darkest Africa, over-spread the flocked wallcovering. There followed, in rapid succession, a second shoe, a silver hair brush, and a stream of pirate-quality invectives.

"Hands up, I say," Granby demanded again.

From the room came an ungodly growl and a stream of foul-smelling liquid. Granby recoiled in horror. Whatever had invaded these quarters had to be expelled immediately. Poor Miss Latham must be terrified. Spurred by duty, Granby set his terror aside, covered his nose, and girded for a frontal assault.

"Never fear, Miss Latham. I shall protect you. Stay down. I'm coming in."

Granby crossed himself and rushed the room. He whirled from side to side, flailing his revolver, seeking the crazed marauder.

The guest suite was in horrifying disarray. Glorious frocks of silk and taffeta were tossed about like casualties of war. Lacy bloomers hung, as if they'd been lynched, from the Venetian glass chandelier. Broken glass and crockery crunched underfoot. Large, ugly spatters marred the walls.

Miss Latham, clad in a fetching blue velvet gown with a full skirt, low-cut bodice, and muttonchop sleeves, sat on the bed. She was ashen and had a stunned air about her. Her maid, a sow-eyed girl, cowered in the corner.

"What's going on in here?" asked Granby.

The maid's fat-lipped mouth fell open, but no sound, save a tiny whimper, emerged. Scullery scuttlebutt had it that the girl was a mute. And from the trapped look in her eyes, Granby took the rumor to be true. He felt a flutter of attraction. After Mother, the notion of a silent woman held considerable appeal.

He knelt beside Miss Latham and gentled his tones. "My dear lady. What happened? Are you all right?"

She blinked. "Who are you?"

"Edgar Granby at your service, Miss Latham. Mr. Buchanan has engaged me to look after you."

Her bosom heaved with an extravagant sigh. "Well done, Mr. Granby. You frightened her off."

"Her?"

"Emily, my hairdresser. She went out the window and raced into the woods."

A meager patch of lawn separated the rear of the house from a dense copse of poplar and beech. The fleeing assailant was out of sight by now. As Granby crossed toward the window to get a closer view, a frigid blast billowed the organdy curtains. "Good God, Rosalie. Close that window before Miss Latham catches her death of cold." Granby tossed his frock coat over Miss Latham's shoulders. "Be quick about it."

The maid shut the mullioned panels and flipped the locks.

"That's better." Striding slowly about, Granby surveyed the wreckage. There was a broken vase, a ragged gash in the portrait of Mr. Buchanan's mother, two legs crudely amputated from a Chippendale chair. All manner of refuse was tossed about. "My word, Miss Latham. What put your hairdresser in such a state?"

"I honestly can't say, Mr. Granby. One moment

she was fashioning my chignon; the next, she was whirling in a fearsome rage. It came upon her suddenly."

"How terrifying for you."

Miss Latham shrugged. "This is not the first fit of violent temper Emily has had. It seems she suffers from some ailment of the mind."

"Is she under the care of a physician?"

"No, but her mother was diagnosed with lunacy and confined to an asylum when Emily was a small girl. I was warned that such afflictions can be mysteriously passed among members of a family. But none of that is of particular interest to me. All I care about is Emily's way with my coiffeur. The girl is devilishly clever. A treasure, really."

Miss Latham patted her glorious hair. The sight inflamed Granby's blood. He had never been so near a lady of such breathtaking visage. Stray ginger curls framed a sculpted face inset with emerald eyes and a full-lipped, insouciant mouth. She was possessed of a lithe neck and comely form. Two hands would have spanned her tiny waistline. A trim ankle peeked out from beneath her lace-trimmed hem. So did a pointed shard of glass.

Granby swooped to retrieve the dangerous spike, scrupulously avoiding accidental contact with Miss Latham's flesh. Surely, he'd fall in a swoon if he so much as grazed that creamy softness.

Granby coughed to clear his voice of emotion. "Thank heavens no harm befell you, Miss Latham. Nor shall it while I am charged with your safety. I shall see to your hairdresser's dismissal at once. And to the immediate restoration of your quarters."

Granby bowed, flaring his waistcoat in courtly fashion. "Now, if you'll excuse me." Turning on his heel, he strode through the rubble toward the door.

"Wait, Mr. Granby. Stop!" Miss Latham cried. "I simply cannot do without Emily, and I will certainly *not* permit her dismissal."

"Be reasonable, Miss Latham. A person given to such capricious behavior cannot be in the employ of the president- and First Lady-elect."

"That would fly in the face of fact, Mr. Granby. Emily *is* in our employ."

"Yes, but you don't understand."

"No, *you* don't. Emily's services are critical to my well-being. If she goes, so do I."

Granby thought to argue further, but her resolute guise froze his tongue. He nodded stiffly.

An odd grin lit Miss Latham's face. "How lovely that we understand each other, Mr. Granby. Have no fear. I shall see to Emily. Most assuredly things will proceed smoothly from here on."

Several days did pass without incident. Then again, Granby was summoned to quash a commotion in the guest suite stirred by the explosive hairdresser. As before, the girl raced off as Edgar arrived and sought refuge in the woods. He had hoped that her behavior could be tempered by a sound dressing-down, but the opportunity was denied him.

Miss Latham sat amid the rubble like a perfect rose. Once again, Granby sought to reason with her. "Please, dear lady. The entire nation would be tossed in chaos should any harm befall you or Mr. Buchanan. As our future First Lady, you must take a broader view."

"No harm shall befall me, Mr. Granby. I am perfectly capable of managing Emily's little outbursts."

"But she is unstable, Miss Latham. You've said so yourself. Persons of such unreliable nature are confined to asylums for a reason, are they not? The safety of the public cannot be placed at risk to secure the freedom of lunatics. And the safety of the president and First Lady most certainly must not. I am sure Mr. Buchanan would agree."

Her lovely face warped with rage. "Mr. Buchanan is to hear nothing of this, Edgar Granby. Do you *hear* me? Nothing!"

"Yes, Miss Latham. Whatever you say, Miss Latham."

"I say you'd best hold your tongue. Or you'll be the one seeking new employment."

For days, Granby agonized over whether and what to tell Old Buck. If he defied Miss Latham's edict, he risked her wrath and possibly, permanent disaffection. But if he kept still, Old Buck's safety, and the rightful course of history, could be jeopardized.

Edgar was tortured by indecision. His appetite vanished. Sleep eluded him. Wrenching pains in his abdomen caused him to seek relief in narcotizing nostrums that left him weary and befogged.

Thankfully, there was no further disturbance from the guest suite. As another week elapsed without incident, then another, and a third, Granby endeavored to put the distressing matter out of his mind. Perhaps, Miss Latham had found some reliable means to contain the hairdresser's moods. Or perhaps, the future First Lady had taken the sensible route and dismissed Miss Emily on her own. In either case, no action on Granby's part would be required. He kept trying to convince himself that the crisis had passed, but still his weight dropped and his exhaustion deepened and his health deteriorated to the perilous brink of debility. Edgar was so wasted and fatigued, he could barely lift the letter that arrived in the weekly post from home.

December 11, 1856
Edgar, my soon-to-be-former son,

I have prayed for you to come to your senses, but it appears that my entreaties have been for naught. At this juncture, your father and I feel duty bound to alter the terms of our final Testament. Dorothea and her delightful family will surely make laudable use of the sizable proceeds of our estate. Given your inexplicable behavior, I fear you would soon fritter our life savings on questionable enterprises, at best.

As I write, Mr. Sparlingame, our attorney, is preparing the changes. Surely, you realize what grief this causes us, Edgar. Yet again, you leave us shattered and bereaved.

Should you decide to return to Mr. Pinkerton's employ, Father and I might be moved to reconsider. Failing that, you shall be summarily disinherited.

I remain, your long-suffering, galled and appalled,
Mother

P.S. I presume you recall your classmate, Jonathan Rediskew, though he was always so clearly beyond your station. I thought it might interest you to learn that he has recently been named president of Maritime Shipping Enterprises, Inc. Of course, we don't

*expect such lofty accomplishments of you, Edgar.
But surely you can manage some morsel of respectable achievement before your father and I go to our
final reward.*

With his last ounce of strength, Edgar groaned.
And so, it had come to this: their money or his life.
Granby read the note again, clutching his abdomen
to ease the searing pain.

For twenty-nine long years he had borne his
mother's vicious swipes and his father's dogged
inattention. For all that time, he had tolerated their
adoration of his beak-nosed, whiny sister with
saintly restraint. How many times had he resisted
the pressing urge to murder Dorothea in her sleep,
not to mention his parents? Three little shots, and
all his problems would be solved. But he had refused, as usual, to take the easy way out. In so
doing, he had more than earned that damned inheritance. And have it, he would.

Mother would not dare disown him once she
learned of his intimate association with the First
Lady. She would be too greedy for the tasty morsels of gossip Edgar would have in his power to
dispense, the lofty favors Edgar would have in his
power to procure. At long last, the sweet fruits of
power would be his. But first, he needed to secure
his present position, and that meant finding a way
to deal with the matter of Miss Latham's insane
hairdresser.

Taking care to disguise his handwriting, Edgar
wrote a note to forestall the crisis:

18 December 1856

Dear Mrs. Granby,

I am writing at the behest of your son Edgar, who is presently engaged in a highly secret mission and, therefore, unable to contact you himself.

Mr. Granby has asked me to convey his deepest regard and affections and to assure you that nothing would please him more than to be in the bosom of his family during this season of comfort and joy. Sadly, this cannot be.

As you are undoubtedly aware, Mr. Granby is a man of extraordinary courage and valor, who now, as always, feels honor-bound to place duty and country above his personal welfare. Hopefully, he shall not be called upon to make the ultimate sacrifice. I encourage you to offer prayers to that effect.

If God wills it so, Edgar will contact you as soon as is humanly feasible. Otherwise, I'm sure you'll be notified so that you can make final arrangements for the disposal of his humble remains.

Wishing you joy, levity, and merriment in your holiday celebrations, I sign myself in all due sincerity,

Edgar Granby's closest friend and staunchest supporter.

The household was consumed with preparations for the forthcoming holidays and the whirlwind of events to follow. At Christmas, Mr. Buchanan was to introduce Miss Latham to family and friends. On the eve of the New Year, two hundred stolid supporters were expected at Wheatland for a champagne buffet. Afterward, a series of receptions would be held, cul-

minating in the betrothal announcement and a matri-
monial celebration of unprecedented proportions.

Several additional retainers arrived at the estate to
attend Miss Latham's lengthy requirements. A coutu-
rier of international repute was ensconced in the garden room, sketching costumes for the future First
Lady's bridal gown and trousseau. The potting shed
was cleared to accommodate a cutter and seamstress.
Tutors in protocol, diplomacy, ballroom dancing, and
etiquette appeared. Miss Latham received them all,
by strict appointment, in her rooms. Only Rosalie,
the silent servant, passed freely and often between
the guest suite and the household at large.

Observing the maid, Granby began to form a
workable plan. Despite her muteness, Rosalie might
prove a useful ally. Obviously, the future First Lady
had found some means to communicate with the girl.
Otherwise, how would Rosalie understand her lady's
needs and desires?

The idea lifted Granby's spirits. His abdominal
pain vanished, and his appetite returned. Color
bloomed in his cheeks, and he felt a surge of energy.
That night, he fell into a dense, dreamless sleep. At
first light, he awoke fully renewed.

Through a driving snowstorm, Granby trudged the
mile and a half to Wheatland. There, he hid behind
the pantry door until the maid, clad in somber gray
frock and shirred bonnet, returned Miss Latham's
empty breakfast tray. As Rosalie emerged, Granby
sprang forth behind her and clamped a hand over
her mouth. "I need to talk to you."

The girl struggled in his grasp.

"Have no fear. No harm shall befall you if you do as I say. Walk quickly, and keep still."

Stiffly, she followed his commands. Granby ushered her through the rear door and across the small patch of lawn to the woods. There, he sat beside her on a frigid stump.

"I need your help, Rosalie. Miss Latham's hairdresser is not to be trusted. Do you understand?"

The maid's bovine eyes bulged.

"Shake your head once if you understand and twice if you don't. All right?"

The maid's head rose and fell.

"Very well. You are to watch the hairdresser carefully whenever she is in chambers with Miss Latham. Miss Latham must not be left alone with that madwoman for an instant. Is that clear?"

Her chin dipped a fractional inch.

"At the slightest disturbance, you are to send Maxwell to fetch *both* me and Mr. Buchanan at once. Is *that* clear?"

Rosalie's look went quizzical.

"I shall tolerate no uncertainty, young woman. You may consider these orders from the president-elect himself. Now, can I count on your cooperation, or must I advise Mr. Buchanan that you've been insubordinate?"

Rosalie pressed her palms together, beseeching Granby to spare her.

"I take it, then, that we can depend on you?"

She nodded vigorously.

"Very well. You are dismissed."

Rosalie backed out of the copse. She scurried across the frost-laden lawn toward the house. Granby watched with mounting delight. A bird in the hand. His personal ears upstairs. A willing wench in the winter White House. Sheer brilliance.

He saw no way the plan could fail. If the maid summoned Mr. Buchanan directly, Miss Latham could hardly blame Granby for violating her wishes. The president-elect would see to Emily's dismissal himself. Granby's position and, through that, his inheritance, would be assured.

Edgar was positively buoyant. The following morning, he braved the bitter cold and walked to the target range. Looking after the First Lady was a sacred trust. He was determined to keep his defensive skills keen.

Granby drew a crude sketch of his family, clipped it to the line, and fed it by pulley to the far end of the range. He emptied several rounds of ammunition from his breech-load revolver, aiming at Mother's rapier tongue, Father's granite heart, and the wretched little hook nose on his sister Dorothea. Every shot hit its intended mark dead on.

Gleefully, he emptied the spent shells and loaded another round. He was about to fire at Mother again, when a shrill voice from behind called his name.

"Emergency, Mr. Granby. Come quickly!"

Maxwell, the valet, looked a fright. His face was nearly purple, and his barrel chest heaved like a storm-tossed boat. "Something dreadful has happened," he rasped. "Make haste."

"Miss Latham again?"

"I'm afraid so, Sir. Please hurry."

Granby sauntered to the waiting carriage. How lovely that his plan should come to fruition so soon.

He settled in, enjoying the ride. Granby imagined Old Buck in a dreadful lather as he observed the wreckage in the guest rooms. Surely, he would banish the demonic hairdresser from Miss Latham's employ forever.

The valet dithered on, making precious little sense. "Woe is me. The end is nigh. Where shall we go? What will become of us?"

"Good Lord, Maxwell. Calm yourself. We'll go to Wheatland and straighten things out. And as for the end of this particular business being nigh, I say, 'Amen.' "

Moments later, the carriage turned in at the gatehouse. The estate looked quite peaceful, Granby observed. Oddly peaceful, in fact. Not a sign of life on the grounds. Farraday, the gatekeeper, was nowhere in sight. Nor was Lester, the groundskeeper and his crew. Where were the delivery wagons? And where were the carriages filled with staff and advisors that normally came and went in a steady stream all day? Not a single horse was tethered near the main house. Most peculiar, indeed.

Percy Maxwell seemed fit to burst as he led Granby through the deserted foyer to the stairs. No Mrs. O'Flannagan. No parlor maid or scullery maids or butler or—

"Where is everyone, Maxwell?" Granby asked.

The valet stalled in his tracks. "They've been ordered from the premises. I'm to fetch you, direct you to Miss Latham's rooms, and be gone myself. That's all I know, Sir."

Granby felt a thrill of fear, but he endeavored to

appear offhanded. "What sort of emergency do you suppose it is, Maxwell?"

"The kind that's none of my concern and shall remain so. I'll be off now, Mr. Granby. Good luck to you, Sir. Godspeed."

The normally sluggish Maxwell was out the door in a shot. Granby thought to follow, but his duty was clear. He climbed the stairs like a condemned man mounting the gallows. If some harm had befallen Miss Latham, he would never forgive himself. Worse, Mr. Buchanan would never forgive him. Granby would be unemployed, disinherited, doomed.

At the second-story landing, Granby froze. There was a harsh chill. Unnatural silence. The house had been occupied by some dark, evil presence.

Granby forced himself to tread the long mazelike hallway toward the guest rooms. His pulse thundered in his ear. His back was beset by a prickling rash of terror.

Miss Latham's door was shut. Granby knocked with a trembling hand. "Edgar Granby here. May I come in?"

"Yes, Edgar. Please. Come ahead." The voice was Old Buck's, firm and commanding.

Granby gripped the knob and pulled the door ajar. He expected to find a dreadful mess, but inside, all was in pristine order. Mr. Buchanan stood beside the bureau, smoothing a silken garment. Miss Latham sat on the four-poster bed, regal in a turquoise taffeta gown.

Granby tittered with nervous relief. "I'm so delighted to find you both well. Maxwell suggested there might be serious difficulty. Obviously, he was mistaken."

"Obviously," said Constance Latham. "Feel free to leave, Mr. Granby. We have no need of your services at the moment."

"Fine, yes. Wonderful. I'll be on my way."

"Not just yet, Edgar," Old Buck said. "There's a little something I need you to see to for me." He turned to his beloved. "Will you be all right for a moment alone, Constance?"

"Certainly, James."

"Grand. I shall show Edgar the little chore I'd like him to attend and return in a moment."

"Splendid."

Granby followed Old Buck down the hall. The president-elect spoke in a rush as they walked. "There's been a—shall we say—incident, Edgar. A matter of some delicacy and urgency. Can I count on your complete discretion?"

"Of course, Sir."

"I have cleaned the better part of the mess myself. But for obvious reasons, I must not participate in the final disposal, as it were. Here's what needs to be done." He handed Granby a written page of instructions.

Buchanan paused at a storage closet. He pulled the door open, and a girl tumbled out. At once, Granby saw that it was Rosalie, the mute maid. And he saw that she was dead. "Oh my, Sir. What happened?"

"A most unfortunate turn of events, Edgar. It seems Miss Latham has had difficulty with this young woman for some time. Sudden outbursts of temper. Fits of destructive behavior. Apparently, there's madness in her family. Unfortunately, Constance did not wish to tell me about it and see the girl dismissed. My darling felt sorry for her, I suppose. Anyway, Constance has been able to contain things reasonably well in the past. But this time, the violence was directed against her, and she was forced to defend herself. The girl fell in the struggle and sustained a lethal blow to the head. An accident, to be sure. But still a terrible trauma for Constance."

"But this is Rosalie, Mr. Buchanan. The temper outbursts came from Emily, the hairdresser."

"You're mistaken, Edgar. There is no hairdresser. Miss Latham allows absolutely no one to touch her coiffeur. She quite stubbornly insists on attending to it herself."

"All due respect, Mr. Buchanan. There's no mistake. Miss Latham told me all about Emily. Her mother was a lunatic. Confined to an asylum. Miss Latham told me she knew such madness sometimes passed mysteriously from parent to child, but—"

"It was Rosalie, I tell you, Edgar."

"Emily, Sir. I'm absolutely sure."

"Boys, boys." Constance Latham stood in the shadows down the hall. "Tsk, tsk. Bicker, bicker."

"You must return to your room at once, darling. Please," Old Buck said. "You've had a terrible shock."

"Nonsense, James. I'm no shrinking violet." She tossed her head defiantly. "Now what seems to be the dispute?"

Old Buck sighed. "It's nothing, truly. Edgar thought he heard you speak of having difficulty with a hairdresser named Emily. I've explained that you have no hairdresser."

The woman's face changed most dramatically. Her lip curled in a snarl and a saucy glint lit her eye. "The hell she don't," she snarled in guttersnipe cockney.

Granby and Old Buck watched in amazement as the refined Miss Latham swaggered about, hips wagging like a common tart.

"I do the bitch's hair, and I do it right. Every three weeks, I dye that mousy mess of hers red. Every day, morning and night, I brush and dress it 'til you'd never know it was fit for hatching chicken eggs and not much more." She ran her fingers through Old Buck's gray forelock. "Seems you could use me as well, Bucky Boo. Care to take me on?"

Buchanan flushed. "I demand to know the meaning of this, Constance."

"Constance my arse. The name's Emily Wicklow, though I guess they'll be calling me Miss Wicklow once these aching dogs are finally settled in the White House." She slipped off her shoes and showed her bare feet in shameless fashion. "Can't freaking wait."

"Constance, please. Stop that at once!" Old Buck implored.

The woman blinked. Her face settled in repose, and she regained her air of dignified restraint. "Stop what, my darling? Oh my. What's wrong with Rosalie? Poor girl looks dreadful. Is she ill?"

Old Buck's face tensed in a mask of horror. He shot a pointed look Granby's way. "Edgar will see to her, darling," he said. "Come now. You must have your rest."

*   *   *

Granby fought the frozen earth to make a shallow grave. After the mute maid was in the ground, he went to fetch Dr. Williamson, Old Buck's personal physician.

The pair spent two hours in the guest suite, while Granby paced, like a caged cat, in the hall. From time to time, he pressed his ear to the door and tried to divine what was transpiring inside, but the voices were too dim to hear. Finally, the physician left, and Mr. Buchanan summoned Granby into the suite.

Miss Latham was sprawled on the bed, snoring lightly. Granby noticed a vial of sedative and a syringe on the nightstand.

Old Buck sighed. "It appears we have a most serious problem, indeed, Edgar. Dr. Williamson finds that Miss Latham is possessed of a rare mental disorder. In effect, she has two minds, one that functions normally and one given to inexplicable violence."

"How dreadful."

"Indeed."

"It's a good thing you didn't marry her, Mr. Buchanan. The country would be sorely burdened to have a First Lady so afflicted."

"The problem is, I did marry her, Edgar. We were joined in a quiet ceremony last summer. Constance wouldn't hear of coming to Wheatland without benefit of wedlock, though she agreed to keep it secret so the nation could take part in our more public union later on."

"You must divorce her then, Mr. Buchanan. Or have the nuptials annulled. Then, you'll be free to find another bride, one the nation will embrace as a suitable First Lady." One *Mother* will embrace, Granby thought. The nation be damned.

Old Buck sat on the bed beside the lovely, loony Miss Latham. Gently, he smoothed her ginger tresses. "I shall not beleaguer the nation with my wife's illness, Edgar. Neither shall I breach the vows I made to this woman in the sight of God. Dr. Williamson will arrange for Constance's commitment to a private sanitarium of excellent repute. Aside from you, the doctor, and myself, no one must hear of this. Ever."

"But, Sir."

"No buts, Granby. It can be no other way."

"Yes, Mr. Buchanan."

"I can rely on you to keep this in strictest confidence, then?"

"Of course you can, Sir."

"Excellent. Now why don't you take the week off, Edgar? Pass the holidays with your family. Surely, they'll provide the comfort you need in this difficult time. When you return, I'll see what position, if any, I can find for you in the administration."

A searing pain stabbed Edgar's abdomen. Grimacing, he said, "Yes, Mr. Buchanan. Whatever you say."

Granby hobbled from the house and made his halting way toward Lancaster. He was accompanied by dark, jeering despair. His hopes had been dashed, his rightful future stolen by some demonic affliction in Miss Latham's mind.

His gorge rose as he pictured the lawyer rewriting his parents' will, replacing his name as a rightful heir with the damnable Dorothea's. There had to be something he could do, some means of redemption. An unseemly illness could not be the end of this.

Then again, perhaps it could. Possessed of a fresh idea, Edgar smiled. An unseemly illness might well prove the perfect remedy to his woes.

Granby fairly flew back to his rooming house at the outskirts of Lancaster. Poised at the desk, taking care to alter his penmanship, he wrote:

December 23, 1856

Dear Mr. and Mrs. Granby,

It is with a heavy heart that I must inform you that your valiant son has been severely wounded in the line of duty. While the doctors hold out slim hope for his complete recovery, there is some chance that, given the proper care and treatment, he may gain some small measure of relief.

A private sanitarium of excellent repute has agreed to assume the monumental task of his rehabilitation. This is a matter of great good fortune, indeed, given the scarcity of space at this outstanding facility.

I enclose an invoice for the first month's fees. Future payments will be required by the fifth of each month and should be sent in Mr. Granby's name to the above-referred postal station. While the amount is not inconsiderable, I can imagine no nobler purpose than to ease poor Mr. Granby's suffering.

As soon as he is able to communicate again, which may take years, I know your devoted Edgar will express his love and gratitude personally.

I shall keep you apprised of his progress.

Warmest regards.

Chief Director, Secret Essential Operations

Granby walked to town and posted the letter. From there, he strolled to the practice range. He fired at a target with the names of his family members. Three little shots were all it took to dispatch Mother, Father, and Dorothea.

How comforting.

Edgar had no doubt that his brilliant scheme would work. But should it not, he was prepared to take the easy way out, this once.

JUDITH KELMAN

—ᴗᴗᴗ—

JUDITH KELMAN is the author of ten suspense novels, including *Fly Away Home*. Her books have been translated into nine languages and one of them, *Someone's Watching*, was adapted as an NBC movie of the week. She is a former director of the Mystery Writers of America and the American Society of Journalists and she is a member of Sisters in Crime.

Judith says: "Jackie's pillbox, Eleanor's overbite—blah, blah, blah. Oceans of ink have been spilled over such First Lady–related irrelevancies, and yet, historians have inexplicably ignored the tragic and fascinating wife of James Buchanan. The fact that she happens to be fictional seems a lame excuse, indeed. Do you honestly believe Nancy's shoulders? Hillary's brownies? Every one of our First Ladies has been an invention. Constance is mine."

LOST AT SEA

———ɷ———

PAMELA J. FESLER

AT HERBERT HOOVER'S *March 1929 Inauguration, Lou Henry Hoover and Grace Anna Goodhue Coolidge rode together from the White House to the Capitol. The two good friends—one a Stanford-trained geologist, the other a teacher of hearing-impaired children—became lost in a sea of officials and guests who were wandering the corridor. The ceremony was delayed until the women were found.*

What happened to the pair while they were missing?

"Are you hurt, Grace? asked the woman with snowy hair and bright blue eyes. She steadied her tall, slim friend who reached down to brush a large smudge from her left shoe. A broad-shouldered young man in a trench coat and a brown, snap-brim hat elbowed his way through the crush of people, not stopping to apologize for the toe-trodding incident.

"I'm fine, Lou. But I doubt these pumps will ever be the same. Cal will have a fit." It was well known that the thrifty Calvin Coolidge had one weakness: He adored buying his wife expensive clothes and he was picky about how she looked in them.

Lou Henry Hoover chuckled. "He'll buy you another pair, Grace, and give people one more reason to accuse the Republicans of being responsible for the proliferation of raised hemlines and women smokers, bathtub gin and speakeasies, and gang wars between the likes of Bugs Moran and Al Capone. I just wish they'd give us a little credit for the strong economy."

Grace's gray eyes left her friend's face and she looked around the crowd. "Did you see the man who stepped on me?" A wave of people pushed them further into the hall.

"I didn't get a good look at him, Grace. High cheek bones. Hair wavy at the temples. I think he was clean cut in a collegiate way."

"Then in this town he could be either a gangster or a politician. It's difficult to tell the two apart any more. You know how to tell the difference between them, don't you, Lou?" Mrs. Hoover shook her head as the two inched through the crowd.

"If he stabs you from the front, he's a gangster, from the back he's a politician."

"Grace? See that scrawny little man in the blue pinstripe suit with built up shoulders? Is he talking to you? The one over there." Lou Hoover inclined her head to the right. "He's looking at you and he's speaking in sign language, isn't he?"

Grace Coolidge cocked her head and narrowed her

eyes. "Let's see, heart, day, pay, back . . ." Mrs. Coolidge paused.

"What else?"

"Nothing else. Lou, look at him." The little man's face twisted into a mask of cold anger.

Suddenly, his right index finger jabbed out from under his left hand. The finger twisted to the left and as it did, Lou Hoover grabbed Grace Coolidge's arm.

"Grace, does that mean what I think it means?"

"If you think it means kill or murder it does. He's by no means fluent, but he knows how to deliver a message."

"Kill whom, Grace, kill whom?" The little man's fingers moved again.

"Trench coat. Kill trench coat? Ouch!" Grace Coolidge looked down at her right shoe. It matched her left, smudge for smudge.

"Mrs. Coolidge, excuse me for stepping on your toes and intruding on your conversation. I think that message was meant for that snaky-looking gentleman across the hall. The one in the overly tailored brown suit." The young man who'd ruined Grace Coolidge's shoes now stood, hat in hand, beside the women.

The women turned and saw the hooded eyes and quivering nose of a politician from a Midwestern state, a legislator whose views and ideals were as different from the president's as the taste of store-bought margarine from fresh-churned butter.

The politician looked from Mrs. Coolidge to Mrs. Hoover as the young man adjusted the bulge under the arm of his coat. The legislator paled and slithered off through the crowd. At the same time, five nattily dressed men, like salmon swimming upstream, followed the lead of the little guy and washed out the nearest exit.

"Do you know the name of a good shoe repairman?" Mrs. Coolidge asked their companion.

"No, Ma'am. I'm not from these parts. If we were closer to the Great Lakes, I'd know just where to send you, but here, no."

"What a shame. I thought anyone who could send that ignorant reptile of a public servant crawling away would know just about everything."

Lou Hoover laid her hand on Mrs. Coolidge's arm. "Grace, I think this gentleman's one of ours."

Grace Coolidge put a hand over the one on her arm. "Of course he is, dear. Has your trip to Washington, D.C., been worthwhile, young man?"

"I'm not sure, Ma'am. Knowing what our scrawny friend said might help me decide."

"He said the words *heart, day, pay* and *back.*"

"Does that mean anything to you, young man?"

"Yes, Mrs. Hoover, it does."

"Well, then, it hasn't been a wasted trip. I take it you know that little man."

"He's an attorney. Outwardly as clean as a whistle, but pop into a dinner party where Bugs Moran's the guest of honor and you'll find his knees under the table. He's been known to act as an intermediary for Moran. If I were a betting man I'd say we interrupted instructions for revenge for the St. Valentine's Day Massacre."

Both women stared at the young man, who shook his head in disgust.

"Guy's from a hard-working family. They own a

grocery store. Probably learned some sign language from his sister. She teaches at the state school for the deaf. Well, ladies, let's find your husbands."

He began to push through the crowd. Lou Hoover scanned the man's broad, khaki gabardine-covered back and nudged her friend.

"Grace, tell him what else you saw."

"Young man?"

"Yes, Mrs. Coolidge?" he said over his shoulder.

"Are you known by a nickname with these gangsters?"

"Probably nothing printable. Why?"

"Do you always wear this?" Mrs. Coolidge pulled on the material of the man's coat as she spoke.

"Most of the time." He turned and faced the women. "Ladies, what's going on?"

"The little man said three other words: *Kill trench coat.*"

The young man's face became still.

"My dear boy, you cannot leave here alone. You need an escort home." The look on her face and her tone of voice were the same ones she used when her sons were boys and she told them they would wear galoshes when it rained.

"I won't argue with you, Mrs. Hoover."

Two square-shouldered men in high collars appeared directly in front of them. Relief spread over the men's faces. Mrs. Hoover whispered in the ear of the taller of the two.

"Where were you, Grace? Your shoes. What happened?" Calvin Coolidge asked.

"My apologies, Mr. President," the young man

said. "I thought I saw someone I knew from back home. Your wife's shoes bore the brunt of my haste."

"To answer your question, Cal, I was swimming upstream against a tide of politicians, trying to get back to you." Calvin Coolidge smiled at his wife.

"If everyone's ready, we'd better get this show on the road," Herbert Hoover said. "Thanks for your help, my boy. I believe we met in Chicago, didn't we?"

"We did, sir. My pleasure, sir."

"What was your name again, son?" Mr. Hoover asked. "Ness, was it?"

"You have a good memory, sir."

"Mr. Ness."

"Yes, Mrs. Hoover?"

"If your people haven't thought of it already, you might consider looking at the tax records as a way to clear up those problems back home." The young man's mouth twitched and formed a semi-smile and a swell of people pulled him away with the two Secret Service men in his wake.

"Take care," Mrs. Coolidge called. "Let us know how you're doing."

Eliot Ness put on his hat and tipped the brim.

"You can count on that, Ma'am."

"The income tax law is a lot of bunk. The government can't collect legal taxes from illegal money."

—Attributed to Alphonse "Al" Capone, who, after years of murder and bribery to avoid prosecution, was sentenced on November 24, 1931, to eleven years in prison for income-tax evasion.

PAMELA J. FESLER

——⟡——

PAMELA J. FESLER is a former advertising copy-writer and magazine editor whose fiction has appeared in *Mystery Scene* magazine, *Rosebud*, *Mystery Forum* magazine, and the well-received anthologies, *Marilyn: Shades of Blonde* and *Mom, Apple Pie and Murder*.

"I read that Grace Coolidge and Lou Hoover were swept into the crowd when they arrived at Hoover's inauguration, and were out of sight for several minutes," Pam says. "What happened to these two intelligent, perceptive women while they were gone? I couldn't find an answer to that question, so I invented my own."

MADAME PRESIDENT

～⁂～

ANNE PERRY

PRESIDENT WOODROW WILSON lay white-faced and motionless in his bed. He might be asleep. On the other hand Edith Wilson knew all too painfully that he might have lapsed into a coma. She had lived in a state of perpetual fear for him since he had been taken ill during his whirlwind tour of the country in September, just six weeks short of a year after the armistice which had ended the most devastating war ever to sweep the world. He had worked so desperately hard to bring about the League of Nations which would prevent such a catastrophe ever happening again. He had traveled all over a ruined and grieving Europe, seeing firsthand the destruction and everywhere the fears and suffering.

Then he had worn himself to even deeper exhaustion on a whistlestop tour of the United States, raising support for so many things which needed to be done. By September 25 he had been too ill to continue and had had to yield to necessity and return to Washington. He had arrived on Sunday, September 28. On the Wednesday Edith had found him collapsed, his left side paralysed. She could still remember the horror of it so vividly it made her skin prickle and her insides churn. She had run immediately for her friend and Woodrow's adviser, Dr. Grayson. They had returned to find the president unconscious on the bathroom floor.

The press had been told nothing, but as might have been foreseen, there was wild speculation. Some even said that he had gone insane. The ugliest, and perhaps the most painful rumor for her, about a man she loved so wholeheartedly, whom she admired and had worked with in such understanding, was that he had contracted some venereal disease.

Of course she knew it was a stroke. The left side paralysed, the gruff, whispering voice, the blind left eye all told her that. What neither she nor Dr. Grayson could possibly know was whether he would ever recover. And apart from her love for him as her husband, as the president, he was the one man who believed far more than anyone else in the creation of the League. There was so much to do! They dared not let his true state be known. Everyone else was kept on the other side of that door, everyone, even his oldest friends and closest advisers. One misplaced word, even a suggestion it was anything more than a very temporary exhaustion brought on by overwork, and Vice President Thomas Marshall would naturally assume the leadership. That was what vice presidents were for.

Only Grayson could be trusted. Edith herself carried all the messages back and forth. It was she who decided what was important enough to take to the president, and what was not. If it was not, she simply declined it and it went to someone else. If it really mattered—and she knew what he cared about, she had worked so closely with him ever since their marriage that she knew what he would have decided—she took it into the bedroom, waited an appropriate while, then signed his name, erratically, like the shaking hand of a sick man. It was not difficult; she knew his writing so well. Then she took it out again and told them the president had approved it.

So far it had worked very well. Of course Tumulty was suspicious; he was always suspicious, and he disliked her. But with Grayson's help she had managed to hold him off.

Now she looked at Woodrow's exhausted face, waited one more minute, then turned and walked out of the room with the sheaf of papers signed, in her hand. She came almost face to face with the secretary of agriculture and made herself smile at him.

"Here you are, Mr. Meredith. The president has initialed them."

"Thank you, Mrs. Wilson," Meredith took them. "How is he today?" he looked concerned, more than merely polite.

What should she say? How close to the truth?

"I think he seems a little better," she answered, forcing a lift into her voice. It was a lie; he looked no better at all.

"I'm glad," he said, a flicker of hope passing over

his face. "Tell him I was asking after him and we all wish him well again soon."

"I will," she promised, turning to leave.

At her elbow was Alvar Brand, one of the regular aides. He looked slim and dapper, and very composed, as always.

"Mrs. Wilson, I wonder if I might have a word with you, as discreetly as possible?"

She did not like Brand very much, but she could not refuse. "Of course," she conceded.

"Perhaps in the study?" he suggested, motioning toward the small, private room where she wrote letters and read.

"Is this necessary, Mr. Brand?"

"Oh, yes," he said firmly, a tiny smile on his mouth. He moved ahead and opened the door for her. She went in before him. Lily, her maid, was inside, straightening and tidying up. She looked startled and excused herself, brushing past them to leave. She was a pretty girl, smart and diligent. Edith caught a suggestion of perfume as she passed. Nice.

"What is it, Mr. Brand?" she asked as soon as he had closed the door behind her.

"How is the president today?"

"Improving," she said tartly. "You could have asked me that outside."

He was still smiling. "I did not think you would care to answer me outside, Mrs. Wilson. You see it was an honest answer I was seeking. He is actually still alive, I presume? Even if he could speak . . . or indeed register anything at all. Does he have moments of awareness, or is he in too deep a coma to respond at all?"

She felt the blood leave her face and her throat tightened until she thought she would not be able to form the words to answer him. She had feared this at the beginning. By now she had thought the danger past.

"He—he is . . . You are quite mistaken, Mr. Brand." She looked at his bright, confident eyes and knew she was fooling no one. "He is far better than you imagine. I am simply protecting him from too many people. He needs to rest."

"I regret to say this, Mrs. Wilson, but I do not believe you. I think he has suffered a severe stroke from which he will not recover. However, if I am mistaken, as you say, it will be easy enough to prove. Allow me in to see him. It will take only a moment. Then I shall never bother you again. In fact I shall be happy to assure all those others who doubt, as I do, and your problems will be over." He smiled, showing white teeth.

If only she could! If Woodrow were well enough for her to be sure he could appear bright and lucid just long enough! But he was too weak, too close to complete collapse.

"Certainly not!" she said sharply. "You will have to accept my word, Mr. Brand. I am not going to allow you, or anyone else, into the president's bedroom to stare at him when he is ill, simply to gratify your curiosity. Now I have things to attend to. Good day." And she made to move past him.

But he blocked the doorway.

"Not everyone feels as you do about the League of Nations. There are some who do not think it is a good idea, and they are prepared to go to some lengths to see that it does not come to pass."

"May I assume that you are one of them?" she said icily. "If you are working against the president, then you have betrayed your trust, and you had better leave the White House immediately. I shall explain to my husband why you have gone."

"Not so quickly!" He held out his hands to bar her exit. "I have no feelings one way or the other. But if you wish it to succeed, you would be well advised to make a friend of me, not an enemy. I can be a very bad enemy, Mrs. Wilson. Consider the Volstead Act—only a few days ago. A very big decision that! Affecting almost every American—prohibiting the sale, trade, and consumption of liquor! A lot of people feel very strongly about that . . . very strongly indeed. It will alter a whole way of life. Many moral issues at stake. The president vetoed it. I saw the papers—his signature scrawled on the borders—but written by you . . . at his dictation? That's what you said. But really, Mrs. Wilson? Can a comatose man dictate . . . can he even understand?"

She remained frozen, horrified.

"And there are other matters . . . Madame President," his tone was now openly sarcastic. "Such as re-privatization of railroads, appointing secretaries of the treasury and the interior, filling major diplomatic posts in Europe and South America. Shall I go on?"

"What do you want?" Her words came with great difficulty, harsh with loathing. She would like to have struck him, squashed him as she would a beetle, and thrown him out, but she knew she dared not. For the moment he held the power. His knowledge of it was in his bright, smug face. Once you give in to a black-mailer you are his forever. She needed time! There was no one else she could turn to. She must protect Woodrow, and all he believed in, all they both believed in! She stared straight back at Alvar Brand.

He saw the hatred in her eyes, and the helplessness.

"For the moment, just a token of our understanding," he replied. "There will be more later, of course. That's a very nice pin you're wearing. Diamonds, I presume? Yes, I thought so. I'll give it back to you one day. I only want to borrow it . . . a keepsake—a token, if you like!" He held out his hand.

She unfastened it with shaking fingers and passed it to him. "Now get out!" she hissed.

When she had composed herself sufficiently to return to her normal duties—at least those which had been normal since Woodrow's illness—she found Tumulty waiting outside.

"Are you all right, Mrs. Wilson?" he asked, looking at her narrowly.

She disliked his gaze; it was always too knowing, and not a little disapproving. He felt elbowed out of position by the president's trust in her abilities and judgment, a trust he did not share.

"Perfectly, thank you, Mr. Tumulty, just a little tired." And she walked away with a brief, rather tight smile.

"You have lost your diamond pin," he added, eyeing her empty lapel. "Do you wish me to ask someone to look for it?"

"No, thank you. It is not lost. The catch was faulty. I took it off myself."

She could tell no one. The day passed with deadly

slowness and she kept up the pretense that there was nothing wrong except the ever-present agony of knowing how ill the president was, and always at the back of her mind, when she was too tired to prevent it, the fear that he would not recover.

She kept waking through the night. The following day she somehow managed to keep her composure, to be polite to everyone and let nothing slip of the thoughts racing in her mind, the seeking of some way, any way, of escape.

She took the papers and drafts of bills from the secretaries and aides who came. She said she would consult the president, and she went into his room. He lay there quietly, looking so old and frail it was all she could do not to weep. But that would help no one, least of all him. She could not even confide in him. If he could hear her, and understand, it would be torment for him to lie there knowing what was happening and be unable to help. She did not know how much he heard. Sometimes she was almost sure it was everything, she had such an awareness of his presence with her. Right now she felt more close to him than she ever had in her life.

She must stop doubting and take command of herself. She read the papers carefully, making notes. She knew what Woodrow would want in almost all these instances. The two she did not know she would hand back and say they were not important enough to bother him with now. She scrawled his name on all the ones in which there was a decision, then went back out again.

Tumulty was waiting for her, and Dr. Grayson and John Trevellyn, one of the nicest men she knew and a loyal friend. She had been sorely tempted more than once to confide in him. She still wanted to. He would understand. He was the one person she knew who would not question her judgment in this.

The other person there was Alvar Brand, smiling and watching her face, and watching Tumulty. His hand was in his pocket, and she knew from his eyes that what he was turning over and over was her diamond pin.

She gave the papers back with a polite word to each person.

Trevellyn looked at her, his eyes clouded. He knew something was wrong.

"I'm glad the president was well enough to read all those," Brand said distinctly, looking at Tumulty, then Edith. "That's a lot of fine print. He certainly is improving." He looked from one to the other of them. "Isn't that wonderful?"

They all answered him nervously, making conversation.

"With this kind of recovery he won't need your special assistance much longer, Mr. Trevellyn," Brand said pointedly.

Trevellyn paled and made no answer.

Edith did not understand, but she caught the pain in Trevellyn, and in Brand's face the same sharp, glittering power she had seen when he had taken the pin from her. It tightened the knot in her stomach.

The following day was even worse. Edith went through the motions while her mind was in turmoil. Woodrow was no better. Brand was gloating. Trevellyn looked wretched. Somehow she got through the afternoon, but by five o'clock she longed to be alone just for a few moments, and to stop pretending.

She went to the study and opened the door.

He was there, lying on the floor, his eyes wide open, his hair matted with blood. Alvar Brand was dead. The statue that had been used to kill him was still beside him, its base partially wrapped in a lace handkerchief.

Her first feeling was of an overwhelming burden being lifted from her. It should have been horror, or grief, or some kind of anger because it had obviously been murder. But she was relieved. He could no longer threaten her—or Woodrow—or all the things they believed in which mattered so much.

She should tell someone. It should be reported. There would have to be a doctor called, and probably police, or at least some kind of authority.

She turned and opened the door again, and came face to face with Tumulty.

"Why, Mrs. Wilson, whatever is the matter?" he said quickly, for once his face full of genuine concern. "You look quite ill!"

"Mr. Brand is dead!" she blurted, her voice choking. She had meant to be in perfect control, but she was shaking so badly she could hardly form sensible words. "He's . . . he's been hit—"

"Brand? Alvar Brand?" He blinked at her. Then as she did not reply, he pushed past her quite gently and went into the room. "Oh, my good God!" he said and stopped abruptly. He stared for several seconds, then swiveled round. "This isn't natural, Mrs. Wilson. I'm afraid there can be no question but Brand was murdered." He looked at her very steadily. There was fear

in his face, and something which might even have been
pity. "Would you like to tell me what happened?"

"What . . . what happened?" she stammered.

"Yes. What happened in here? How did Brand
come to meet his death?"

"I don't know!" Dear God! Did he imagine she
had done it?

Then it dawned on her: Of course he did! The
lace handkerchief around the base of the statuette,
Brand's remarks the day before yesterday—the way
he had threatened her, obliquely, but enough to see
now, in hindsight; and they would find her diamond
pin in his pocket. No doubt it was still there.

"I do not know what happened," she repeated as
steadily as she could manage. "I opened the door
and came in . . . to be alone for a few moments. I
found him . . . just like that."

"Where did you come from, Mrs. Wilson?"

She did not immediately understand him.

"Where were you . . . before you came to the
study?" he repeated.

"I . . . I was with the president—"

"Was he awake?"

"Well . . . no—"

"Was anyone else there?"

"No . . ." Then she realized. Of course. He was
trying to protect her, but he was thinking what others
would think, especially when they saw the evidence.
Heaven only knew what motives they would reach
for! Tumulty was suspicious of her already with regard to her signatures, and Woodrow's real state of
health, and how much she was keeping from them.

"I see," he said slowly, and there was regret in

his eyes. Much as she disliked him, she believed it was real.

The farther door opened and Dr. Grayson came in. He stared at them both, then past them at the body of Alvar Brand on the floor. Without speaking he went over to it and knelt down. Quickly and professionally he examined the wound, the blood still wet, the way he was lying, and the statuette close by. He turned to look up at them, his face pale.

"What happened?"

No one asked about an intruder. This was the White House. The idea of a burglar, a break-in, was preposterous.

"We don't know yet," Tumulty answered. "Obviously, it was murder."

"Obviously!" Grayson agreed, climbing to his feet and glancing at Edith, then away again. "Who was around here within the last hour?"

"Is it as recent as that?" Tumulty asked.

"Yes. The blood in that wound has hardly congealed at all and he's still very warm. You didn't answer my question."

"I have no idea. I passed Trevellyn as I came in. I haven't seen anyone else . . . apart from Mrs. Wilson, of course."

Grayson opened his mouth to say something, then changed his mind.

"I'll send for him." Tumulty opened the door and called Trevellyn's name. The maid, Lily, was in the hallway. He told her to go and find Trevellyn, then as an afterthought, asked her who else she had seen. Edith did not hear her reply, but he repeated it when he came back: only a messenger, and the assistant to the secretary of the interior.

Edith waited in growing horror for Trevellyn to come. The issues at stake were momentous. Europe had been devastated by war. An entire generation of young men had been slaughtered, and no one could count the crippled, maimed, homeless, and bereaved. There could not be a family anywhere which had not lost at least one member. America itself had been scarred in a new and fearful way. Too many had mourned a young man who would never return. The League of Nations was the greatest single step toward seeing it never, ever happened again. How could any sane man or woman be against it? And yet there were some—and they were powerful.

Involuntarily she glanced at the figure on the floor. She could not be sorry he was dead. He was the worst of all possibilities: not even a man who disbelieved in the League, but one who did not care either way, was simply willing to foil the plans for his own political or financial advantage. She had not killed him, but she could certainly have wished him dead.

Had John Trevellyn killed him? For her? She was not unaware of his deep regard for her, deeper perhaps than he had thought it appropriate to say. It was his loyalty to the president and his profound belief in the same causes which had stilled his tongue. Could they also have motivated such an act? After the carnage of the war, which he had seen firsthand, might he consider one man's death an acceptable price to pay? Was this a final act in the war itself?

The door opened and Trevellyn came in. Tumulty showed him the corpse. He looked startled, but not grieved. He made no pretense, but he did seem acutely worried, even frightened. She knew him well enough to see it through his outward composure. His hands were clenching and unclenching. Twice he rubbed clammy palms against the sides of his trousers. He would not deny knowledge of it. He would not commit himself at all, and all the time he never once looked at Edith.

She left at last, feeling more wretched than she could have imagined. Of course word had spread like fire. Everyone was shocked and afraid. Tumulty had done his best to conceal the nature of Brand's death, but he could not keep the anxiety out of his voice, and Trevellyn looked like a ghost, as if his own personal happiness had somehow ended. Of course the pin had been found in Brand's pocket. She had lied about it, and Tumulty knew it, and she had no explanation that did not make it even worse. No one on earth would believe she had given it to Brand to have it mended, which was the only answer which would be excusable.

For once there were no papers to take to the president. She went into his room simply for the comfort of being near him. The November sun shone through the high windows and she stood for a moment staring out over the lawn, past the bare trees toward the wide, gracious streets beyond. Did anyone out there have the faintest idea of the love and the pain and the fear which was closed up behind these beautiful walls?

She turned to look at her husband. He looked so old and so terribly tired in this harsh, clear daylight. She wished she could tell him all about Alvar Brand, and Trevellyn, and what had happened . . . ask his help. He would know what to do.

But he was fighting his own tremendous battle just to survive, and he needed every strand of strength he had—and even that might not be enough. That thought was worse than all the rest: a loneliness she could not bear even to think of.

She went over to him and knelt down beside the bed, taking his limp hand in hers, and holding it, blinking back the tears. This battle she must fight by herself . . . and win.

An hour later she was in her own room. Lily had just come in with some clean, pressed clothes and hung them up. She really was a pretty girl, and nice. Still, Edith was glad when she went and left her alone. She needed to think.

Who had been in this part of the building when Brand had been killed? Herself, Tumulty, Grayson, and John Trevellyn. The messenger and the aide hardly counted. They would have no reason to kill Brand; they probably did not even know who he was. And they would certainly not have had her lace handkerchief to hold the statuette to avoid leaving fingerprints. Or worse than that . . . far worse, to incriminate her!

This was no time to lose her self control! She must not let fear take over and numb her mind! It was a hideous thought, that one of these men she knew, or thought she knew, should have done such a thing! Not only had they murdered Brand, which she could not entirely condemn, but they had taken the trouble to make it look like her crime. Why? Simply to remove suspicion from themselves, or more than that?

If she were convicted of murder, or even suspected of it, it would ruin the president.

She sat on the dressing table stool and stared at herself in the mirror.

"Come on, Edith!" she said sharply. "Think!"

Grayson would never frame her. He was her one loyal, absolutely trusted friend. He alone knew of the president's true state. Dismiss him from the thought. He might loathe Brand, but he could never have laid the blame on her. It would destroy all he believed in.

Tumulty? He did not like her much, and he did not trust her judgment, but he was an honourable man, and loyal to the president. He might very easily call her bluff—in fact she thought he had been on the edge of it two or three times—but he would do it openly, face to face, not by murdering Brand.

That only left Trevellyn, and the thought she had been trying to avoid. Had he done it for her, or for some reason of his own? Was Brand blackmailing him too? Over what? He was a trifle extravagant, she knew that. Had he allowed himself to get into debt?

She looked very pale, and far older than she would have wished. Perhaps vanity was foolish, but it was part of her, probably of most women. She should do something about her white cheeks. She reached for a small pink scarf she liked to wear. It was flattering; it lent color without seeming artificial.

It was not where she had left it. She opened another drawer and another. Nor was it in any of them. It was nowhere to be seen. How annoying! A little perfume? She took the stopper off the bottle. That was emptier than it should have been too! Although she had not used it lately. It was very expensive—something of an extravagance, even for her.

Then she remembered where she had smelled it

only a couple of days ago. Lily! Lily, her maid. And there was only one place where she could have got it! Right here on Edith's dressing table.

It was a small thing; a tiny theft by a pretty girl who was surrounded by lovely, feminine things she could never afford. It was only too easy to understand. A dab of perfume, a pink scarf . . . a lace handkerchief!

Had Alvar Brand noticed it too, and deduced what had happened? Had he also tried blackmailing Lily? Was that really worth killing him for?

Surely not!

She started going systematically through all the drawers, checking everything. There was also a small decorative pair of earrings, not valuable of itself, and almost certainly a sachet of lavender and an embroidered case for hosiery.

She went to the door. "Lily?"

It was several moments before she came. She looked flustered, but then everyone did. There had been a murder.

"Yes, Ma'am?"

Edith closed the door and faced her. "Lily, I know you have been using my perfume, and I believe you may also have borrowed one or two of my belongings . . . a pair of earrings, a kerchief . . ." She did not need to continue; Lily's scarlet face was witness of her guilt. She was ashamed. She was also terrified. Her eyes were hollow and her body was trembling.

"I didn't mean to!" she said hoarsely. "It was an accident, I swear!"

The perfume could not be an accident, nor the thefts. Edith steadied herself with an effort.

"I think you had better tell me what happened, Lily.

Sit down on the chair, before you faint. Here . . ." She guided her backward onto the seat. "Now, explain to me. Was Mr. Brand blackmailing you, Lily?"

She kept her voice firm, in command, not to be defied in any circumstances, above all, not to be lied to.

"Yes," Lily answered with a barely audible whisper.

"What did he want from you? Tell me the truth!"

Lily looked straight at her, her face hot but her eyes unblinking.

"He wanted me to make love with him. I said no, he could tell you everything, but I wasn't going to do that! There's somebody else I . . . I have feelings for. I couldn't do it, no matter what."

"I see. Then what happened?"

Lily lowered her eyes at last. "Then he tried to force me, Ma'am. That's when I hit him. I didn't mean to kill him. An' I'm terrible sorry I used your handkerchief to wipe my fingers off the statue. I know fingers leave marks. I'm always wiping them off things myself when people touch mirrors and glasses and the like. Will they hang me, Ma'am?"

"No, Lily, they won't hang you," Edith said firmly. "You put my things back, except the kerchief. We'll say I gave you that. And just tell Mr. Tumulty that Mr. Brand tried to force himself on you, and you defended yourself. You hit harder than you meant, because you were afraid. I think it would be a good idea if you didn't mention wiping off the finger marks, unless you have to."

"Will they believe me?" Lily still looked horribly afraid.

"I believe you," Edith said quite sincerely. "I think Dr. Grayson will as well."

Lily unbuttoned her blouse slowly and slipped it off her shoulders. Purple bruise marks were clearly visible where somebody's fingers had gripped her. They need not have been Brand's, but they were fresh, and looked painful.

"Thank you," Edith said with a very small smile. "I am grateful to you for owning up. It was very . . . responsible."

Lily looked close to tears.

Edith had been too aware of fear and loneliness not to have a real compassion for the girl.

"Don't worry," she said again with conviction. "I shall look after you!"

Two hours later she was back in the president's bedroom. It was dark now, the swift November evening closing in. Woodrow still lay propped up on the pillows, but his eyes were open.

"How are you, my dear?" he whispered to her gruffly. "You look tired. Is everything all right?"

"Oh yes," she said decisively, smiling at him and reaching for his hand, her heart racing with excitement at the sound of his voice. "Everything is fine. There is nothing whatever that I can't take care of . . . until you are well again."

His lips curved very faintly on the unparalysed side of his face, and relaxed again, the anxiety slipping away from him.

"Well done, my dear. I knew I could rely on you."

ANNE PERRY

~~~

ANNE PERRY lives in the northern Highlands of Scotland, in a stone house by the sea, and loves the garden, but does no work in it because she is busy writing mysteries, mostly set in Victorian London. They usually concern either Charlotte and Thomas Pitt, or William Monk and Hester Latterly, and they are beloved by millions of readers the world over.

Anne says: "I chose Edith Wilson among the First Ladies because her predicament caused by the president's incapacity seems to invite opportunity for mystery. The period just after World War I is one I thought I would enjoy researching and writing about—and I did."

THE MOTHER OF OUR COUNTRY

—◈—

LINDA GRANT

THE SUN WAS warm on the porch in early September. Elizabeth Brandon pushed the gray wool shawl off her shoulders and leaned her head against the high chair back. She closed her eyes and watched dark shapes float on a red screen.

Her inner eye was sharper than her outer one, these days. The world had become fuzzy and indistinct as she moved into her seventh decade, but her memories were clear and sharp. Questions about the past were always referred to her, and she prided herself on being able to answer them more often than not.

Life had taught Elizabeth that the gifts of providence were rarely simple. For every joy a man might relive, remembrance offered a pain to trouble his serenity. In her experience, those who thought most highly of themselves usually had the poorest memories.

She sensed her own troubling memories gathering like storm clouds and wished that she had never responded to the man from the college. He had written twice explaining that he was preparing a book on women of the revolution and had professed he would be most grateful if she would share her reminiscences.

His letter was extravagant in its enthusiasm for "the brave heroines of our nation's battle for liberty," and the first name on the list of those illustrious women was Martha Washington. He's sure to ask about Valley Forge, Elizabeth thought.

Even in the warm September sun, she felt a chill. It was as if she carried the cold of that winter in her bones, waiting only for memory to summon it. She drew the shawl around her shoulders as she recalled how the wind cut through the warmest coat and a deep breath seared the lungs with air so cold it burned.

Physical cold was bearable. She'd known worse in Massachusetts. It was the poisonous mix of cold and fear, misery and desperation, that had made Valley Forge such a bitter place. She'd often wondered if the events of that winter might have unfolded differently in a less hostile setting. If mercy might have tempered justice. If betrayal might not have been the only solution.

Elizabeth Brandon was a practical woman, widely regarded for her strength of character. She'd borne eight children, and buried five of them, along with two husbands, her brothers, and all but one sister. She'd made hard choices and suffered the consequences, and while there were many things in her life that she regretted, it was only her actions at Valley Forge that haunted her with guilt.

She saw, in memory's eye, the high ground with the land around it bare of trees. The row upon row of log huts capped with snow. They seemed to form a spreading village. From a distance, it was a pretty sight. But up close, you saw the men, many of them little more than boys, in ragged, threadbare clothes that wouldn't protect them from a summer shower much less the biting wind and freezing snow. She'd laughed when her coach pulled into camp and she passed a sentry standing in his hat. Only later had she learned that the hat was the poor man's only protection from frostbite for his shoeless, rag-wrapped feet.

Her husband had found them quarters in a farmhouse, a room upstairs and a parlor they shared with two other officers and their wives. Not nearly as fine a quarters as those of Sarah Calvert and her husband, who had a cottage all to themselves, but cozy enough.

Sarah Calvert. Her sad-eyed, anxious face was etched in Elizabeth's memory. The mention, even the thought, of Valley Forge called it forth. As did certain smells: the acrid smoke from a green-wood fire, the stench of human waste, the odd combination of sweat and sickness that was everywhere that winter. Memory was like a string of beads. You might pick up a single bead, but the rest came with it, whether you wished them to or no.

Martha Washington's face was another bead on that string, always awakening regret that the happy memories of Morristown were tainted by the bitter ones of Valley Forge. Elizabeth had missed joining her husband at winter headquarters that first year in Cambridge because her son had just been born, but she'd left the children with her mother and journeyed to Morristown the following year. For her, as for the soldiers and the women who joined them, the general's wife had been a great source of comfort.

She was a small woman, plump and motherly. Seeing her in her homespun dress and speckled apron, Elizabeth would not have guessed her to be the wife of the commander-in-chief. The matrons of Morristown had been humbled when they put on their finery to pay a call, and she pulled out her knitting and worked on socks for the general while they sat with idle hands.

Everyone applauded Mrs. Washington's gentle kindness. She knew exactly what was needed to soften the harsh realities of the winter camp, to bring people together and help them feel at ease. The younger women, like Elizabeth, looked on her as a second mother. We find what we seek, Elizabeth thought. And we are blind to what we would not see.

Life in Morristown was difficult, but Elizabeth had enjoyed the daily sewing sessions Mrs. Washington organized and the social evenings at headquarters. She had often accompanied the general's wife on her visits to the hospital to cheer the unfortunate soldiers.

The next year, winter quarters moved to Valley Forge. John Calvert brought his Virginia riflemen, and Sarah joined the wives there. They were an odd couple. She was quiet and serious, with a face too long to be called pretty, while he was darkly hand-some with a gay, outgoing manner that made him an instant favorite with the ladies. She was tall for a woman, several inches taller than her husband, and walked with a limp from a riding accident. While both were from Virginia, Sarah came from the older gentry of the Tidewater and John from the newly wealthy upcountry landowners.

Coming from Massachusetts, Elizabeth found all southerners a bit strange. She was well aware of the conflicts between soldiers from different colonies, but she was surprised to learn that there were divisions *within* Virginia.

Mrs. Washington took to Sarah immediately, for they had much in common. Both were Virginians, widowed early with two young children, and both had remarried soldiers. When the general's wife learned that Sarah's daughter, Margaret, suffered from the same infirmity that had claimed her daughter Patsy, a deep bond was forged.

Sarah also shared Mrs. Washington's concern for the sick and wounded soldiers suffering in the camp hospitals. Conditions were much worse at Valley Forge than they'd been at Morristown. The lack of good food made many sick; and without adequate clothing, others fell victim to frostbite that cost them fingers and toes. Medicines were in such short supply that there was often little the doctors could do to ease the suffering, and the hospitals increasingly became places men went to die.

Sarah had arrived in camp with bundles of dried herbs to treat everything from fever to infections of the skin. Her mother had been skilled in the arts of healing and Sarah's knowledge of plants impressed even the doctors. Her husband seemed irritated that she insisted on working at the hospital, but the soldiers were grateful for her teas and potions, and for her quiet smile and cheering conversation.

The herbs were gone within the first month, and the number of sick only increased. Even outside the hospitals, one could hear the screams of men whose limbs were being cut from them with no palliative but whiskey to ease the pain. Other wives came once and could not bring themselves to return to the wretched place. Sarah and Mrs. Washington were among the few who continued to visit.

Misery takes a toll and pain that is bearable for a day or a week erodes the soul when it fastens on a body for too long. As the months passed, Sarah's eyes grew sad and anxious. Her face thinned and her mouth seemed to have forgotten how to smile. Then, one afternoon, when new snow followed by strong winds had kept most of the sewing circle at home, Sarah arrived looking so pale and gaunt that Mrs. Washington immediately expressed concern.

Sarah burst into tears, long wracking sobs that took several minutes to subside. When she'd finally calmed herself, she told of seeing a boy at the hospital who could not have been much older than her own son, a boy who had lost a leg and whose raging fever meant that he would almost surely die.

"He looks so like David," she repeated. "It could have been David there in that bed."

"You mustn't do this to yourself, my dear," Mrs. Washington said. "You'll make yourself sick, then you won't be able to help anyone. Stay home from the hospital. You need your rest."

Later, after the other wives had left and only Sarah and Elizabeth were still there, Elizabeth had mentioned that she'd had a letter from her mother and that her son had taken his first steps. To her surprise, Sarah dissolved into tears again.

Mrs. Washington tried to comfort her. "I know how hard it is to leave the children at home," she said. "Especially the babies. You have a young son, too, haven't you, Sarah?"

"I have two sons." The sharpness of her tone surprised them. "One by my first husband and one by Mr. Calvert." She struggled to control herself and said finally, "I'm sorry to burden you with my problems."

"No, no, my dear. Burdens are easier to bear when they are shared. What is it that distresses you so?"

"I fear for my son, David," Sarah said. She stared at her hands and seemed unwilling to go on.

"Is he ill?" Mrs. Washington asked.

Sarah shook her head. Finally, she said, "Oh, Mrs. Washington, you are fortunate indeed, for the general has room in his heart for another man's children. Sadly, not all men are so generous in their affections."

Elizabeth was shocked by Sarah's reference to Mrs. Washington's situation. The wives understood that it must pain the general and his wife that they had never been able to have children of their own. It was never mentioned.

"It's natural for a man to favor his own children," Mrs. Washington said. "Especially the first born."

"Mr. Calvert hates David," Sarah said. "He was

always harsh with him, and since the baby came, he's been much worse."

"He probably feels that the boy needs a firm hand," Mrs. Washington said. "A child needs both a mother's tenderness and a father's sternness."

"I understand the need for firmness," Sarah said, "but Mr. Calvert goes too far. He's ordered David to join us here in Valley Forge."

Both women gasped. It was still deep winter. The trip to Pennsylvania from Virginia was dangerous at best. A storm could catch a traveler on the road with no shelter at hand.

"He is writing to his brother Michael to take David from my mother and bring him here. I fear he'll not survive the trip." Her lower lip trembled and she twisted her kerchief in her hands.

Mrs. Washington looked perplexed. "But why?" she asked.

"Mr. Calvert says it's time David learned to live with men," she said. "That it will build his character. But I fear he means to kill him."

"Oh, no, my dear," Mrs. Washington said. "Surely not."

Sarah sniffled and bit her lower lip. "It's not only I who fear for David's safety. His uncle, my first husband's brother, Colonel Richard Layton, distrusts Mr. Calvert's motives. He suspects that Mr. Calvert desires that David's inheritance should pass to his own son."

She fought back tears. "I should never have married again. When I was a widow I could protect my children. Now they belong to Mr. Calvert. He can order David to do whatever he wishes, and I must stand by. If my mother refuses to send him, the law will compel her."

Mrs. Washington nodded gravely. The law regarded a married couple as a single person and that person was the husband. Children belonged to their father. A wife who ran away might be fetched home by an officer of the law and could be charged with stealing since even the clothes on her back belonged to her husband.

In Elizabeth's experience few husbands acted the tyrant, but the law certainly allowed it, and listening to Sarah, she was chilled by the realization that if John Calvert did truly wish to harm his stepson, his wife could do little to prevent him.

Mrs. Washington looked deeply troubled. A word from the general would put a stop to the nonsense of bringing the boy to winter quarters, but if Mrs. Washington meant to speak that word, her face did not betray it. That look was the first sign Elizabeth had of Mrs. Washington's other side.

An aide had interrupted them, warning that they best return home at once since the wind was rising and a blizzard might soon be upon them. Elizabeth left with a heavy heart, her mind so burdened by Sarah's story that she was scarcely aware of the icy winds that tore at her all the way home.

By dinner, her throat ached and she realized that her chills were the product of more than a troubled mind. She remembered little of the fever that gripped her for three days, then passed, leaving her weak and aching.

When she was sufficiently recovered to receive visitors, she learned that the camp was abuzz with tales of Richard Layton's confrontation with John Calvert. So bitter had been their meeting that only the intervention of a third officer prevented them from coming to blows.

Both regiments had immediately taken up their officers' causes as their own. Misery easily breeds anger, and an empty stomach fills quickly with bile. The bored, starving men were spoiling for a fight, and the rest of the camp waited eagerly for the spark that would ignite it.

General Washington had put a stop to the feud, the women told her, but though the two Virginia colonels had shaken hands and sworn to avoid any future conflict, there was clearly no love lost between them.

Elizabeth was grateful to hear that the general had ordered Calvert to leave his boy at home, but she knew that if Sarah's suspicions were correct, he might still find a way to do the child harm.

Her illness kept her housebound for another five days. Her husband reported that an uneasy truce prevailed between the colonels and their regiments. The officers spoke to each other with such elaborate courtesy that no one could mistake the hostility behind it. It was rumored that some men were taking bets on how long before the quarrel erupted into the open again.

Elizabeth was looking forward to returning to the sewing circle on Wednesday, but a heavy storm blew in late Tuesday night, leaving deep snow that kept her home. When her husband returned at noon, he brought news that John Calvert was dead.

Calvert had been struck from behind, a blow that cracked his skull. Sarah had found him in the morning, almost buried by snow in front of the stable near their house.

The general ordered a thorough investigation to determine the identity of the murderer, but Calvert's men were convinced their leader had been killed by his wife's brother-in-law and demanded that Layton be arrested at once. Layton's soldiers were quick to threaten action should anyone lay hands on their leader. Anger and distrust spread through the ranks like infection from a festering wound.

Elizabeth had hurried to Sarah's house as soon as she could that afternoon. Fresh snow covered last week's mud and filth, making the camp appear clean and hopeful. It troubled Elizabeth to realize that she could not summon sorrow for John Calvert's death.

She found her friend dazed, her eyes red from crying. The small cottage was immaculate, not an item out of place. Both Elizabeth and Sarah hired local girls to help with the cooking and other work, but when it snowed heavily as it had done the night before, the girls didn't come. Sarah must have done all the cleaning herself. Probably a good thing, Elizabeth thought, busy hands calm a troubled mind.

Elizabeth had visited the cottage several times, and each time she'd been impressed by Sarah's skill in giving it the feeling of a home. She'd brought a few pretty things from Virginia—two small embroidered pillows, some decorative plates, a copper bedwarmer. Others might have considered them frivolous, but they gave the place her personal touch.

"I feel as if I bear some of the guilt," Sarah said

as they sat down near the fireplace. "I must confess, I wished him dead more than once."

"You mustn't think of it," Elizabeth advised.

"They say Richard killed him, but I know it can't be so," Sarah said, as she sat twisting her kerchief in her hands. "I know he was angry, but he's not one to strike a man from behind. These are desperate times. It could have been anyone—a thief, a Tory."

A rap at the door startled them, and Elizabeth opened it to find Mrs. Washington herself. The general's wife bustled in and enveloped Sarah in concern.

Food was scarce, but Mrs. Washington had brought soup and bread and when she learned that Sarah had not eaten that day, she insisted she sup immediately.

"You should not be alone at this time," Mrs. Washington said, taking her knitting from the bag she carried. "We'll sit with you awhile."

Sarah looked confused, even distressed, but she could hardly refuse the older woman's kindness. Mrs. Washington was widely admired for her ability to put others at ease and draw them into conversation. Elizabeth herself had once observed that the general's wife could draw speech from a stone, and a friend had added that they'd have had the stone's life story before an hour's end.

So it was with Sarah. Mrs. Washington gently drew her out until she was even able to talk about the events of the night before. "I hate to think that he must have lain out there all night in the snow, only a few steps from the door. If only I'd gone out—"

"You couldn't know, my dear," Mrs. Washington said. "Do you know if he was struck when he was leaving or on his way home?"

Elizabeth thought it a strange question. Surely, the general's staff could have provided a better answer than the widow.

Sarah shook her head. "He left after dinner, before the storm arrived. I heard no sound that might have warned me."

"And you saw no one nearby?"

"No. It was already full dark. I didn't even look out the window."

The conversation continued, a strange mixing of the details of John Calvert's last night on earth with the minor camp gossip and news from home that were a usual part of sewing circle gatherings. And when Mrs. Washington finally put her knitting away, both Sarah and Elizabeth were relieved.

As she rose to go, Mrs. Washington complimented Sarah on her house. "Such a wise thing to bring a few touches of home," she said. "They remind me so of things I left behind at Mount Vernon. But where is your lovely copper bedwarmer?"

Elizabeth looked toward the stone fireplace. The bedwarmer that usually hung from the wall next to it was missing. She had admired it for the intricate floral pattern worked on its copper lid and the carved rosewood handle and thought each time she saw it how wise Sarah was to bring objects that combined beauty with utility. Climbing into her cold bed at night, she'd wished she'd thought to bring a container in which to put coals to heat the chilly sheets.

As she looked back at her friend, she was surprised to see that she looked quite distressed. "I . . . it's in the bedroom. I couldn't bear to look at it. It was a gift from Mr. Calvert in a happier time."

Mrs. Washington patted her hand and tried to comfort the distraught woman, then she and Elizabeth departed.

"You must ride home with me," Mrs. Washington said, leading Elizabeth to her own conveyance. "We'll send someone back to fetch your buggy home."

She would rather have gone home to rest. She was still not fully recovered from her illness and the emotional strain of the afternoon had left her quite exhausted, but the request felt more like a command than an invitation.

On the ride to headquarters, Mrs. Washington said, "I must ask you not to speak to anyone of our conversation this afternoon. Not even to your husband."

Elizabeth was so surprised that she quite forgot herself. "But why?" she demanded, before realizing that it was not her place.

"Because, my dear, it relates to Colonel Calvert's death and must be restricted to those investigating that unfortunate affair."

"But surely you can't think—" Elizabeth objected.

"I am as fond of Sarah as you are," Mrs. Washington said, "but I cannot shield her from lawful inquiry."

"But why? What could possibly make you suspect her?"

Mrs. Washington paused, then said, "You are a woman of sound judgment, Elizabeth. I will tender you my trust and hope that I may obtain yours in return. May I have your word that you will not repeat what I am about to tell you?"

"I give you my word," Elizabeth had said.

"The doctor's examination of Colonel Calvert's

body revealed that the hair around the wound was singed. From this, he infers that the colonel may have been struck by an object that was hot enough to burn his hair.

"The men are quite confounded by this finding, but it suggested to me that a household contains several heavy objects that are heated in the course of a day or night. The missing bedwarmer would have been full of coals last night, hot enough to singe a man's hair, I think."

"But you can't think that Sarah—"

"She wouldn't be the first wife to kill a husband," Mrs. Washington said. "And she was not without reason."

"But—"

"The provost will decide when he has seen the bedwarmer. Copper would dent, I should think, if it were used to strike such a blow. If no sign of damage be found, there'll be no evidence against her."

Elizabeth felt a lump grow in her throat. "And if there be damage?"

"Then, she must be charged," Mrs. Washington said flatly. "It will be left to a judge and jury to decide her guilt or innocence."

"No," Elizabeth cried. "They'll burn her if they find her guilty. It's not fair. He would have killed her child and walked free, but she must burn for saving him. Surely you can't—"

"Look around you, child," Mrs. Washington said sharply. "Is it fair that farmers sell precious food to the British and deny it to their own countrymen? War is not fair."

"Oh, madame, pray, be not so harsh. As a mother, you must understand."

"As a mother, I know that one must do what is necessary even when it causes pain," Mrs. Washington said sternly. "We are at war. This murder threatens to set our soldiers against each other. It is a hard justice, but hard times demand it."

Mrs. Washington's face might have been stone for the emotion she showed. Elizabeth would remember it for the rest of her life. There were many paintings of the woman who became first lady, but none ever showed what Elizabeth saw that day.

"Now, we'll speak no more of it," the general's wife said. "You must leave this to me. I want you to give me your word that you'll not speak to Sarah."

Elizabeth remembered the moment bitterly. She could not speak the words but merely nodded. But Mrs. Washington demanded more. "Say it, Elizabeth, swear to it."

And she had. She had pledged her word to a woman she loved like a mother, though she'd felt she must surely choke as she spoke.

And not one hour later, she had sneaked back to Sarah's house and broken her word.

Another storm blew in that night, and Elizabeth lay awake all night listening to the wind howl around the farmhouse. If Sarah had fled as she warned her to do, she would be out in that storm, and Elizabeth feared she'd never survive it.

The provost found the Calvert house empty when he came to interrogate Sarah the next morning. Her confession, which she'd left on the table with the dented bed warmer next to it, told how John Calvert had sat at the same table and written to his brother to take the children from her mother and deliver them to his sister's home where they could be raised according to his instructions. He had laughed at her protests, boasted that there was nothing she or Charles Layton could do to thwart him. Then despite the threatening storm, he'd headed for the stable to take the letter for posting. She'd just finished filling the bedwarmer with hot coals, and she took it up and followed him.

"I make no excuse for myself," she wrote. "I knew when I struck him and left him in the snow that he would perish. I know it is an evil thing I did and God will judge me for it. But I could not permit him to kill my son."

The men of Calvert's regiment organized a search. Though Sarah was an excellent horsewoman, no one expected her to get far, especially in a heavy storm. When they could find no sign of her, it was assumed that she had perished in the snow, in just retribution for her foul crime. Elizabeth hoped her friend might have made it to Philadelphia to seek asylum with the British, but spies in the city reported no sign of her.

The hard feelings between the Virginia regiments died down, and signs of spring as well as fresh supplies made life in camp more bearable. The sewing circle continued to meet every morning.

If Mrs. Washington suspected that Elizabeth had broken her word and warned Sarah, she never gave a sign of it. If anything, she was even kinder than before. Elizabeth thought reproach might have been easier to bear than the undeserved tenderness. Each kind word pricked her conscience, and she found the guilt a heavy burden.

That was the last year Elizabeth joined her husband at winter quarters. She missed him mightily, but she could not face Mrs. Washington, knowing how she had betrayed that great lady's trust and caused her friend's death. When her husband was killed just four months before the end of the war, she regretted bitterly that she had missed the time with him and believed it God's punishment for breaking her oath at Valley Forge.

She did not blame Mrs. Washington for her harsh decision, any more than she blamed the general for the deaths of the men he sent into battle. She never spoke of it. And when the General became President and others talked of the sweet and gentle woman at his side, she kept silent. She will do what's necessary, Elizabeth thought, and only those close to her will know the cost.

The young man came to visit the next afternoon. He was tall and thin, wore a suit a size too small, and had the distracting habit of peering at her as if to see if she were still alive. He overflowed with enthusiasm and reverence for his subject, and Elizabeth thought his effusive comments on her character to be more appropriate to a eulogy than a conversation.

Though he'd come for her reminiscences, he talked more than he listened, which suited Elizabeth fine. He reeled off the names of his famous subjects, beginning with "that great lady, Mrs. Washington, the wife of the 'Father of our Country.'

"I'm also including some who were less famous

and whose deeds of heroism deserve recognition," he continued. "Women like Sally Cavanaugh."

When Elizabeth gave no sign of knowing the woman, he said, "Why, her story alone might occupy a whole book. She was quite a mystery. She appeared one day out on the frontier at the fort at Cherry Valley and offered her skills at nursing. She was a tall widow woman, walked with a limp, said her husband had been killed by the British. They say she spoke like a lady of the South, though those settlers who made it as far as Cherry Valley were generally from New York."

Cherry Valley. The name was familiar. More than familiar. Elizabeth closed her eyes and tried to remember why it had stuck in her memory.

Watching her sink into reverie, the young man was afraid he was losing her, that she might be drifting into sleep. "She was a very courageous woman," he said, raising his voice a bit. "When the fort was under attack, they say she was right there among the soldiers, where the bullets were flying, brave as any man."

But Elizabeth had shut out his voice. Cherry Valley was where the courier was bound the morning Sarah Calvert disappeared. She remembered it because he'd left early, during the night, and the Dutchman's wife, Mrs. Van Hook, had lost the chance to send a letter to her brother and was deeply distressed.

The courier left early for Cherry Valley and some time later a tall woman with a limp and a particular skill at nursing had arrived at the same fort.

Couriers didn't come and go at their own will. Someone had to order the courier to leave early. Or someone had to ask the general to send him early.

Her eyes opened wide as the truth hit her. Sarah

had lived. Her warning had not caused her friend's death. And Mrs. Washington was not the cold-blooded judge she'd thought. A smile spread across her face, and Elizabeth let out a deep, resounding laugh that startled the young man.

A country needs a father and a mother, she thought. A mother who knows how to do what is needed.

LINDA GRANT

~~~

BERKELEY RESIDENT LINDA GRANT is a former president of Sisters in Crime, and the author of the popular and critically acclaimed Catherine Sayler mystery series. Sayler, a San Francisco private investigator specializing in high-tech crime, takes cases that range from sabotage in a genetics lab to sexual harassment in a software company.

"Martha Washington was one of the few women mentioned in history books when I was in school," Linda says. "She was always portrayed as a comfortable, motherly figure, with cap and apron. I wondered at the time what kind of woman she was, this Virginia widow who married a young militia officer and found herself thrust into war and the birth pains of a nation. I always suspected there was more to her than the Hallmark-grandma image I had absorbed in school. The research I did for this story convinced me that our first First Lady was a remarkable woman in her own right."

161

DOLLEY MADISON AND THE STAFF OF LIFE

———— ✦ ————

BARBARA D'AMATO

"**A**MELIA, WOULD YOU pass the president the condiments?" Dolley Madison said. She had observed her husband's slightly impatient glance as it swept the luncheon table. He could be irritable when his gastronomic needs were not met. As the girl carried the cruets to James' end of the table, Dolley added, "I'm quite worried that the ambassador will find us provincial here."

They were expecting the new Russian ambassador, just assigned to Washington, at a dinner this evening.

"They may find many things provincial here, Dolley. And about that we can do nothing. But one thing they will not find provincial is you."

She smiled. Really he could be quite delightful.

James returned to a subject on which he had been speaking earlier. "It is all very well for the Northern states to criticize the slow growth of trade and industry. It is always easy to complain. But the development of a nation's industry follows its own course, to a degree. It grows at a natural pace, from elements such as the availability of raw materials and skillful workers which develop together. It cannot be rushed more than a judicious amount. It requires a proper passage of time to mature."

"I'm sure that's true, James," said Dolley, sighing faintly.

"Where is my cider?"

"The cider is not ready, James."

"I wanted cider."

"This is October first, dear. We always make the first pressing in early October when the winter apples are ripe. As you have said yourself, summer apples make a cider that's not worth drinking."

"I like cider with my luncheon."

"And after the pressing, it requires three days in a cool room for proper fermentation to take place. Like the industry of a nation, it requires a proper passage of time to mature."

"How much longer will it be?"

"Well, I did have six barrels moved to the warm room, so as to mature more quickly. They should be drinkable tomorrow."

"I suppose that will have to do."

Dolley sighed a second time.

Then she noticed a tear splash on the polished table.

Amelia stood there with the platter of smoked fish. Dolley looked up at the girl. Tears were welling in her eyes, even though she bit her lip and tried to appear composed. "Why, child, what's wrong?" Dolley said.

Amelia burst into sobs.

James said, "Dolley, the conduct of the household staff is your responsibility."

Amelia ran from the room.

Dolley Madison drew Amelia into a corner of the service pantry. The silver and china were stored here. There were no kitchens inside the White House. Kitchens, ovens, rooms to hang meat, rooms to ferment beverages, to allow bread to rise, or to store vegetables, were all outside the White House in small warm rooms or cold rooms so that neither their odors nor the heat of ovens in summer would seep into the mansion itself.

"We can't have this, Amelia," Dolley said.

"Oh, I am so sorry, Ma'am," the girl sobbed. Service at the White House was a choice position, and she didn't want to lose it. In addition, she liked the First Lady, even if the president frightened her.

"What has so upset you?"

"I have accepted George's proposal of marriage."

"I see. When?"

"I told him just a few minutes ago."

Dolley cocked her head and thought. George Fredericks was an unpleasant, hotheaded young man, but he was head butler, in charge of the White House silver. Amelia truly loved Henry Poole, who was a lowly supplies porter. Amelia's family, over the last several weeks, had remorselessly urged her to accept George, and in the last day or two had virtually ordered her to do so.

"It is not my place to interfere with your parents'

counsel, dear," Dolley said at last. But she contrived to add, "Possibly a long engagement might be wise."

It was an hour and a half later when the head ostler and the chief of White House staff bustled into the entry hall. They wished to see the president, but he was closeted with a delegation from Massachusetts and Dolley intercepted them.

"Henry Poole has been found dead, Ma'am," the chief of staff said.

"Oh, no! Where?"

"Near the grape arbor. Not far from the stables."

"Show me."

They hesitated, but as she held firm, they finally complied.

Henry Poole lay on the turned earth near the roots of a grape vine. "How long do you suppose he has been dead?" Dolley asked.

"It's warm here in the sun, Ma'am. Therefore, the temperature of the body is not a good guide. And he has . . . ah . . . has—"

"Become rigid?" Dolley asked, wondering yet another time how it was that men thought women had no idea of the facts of life.

"Yes, Ma'am. But that is quite a variable effect. I should say between one and three hours, Ma'am."

"You have noticed the injury on his forehead?"

"Yes, Ma'am."

"It suggests a murderous attack. Notify whatever authorities are appropriate. Keep me constantly informed."

Dolley Madison, of course, was thinking of George Fredericks. One could hardly think of an attack on

Henry Poole without thinking of George Fredericks. But the circumstances were certainly very peculiar.

She found George in the pantry and immediately taxed him with it.

"I never attacked Henry," was his first response.

"You have reddened knuckles. There is an abrasion on your chin. There was bad blood between you. Don't make me impatient with you."

When Dolley Madison became emphatic, it was hard to resist her. She watched George think, his jaw working unattractively for half a minute. Then he said, "He attacked me, Ma'am. I was only defending myself."

"Tell me the circumstances."

"Amelia accepted my proposal of marriage. I had gone out to the supplies shed to see if the soft polishing cloths had been left there by mistake. He saw me cross the yard. He began to berate me about the betrothal, and we went into the warm-room outbuilding to argue. He attacked me there. We fought. We bumped into the table where the bread was and knocked some pans onto the floor. We bumped into two of the cider kegs and knocked them over. During the course of the fight, Henry struck his head. But he was not unconscious, and he walked away, only staggering somewhat. I remained behind to pick up the bread pans and set the cider kegs upright. No cider was spilled, Ma'am. I can say that. Henry must have walked some distance and collapsed and died, for I swear I never saw him after he went out the door. And I didn't wish to see him anymore, so I did not look for him."

* * *

Dolley immediately went to the warm room.

It was a long, separate outbuilding, kept warm with a small Franklin stove. Down the center ran trestle tables on which bread was set to rise, or, in the winter, on which frozen supplies from unheated outbuildings were set to thaw. The kegs of cider that she had designated were next to the tables, fermenting a bit faster than was truly advisable. The pans of bread had already been removed, no doubt to the ovens for baking. The dinner for the Russian ambassador was now just a few hours off.

Understanding all of what had happened, Dolley decided it was time to tell the president. It was their custom to take tea at midafternoon. This would be a good opportunity.

Amelia was not serving at tea. Dolley had given her leave to spend the afternoon in her room.

The president listened as Dolley explained the circumstances of the death. "George says he was defending himself against attack, which is less reprehensible than attacking Henry, of course," she concluded.

"Indeed it is. Far less. The second is murder."

"But it cannot have happened as he claims."

"Certainly it could. It makes perfect sense in view of the individuals involved. George is hotheaded, and surely would strike back if attacked. And it makes no sense that *he* would instigate an attack on *Henry*, after Amelia had accepted him and made him the victor in their suit for her hand."

"She accepted him just before serving our luncheon. But Henry cannot have been killed after that."

"Why not?"

"His account of the fight is wrong. As I see it, Amelia met Henry before luncheon, probably in the warm room, to tell him she planned to accept George, as her family wished. Amelia and Henry were in love, and they parted with great sadness, perhaps a gesture or two of affection."

"They ought not waste working time—"

"Please, James! I think George must have come upon them—or perhaps followed her from the house—and, not knowing she planned to accept his suit, seeing them together became enraged. He must have bided his time, though, until Amelia left, because she did not see him attack Henry, and later told him she would marry him. But as soon as she was gone, he struck. He is, as you say, a hothead. In any case, he did not strike in defense of himself."

"But equally a hothead before luncheon and after. You cannot possibly know, Dolley, which time it was."

"Yes, I can. The bread pans could only have been knocked off the table without the bread being ruined before luncheon, while the dough was still dense and low in the pan. By early afternoon, it would have risen over the top. And indeed it had already gone to the ovens when I went to inspect the warm house. Even tipping a pan on its side once the bread is risen and fragile, would have ruined the loaf."

"I see."

"Bread, like industry and cider and love, is a commodity that requires the proper passage of time to mature."

BARBARA D'AMATO

———

BARBARA D'AMATO has given mystery lovers two wonderful series set in the Windy City: one starring reporter Cat Marsala, and the other starring two Chicago cops, Suze Figueroa and Norm Bennis. Her novels and short stories are frequently to be found on awards lists, and she has won both the Anthony Award and Agatha Award for true crime writing.

"Dolley Madison is one of the First Ladies I would most like to meet," says Barbara. "Smart, an incisive, iconoclastic thinker, she was also able to be stylish and politically, socially savvy."

ALICE HOLDS THE CARDS

―⟨∾∾⟩―

CAROLE NELSON DOUGLAS AND
JENNIFER WADDELL

> I can do one of two things. I can be President of
> the United States or I can control Alice. I can't
> possibly do both.
>
> —THEODORE ROOSEVELT, 26th president
> of the United States,
> on his oldest daughter

Washington, D.C., 1917

PRIDE REINCARNATED IN the flesh stood at my
door with a self-satisfied face that offered all the appeal of a mustachioed head of cabbage.

"Mrs. Longworth?" the vegetable-faced gentleman
asked.

"Yes?"

"Colonel Marlborough Churchill, at your service."

Of course, he wasn't *the* Marlborough Churchill of
Glorious Revolution or Spanish Succession fame, but
judging from the altitude of his nose and the swell
of his chest, *he* thought he was. It has often been
my observation that people who always try to look
important invariably never do, and such was certainly the case in this situation.

"Mrs. Longworth—may I call you Alice?"

I raised one eyebrow in an expression my terminally sophisticated husband, Nick, has always considered unladylike. But at age thirty-three I do not worry overmuch about my husband's opinions.

"No, you may *not*," I snapped. As a Washington matron of the advanced age of thirty-three, I felt entitled to say who may call me by what title.

Both of the colonel's brown, fuzzy caterpillar eyebrows wiggled their way up his massive furrowed-cabbage forehead just as my aberrant single one settled down.

"The cook, the maid, and the chauffeur may call me Alice," I continued, "however, to *you*, I am Mrs. Longworth. Or Mrs. Roosevelt Longworth, whichever you prefer. But do come in if you feel you must. Would you like some hot tea?"

The colonel engaged in a series of overdramatic, gravelly coughs in an attempt to hide his discomfort and nodded.

I smiled. "Pity. I'm afraid I haven't got any tea. Perhaps it would be best if you simply tell me what you want and go on your way," I said as he followed me into the parlor. "There's a war on, you know. So much to destroy, so little time!"

The colonel, whose complacent cabbagelike countenance had turned to sauerkraut, settled so deeply into my blue, flower-printed living room sofa that I feared I would have to uproot him to be rid of him and replace the springs after he left.

"Franklin warned me about you," he said.

"Oh, *really?* How delightful! Being someone to be

warned about is so flattering. And you came any-way—brave soul."

Churchill's nondescript brown irises sank into pale folds of flesh as he narrowed his eyes and leaned forward.

"Mrs. Longworth," he went on, "I am here to offer you a chance to serve your country."

I sat back and folded my arms across my chest. Currently, the press was criticizing me for *not* serving my country. Oh, I served quite literally, dishing out ice cream for soldiers coming through Washington, and social niceties like that, but I never did anything that could be considered a serious contribution to the war effort.

Frankly, I had no desire to do any such thing. War, in my opinion, is one of the male gender's duller avocations, excepting golf. There is so much method in all the madness that one cannot appreciate the madness behind the method, which, after all, is what war is all about. Spontaneity is the spice of life—and *hopefully* of death, I think.

"You have a patriotic assignment for me. So I've been told by Feather Duster," I said.

"Feather Duster?"

"That's what we call Franklin in the family. I don't believe it's because we find him flighty. Who knows where these Roosevelt family traditions start—or, worse yet, will end? What do they want me to do this time?"

"Well, I'm afraid it's not the sort of activity a lady ordinarily would wish to engage in—"

"Fortunately for you, I'm not in the business of being ladylike."

Churchill's eyes widened. (At least, I assume they did; hard to tell with all that flesh drooping like bee's wax all over the place.)

"Out with it, now!" I snapped my fingers a couple of times in his face. "What do you want me to do?" It's such great fun to intimidate decorated military leaders!

"As you know, Feather . . . er, Franklin sent me. He wants you to s-spy." Churchill's stammer hardly befitted a man presumably used to barking out orders.

"On whom?"

"Mister Bernard Baruch and Miss Eugenia Leigh."

I leaned forward in my chair to look my uninvited guest in the eye.

Bernard Baruch was one of the most eligible bachelors in Washington whose only physical fault was deafness in his left ear. He was currently keeping himself rather busy advising President Wilson as to which resources should be sold (or traded) for how much, to whom, and when, now that the United States had entered the war. He really was a dear. His dark, glossy hair and strong jawline, not to mention his bank account, attracted scores of women; however, he had the unfortunate habit of never saying anything bad about others behind their backs, which was rather disappointing.

Eugenia Leigh was one of Washington's most beautiful brunettes and was smooth as ice on a summer day, capable of doing all and saying anything about anybody. She was currently keeping *herself* rather busy occupying Bernard Baruch's otherwise free moments. The two people in question were both good friends of mine, and I wanted to make sure that Churchill knew what he was asking of me.

"You're suggesting that I spy for you? On my friends and neighbors?"

The colonel looked apologetic, and apoplectic. "I'm afraid so . . ."

He positively cowered under my glare. I waited a few more seconds more before I spoke.

"Splendid! When can I start?"

It didn't take long for Churchill to brief me, despite his stuttering. Apparently, sweet Eugenia had an uncle in Bucharest who handled her estate and more or less stuck his nose into her day-to-day affairs, which made my cousin Franklin, who was serving as assistant secretary of the navy at the time, a wee bit nervous.

Now, in all fairness, I must say that I don't think Franklin considered spying on the woman justifiable merely because she had recently taken a house conveniently located just down the street from Bernie. However, when Eugenia and Bernie began seeing each other in a romantic context, Franklin then decided it was time to take action, and rightly so. If Eugenia managed to find out and relay to her uncle . . . say, for instance, that the Chilean government had its gold reserve in Germany (which the Germans refused to release to Chile), that Germany had 200,000 tons of nitrates in Chile (which the Chileans refused to release to Germany), and that Bernie proposed to buy all the German nitrates from Chile at four and a quarter cents a pound and pay for it in gold, the United States could be seriously compromised.

So, not three days later, here I was, slinking around inside Eugenia's house while she was out, having intimidated the foreign maid with the name of Roosevelt to get in. I was looking for nooks and niches in which to hide listening devices—all in the name of "serving my country." That phrase was becoming so overused of late, one would think one's native land was a dessert!

I had no illusions about why I had been drafted for this delicate task. A woman was expected to know better than a mere man where within her lair another woman would lure the male of the species to extract illicit little nothings from him.

Such little nothings might be mere jewels or more deadly gems of international information. Even a supposedly respectable woman—and although I was notorious in myriad small ways, I was still considered an upright pillar of the community in the larger picture (as much as Washington may claim any upright pillars among its society)—even a supposedly respectable woman is assumed to have special insight into the wiles of a Delilah. I cannot say that I felt much sympathy for the women who made a hobby of dallying with other women's husbands, though, of course, the dallying men are always the more to blame, being such utter hypocrites. The Washington breed of the beast is the most amusing to hunt and trap.

But Bernard Baruch was not married to anything but money, so I knew poor Eugenia was probably in a perfectly dreadful situation—in the worst case, she would have to spy for her foreign uncle or have her income cut off. The lady must choose between the lion or the tiger: betray her country or starve to death. Women are always being put into such unfair positions, hence the many dreadful melodramas that haunt the stage these days.

Frankly, I am more admiring of farce than of melodrama, but I found this particular situation perfectly delicious. The stuff fiction is made of! And I was having so much fun playing Mata Hari at the time that I didn't even stop to remember how that particular Delilah had recently ended her career or wonder whether or not Eugenia could be executed for treason!

I had just discovered the most fabulous hiding place on the north balcony (we could place a microphone in the potted fern by the hammock-bed, its cord threading down the wall behind the ivy, across the grass and into the large studio at the rear, making the whole apparatus practically invisible) when I felt a hand on my shoulder.

I jumped, whacking my head against the pole-support for the hammock's mattress before I could turn around to see who had discovered me.

"Alice? *Alice Longworth!* It *is* you! How did you get in? And what *are* you doing here?"

Pale blue eyes, teacup-wide, stared down at me in astonishment. I mirrored their gaze with an equally surprised stare of my own.

Instead of Eugenia Leigh's creamy peach visage, which I had expected to see, I found myself face to face with her young friend, Mattidale Johnson, whom

I had known for a full three years before I ever met Eugenia.

She was a delightful girl—the kind who still approached life with a sense of wonder and who always spoke in italics. I hadn't seen her in ages, but I heard snippets of her whereabouts and activities every now and then. She was a distant relation on my father's side of the family, I think. But who could be sure? Relations had come out of the woodwork when Father was elected president. Whether or not all of them were actually blood-related remained for time to tell.

"What am I doing here?" When caught in the act, I always tell the truth because it's the least likely explanation to be believed. "I'm conducting a top-secret government investigation! What does it look like I'm doing?"

I stood up, smoothed my hair, and straightened my blue gown. The press would have called it an "Alice Blue" gown, I suppose, but I knew better. My tailor was Italian, didn't speak any English, and had never heard the song "Alice Blue Gown." Besides, the fabric was at least three shades lighter than my eyes, which the famed blue was supposed to match.

"Really, Alice. If you don't want to tell me what you're doing, you should just say so. Lying isn't ladylike."

"Ladylike! The next person who says that word to me is going to get smacked."

Mattidale gasped. "But that's not the sort of thing a la—" She stopped short and giggled. "Oh, Alice! I'd *forgotten* how *wicked* you are! Such *fun!*"

I pulled a cigarette from my handbag, lit it,

propped my foot up on the edge of a vacant plant pedestal, and inhaled. "But what are you doing here, Mattidale? I dare you to come up with a better explanation than mine."

"Me? Oh, I live here."

"Ha! That's what Nick's last midnight fling said to me the morning I tripped over the two of them together in the park. I trust you mean it in a more honorable way."

"Naturally!"

Mattidale, trying not to look aghast, tucked a wisp of loose, amber hair whose color almost perfectly matched my own back into her hat with a characteristic flip of her wrist. She was always on-the-go and was thus always trying to rearrange her hair into some semblance of order after it had been whipped out of shape by her constant tornado of activity. "I'm staying with Eugenia for a while until my husband comes back from Europe."

"Gregory's fighting?"

"Afraid so."

"But I heard that you two just got married!"

Mattidale lowered her eyes. Hell's belles! The child was going to cry on me. This would never do. If there's anything I hate worse than a sobbing sophisticate, it's a soggy shoulder. I have never cared to have my dresses ruined by tears. I had to come up with something to stop this, and quickly. How to distract a sorrowful nineteen-year-old newlywed . . .

"Mattidale, would you like to know what I'm really doing here?"

Interest flooded the girl's face instead of tears. She blinked expectantly.

I put out my cigarette and flicked it over the edge of the balcony before I leaned forward and whispered *"Spy work"* into her ear.

"For the president? Really, you weren't lying when you said you were working for the government?"

I laughed. "No, you silly goose! Not for the government! For myself. What do you think I am? Some kind of secret agent?"

"You are the president's daughter—"

"Former president's daughter, thank you very much. I wouldn't claim a relationship to Woodrow Wilson even if one existed!"

Mattidale waved my denunciation aside. Her pale blue eyes deepened to lapis lazuli with excitement. The color was really quite striking with her fair complexion; anyone who had ever said the girl was never beautiful should have seen her at that moment. "So who are you spying on? Eugenia?"

"Of course not," I said. "She's not interesting enough to care two figs about—otherwise your family would never let you stay with her!"

"Then who?"

"Well, if you promise not to tell—"

"Oh, I promise! You can trust me!" Mattidale was breathless with anticipation. This was going to be too easy.

"So, I have your solemn oath on it?"

"Cross my heart and hope to die!"

For effect, I leaned back on my heels, looked over the balcony, then turned and looked inside the house in a show of making sure no one was listening to our conversation. "No need to go that far. I trust you. Look—watch my hand! I'm going to write it so no one can overhear."

Mattidale bent over my shoulder and watched as I traced out the letters N-I-C-K with my finger on the green and white striped mattress of the hammock-bed.

"Your *husband?*" she gasped in a stage whisper.

I clapped my hand over her mouth. Good thing I wasn't trusting her with any real secrets. "Shush! Now, I'm going to remove my hand. No more exclamations?" She nodded, and I took my hand away from her face. "I'll tell you what I'm going to do. I could use your help, so if you like, I'm going to let you spy on him with me."

"Oh, Alice, I'm not sure that's a ladyli—proper thing to do, I mean."

"If you're going to turn Victorian on me—?"

"No! Of course not!"

I stifled a smile. One of the benefits of being a national figure is that you can manipulate the not-so-famous into doing what you want them to do just by asking them to do it. And what the power of a name won't do, a forceful personality will. I had both at my disposal.

"Well, then. In that case, here's the plan. Bernie Baruch and I have both been invited to a dinner party tomorrow night given by Franklin and Eleanor Roosevelt, but I'm not going to go."

"No?"

"No. I'm going to play sick and tell Bernie to take Eugenia to fill my place."

"But wouldn't she have to go with Nick to do that?"

"Oh, Nick isn't going."

"Why not?"

I sat down on the edge of the swinging bed, crossed my legs, and leaned back on my hands. The word *unladylike* threatened to burst from Mattidale's lips as she looked at my posture, but the girl's self control was improving. "Nick and I don't go to the same parties anymore. If he prefers to keep company other than myself, then let him."

Mattidale opened her mouth, then shut it again without saying anything.

"Don't look so astonished—it's really not all that awful. I wanted to divorce him five years ago, but the family . . . Roosevelts in politics don't divorce, you know. And if you're a Roosevelt, you're in politics. And if you didn't know, they would tell you, believe me."

What I didn't tell the innocent young thing was that "Princess Alice Blue-gown" had been twenty-two and in danger of becoming Washington's most famous old maid, and Nick was of the right party, if somewhat older; even if his hair was rapidly becoming a fond memory, men do wear hats so much. And it did permit a White House wedding, though I knew nothing of Nick's wandering ways at the time; brides usually don't, although all of Washington did. That's why I made certain to be outspoken now. Women should know these things. There are advantages in being young and ignorant no longer, it frees me to do what I like.

"But you don't let him get away with it scot *free*?"

"Of course not! Why do you think I'm spying on him?"

"Oooohh, of course! What do you want me to do?"

"Wait a moment, I haven't told you everything yet."

I leaned over, grabbed my handbag, and pulled out another cigarette. It was easier to wax creative amid a haze of smoke. "Now. I happen to know that Eugenia and Nick have an understanding." This, of course, was a *complete* fabrication.

Mattidale sat down with a thump on the green and white cushion of a wicker chair backing onto the balcony door. "She never even let on that she knew him!"

"Of course not. That's part of the understanding: utter secrecy, et cetera, ad nauseam. The arrangement is, when she goes out, Nick gets the house."

"But what does he *do* with it?"

I shot the girl a mildly deprecating glance. "Really, Mattidale. You're a married woman now—you know about the kinds of things men and women do in private."

Mattidale's hand flew to her mouth.

"So," I continued, "what we're going to do is have a little fun. We're going to listen in!"

"For *blackmail?*"

"Don't be ridiculous. Nothing quite so bourgeois as that."

"Then what for?" Mattidale was practically drooling.

"Well . . ." I lifted my eyebrows twice in succession and lowered my voice. "I was thinking of something on more of an operatic scale. Grand drama, you know?"

"I hope you don't mean you're going to sing!"

"Ha! The day I serenade my husband while he's entertaining another woman will be the day Taft sees his shoes! Of course I'm not going to sing." I reached into my handbag, pulled out the revolver I always carried and dangled it in front of Mattidale's face. "You ever pointed one of these things at somebody?"

Mattidale, wide-eyed, shook her head.

"Oh, it's quite a thrill, I can assure you."

"Alice, you can't *shoot* someone for being unfaithful, even if you are the daughter of a president."

"I know *that!*" What an innocent the child was! "Don't worry—we're not going to shoot anybody. Look. Here's what we're going to do. There's some new listening equipment that's been developed for the war effort, and I've got access to it."

"How?"

"Never mind that—that's classified information. Only presidential families know about it." Of course, it was a ridiculous answer, but I couldn't be bothered for details, and Mattidale was just gullible enough to accept it. "What we're going to do is run the microphone cords from strategic spots in the house to the studio out back. Then we're going to listen to what goes on between Nick and whoever he shows up with tomorrow night, and at precisely the right moment, we're going to rush in and surprise them!"

"How perfectly dreadful!" Mattidale frowned for a moment, then burst into smiles. "And then what?"

"And then we're going to intimidate the hell out of them by shooting some bullets in their general direction."

"Oh, Alice, you shouldn't swear! It's not lady—I mean . . . oh, never mind! What if you miss and hit somebody *else?* And what if the newspapers find out?"

I stood and drew myself up to my full height: five-foot-eight in the low-heeled boots I was wearing. "I never miss, and who cares? Nick'll be too embarrassed to tell, and his hussy of the evening won't let him closer than the length of her parasol ever again. Thus, I win twice over! One humiliation and one elimination—and you'll be there to see it."

Of course, I wasn't *really* going to shoot at anybody, especially at my husband. I have seen domestic violence, and it's nothing I would ever seriously consider engaging in (tempting as it was), even within the context of my own nonmonogamous marriage, which Nick was making so obvious that the general public had begun to describe it as "open."

However, if the mere prospect of firing bullets from a gun distracted Mattidale, then the bluff was good enough for me. Tomorrow evening, we'd just meet in the studio, Mattidale would get to see the brand-new listening equipment, I'd teach her how to play poker by candlelight, or something, and she'd forget all about her troubles for one night. Additionally, she'd be utterly misled about the true purpose of my prying expedition.

But best of all, I wouldn't have to go to another one of my cousin Eleanor's dull dinner parties.

I'd just have to talk to Colonel Cabbage-face after dinner and get him to lay out the wires by tomorrow night without actually turning the whole system on. That way, we could sit down there without hearing anything, which, no doubt, would relieve Mattidale. She seemed absolutely terrified of guns, but I had joined my father's expeditions since I was a girl.

"So what do you think?" I asked.

"I think the whole scheme is outrageous!"

"Fabulous! That means it's worthwhile. Now be a good girl and escort me down to the door so I can escape before Eugenia comes home and sees me."

Mattidale dutifully took my arm, and we pranced down the stairs in a ridiculously girlish fashion until we reached the bottom and my shoe came down on something small and hard, which caused my foot to slide out from underneath me. Before I knew it, I was in the splits position on the pale porcelain tile floor. I let loose with an unprintable word, much to Mattidale's dismay.

"Goodness, Alice!" Mattidale's head twisted around to face the kitchen. "Frieda!" she called. "Bring some ice! I think my guest is hurt!"

Instantly I forgot all about my aching joints. "Frieda? Who's that?"

"Eugenia's new maid. Her uncle sent her all the way from Bucharest to take care of her. Wasn't that thoughtful?"

"There's a *German* in the house? Does Bernie know?"

Mattidale nodded—in answer to which question, I couldn't tell. "*Frieda!* Come quickly!"

"How'd she get in the country with the war on?"

Mattidale frowned at me. "I don't know. I think she arrived before we entered the conflict. And I think Eugenia's uncle has some kind of government connections, which helped. Alice, are you quite all right?"

I realized that I must have gone pale.

"*Frieda!* Hurry! I'm afraid she's going to faint!"

A short, blond-haired woman with a plain face and

wearing an even plainer black skirt emerged from the kitchen, ran through the parlor and slid to a stop on the slick, porcelain floor. I waved her offering of a cube of ice wrapped in a pastry cloth away, suddenly more interested in a small square of another kind of ice that had just caught my eye. All other thoughts had fled.

"What is it?" Mattidale demanded.

I slid over the tile on my posterior to pick up the offending object responsible for my fall, not believing what I saw, then finally looked up at Mattidale and shook my head for a moment to clear it before I spoke.

Once again Nick had exceeded even my cynical expectations. "It's one of the diamond cufflinks I gave to Nick for his birthday last year. Do you see? The setting is engraved."

I do so hate coming up with an elaborate lie and then finding out that I was wasting my time because my creative falsehood is only too true.

The following evening Mattidale sat cross-legged in front of me on Eugenia's studio floor. The ecru dress she was wearing had a tremendous amount of material in the skirt so that when she sat, all the fabric pouffed out around her, making her look rather like an inverted mushroom. I had shocked her by showing up in trousers, and to her credit, she never even breathed the word *lady*. Dear child—she was learning. Perhaps she would amount to something someday. Maybe I'd have to introduce her to Margaret Sanger—now *there* was a woman with some sense.

Naturally, she was fascinated by the listening equipment. Colonel Marlborough Churchill, for once, had lived up to his illustrious name by setting up the microphones and wires just where I wanted them to be, but only after much begging and pleading. Thankfully, he had no notion about what I was really up to tonight or he never would have agreed to help me out.

Even so, he still refused to tell me where the "on/off" switch was, which made me furious. What if it accidentally got flipped on? How would I turn it off? What if Nick were really up there?

I didn't want to know, I didn't want to hear, and I definitely did *not* want to see, despite my earlier bluff.

Mattidale was fingering the heavy, black wires that had been threaded from the house, across the lawn, under the crawl space of the studio out back, and right up into the spacious, well-lit, multipurpose room we had appropriated and claimed as our new poker-playing territory. Mattidale had been unable to locate the key to the place, so I had picked the lock using two hat pins and an ice pick. It was a skill I had mastered during my White House years when I wanted to see behind doors that happened to be closed.

We hadn't turned on any of the electric lights, choosing candles instead, as we didn't want to draw any attention to the house.

"Are *all* of these wires attached to microphones?" Mattidale's changeable eyes looked like a star-studded midnight as the candlelight flickered in them.

"Every one."

"And these things will let us hear what people are saying inside the house?" An arched metal contraption attached to a flattened oval earpiece dangled from Mattidale's delicate fingers.

"Those are the headsets, yes."

"There are so many!"

"Eavesdroppers often travel in hordes—especially if they're government employees. Everything takes a committee! Despicably inefficient way to run a railroad, if you ask me."

Mattidale laughed. "Which rooms of the house can we hear?"

I put down my candle and stalked, catlike, to the window. "We can hear anything that occurs on the balcony, in the parlor, the kitchen, the three bedrooms, the living room, or the library." I could see the balcony with that hideously striped hammock-bed on it from here. Had Nick been lying there recently, I wondered? Why is concrete evidence of a known fact harder to live with than the fact itself?

Mattidale giggled and clapped her hands. "Why, that's quite a lot of area we've got covered! It's better than slinking around in the actual house! We'd only be able to hear *one* room if we did that!"

"Yes, I suppose you're right." I whirled around. No sense in dwelling on things I couldn't help. "But come now. I'm going to teach you how to play poker." Mattidale watched as I whipped a deck of cards from my trouser pocket, shuffled them in the air, bridged, and let them cascade in waterfall sequence from one hand to the other.

"But that's absolutely *marvelous!*" she cried. "How on earth do you do it?"

"I'll teach you later. First . . . the game." After we both donned thankfully silent headsets, I proceeded to lay out rules and strategy of five-card draw over the course of several practice rounds. Although it was obvious Mattidale didn't consider cards very ladylike, she seemed to enjoy herself in spite of the fact and had even picked up some slang.

After about forty-five minutes playing-time, she suddenly looked up from an obviously distressing hand. (Although she had gotten the rules down by now, her poker face left a lot to be desired. I'd have to teach her the fine art of dissembling before I sicced her on the men in my poker-playing circle.)

"Alice!"

"Yes?"

"The sets are so *awfully* quiet! Do you suppose they're turned on?"

"Absolutely," I said. "This is the newest, most secret equipment! No noise, no static."

"Precisely! I don't think they work! Hit me with three, by the way."

I dealt Mattidale the three requested cards and took two for myself. "Of course they work. You don't think Wilson would spend government money on them if they didn't, do you? Granted, the man is about as intelligent as a monkey in a barrel, but even monkeys aren't *that* ignorant. Your bet."

"I check."

"Coward," I teased. "We're only playing with matches."

"What if I want to start a fire? I'll need some matches! But no fair changing the subject. If the equipment works, shouldn't we have heard something by now?"

"Maybe nobody's home."

"But Alice, there's a light on in the balcony bedroom! Don't you see it?"

I twisted my head around to look. Sure enough, the infernal thing was burning. "Well," I said, turning back around, "if you're going to check, then I'm going to bet. Five matches. You in?"

"I'll call. And—oh, why not? I'll raise you ten big ones."

"Ten! First you're too yellow-bellied to bet, and then you're raising me half of what you've got left? Get some sense!"

"I *have* sense! *You're* the one who's acting crazy! If you insist on playing cards, I want to hurry up and finish the game so I can go inside and see what's going on!"

"You can't do that! What if someone's up there?"

"Then you pull out your gun and shoot at them! Remember?"

So maybe the child wasn't gun-shy after all. "I'll tell you what—"

Before I could tell her anything, a loud popping noise exploded in our ears, and the next instant, disembodied voices swathed in soft static crackled into life.

Mattidale screamed. "Poltergeists!"

"Wrong. Modern military science," I said. "Pick up your cards—I can see your hand. Believe me, a king high is not worth your bet."

Mattidale wasn't listening to me.

"*But, darling, General Pershing needs mules to haul*

guns to the front," a woman's voice purred over the speakers. *"Spain's not giving them away for the asking. What do we have to trade? What happens if none of our soldiers have guns?"*

The two of us rushed to the window to peer up at the balcony just in time to see the light in the bedroom dim.

"Why do you care about the war when I'm here?" The second voice was male, and it was definitely the voice of a man who was in love. Nick? Was it him? I couldn't tell through the muffling static. *"Everything you need, and everything you need to worry about is right here—"*

"Egotist," I muttered.

"What?"

"Shhh. Listen."

Mattidale cocked her head and listened for a few moments. The two voices had ceased talking. "I don't hear anything."

"Exactly."

"Oohhh! Now, Alice! Now! Let's go get them!"

"Mattidale—"

Something crashed behind us. We whirled around and braced ourselves against the wall just in time to see a middle-aged, more or less handsome bald man with a mustache burst into the studio. He had thrown the door open so hard the handle embedded in the wall.

"Nick!"

Nick, fully clothed, tripped over a black wire and stuck his hands out in front of him just in time to keep himself from kissing the hardwood floor. "Alice? *Alice!"*

Before I could say a word, Colonel Cabbage-face huffed and puffed his way through the door, turning our astonished trio into a quartet. He pointed a chubby, accusing arm at Mattidale. "Who's that, and what is she doing here?" Then he waggled a finger at me. "And what are *you* doing here! How did you get in?"

"Same way you did when you installed the wires, no doubt," I snapped. "Illegally. Mattidale is my guest."

"Your . . . your g—! Alice!" Nick ran his palm over his forehead, then flicked a drop of sweat to the ground. "This is not your affair! You can't *entertain* people with government business!"

"*Really?* Then what else is government business good for?" I demanded.

But Mattidale was having none of this political repartee. She stepped in front of me and stomped her foot. "We haven't got anything to do with your nasty old government, we just came to spy on *you!*"

"Me?" Nick's eyebrows crawled halfway up his bald head.

I pushed Mattidale aside and waved the issue away with a gesture of dismissal. "Never mind, I'll explain later. Meanwhile, I demand an apology. You've ruined a perfectly lovely poker game."

"Not now!" Nick, who, like the colonel, had already grabbed a headset and clapped it over his bald crown, was speaking through clenched teeth. "Churchill! I thought you said this damned device worked!"

"It does!"

"I don't hear anything."

My toe started tapping involuntarily. "That's because," I said, "both parties upstairs more than likely have better things to do than palaver."

Mattidale and Churchill's hands flew to their own mouths at my assertion, but I didn't even startle Nick.

"What did you hear?" he demanded.

"Nothing I haven't heard before, nothing I've heard very recently, and nothing I'm going to tell you."

I put one hand on my hip and pointed at Nick with the other.

"What are you doing mixed up in my business, and how the hell did you wind up losing *this*"—I pulled the diamond cufflink from my pocket and held it out before me—"in the house of a woman you don't even know?"

Nick looked shocked. Whether or not it was pretended shock, I couldn't tell.

"So that's what happened to it!" he said. "Bernie borrowed them last week because—wait a minute! This is absurd! I don't have to explain anything to you, and I'm not going to! Now tell me what you heard. It's important!"

I rolled my eyes, which I knew was bound to infuriate the ever-sophisticated Nick. It wasn't the sort of thing he liked to see a wife of his doing. Not ladylike. "First, you tell me how you got here and why."

Churchill answered that one. "Bernie didn't arrive. We knew something was up."

"Arrive where?" I asked.

"At Franklin and Eleanor's."

"You were at Eleanor's dinner party?" I couldn't

believe it. "I had no idea her tastes were so plebeian And *you!*" I pointed at my husband. "How did you get involved?"

"Cornered Churchill, who had been seen sneaking around my house—and my wife—a couple days ago and demanded an explanation."

"Nick! For crying out loud!" I threw both my hands in the air. "He's not even my type!"

Churchill was getting ready to be severely offended, but Mattidale cut him off at the pass. "Will someone please tell me what's going on?"

All three of us whirled on the nineteen-year-old. "*No!*" our trio shouted in unison.

"We don't have time for this!" Churchill tapped the earpiece on his headset with a fat finger. "I don't hear anything. Eugenia could already be cabling top secret information to that uncle of hers in Bucharest! We've got to stop her!"

"No need to," came a new, female voice from the door. "I haven't got an uncle in Bucharest. He died three months ago. Although the discussion you've been having out here could possibly wake the dead, even in Europe."

All four of us whirled around to regard a complacent Eugenia. She stood in the doorway, one hand on her hip, the other hand propping her up as she leaned against the frame for support. Her loose dressing gown of white silk chiffon floated, cloudlike, in the breeze. Reflected candlelight made shadow and highlight flow into one another with every billow of the fabric, making her look less like the person she was and more like a ghostly visitation—maybe sent from her erstwhile uncle. Handsome Bernard

Baruch stood right behind her, looking like a phantom shadow in dinner dress, buttons awry.

I pounced, apparently the only one not momentarily daunted by the sudden presence of wraithlike Eugenia and her male counterpart. "But you *do* have a German servant!"

"You *do?*" Churchill asked.

"You *do?*" Bernie echoed.

Churchill ripped the headset from his ear and threw it to the ground, then glared at me. "You didn't tell me that!"

I shrugged. "You never asked."

"Calm down. Frieda is *not* German." Eugenia strolled across the studio floor, her dressing gown nipping at her bare ankles, to look Churchill squarely in the eye. "She's Romanian. She's on our side."

"But *you* said she was German!" Mattidale insisted.

Eugenia, who seemed to notice the presence of her young houseguest for the first time, looked surprised at the accusation. "I said nothing of the kind! You all just assume that since the Central Powers are occupying Bucharest at the moment that Frieda must be German."

"You mean with a name like Frieda she's *not?*" I demanded.

"Certainly not! Her last name is Bukov, for goodness' sake."

"And your uncle didn't have any government connections?"

"Oh, Alice! Don't be ridiculous. He knew the American ambassador at one time, if that's what you call connections. I can assure you he never gained anything by the acquaintance. Where do you get such absurd notions?"

Nick, Colonel Cabbage-face, and Bernie all stared at me. I, in turn, stared at Mattidale until at last all the other eyes in the room mimicked the direction of my own gaze.

"What?" the child asked. "I didn't do anything. You look at me like *I'm* the crazy one! *You're* the ones standing around in the dark yelling at each other like fools—and all for nothing."

"She's right," I said. "Turn on the lights. No need for concealment when the eavesdroppers have already been caught. Might as well stand around yelling at each other like fools in broad daylight—or the semblance of it, anyway."

Eugenia strode across the studio and flipped three switches, leaving all of us blinking as our eyes adjusted to the light that filled the room and spilled out the door into the dark night beyond. Ebony blotches swarmed in and out of my vision field; one even looked strangely like a body in motion. I blinked some more and then squinted. It was still there. Doing something. Writing, maybe. I grabbed Mattidale's arm and pointed. There, outside, cast in shadows but visible nevertheless (thanks to Eugenia's electric lights), a figure was hunched over a small tablet, scrawling all over it.

I was out the door and on top of the figure before it even looked up. (Trousers do wonders for a woman's maneuverability.) "Bernie! Nick!" I yelled. "Somebody's out here!"

"Nab him!" Bernie's deep, unperturbed voice called back.

"Already did. Only it's a *her!* It's Frieda! And she's written all over this tablet in—I think it's—yes, it is! It's German!"

"So what you're telling me," Colonel Cabbage-face said after some of his on-call minions had taken our captive away and we were seated in Eugenia's Victorian-styled parlor, "is that Frieda is Romanian *and* German?"

"Yes," I said. "I just got off the telephone with Feather Duster, who in turn just got a return cable from the Romanian government. Her birth record listed her mother as German and her father as Romanian; turns out she was named after her mother."

"Which would explain the German first name and the Romanian last name." Nick scratched his head. "But Eugenia's uncle hired her and sent her here, which must mean he was a spy after all."

Eugenia made a sound of disgust. "That's preposterous. My uncle hired her off the street! How was he supposed to know she was a spy?"

Nick looked unconvinced. "That's what he told *you*, but how do we know whether or not it's really true?"

I glanced at Eugenia. Although Bernie's arm was wrapped around her in a gesture of moral support, she still looked ready to burst into tears. "Leave her alone, Nick. It doesn't matter now, anyway. He can't do any more harm, if he ever intended to do any in the first place."

Churchill shrugged. "At any rate, we'll never know. The good news is that Frieda didn't hear anything tonight worth reporting back to Bucharest, thanks to the studio farce out there."

I sighed. "So it's settled. And now—on to more important matters." I pointed a long finger at Bernie. "Like discovering what you were doing with Nick's diamond cufflinks. Out with it!"

Bernie hung his head, shamefaced. "There was a White House Ball a week ago, and I couldn't find my own formal pair anywhere, so I borrowed Nick's, then lost one of them. I had no idea where it went until tonight."

"A White House Ball? And I wasn't invited?" I confess to being a bit taken aback. "I'll just have to remember that the next time I throw a party of my own."

Nick laughed. "Would you have gone if you *had* been invited?"

"Certainly not! Of all the presidents I've known, Wilson is the one whose face is most likely to wind up on a dartboard. Probably mine."

"Alice, half the faces of America would probably wind up on your dartboard at one time or another, if you had one!" Bernie said good-naturedly. "But never mind that—now you've got to satisfy my own curiosity. What were you doing slinking around in Eugenia's studio?"

"Yes indeed. What?" Eugenia's otherwise lovely face was so contorted with rage that I almost wanted to laugh. Whoever said beauty wears anger well was gravely mistaken.

I shrugged. "Defending my country from enemies foreign and domestic."

"But Alice!" Mattidale, who was sitting next to me

on Eugenia's red velvet sofa, tugged on the sleeve of my blouse. "We weren't on government business! We were going to—"

"Have a little fun," I interrupted. Sometime in the very near future, I was going to have to teach the child how to keep her mouth shut. "A poker game was in order, and the studio seemed as good a spot to play as any other."

Bernie regarded me through skeptical, narrowed eyelids. No doubt I'd be pressed for the true explanation at the next possible convenience.

"And so you stood me up for a poker game!" he said. "That's why I didn't go. I hate going to parties alone—so dull! You know I've got a low boring point!"

"Mine's lower," I said. "And besides, I distinctly remember telling you to take Eugenia along."

"She was engaged elsewhere."

"Really?" I couldn't ever remember a time when Eugenia didn't drop everything to accompany Bernie to this party or that. "Where?"

Eugenia blushed.

Bernie shifted positions in his chair and said nothing for a moment. "Ah . . . *chez elle,* you might say."

"I see," I said. And I did. Indiscretions always seemed more respectable when discussed in French, and they were inevitably more interesting than one of my cousin's dinner parties—language irrelevant. "So you *both* stayed home to . . . discuss the role of big guns in the invasion of Germany."

"*Alice!*" The tiny capillaries in Eugenia's face looked ready to burst. "For Heaven's sake!"

"What?" I spread my arms in a gesture of innocence. "I heard two voices over the headset discussing what would happen if General Pershing didn't have mules to haul guns to the front. I just assumed it was the two of you."

"Mattidale's husband could be on that front!" Eugenia said. Mattidale gasped. "I was just concerned, that's all!"

Colonel Churchill's flabby forehead scrunched into a series of bewildered wrinkles. "So you weren't pressing Bernie for information your uncle in Bucharest might find useful?"

"Of course not!" Eugenia looked ready to shed her voluminous dressing gown like a snakeskin—a boa constrictor's, say—and strangle Colonel Cabbage-face. "As if Bernie would share that kind of information with me! And I already told you my uncle is dead! Died of a heart attack. Not that he was ever dangerous in the first place—he wouldn't have hurt a . . . a *German!* You've wasted your time and your money eavesdropping on me."

Churchill pulled a toothpick out of his coat pocket and began to pick at his teeth. "Never know unless you do," he said through the thin splinter of wood.

I yawned. I'd had enough of finger-pointing and pointless espionage for one evening, so I stood up and prepared to go on my way. "Well, it's been a charming evening and all, but other business beckons."

"Like what?" Nick asked.

"Like more poker," I said.

Colonel Cabbage-face stood and rearranged his pants. I could have made curtains from the amount of material that was draped from his waist. "Playing for high stakes?"

"Of course," I said, and winked at Mattidale.

"And what," Eugenia demanded, "are you going to do with your winnings?"

I propped one foot up on a footstool that matched the red velvet chairs, slid a cigarette out of one of my trouser pockets and a match I had won from Mattidale out of the other, then executed a one-shouldered shrug.

"Smoke," I said. "Naturally."

And no one even breathed the word *ladylike*.

CAROLE NELSON DOUGLAS AND
JENNIFER WADDELL

~~~

CAROLE NELSON DOUGLAS, a former newspaper writer/editor, is a veteran multi-genre novelist who writes two award-winning mystery series: the historical adventures of diva/detective Irene Adler, the only woman to outwit Sherlock Holmes, and the contemporary Las Vegas capers of feline supersleuth Midnight Louie. Jennifer Waddell is an award-winning recent graduate of Texas Christian University, who aspires to a fiction-writing career. She has been Carole's part-time personal assistant since 1995, and this is their first collaboration.

"Why Alice Roosevelt Longworth?" the writing duo ask rhetorically. "Whyever *not*? When the twentieth century was in its infancy, Theodore Roosevelt's irrepressible daughter was a lovely Gibson-girl debutante, America's Princess Alice, married in her father's White House. She traveled, campaigned, smoked, and played poker with her father's cronies. A cousin of Franklin Delano—and a closer cousin of Eleanor—Roosevelt, Alice survived the betrayals many women associated with political men faced during her long era, took on rearing her orphaned eleven-year-old granddaughter at age seventy-three, and lived into her nineties. She died at the brink of the Reagan era, remaining to the bittersweet end America's tart-tongued girl–turned–grande dame, a Washington institution as venerable, varied, and surprising as the Smithsonian itself."

JACKIE-O

KRISTINE KATHRYN RUSCH

S HE NEVER USED the word "murder." Not casually as in "I could murder him for this;" nor seriously as in "A man was murdered on Fifty-Second and Broadway." She watched little television, and avoided editing books that used the offending word.

She never thought about death or murder or assassination until her final months, alone in her fifteen-room Fifth Avenue co-op, those nights when sleep eluded her.

Then she faced it.

All.

Sleepless nights brought to mind other sleepless nights, in '68, and in that horrifying, grief-filled year of '63. She had lost her tiny Patrick that year, and then Jack.

Jack.

He had been president, but she had made him
great. She had understood how much of politics was
perception, even unto the end. That was why she—
a self-absorbed woman with few charities and even
fewer charitable interests—had become America's
most popular first lady, instead of more deserving
souls, like Eleanor Roosevelt. She had made the
country worship her. She had been their queen, and
the cost had been so great she could barely fathom
it, even now.

Jack. On those sleepless nights, she saw him,
lounging in his rocker, smiling at her as if he had
been caught with another woman, and she could almost hear him say, as he so often did about his
rocker—*it gives you a sense of motion without a sense of
danger*. She used to laugh at that. Her Jack, who always had a sense of danger, finely tuned. So finely
tuned that it saved him—not from getting into trouble, but from getting caught.

She did not keep the chair in her co-op because
she could not bear to look at it. And yet, whenever
he appeared, he was sitting in that chair.

Except in her dreams. In her dreams, she saw him
in slow motion, waving, the breeze in his hair. And
she would know, she would know in an instant he
would be gone. She would try to warn him, and
wake up, the words still trapped in her throat.

Mornings she would stand before her bathroom
mirror and study her face. Gaunt and hollow, skele-
tal, cigarette lines around her mouth, eyes too big,
skin yellow from cancer and tobacco. She only had
a few months, the doctor said, and those months she

would spend with her grandchildren. Children had been her only joy, her only hope. She had felt if she could protect them she was doing the best she could.

She had used Ari to protect her own. First Ari's bluster and Ari's strength, and then finally the small percentage of his wealth she had managed to carve away for herself. Still, her children were too much in the public eye, too much a center of attention. Teddy said it was because she had tried to protect them, to hide them, but she knew better.

She knew.

It was because she had made their father into a myth. The King of Camelot. If she could take those words back now, she would. Spoken to Ted White only weeks after Jack had died. She had taken the idea from the musical he had so loved, the line that he had often misquoted to her when she complained about something, again with that impish smile. *These are the days of Camelot*, he would say. *They will not last forever.*

And they did not. And by quoting them to Ted White, and by having him use them, first in that *Life* magazine article, and then in his *In Search of History*, she had sealed her children's doom. Because Camelot's King was dead, all eyes turned to its prince. Her John. There were the brothers, Robert and Ted, and they would hold the throne until John was ready.

Then when Bobby died . . .

When Bobby died, she knew her children were next.

The country had hated her—hated her—its queen, for betraying its king, for marrying a coarse foreign commoner for his money. She had said nothing publicly, but privately she could not keep quiet.

"If they are killing Kennedys," she would say, "my children are number-one targets. I want to get them out of this country."

Her children were, now, as safe as she could make them, through all her mistakes, all her miscalculations. Her pride, her joy, were her grandchildren, Caroline's children: Rose, Tatiana, and Jack. For they were the safest of all. The country did not watch them. The public did not even know their names. They would grow to have their own lives, not the lives the myth had made for them, the lives they were expected to have.

Her grandchildren gave her a feeling of safety Ari never had.

During the daytime, in the sunlight, in the park. Feeling their soft baby-fat skin and listening to their idle chatter.

But at night, at night while Maurice slept, she was left alone, with her thoughts.

And the ghosts.

Jack did not want vengeance. Bobby did. Bobby, who had been her strength in those days after the assassination. Bobby, who had held her arm, been at her side. Bobby, whose eyes revealed the depth of his sorrow.

Bobby. At the time, she had thought Jack's death had broken him.

Instead it had made him stronger. Bobby always felt things more intensely than anyone else she had ever known. He hated harder, loved fiercer, grieved deeper than the rest of the family combined.

And when he emerged from the grief, when he ceased the self-pity that had led him to believe that he, somehow, had caused his brother's death, he had come to her. He had sat across from her in her co-op, their knees touching, hands inches apart.

I need you to remember, Jackie, he had said. *I know it's hard, but I need to know.*

She had tried for him. She had. She could remember getting off the plane at Love Field, the smell of roses—she could never smell roses again without thinking of that flat Texas sunshine—the feel of her hat on her head, and the weariness she felt, weariness she had carried since Patrick's death, since she had lost her last, and somehow, most precious child. She remembered smiling, though, despite the exhaustion, and the taste of that strange breakfast on her tongue. She even remembered Jack's speech, although she had heard it a dozen times. He had sounded particularly warm that morning, particularly enthusiastic, and she had thought that his enthusiasm would get them both through the new campaign season.

She remembered it all for Bobby, dry-eyed, voice calm. The convertible, top down. The sound of the crowd, the aching slowness around Dealy Plaza, the perplexed look on one Secret Service man's face as the rhythm of the motorcade changed. Then the popping. One shot, two, she couldn't remember. Everything blurred. She'd seen the tape—once—herself on the back hood, the Secret Service forcing her down, but she remembered none of that. Only Jack's expression—the single wince of pain—and the warmth of his blood as it splattered her.

She remembered—the decisions, the wait at Parkland Memorial Hospital, the ride to Air Force One, and Lyndon beside her, Lyndon!, taking the oath—all of it, except the things Bobby wanted her to recall.

How many shots?

A puff of smoke near the grassy knoll?

Any guilty looks?

If Bobby had been there, he would have seen everything. He would have counted the muzzle flashes, heard the shots, known then and there who had done it and why. If Bobby had been there, he would have thrown himself in front of his brother and died with him, not fled to the back of the limo as she had done.

If that was what she had done. In her dreams, she chased a bit of skin, a bit of brain, thinking somehow that if she caught it, he would live, they all would live.

Vain, vain hope. For, in the end, they all would die.

Maurice was her mainstay, her rock, the only person she had allowed herself to lean on since Jack, perhaps even before Jack. Maurice organized her, rescued her, helped her when she didn't even know she needed saving. And now that the cancer diagnosis was in, she knew that for the first time in her life, she would die before a man she loved.

She found no comfort in that. She knew what it was like to be the survivor.

She knew that being a survivor sometimes meant

closing your eyes, and moving forward, no matter what the consequences.

Bobby had told her once that she lived in denial. She agreed, for denial was easier. Easier than blaming her chain-smoking for the flaws in Patrick's lungs. Easier than wondering if her lack of observation had let a murderer go free.

On those nights, surrounded by her ghosts, she sat in the darkness of her living room. Sometimes she would have a fire in the grate, her possessions shimmering in the flickering light. And she would review:

The look on Lyndon's face as he took the oath. Eyes swimming, his craggy features already lined, the weight of the world suddenly on his shoulders. She had stood beside her husband on a cold January day when he took that oath, and she had stood behind Lyndon on a warm Texas afternoon, her bloodstained skirt clinging to her thighs, as he did the same.

Bobby had always blamed Lyndon. It had happened in his state, and he was next in line. But Lyndon, coarse as he was, grieved that day, not for Jack—he had never liked Jack—but for the country. Lyndon had never wanted the nation to go through such grief, such turmoil, such trauma. And it would go through more, all under his watch.

Bobby was wrong. The culprit was not Lyndon.

Nor was it Dick Nixon, much as they all loved to hate him, nor the FBI, nor the CIA.

The culprit was time itself.

Some nights, she would awaken to gunfire. One shot, two, three shots, four. The screams of the crowd, the shouts of the Secret Service. She would crawl out of bed gingerly, careful not to disturb Maurice, and put on satin slippers to protect her feet from the cold wood floor.

Getting up would calm her. The co-op was her safe place. She bought it in '64, as the first initial anger of grief waned. She had her children to think of, and she wanted them to get through the tragedy of their father's assassination and move on to their own lives.

She wished she could still hear them giggling in the corridors, playing in their rooms.

Instead she heard gunfire and the voices of men long dead.

She could not tell Maurice. She, who told him everything, could tell him nothing about Jack, about the ten years together, about the death. In that silence, Maurice once said, he learned how much she had loved Jack and how, in the end, his loss had devastated her, and changed her.

For she hadn't been Eleanor Roosevelt. Her focus in the White House had been fashion, furnishings, and adding a sense of grace. She hated going out in public, hated thinking of the disadvantaged and the poor. She did her duties in that area, but saved her passion for the look, the appeal, the glamour of the place.

It was only later, after the deaths, after the fear, that she came to terms with life. "Life is what matters," she would say. *Life.*

And the children.

If that was denial, so be it.

For Jack was dead. Had been dead for nearly thirty

years. And in dying, as in living, he had changed the world.

What she would say to Bobby now, if she could, if he—and not his ghost—were sitting before her, was that it did not matter if there had been one assassin or two, three assassins or four. What mattered was the fact of Jack's death. He never had his chance at a second term. He never had a chance to place his stamp upon the country. No one really knew what he could have done, except maybe Bobby. And her.

For Jack had an intellectual grace, an ability to be a political chameleon, and yet to somehow keep the people in mind. The rich boy who never carried money, the man who didn't understand—just as her father hadn't understood—why sleeping around pained his wife, instinctively knew how the poor and the disadvantaged felt.

She had gone to dinner after dinner at the Kennedy compound and listened to the old man prattle about how Jack would never measure up to Joe Junior, and she had known that the old man was wrong. For Jack had the compassion that Joe Junior lacked.

And Bobby, in his intense way, learned that compassion on the day his second brother died.

She had hope while Bobby lived. It was only after the second assassination that she turned her back, became Jackie-O, suffered the ridicule and the outrage, all in the name of her children.

And on those nights of remembered gunfire, she would stand by her denial. For the focus was wrong. The focus did not belong to Oswald, patsy or assassin. The focus belonged to Jack, who he was, who he would have been, and all that he had lost.

All that they had lost.
All that the world had lost.
Together.

It was a mystery that would never be solved, a mystery that broke her heart, a mystery that she could never discuss, because within it lay too many dreams, too much hope.

In the end, Camelot was her metaphor. A place that she could never return to, a place that glittered in hindsight, but had, in life, been filled with all too human loves, all too human betrayals.

All too human grief.

On those nights, she faced the past, faced the assassinations, faced the deaths. She listened to the ghosts, heard the shots, felt the blood. She remembered, and she spoke of it to no one.

And then, as night faded, and dawn crept over the New York City skyline, she would slip back in bed, and wrap her too-thin arms around Maurice, holding him, holding him, breathing with him, enjoying his warmth.

In the sunlight, she would play with her grandchildren, speak to her own children, and edit a few books. She would look at flowers and smile at birds and hug those closest to her. She would cuddle them close and feel the precious fragility in their bodies. And she would remember only this:

Life mattered.
Life and love.
And the ever-present specter of death.

KRISTINE KATHRYN RUSCH

~~~

KRISTINE KATHRYN RUSCH is an award-winning author and editor who has published more than thirty novels and more than one hundred short stories, many of them appearing in collections of the "year's best" fiction. Her most recent book, *Hitler's Angel*, is an historical crime novel set in Munich in 1931.

"I still remember her," Kristine recalls, "standing beside her tiny son on the day of the funeral, looking grim and sad and in control. I've always been fascinated by the Kennedys, partly because I am the same age as John Jr., and his little salute tied me to that funeral, and partly because I had experienced my first death that same month, the loss of my nephew who was only a few weeks old. I don't remember my family's grief; I do remember hers. So it was a natural to choose her as my First Lady. When I decided to write a story, I realized I had given myself a huge problem. There is only one unsolved crime in Jackie Kennedy's life. Anything else—from the theft of the White House china to the death of a friend—would pale by comparison (especially to a reader). So I had to address that, and I came up with 'Jackie-O.' "

GOOD-BYE, DOLLEY

―――∞∞―――

GILLIAN ROBERTS

"**H**AVE A GOOD nap, Grandma, and get yourself
right as rain again. And let's think of somebody else
to talk about. No disrespect meant, but Dolley Madison isn't the kind of Colonial woman I want. She
was okay, I guess, but typically feminine, concerned
with dresses and dinner parties. I know she saved
the Gilbert Stuart painting of George Washington
when the White House burned, but really, that was
just about holding on to some of the decorations,
wasn't it? I'm looking for somebody less traditional."
She double-checked that the shades were drawn,
then tiptoed out.

I didn't nap. Why would I? Soon enough, that'll
be my permanent vocation. Instead, I decided that
this nonsense had gone on long enough. Looking
sideways when the truth staring me in the face was
giving me a pain in the neck.

Patricia, I'll say when she comes back, I'm dying and it's not a tragedy. Stop pretending I'm going to bounce back from old age.

I'm sure she thinks her sunny act is therapeutic. She wouldn't do it otherwise. But the truth is, it's killing me off faster than I need to go. It's enervating. I don't have strength left for games. It isn't the whispering about me that's making me crazy. I hear it, all right, even though they think I don't. I've encouraged everybody to think I'm much deafer than I am. You can't imagine how much I've learned that way, and how many annoyances I've been able to ignore. No, it isn't hearing their real concerns, or speculations, or even the funeral plans they've made. What's driving me around the bend is the lethal cheeriness. The unbendable optimism, the downright perkiness when we're together. The way our vocabularies have to be expunged of any dark ideas or less than happy words. Talking has become treacherous, like sweeping for potential land mines, lest the truth be stepped on and explode. Let me tell you, it's both exhausting and boring. I don't want my cause of death to be tedium!

Patricia, I'll say, I know I'm dying, the doctor knows it, and you, as an almost Ph.D. at a prestigious university, surely have the motherwit to look at my ninety-six-year-old self and see that most of my cells have already dried up like potato chips. I have a few still functioning in my brain. Let's use them and really talk, make nothing off-limits. I need to tell you my stories so they'll keep on breathing when I don't.

Although, to tell the truth, given that the girl's collecting them for a thesis, she'll most likely eviscerate them, analyze every bit of life out of them till they need artificial resuscitation.

Of course, Patricia will interrupt me right away and say I shouldn't talk that way. She'll shake her head and repeat that damned meaningless cliché of hers that "In a few days you'll be right as rain." I keep meaning to ask her what's so right about rain and why would I want to become all wet?

Once the air is cleared, I'll tell her how wrong her reading of history is. I don't care what her feminist studies says. She's wrong. They're wrong. Makes me damned angry, too. Just because a woman's clever doesn't mean she's nothing more than a standard issue pretty face and delightful hostess—even if she's those things, too. That just maybe Dolley saved the United States, and not in the most feminine—or legal—way. Let's see what Patricia the deadly serious Ph.D. does with that.

Patricia's hoping for a new slant on how it was to be a woman in Colonial times. She's looking for "rebels and wise women" she told me, and she figures that somewhere in the family stories there'll be somebody for her to "discover." Certainly not somebody famous like Dolley Madison, not even when I started talking about how she'd be great for the dissertation. That's about when she told me to take a nap and think of somebody else.

The women of our family used to tell each other damn near every detail of their lives and the lives of everybody around them, too. That was in the days before TV, and movies, and telephones, and e-mail, and getting Ph.D.'s, and having jobs instead of front porches, condensed talk down to messages. I'm the ancient one, the last of the old-time women who had the time and interest for stories. Except the way Patricia wants them, of course, which is completely different.

Our stories were fun, kept alive because they were interesting. Patricia's dissertation requires *significance*, and by the time she's done with a tale, it's so weighted and stuffed with *meaning* of the right sort, it's no fun at all.

It's interesting to think that either this country's so young or I'm so old that our family stories go back to the Revolution. (Not that we were first families, mind you. We were here early, all right, but only because we were debtors who were asked—or told, for all I know—to leave the old country. But we were here to witness whatever was going on.

I actually remember my great-great-grandmother. Imagine that—I knew a woman who knew Dolley Madison. A woman who was there when the Brits burned Washington. Of course, great-great-grandmother was ancient by the time I remember her—probably around the age I am now. Wonder who I scare, because it scared me to look at her—her eyes all filmy with cataracts, and she so stooped over and tiny. But her voice was all right, and she'd tell her stories—or ask her daughter, my great-grand-mother, to tell them. And the most important one was about the night the White House burned down.

Maybe it's her daughter, Great-grandma, I remember. Can't tell anymore, all their faces have become a single blur of wrinkles and crepe skin. The same blur I see in the mirror, when Patricia or the nurse allows me to look at myself, that is.

Great-great grandmother was practically a child

back when the war was raging. The Second War of
Independence they were calling it because we were
fighting for freedom from England all over again.
This time, it had to do with money freedom, with our
right to trade with anybody we pleased, including
England's enemy, Napoleon. At least I think that's
what it was about, although at my age, I've come to
believe that no matter what fancy justification and
reasons they tell the rest of us, the only thing war's
about is somebody itching to bash somebody else.
That war, in 1812 and thereabouts, was for freedom
of trade, or so they claimed. If people are mixed up
about it now, it's because people were damned confused about it then. We were sucked into Napoleon's
fracas with Great Britain—and please do not ask me
what *that* was "for"—and we gave England an ultima-
tum. And they agreed to our terms, so there was no
need for a single shot to be fired. Problem was, we
heard that they'd agreed a day too late—no e-mail
then—and by then, we were already at it again, so
we kept going.

Some people were happy the war had happened
because they figured that if we beat England, we'd
grab Canada, a nice piece of real estate. And other
people decided that hey, while we were at it, we
could get rid of more Indians and use their land, too.
It was not a nice or a popular war.

Only thing we actually got out of it was "The Star
Spangled Banner," written in the rockets' red glare
after the Brits had burned the capital and were on to
Baltimore. Can't even sing the song. Surely not a
prize worth the candle. Or the rocket.

So we were having an unpopular war that was all

over the place with murky or downright despicable reasons for existing, and we had this unimposing President Madison, according to Great-great. Little bit of a fellow, she said. No personality. Way older than Dolley, and a lousy politician. A good mind, because that was a pretty fine Constitution he helped make up, but none of the charisma, we'd call it now, that could lead a country, get Congress to cooperate, make sense of the muddle of a war. And the country needed lots of personality.

That's where Dolley came in. She was the Madisons' personality. She was the sparkle. She was all the color in the both of them. I find this interesting. Not only was it a time when a woman's place was in the background, but this woman by all rights should have been even more unnoticeable, because she was raised a Quaker. A plain person.

But he was the plain one—old, odd, small, quiet Jemmy Madison, who'd never married once his first girlfriend jilted him. Not exactly a lusty man. And a very surprising choice for Dolley Payne Todd, a grieving, penniless Quaker widow living with her mother after she lost her husband and one of her two baby boys in the yellow fever epidemic.

The Paynes had once been wealthy but, acting out of conscience, Mr. Payne became a Quaker and freed all his slaves after the Revolution. Had to pay large fines for doing so. He sold his lands and his livestock and moved his family to Philadelphia, in the only state in which slavery was outlawed.

Unfortunately, his business ventures failed and Dolley had to drop out of school and do what slaves had formerly done for them. Plus, she sewed and took care of her younger brothers and sisters until she married. Eventually, the Paynes turned their house into a boardinghouse and that's where the widow Dolley and her son returned. Not a bed of roses.

Still, Dolley half-dead was more alive than most, and I do believe that dried up Jemmy Madison, who'd come to the boardinghouse to visit Mr. Jefferson, couldn't believe his eyes when he saw this effervescent creature. And maybe after all her ups and downs, she just needed someone with common sense instead of flash.

In any case, Jemmy and Dolley found each other, and a true and lasting love match—hard as that is to believe—it was.

Great-great grandmother, who the family calls G.G., or Gigi, said that Dolley Madison was as pretty as could be. Plump, which wasn't a crime in those days, voluptuous, with dark curly hair and a quick wit. A magnet, pulling people to her. The Quakers threw her out, you know, when she married Madison, who wasn't one of them. And maybe, with no reason anymore to look like a mousekin and not be allowed to dance, she turned up the bubble machine as high as it could go and became anything but plain—from a gray-cloaked creature to the first Queen of Fashion.

She became the most famous party-giver and hostess in the United States. It was her idea to have an Inaugural Ball, and that was only one of her entertainments. And Lord but she dressed the part, which is where Gigi comes into the picture, in case you were wondering. My great-great grandmother was a milliner of great talent. Dolley was particularly fond of turbans, if you can imagine how outrageous a look that'd be in a room full of Colonial dames. Turbans with jets and sequins, turbans with flowers in the creases, with great feathered plumage. Gigi and Dolley had an important quality in common. Both of them knew how to take almost nothing and whip it into something splendid. With Dolley, it was supplies for parties and dinners and ideas for gowns she'd sew herself. With Gigi, it was hats that framed Mrs. Madison's curls and face perfectly, that made her look the part of the most important woman in the country and that used old materials, recycled odd pieces and found items, and cost next to nothing. They spent so much time together, that Dolley treated her milliner more like a younger sister than a hat-maker.

"I am so very sorry that I must delay payment a while longer," she told Gigi one day, and not for the first time. "I hope that within a few days . . . but the war . . ."

There was no money for running the White House and the affairs of state. But Great-great understood that it wouldn't do for the First Lady to look as poor as she actually was. It wouldn't do for the White House to look as if it were about to collapse, as if the United States of America had been a brief flash in the pan. Shabby poverty would make foreign dignitaries wary of the new country, would drain the last symbolic reservoirs of strength.

And so, like so many other tradespeople, Great-great worked on credit, staying alive through the bundles of state-dinner leftovers Dolley gave her.

Dinners made of other people's extension of credit. It was an exhausting juggling act, but they held on and hoped life would soon improve, and the two women, despite the difference in their ages, spent as many afternoons as possible sewing and laughing together.

But one day, Gigi decided that she had to interrupt the laughter and speak about unpleasantries. Things much worse than poverty and scrimping.

"Meaning what?" Dolley asked. They were sitting and stitching—Gigi replacing a spray of artificial rosebuds with a strip of multicolored ribbon, and Dolley reworking a bodice so that it looked new.

"The talk," Gigi said. "I've refrained from mentioning it because I hate to, but—"

"Talk," Dolley asked. "Surely not gossip?"

Gigi nodded.

"About me?"

Gigi nodded again. She couldn't bear saying the words, although nobody else in town seemed to have trouble doing so. And could you actually blame people who were already so anxious and fearful about the future? Here was their future in the hands of this stick of a man with a colorful, outgoing, party-loving, bedangled, and bedecked wife. As much as Gigi loved Dolley, even she privately thought the president's wife could have toned down her costumes out of respect for the war and the general suffering. But Dolley thought that would signal defeat, and that was that.

Dolley and Jemmy had produced no children of their own, for which fact people made up their own unkind reasons. Add to that Dolley's love of admiration, of flirting, bantering with a good-looking man. Gigi knew that was how the president's wife smoothed her husband's rough corners. That was how she made him look better than he'd otherwise have appeared. She was the oil moving the wheels for Jemmy often as not. She was the one put good ideas about human psychology in his ears and used the same psychology on the people he needed to have help him. She was such an excess of color and movement and light that her brightness spilled onto him and he didn't appear quite as drab or inconsequential.

She was a diplomat, perhaps the most important one we had—but we didn't approve of strong women back then either. Dolley had to do her job like a woman, the president's wife, and stealth and feminine wiles were the only weapons allowed women.

"You'd think people would have more important things on their minds with the war nearly at our front doors," Dolley said. "Don't let it trouble you. Don't pay evil talk any heed."

Gigi said her throat all but closed up for having to say harsh words. "It's . . . it's not nice, Ma'am. Not right, the lies and insinuations."

Dolley put down her needle and thread and waited while Gigi thought about the women who were talking. Women to whom nobody paid Dolley-doses of attention. Women whose pockets were as empty as Dolley's, but who weren't first ladies and for whom nobody invented costumes so they could still shine. Men in high boots and medals did not click their heels to address them, or kiss these women's hands and smile as they spoke to them.

And those women found each other, and together,

resented Dolley. And they spoke to one another in front of people who didn't matter much to them, like my great-great grandmother. So Gigi knew a lot more than Dolley did about what was happening outside the protected diplomatic and political circles.

And what else Gigi knew was that if a word of the suggested improprieties had been true, or even if not true, if believed as if it were true—the White House could come crashing down like so many cards. Would have destroyed Madison, who adored his wife, given his enemies a real "in," pulled apart the fabric of society, maybe changed how the government was run—lot of squabbling about basic philosophy back then—and who knows what else?

The rumors that had begun with slurs on Dolley's extravagant taste and style, had escalated to charges that she was bankrupting the country, then expanded to include the idea that she was dictating government policy, that her quiet husband relied entirely too much on a flighty and uneducated woman's observations and suggestions.

Great-great Grandmother, knowing what disdain Dolley had for malicious gossip and idle tongues said nothing for a long time. But now, the rumors had taken a turn for the worse and had grown to link Mrs. Madison with a specific military officer. A young, handsome, tall man with a temperament very much like Dolley's. He was merry and quick witted. And married. And now whispers were added insinuating that he was committing treason and Dolley was colluding with him, and Great-great could no longer keep silent. "Oh, Mrs. Madison," Gigi finally cried. "Mrs. Madison? This must be gravely serious, then." Dolley put her finger under Gigi's chin and made her face her. "All right," she said, "Tell me. Who is saying what?"

It worried Great-great, because although everybody's tongue was clacking, the true instigator was a woman who had gone out of her way to be close to the First Lady, to be helpful and trustworthy, to be everywhere that Dolley was. A woman everyone thought of as sweet. "Miss Prince," Great-great finally, reluctantly, whispered. "She began it and she feeds it."

"And of what great sin am I accused?" Dolley's eyes could flash without merriment, too. "The pies I'm serving aren't fresh enough? The ballroom needs a fresh coat of paint? What?"

"The suggestion has been made that Captain La-Farge and . . . and you . . ." Gigi was terrified, sure that even good-natured Dolley Madison would be infuriated by the suggestion.

But instead, Dolley looked startled, and then she laughed. "I should have known. The poor thing. A woman scorned. Once upon a time, Lydia Prince set her cap for Henry LaFarge. He never noticed her, and then he found his Maria and married her."

"Guess she should have set more than a cap for him," Great-great said. "If she'd set one of my turbans, maybe she'd have caught him." And they both laughed, although it was not a joke at all, because under her boring headgear, Miss Prince was filled with venom. "Remember," Great-great said, "hell hath no fury like a woman scorned."

"I wondered why she's been so solicitous of me

lately," Dolley said. "But it isn't me she wants—it's the captain."

"But it isn't the captain she talks about—it's you," Gigi said.

Dolley shrugged and shook her head, making her black curls jump. "Jealousy is so sad. It eats a person up. She's upset because Henry and I are friends. She hates that, hates anyone else to be happy if she isn't. There's nothing to her stories, of course. Henry is an upright man and a patriot and I . . . it's rank nonsense and I won't dignify it with my attention." She smiled, and dimples played next to her mouth. "The truth is all that matters," she said. "Why listen to trivial and malicious lies? Feel sorry for the need that prompts them, but don't let them trouble you, whatever you hear. I surely won't."

It was easy worrying over other things. The British were close to Washington and there were not enough troops to defend it. The president himself was off at the battlefield. Unfortunately, Henry LaFarge had been assigned to protect the White House and its mistress, so if anything, the talk grew worse.

Lydia Prince, nice as she could be, put herself in the position of protector and good friend, worrying about Jemmy, about the future of the White House. About everything. Gigi tried to follow Dolley's advice, tried hard not to listen, not to care, but she still worried all the time.

Then one day, she saw Dolley and Miss Prince admiring the Gilbert Stuart portrait of George Washington that hung at the foot of the staircase. "It gives me courage and comfort," Dolley said.

Lydia Prince nodded. "A treasure," she murmured, and she stood attentively studying the portrait.

While Dolley studied her.

And Gigi studied Dolley. Later, Gigi said that the expression in Dolley's eyes was something to behold, as if some grave and frightening decision had been reached. But then it was gone, like a lightning flash, and all that was left was Gigi's new understanding that no matter how much she had said about ignoring gossip, Dolley Madison was paying close attention to her secret enemy. Listening and watching and, most of all, thinking.

And then the day came when the British smashed their way up into Washington. Dolley was at first nowhere to be found, and it was assumed that she'd come to her senses and left the city for Philadelphia and her parents.

But suddenly, while the city began to burn, there she was, running through the presidential palace with Gigi.

You could smell the fires that had been started in other buildings already, and the sky was turning the color of blood from the flames. The Brits would be at the White House any minute. Great-great wanted nothing more than to run all the way to Maryland, and as soon as possible.

"We have to hurry," she said. "Why are we here? Is there something you want me to help you with? Gathering up your hats—or dresses?"

Dolley pulled back, looked at her as if she'd said something obscene, and shook her head so hard the turban nearly fell off. "Clothing?" she asked, sounding as incredulous as if she were still a Quaker in a gray dress. "Not clothing! They want to erase us. They're going to burn our memories so that we don't remember who we are. We're here to make sure that doesn't happen."

Outside, something that had been stored in a flaming building exploded. "Then, please—let's just go," Gigi begged. "No point staying. We can't carry all the furniture, Mrs. Madison."

Dolley nodded. "Let me think," she said, putting a finger up to her mouth. "Do you hear anybody yet?"

"No," Gigi said, "and I want to be out of here before I do!"

Dolley continued to eye the room and then, glancing at the doorways now and again, singled out a drawer and extracted a roll of papers. "This," she said. "Put this in your sewing bag. They won't be suspicious of you. Everybody's been made to think I'm such a ninny they'll believe I was having a chapeau designed while my home burned."

Gigi couldn't resist a peek, even though the truth was, she couldn't read.

"It's the original Constitution you're holding," Dolley said gently.

"Ah," Gigi said. "Your husband's work."

"Not because of him, because it's *us*. That's the backbone of our country, and the British aren't going to turn it into ash."

Great-great said her own backbone turned to jelly with that. She was a sixteen-year-old milliner carrying the Constitution of the United States while the country went up in flames. She felt as if her bag held the weight of the world. "Let's run, then, please," she said. "It's good that you saved this, but now, the soldiers—"

Just then, a soldier—but one of our own—Captain Henry himself came in top speed. "Mrs. President!" he said, "I thought I heard you, but I was told that you'd left the city. I was, in fact, dispatched to retrieve your personal effects in a satchel up in—what are you doing here? It isn't safe! You must leave immediately."

"A satchel?" Dolley rocked back on her heels for a moment. "Of course. I've been waiting to understand what it was to be, then. I supposedly left a satchel—could it have been on my bed, perhaps?"

"Supposedly? Ma'am, I'm confused. Isn't that the message you sent?"

"I never sent any message."

"Then who . . . why would . . . ?"

While this exchange was made, Dolley's eyes darted over the floor, the walls, and alcoves. Gigi knew that look—she was planning something, and this time, it wasn't a party on her mind.

Great-great clutched the sewing bag to her side. She could smell the acrid stench of the city being destroyed and she knew they had minutes, if that, before they were burned alive. "Please, Mrs. Madison," she said. "You've gotten what you wanted. Now, we have to—"

"In the bedroom! That isn't very subtle, is it?" Dolley asked. "Excuse me a second—there's something else I need to save."

"I'll get it—what is it?" Henry LaFarge said.

"The country. I—we are saving the country," Dolley said with none of her customary dimpling and smiles. "Please wait for me—unless you find yourself in danger. In which case, I insist that you leave." And she was gone, out of the room and up the stairs.

"No," Captain LaFarge protested. "That isn't done—allow me to . . ." He looked at Great-grandmother, at the bag she carried. "And you? Are you saving things, too?"

They were moving, almost unconsciously, toward the great hallway, the stairs up which Dolley had raced. Gigi noticed with a start that the portrait of George Washington, the one that so inspired Mrs. Madison, was no longer on the wall. She tried not to show the rush of alarm—and comprehension—she felt.

"My supplies," Gigi said. "Mrs. Madison was having her hat refitted."

"A hat," he said. "Refitting a hat when . . . well, I suppose women have their reasons."

Something outside but close exploded. Gigi trembled and even the captain had a frantic look in his eyes.

Gigi knew there wasn't anything to retrieve upstairs. But there was something up there. Someone who had told Captain LaFarge to go to the president's wife's bedroom and who was waiting for him to follow directions and appear.

Great-great felt a shudder that was so fierce, even the captain noticed. "What—" he began, but now, Great-great heard scuffling above her, and perhaps a high shriek, and she doubled over and coughed and choked until the clunks and thuds stopped. Until there was silence above. "Sorry," she said, "I—something was caught and I—"

The captain waved off her words. He looked at his watch, and shook his head. "I must get her back down—she'll be killed in all this if we don't—"

The red-seared air came closer. Everything was on fire and, any instant, so would they be.

"She'll be down in a second," Great-great said, praying that was, indeed, who would still be able to walk down the staircase. "Why don't we—" They moved closer to the great doorway.

"Saving the country indeed," he said. "Saving her dresses!"

"The country. You'll see."

And then he did, or thought he did, as Dolley descended the stairs, two at a time, her brow beaded with perspiration, the turban at an angle, nearly falling off by the time she reached them and they all raced out the door. They could see, then, that a wing of the White House was already on fire.

When they were safely in a carriage that had been waiting for Captain LaFarge, Dolley removed her turban. From inside of it, she unrolled a piece of canvas with fresh-cut edges. She was still breathing hard.

"George Washington," Henry LaFarge said. "You saved his portrait."

"The father of our country," Dolley said.

He gave her courage, she'd always said. And inspiration. And he had this time, when she'd needed both in great amounts.

"But what made you take it upstairs with you?" Captain LaFarge insisted in his amiable but rather stupid manner. "Such a heavy painting when it was in its frame."

"I was in a hurry," Dolley said, with the right

amount of imperiousness to assure that he'd accept it as an answer, although it made no sense.

"And you brought not an article of clothing down after all that risk," he continued. "What happened? Did you hear the British?"

"I realized there simply wasn't time," she said quickly.

"And the painting's frame?" he asked. "What happened to it?"

The big, heavy frame, Gigi thought. With solid corners that could stun or worse. Not the most common weapon for self-defense—or country-defense, but one that was available. And one that would leave no evidence after it burned in the fire.

"Too bulky. That's why I went up—to cut the painting out with my sewing shears."

And how would a sweet, not overly bright man know that all Dolley's sewing supplies were kept in the dayroom where the sun poured through the long windows. Downstairs and nowhere near her bedroom.

"But . . ." he said, and then he gave up. Poor, befuddled Captain LaFarge. He never had been too observant, never had even noticed that Lydia Prince was in love with him, even when everyone else in Washington knew. He was either too polite, or too dim, or too convinced that women were beyond explanation to ask why running upstairs with a large painting didn't make sense. He'd never have any glimmer of an idea that there was more than method to the First Lady's seeming madness. Or that she'd just saved his life.

Or George Washington had. It's ironic, Gigi thought,

how Dolley saved the Washington portrait—and it, in its own way, saved her, the captain and, just maybe, the country.

Captain LaFarge, handsome and thick-skulled and blinded by the conviction that women seldom made sense, would never suspect that if he hadn't heard Dolley's voice coming from that stateroom, if he'd instead gone straight upstairs, the woman he'd scorned and her knife would have been waiting for him, just as they were waiting for Dolley when she entered her room.

Lydia Prince's crazed rage had gone so far that if she couldn't have the captain, then no one would. And although Dolley "had" him only as a friend, Lydia was ready to destroy even that. In fact, she was ready to pull down the fledgling country, if possible.

Henry LaFarge would have been so unaware, so taken by surprise, she would have done her work with her knife, although nobody would ever know that. After the fire, the body of the handsome young soldier, subject of a relentless campaign of rumors, would confirm their worst fears by being found where it never should have been, on the First Lady's bed.

No one would have known about the false request for a satchel of clothing. No one would have realized that there never had been a basis to the rumors. And of course, sweet Miss Prince, so close to the president's wife, would have been only too glad to confirm that all the rumors now seemed proven true.

Dolley and therefore James Madison would have been compromised, integrity lost at a time of a crushing and humiliating defeat, and who knows what else besides the White House would have been destroyed that fateful day?

Gigi reached over and put a dampened cloth to Dolley's hand and rubbed gently until the bloody mark she'd seen was gone. There was no scratch below it on the First Lady's hand, but the hand itself trembled. Dolley was doing her best to appear calm, but she was just barely holding together. A Quaker pacifist at war.

There were more bloody stains on her skirt, and Gigi, trying not to imagine the scene upstairs at the White House, deliberately dragged her cloth over the side of the carriage, now filmed with the ash of Washington's burning, and smudged the skirt until the bloody evidence was barely noticeable. "You were slightly smudged, Mrs. Madison," Gigi said. "But I fear I made it worse."

"Soot," LaFarge said. "All over the place. No point trying to get rid of it. It's only going to get worse."

Dolley looked placidly at the milliner. Neither had to say a word to the other, not then, and not ever.

"Well," Captain LaFarge said as they rode toward safety outside the city. "A pity you didn't get to save any of your treasures."

And Dolley smiled, flashing her deep dimples. "Not true, Captain," she said. "As immodest as it sounds, I prefer to believe I saved the country's honor. A treasure of immeasurable value."

"Honor? Ah, you must mean the painting," he said.

"And the Constitution," Great-great-grandmother said, pulling it out of her sewing bag and displaying it—just so he'd know he wasn't dealing with complete ninnies.

"Ah, yes," Dolley said. "I'd nearly forgotten. The painting and the Constitution. Yes, we saved those, too."

And that's how she told it, word for word, but it wasn't the sort of story you told a lot of people. After all, the president's wife had murdered a seemingly respectable woman. All the rest would seem hearsay or worse, given that bedrock of rumors.

Great-great grandmother herself didn't breathe a word until both Dolley and her son Payne were dead. And she told her daughter and late in life her daughter, my grandmother, told me. It was always the one story that was held back. As I have. Never got to tell it to my daughter, who wasn't much interested, and then, when she might have been, she was dead.

So now I'm the only one left who knows it, and it's my turn to set the record straight, which will be my pleasure since Patricia's got my hackles up with her talk of how Dolley's heroics boiled down to nothing more than feminine wiles. Wait till she hears the truth, finally.

Wait till I do. I was lying even as I had those thoughts. Not about the story, but about what I'd do with it.

I heard myself sigh, and it sounded as if all the voices of the family, back to Great-great's and maybe Dolley's were sighing, too.

I wasn't going to tell Patricia. I wasn't going to pass on my best story.

It wouldn't do. Didn't matter how the times

changed, how we were into honesty these days. How nobody would condemn a woman for defending herself and her life and her country.

What mattered was Dolley. This was her story, not mine to give away. With all her wiles and gift of gab—if she'd wanted anyone to know this story, it would have been public. It would already be in the history books. Till now, the women in my family had treated it with all the respect it deserved. It was our secret, partly our story, too, because of Gigi.

But if I gave it to Patricia, she'd do an autopsy, pull out its guts and put them on display for anybody who wanted a peek. I like to think of Dolley in her turbans, startling fabrics, and vivid colored gowns. I like to think of her transforming a tablecloth into a skirt and creating White House banquets when there was barely bread for the table. I like that she fashioned herself into the woman she'd decided to be. The woman the country needed right then.

But at heart, she was a Quaker lady, not a tell-all star, and I can't bear to think of her as a naked and exposed display.

So, with another sigh, I closed my eyes and knew I wasn't going to tell Dolley's story. Let her keep her secret. Forever. It would end with me.

When Patricia returned, I said I'd had a good nap and felt ever so much better. In fact, my cold was just about over and I'd be as right as rain in a few days.

GILLIAN ROBERTS

～～

GILLIAN ROBERTS is the criminal alterego of Judith
Greber. As Gillian, she is the author of the Amanda
Pepper/C. K. Mackensie mystery series set in Philadelphia, and the Emma Howe/Billie August mystery
series set in northern California. As Judith, she is the
author of four mainstream novels, including *As Good
as It Gets*. Greber, and possibly the mysterious Gillian, is a former Philadelphian and a current
Californian.

She explains: "The two things I thought I knew
about Dolley Madison were that she served as First
Lady when the capital was still in my hometown of
Philadelphia, and that she invented ice cream. Neither of these 'truths' proved to be even close to accurate! However, by the time I figured that out, it didn't
matter. Dolley, herself, was sufficiently captivating.
She was a brave, intelligent, creative, and complicated woman—even in Washington. Even without
ice cream."

PORTAL

❦

T. J. MACGREGOR

I

SHE ALWAYS FEELS lightheaded after a seance, not quite herself. It's as if the power of the unseen somehow crosses the invisible threshold between there and here and rides into this world through her.

Right now, she's alone, it's quiet, everyone sleeps. She can hear the distant hoot of an owl as clearly as she hears the beat of her own heart. Her body seems to creak when she moves. Her fingers feel thicker, stubby, and when she flexes them, they don't seem to belong to her. Her skin is damp.

Only once has she mentioned this to her husband. In his soft, practical voice, he bypassed the issue of her fingers, of the lightness in her head. He told her that she must put an end to the seances.

But she can't. The seances are her only contact with Willie. And yes, she is sure it's her dead son who comes through, her last born, her precious baby. Her

239

heart aches just at the thought of his beautiful face. When she closes her eyes, she can almost see it, his face, those exquisite features. Willie, who was the most like her.

Mary rises from the bed, body creaking. The lightness shoots through her skull, black stars explode inside her eyes. Water, she thinks. She needs a glass of water.

But before she reaches the basin, the wall directly in front of her seems to burn with color. To glow. She throws up her hands to shield her eyes from the strange, luminous light. Her head pounds, her feet seem to move forward of their own volition, her stomach heaves.

She stumbles and falls into the light. A scream tears up her throat and lurches into the air as a stifled sob. Then the light is everywhere, glowing but dissolving, pulsing yet silent. Mary can't breathe. Mary can't see.

Mary, Mary, quite contrary . . .

She blinks, her vision clears. She's on her knees, hands gripping the layers of her skirt, her breath heaving in her chest. Directly in front of her is a small child with gold hair, a girl softly singing a song Mary has never heard. *Mary, Mary, quite contrary, how does your garden grow?* She is skipping, her arms swing, her small, dainty feet seem to dance against the floor. And then she stops, her eyes grow wide, the song dies in her throat.

"Who . . . who're you?" the girl stutters.

Mary tries to speak, but her throat closes up. She tries to move, to get up; her legs refuse to work. She and the golden-haired child stare at each other, the moment frozen in time.

"*Caroline . . .*" calls the voice of a man Mary can't see. "*Caroline, ready or not, here I come . . .*"

The girl's head snaps around, she twists her body. "*Daddy!*" she shrieks, and runs down the hall toward the man who has appeared.

Mary, Mary . . .

The light burns around her again, the air pulses, and Mary wrenches back, hands flying to her face.

When she comes to, Abraham is leaning over her, saying her name again. His beard looks odd from where she's lying, sort of fuzzy, with streaks of gray beginning to peek out here and there. "Okay, I'm okay," she says, and presses her palms against the floor, pushing up to a sitting position.

Mary doesn't have to look around to know she is in the room where Willie died, the room where everything has been the same since February 20, 1862. Until today, no one, not even her husband, knew that she has entered this room many times in the months since his death. The rest of her life goes on around her, as though she's merely a spectator at a play. Even though she smiles and shakes hands and does what is expected of her, she knows her real life is here, in this room.

"What were you doing in there?" Abraham asks. "I thought . . ."

The rest of what he says drifts away from her. Her heart remains in Willie's room. One night, she even fell asleep in here, curled up on the floor near the bed, Willie's voice whispering in her ear. But these are her secrets and hers alone.

Her husband helps her to her feet and doesn't release her arm even after they've left Willie's room. The hallway is cold, much too dark. The flames of the lanterns flicker along the wall, casting eerie shadows. Mary is suddenly so exhausted she can barely make it into their bedroom.

Her awareness seems to blink off and on, here one moment, elsewhere the next. Abraham, tending to her. Abraham, fixing the quilt over her. Abraham, now speaking in the dark about the trouble in the South. About what he should do or not do.

She realizes he is asking her opinion in that way he usually does, as though he's merely relating events and not asking at all. He wants to know what she thinks because she's from the South, from Lexington, Kentucky, and he seems to have it in his head that her thoughts on the subject reflect the thoughts of all southerners.

Yes or no for slaves.

Yes or no for intervention.

Yes or no.

Yes.

No.

The last thing she hears is her dead son's voice, whispering that he loves her.

II

It's five days later. She knows because she has counted each sunrise and sunset. She knows because she needs to know. She stands at the closed door to Willie's room. The Death Room. She reaches for the knob, her hand begins to tremble, then to shake.

Mary jerks it back and hides it in her skirts, then glances quickly up and down the hall.

No one.

Nothing.

Just the uneasy silence.

Do it, she thinks, and brings her hand out from the folds of her skirt and thrusts it toward the knob. Her fingers brush the metal. *Willie, are you here?*

Mary turns the knob.

The door creaks.

She slips into the twilit room and shuts the door fast, very fast. Then she stands with her back against it, breathing hard, eyes darting left, right, left again. Nothing here. Of course not. There was no seance tonight. There may never be another seance.

Abraham won't tolerate it.

People talk, he says, they think you're odd. You must contain your grief, he says. And oh, he adds, you're spending too much money. The gloves, the clothes . . . He shakes his head. Too much. Four hundred pairs of gloves and $27,000 on clothes are way too much. Mary fails to understand how these details about her spending habits are connected to the seances.

She doesn't know what to say, she never does. So she presses her hands to her ears to block out the sound of her husband's voice. She catches the scent of Willie's freshly washed hair, of his clean, innocent skin, and her knees buckle and she begins to weep.

III

Mary raises her head. She stands in a room where she recognizes the long, wooden writing table, but nothing else. And yet, she knows she's in the mansion because of the view through the window, a view from the second floor, facing away from the main road. But the rest of it is all wrong.

The writing table is long, cluttered at one end with stacks of paper. Framed photographs adorn it. Of a boy. A beautiful woman. And the girl that she saw, the girl named Caroline. Between two of the photographs is a rectangle of wood with words engraved on it: *John F. Kennedy.*

Mary runs her fingers over the letters, repeating the name silently to herself, frantically searching her memory for someone named Kennedy. The only name that is the least bit familiar is John, the name of Abraham's secretary.

She hears footsteps, then a door opens and a handsome, oddly dressed man hurries in, flipping through papers, a book tucked under his arm. *"I'll need that file on . . ."* He glances up and they both freeze.

"My God, what . . ."

Mary wrenches back. "I . . ."

The man flinches and the book in his hand crashes to the floor. The noise echoes in Mary's skull, pounds hard and fast, and she charges for the door, running so fast that everything blurs around her. She runs until she can run no more, runs until she crashes into something.

"Mary, what is it . . ."

Abraham grips her forearms, shakes her gently. She pulls her arms free, runs her hands nervously over her skirt, glances back down the corridor. It looks like home. She laughs quickly, sharply, then looks at her husband.

"The mansion is haunted," she says.

Haunted.

The word seems to echo between them, a threat or a promise, she isn't sure which. Abraham's frown deepens; his eyes flare with anger. "Seances." He spits the word in disgust and turns away from her.

IV

"Mama?"

Mary glances down at her son, eleven years old and as gangly as his father. She doesn't know what he has asked her. "What is it, Tad?"

Tad rolls his eyes, indicating that he has already repeated his question several times. "Papa says that Willie died because he was tired. Do you think that's true?"

Her son's face blurs. She reaches out blindly to touch his head, his hair, wanting desperately to say the right thing, the correct thing. But she doesn't know the answer.

That word, *tired*, bounces against the inner walls of her skull, harder and faster until her head feels as if it will explode. The June heat pours over her, black dots explode inside her eyes, a dizziness seizes her. She stops, leaning against a tree, where the full shade falls over her.

She rubs her hands over her face, smelling summer on her skin. Summer—grass, trees, greenery. But just blocks from here, soldiers lay dying in the hospital. That's where she and Tad are going, to the hospital to visit the wounded, the dying, the victims of the war. Yes, she remembers now.

"Mama?" Tad says softly.

Her hands drop away from her face. "He's not really dead," she replies finally. "We just can't see him."

"Papa says—"

"Papa doesn't understand. Let's hurry now." She grabs his damp little hand and moves quickly forward, toward the hospital and the stink of rotting limbs.

V

The July warmth drifts through the carriage windows, washing over her. Mary shuts her eyes, losing herself in the rhythmic noise of the horse's hooves, clattering in the darkness. She tries to imagine what tonight's seance might bring and hopes desperately for a message from Willie.

She's trying a new clairvoyant tonight, a seance at the woman's house, not the first time she has left the mansion for this purpose. Perhaps this woman can accomplish what others have not, a materialization, an apport, something tangible, something . . .

Suddenly, the rhythm of the horse's hooves changes and a moment later she's thrown free of the carriage, her body flying through the darkness as though she has sprouted wings. She crashes to the ground, her head slams against something, and the darkness claims her.

When she opens her eyes, she's lying in her bed in the mansion. The excruciating pain in her head has swallowed every other sensation, every thought, every desire. Her body feels as if it's being consumed by fire. She tries to push up on her elbows, but doesn't have the strength. When she turns her head slightly, the pain rolls from one temple to the other.

She squints. There. She can just make out Abraham and another man on the other side of the room. The doctor. Abraham and the doctor. With considerable effort, she catches a word, a phrase, of their conversation.

"Infection . . . delirious . . . concern . . . someone with her . . ."

Mary doesn't want to hear anything else. She wishes the doctor would leave so she and Abraham can be alone. There are things she needs to tell him, the pressing secrets of what she has seen and experienced in this room. She must tell him about the glowing wall, a portal to that other world.

But her husband walks out into the hallway with the doctor. Mary aches with disappointment. He belongs first to other people. It has been like that as long as she has known him. Even when he comes to her, he brings the multitudes to their bed. He brings the war, the chaos of the country, the needs of the whites, the Negroes, the North, the South. And he attends to everyone's needs, but rarely to her needs.

Hot, stinging tears gather in the corners of her eyes and finally spill over. Mary turns her head to the side and squeezes her eyes shut. Distantly, she hears the voices of that other place calling to her. She knows that if she opens her eyes, she'll see the glowing wall. Perhaps Willie lives now in that other place, with the pretty little girl named Caroline.

VI

She wakes suddenly, inexplicably, her nightgown wet with perspiration. She blinks hard and fast against the dark. Why isn't the gas lamp still lit? Why isn't someone in here with her? Where are her sons? Her husband? Why is the mansion so deeply silent?

A scream rises in her throat and falls into the air as a pathetic little whisper. Mary pushes up on her elbows, her heart slams against the wall of her chest, her mouth tastes like sand, is as dry as sand. She may die of thirst.

Or maybe she is already dead.

She drops her legs over the side of the bed, pinches her arm. Alive. Okay, she's alive. She sits for long moments, motionless, her eyes gradually adjusting to the darkness.

The wall isn't glowing.

She feels her bare feet against the floor.

Water, she thinks, and pushes to her feet. She weaves across the room, toward where she's sure the pitcher and basin are. But the door suddenly opens and the girl with the gold hair runs in, laughing, a little boy trailing after her. The girl, Caroline, sees Mary first, and stops. Her brother slams into her from behind, falls back, hits the floor.

"I see you," Caroline whispers. "You're Mary Todd. Daddy saw you. I'm not afraid."

"You . . . I . . . ." No, she must be coherent, she must . . .

"I'm sorry about honest Abe . . . I'm sorry . . . the theater . . ."

Her words echo horribly in Mary's skull, she doesn't hear it all. The air quivers, blurs, and she struggles desperately to hold on to the connection between them, the link, the *magic* that allows them to see each other, to speak. And for moments, she sees the girl's face clearly, the promise of extraordinary beauty, the hair like sunlight on snow.

Her arms jerk upward and she extends them toward the girl, her mouth moving, articulating nothing. Then the little boy begins to cry, to wail, "Ghost, Mommy, ghost!"

The air ripples again, as though a curtain of shimmering rain lies between them and Mary, and they vanish. Only the light remains. Mary stumbles toward it, toward the light, certain that other people lie beyond it.

But before she reaches it, before the light grazes the tips of her toes, her husband appears, his tall, lanky frame silhouetted in the doorway.

"Mary, my God, you shouldn't be out of bed. The doctor said—"

"The girl, I saw the girl, she said she's sorry about you, about—"

"Ssshhh," he says, and puts his arms around her and helps her back into the bed. "Your gown is soaked. I think your fever has broken." He runs his hands over her face, through her hair, down her arms.

His touch ignites a desire she hasn't known since Willie went away and she pulls him toward her, whispers to him, presses her mouth to his. He tries to pull away from her, but her need is stronger than his resistance and he gathers her in his arms and his body molds against hers. For now, for these few moments, she shares him with no one.

VII

The chill in the mansion surpasses anything she has ever known here. It eats away at her feet, her legs, her hands and face. It slips up her legs, an insidious insect that even the fire in the hearth can't kill.

Tad fell asleep with his head in her lap and now she lifts it carefully and slips a quilt under it. She doesn't have the heart to wake him. She brushes her mouth to his forehead and he stirs in his sleep, perhaps dreaming of summer.

Mary rubs her hands together and gets to her feet. Abraham is out of the city for the next few days and has taken their other two sons with him. She can't remember exactly where they've gone. Such details elude her more frequently these days. They don't seem to matter as much as the portal in the magical wall.

She lights a lantern and hurries upstairs, through the flickering light of the gas lamps. Already, her head feels lighter, the way it has so often since the accident. Her face is damp, too, damp despite the chill in these rooms, and her fingers seem to be shorter, thicker. She has come to recognize the symptoms, to realize they have recurred every time she has traveled to that other place. In moments, as soon as she crosses the threshold into Willie's room, her body will no longer feel as though it's her own.

She pauses outside the room, her heart drumming, beads of perspiration rolling down the sides of her face. She digs into the pocket of her skirt for the key, slips it out. Her hand is so unsteady she drops the key. Its clatter against the floor seems to echo endlessly in the shadowed, cavernous hall. She gets the key in the lock, turns it. The door swings open, creaking softly.

For moments, Mary simply stands there, unable to step into the room, but unable to move away. She holds up the lantern, trying to illuminate shadows in the distant corners, to make out the foot of the bed, the shape of the water pitcher. But the light doesn't reach.

Go.

Can't. Abraham wouldn't like it.

He isn't here.

Can't . . . can't . . .

Go.

Mary squeezes her eyes shut and hears the whispers of that other world. She steps quickly into the room and only then do her eyes flutter open. The whispers cease.

She pushes the door shut with her foot and forces herself to move toward the magical wall. She passes the end of the bed where Willie died. She passes the darkened windows. Then, a foot short of the wall, she stops, sets the lantern on the floor, and sits beside it. Now, she thinks. Now she will wait.

She waits for a very long time, her body motionless on the floor, the lantern's flame tossing light and shadows against the magical wall. Nothing happens. Her eyes begin to burn, her spine aches, her stomach knots. Maybe what they're saying about her is true, that she's a little crazy, not all here, that Willie's death and the fall from the carriage months ago affected her mind.

Mary fights back the wave of despair that crashes over her. Silence clamps down over her, a thick, terrible silence. But then, in the heart of it, she hears something. Voices. Weeping. Drum rolls.

Her head snaps up. Willie's room is gone. The darkness is gone. She finds herself at the edge of a crushing crowd outside a tremendous cathedral. Everyone around her is weeping, watching the front of the cathedral. Mary slips through the weeping throngs, certain that Willie is here somewhere, that he's hiding from her. She calls his name, panic swelling in her chest, and hurries as fast as her legs will carry her.

She reaches the front of the crowd and stops. There, a few feet from her, stands the girl with the golden hair, Caroline. And the young boy. Between them is the lovely woman from the photograph, her body draped in black, a thin black veil covering her face. She's holding her children's hands. But as a casket is carried from the cathedral, the boy releases his mother's hand and brings his fingers to his brow, a solemn salute.

Their sorrow washes over her, a crippling tide, and she runs away from them, from the mother and her two children, from the endless crushing tide of sorrow. She trips, she falls, she scrambles on her hands and knees, her sobs slapping the quivering air. Darkness clamps down over her, a thick, terrible darkness in which she hears a voice say, *"The President . . . shot in Dallas . . ."* Then, another voice: *"On board Air Force One . . . Johnson was sworn in . . ."*

Her head explodes and her hands fly to her skull, gripping it as if to contain the blood and bone. The room spins, the crowd blurs, the light dims, then everything goes black.

VIII

"I saw . . . I heard . . . Johnson as president . . ."

She stammers, chokes, sobs what she has seen, what she has heard, what she has experienced. And although Abraham listens intently and holds her tightly, she glimpses something disturbing in his eyes.

Only later does she realize that he blames himself for these "episodes," that's how he refers to them. *Mary's episodes,* like the title of a chapter in a book about his life.

Perhaps it's guilt that urges him to suggest a seance. It catches her off guard, the way he utters it so quietly over dinner, when it's just the two of them at the table. *"I think we should try to talk to William . . ."* But maybe it isn't guilt at all; maybe it's just a need he has never spoken aloud until now, the need of a father who has lost a son.

And of course she arranges it, secretly thrilled that his desire is so close to her own.

The clairvoyant who conducts the seance is the one Mary was to see the night of the carriage accident. The room where they sit is crowded with mementos of her childhood in Kentucky. Candles flicker. A cat slips in and out of the eddying shadows, its movements so graceful that Mary isn't quite sure whether it's real or not.

They sit, the three of them, at a round table in the center of the twilit room. The clairvoyant's hands cup the sides of a large glass ball in front of her. A breeze blows through an open window, filling the curtains like sails. Now and then, some noise from the street reaches her. Or Abraham shifts in his chair, as restless as a child. But mostly, it's quiet in the room, peaceful.

Mary watches the glass ball, mesmerized by the reflection of the flickering flames. Her eyes get heavy, she can barely keep her head up. Abraham leans over to her and whispers, "I think we should go, Mother. Nothing is going to happen here."

She shakes her head, unable to speak because images are forming in the glass ball, clear, crisp images that flicker through the sea of glass like pieces of a dream. She wants to wrench her eyes away from the glass, but she can't. Her mind seizes the images, clarifies them.

A stage, she sees a stage. She sees a man and a woman watching a play, sees them from the back, the man in a rocker, the woman close beside him. She realizes they are in a private box in a theater. And there, farther back and deep within the shadows, she sees a crouched figure moving slowly and silently toward the man and the woman. He has a gun.

Mary struggles to shut her eyes, but her lids refuse to close. She begs her feet to move, demands that her body rise from the chair, screams within herself to get out now, to get out and not look back. But her body doesn't hear her pleas. Something inside her has broken down, she is frozen to this chair, her eyes riveted to the glass ball.

An explosion echoes through the room, a gunshot, chaos erupts. She screams. And screams.

IX

Then, suddenly, the world goes still again. She moves through a corridor, through an exquisite silence, and sees the golden-haired girl playing with a doll. The girl looks up, eyes wide and startled. Her delicate mouth forms an O shape; she hugs her doll tightly to her chest. This time, Mary speaks first.

"*Your father, you must warn your father . . . He cannot go to—*"

"*Daddy and Mommy went to Dallas . . .*"

Too late, it's too late. "*You must get word to him—*"

The child frowns. "*About what? I don't understand.*"

"*Danger, he's in danger in Dallas . . .*"

But the child is gone.

X

The windows in her bedroom are thrown open to the April night, to the fresh, green scents of spring. Mary hums as she dresses for the theater, the air like a promise of dreams to be fulfilled.

She doesn't really want to go to the theater tonight, but Abraham insists on seeing "Our American Cousin." And because he thinks it's good for them to get out, she consents to go. After all, if she resists, Abraham will think that her madness has returned, that she's holding seances, that she's stuck back there in the black miasma of so many months ago. He needs to believe she's better now.

The thing she saw, the golden-haired girl . . . all of it was a product of her madness.

She is no longer mad.

So they are escorted out to the carriage by men from Company K, the men who guard her husband when he is in the mansion or at the Old Soldiers' Home. They enter the carriage alone, just the two of them, and tonight Abraham sits next to her and takes her hand in his and kisses the back of it and whispers, "You know I love you, don't you, Mary?"

And she touches the side of his face, drawing him toward her, and kisses his mouth, a kiss that deepens, that will last forever.

T. J. MacGregor

———◆◆◆———

T. J. MacGregor is the author of eighteen suspense novels, ten of which feature married private investigators Quin St. James and Mike McCleary, a series set in south Florida. *The Hanged Man*, a psychic thriller, grew out of her interest in the tarot and things that go bump in the night. She has also written five nonfiction books—on tarot, astrology, and dreams. Her next thriller will be *The Seventh Sense*.

"I chose Mary Todd Lincoln because her mental problems intrigued me," T.J. says. "Was it possible that the so-called problems were simply the ways her consciousness allowed her to glean information in nonordinary ways?"

Adams and Evil

———

Sarah Booth Conroy

THE WASHINGTON POST   DECEMBER 10, 1885

Enveloped in a Fog
Washington Enshrouded for Several Hours in Mist

For several hours last evening the city was enshrouded in a fog, which could be felt as well as seen. The gas in the street-lamps did its best to dissipate the darkness which surrounded everything, but finding its attempts vain settled down to its usual condition of feeble glimmer. Even the electric lights, generally so brilliant, were hardly more successful, and looked like stars in a cloudy sky. . . . It began to settle over the city about five o'clock in the afternoon, and soon after that it was impossible to distinguish objects more than two or three feet away. To add to the discomforts of the day, the rain of the early morning had brought the frost out of the ground and made the streets sloppy and dirty. It was just the kind of day which any one would like—as far away as possible.

Sunday, December 6, 1885
The White House, North Study

NEITHER MY MIND nor my hands are thawed enough to write after my walk across Lafayette Square. The effluvium, rising from depths of the Potomac swamp, casts a shroud over the Square—and the conundrum of Clover Adams. Her death sent an avalanche down my spine—and life.

Only once before did I see such miasma—on All Saints Eve—a nebulous night like this one. Through the fog, Clover echoes in my memory, describing what she saw in the vapor—or thought she saw. I wrote in my diary what she told me on All Saints Day:

> As I felt the damp reaching me—poking my dress, chilling my spine—a white and gold hearse, a large bonbon on wheels, rolled across the square. A line of black-coated men respectfully followed the black bier. Fog disguised as smoke rose from their stovepipe hats.
>
> Did the corpse before me order haze to conceal his essence from the devil? Would his soul reach safe haven in St. John's? The gilded spire atop the church of the presidents shines through the mist, like an honest human in the murky morality of the capitol.
>
> The mourners tread where once was the Pearce plantation burial ground. Recently, the square was plowed and leveled, turning up bones, hair, and other remains.
>
> In the park, the shadows grew deeper and longer, sinking strange hollows in the ground. I felt a shudder begin at my toes and rise to the top of my head, a chill vortex whirling around me. I shook myself free, set up

*my camera, and photographed the hazy square, though
the cortege was gone.*

When Clover told the story at tea, Henry's face
turned a ghostly gray. In a low, threatening voice, he
sternly cautioned Clover: "You dig for a graveyard
humor. I'd not make light of such a portent. 'There
are more things in heaven and earth, than are dreamt
of in your philosophy.'"

I was not the only one who heard the Shakespeare
admonition and saw Clover's hand shaking—oh so
slightly—as she poured tea, changing the discussion,
to everyone's relief.

As we left, Mrs. Hay confided in me that she
was surprised at Mr. Adams. "For shame, it's been
hardly a year since her father died. Mr. Adams told
my husband that she has been depressed since
then. She worshiped Robert Hooper. Their correspondence was a mutual joy."

Later, in confidence, Clover explained her husband's strange forewarning. "A few years ago, Henry
was entranced—if that's the right word, *mesmerized*
might be better—by a Boston said-to-be clairvoyant.
For an exorbitant fee, she claimed to call up the dead,
and make pronouncements for the future."

At first Clover laughed at the medium—until
Henry was entrapped by the supposed specters of
his great-grandfather, John Adams and his grandfather John Quincy Adams. The ectoplasm (or whatever the manifestations) in grating voices shamed
him for being a good-for-nothing, a disgrace to the
family because he held no high office nor political
post. Henry, who'd always felt he had disap-

pointed his family, hardly spoke for days. At least, Clover said, he did not go back to the seances— but he was still half persuaded.

Henry was at the Cosmos Club on my next call to Clover. With the final cup from the silver Viennese teapot, Clover told me—with a wry smile—that Henry had warned her again that the cortege might be a premonition of death.

"My death?" she had asked her husband in a light voice. "Pallor spread across his face, as though he'd dipped it in vanilla icing. He left the room without saying a word."

We both laughed at such foolishness.

We laughed too soon, as I discovered a few hours ago.

We had guests, as usual. Since my brother Grover was inaugurated last March, I had to suspend my own intellectual pursuits to serve as "First Lady" (*what a noxious term!*) for the constant round of hospitality.

After Grover's guests left the White House, I bundled up and walked across the square to Clover's house. I knocked on the door for an eternity, realizing that on Sunday, their six servants had the day off. Henry sauntered up as I turned to go. I wish now I had left before he returned.

"Greetings, Miss Cleveland. Have you come to discuss with Clover the arming of Daughters of Pallas Athena? You suffragettes are doubtless drafting a battalion of Amazons to conquer Congress and win the vote."

Henry's sardonic slurs, belittling our rights, were his usual conversational topic with me.

He added, "I'll see if Clover is receiving. She complained of her sinuses, before I took my toothache to the dentist."

With that, he swooped up the stairs, leaving me fidgeting in the parlor, studying William Blake's drawing of Nebuchadnezzar gamboling on all fours eating grass. Sounds of dragging came through the ceiling. I started to go up, invitation or no, when Henry flew down and out of the house without a word, slamming every door including the front.

What had he found? Was Clover ill? Had he gone for the doctor? Why didn't he call me? Presumptuously, I hurried up to her boudoir and saw Clover's limp limbs falling from a low chair, her head lolling on her shoulder, jaw hanging open. Her eyes staring straight ahead with a look of pain? terror? surprise?

I touched her neck, her wrist, without finding a pulse. Though she was still warm, there was no question—life had fled.

I covered her with the blanket from her bed in the next room, and pondered if there was aught I could do. The answer was no, Clover was beyond my help.

I sat and cried in the only other chair. Clover is—was—one of my few Washington friends—as opposed to political hangers-on. She and I have—had—some proficiency in Greek, a mutual respect for intelligence and a disdain for the usual attitude—shared by her husband—that women are only fit to pour tea.

Clover rarely received in her boudoir—as the French would have it, "a place to sulk." The antique desk is my favorite of her furniture, bought from a diplomat's widow fallen on hard times. A fire burned, or rather smoldered, under the marble mantelpiece, adorned by the handsome French clock. The hearth rug was rumpled, awry, as though something substantial had been removed from it. Clover?

The walls were covered with books, two handsome paintings, and three framed photographs of friends holding *Democracy*. That acid anonymous novel, published in 1880, caused a never finished guessing game—Who was who? The capital still seethes with surmises about the author's identity. Henry, John Jay and Clover herself were all accused. I have no doubt Clover wrote the bitter book.

Clover steadfastly scoffed at the accusation. Henry sneered, "My wife never wrote for publication in her life and could not write if she tried."

Henry ranted on one tea time disparaging his wife's photography. By what right, I do not know. A few days later, when I visited Clover, I found her furious. A foul miscreant violated her darkroom, smashing her glass slides, pouring out chemicals, and destroying her cameras.

Where was Henry now? More to the point, where was the doctor? Clover and I were still alone. No signs of injury—presumably she'd had a heart attack, though hers was a stout organ—necessary to put up with Henry.

I looked carefully around, but my eyes returned always to the shape under the cover. The desk was locked—I had the nerve to try it—though unsure what I expected to find.

Finally, steps sounded in the hall. Hastily I assumed my most regal expression, hoping to be allowed to stay. Henry came in, rudely asking, "What in heaven's name are you doing in this room?"

"I am sorry to offend you," I said, "but I thought

perhaps I could be of service to your wife. When I couldn't, it seemed a pity to leave her dead eyes staring into loneliness."

Henry, his face red with barely contained fury, turned to Dr. Hagner, going about his profession, with his usual knowledgeable manner. He removed the coverlet, felt her wrists and throat, and shook his head.

"I am sorry, Mr. Adams, she is indeed dead. I have no idea how long ago, because of the fire. Where did you find her?"

"On the rug, I couldn't leave her there. I moved her to the chair."

When his back was turned, I straightened the rug, pointing out a protruding lump to Dr. Hagner.

Mr. Adams wheeled around and almost shouted, "Miss Cleveland, this is not your classroom, nor your White House luncheon table. I would thank you to return to your side of Lafayette Square and let Dr. Hagner go about his examination without your interference."

I am not easily subdued, not even by an Adams. Without answering, I stood my ground. Unable to frighten me, he ignored me.

Despite Henry's obvious displeasure, the doctor uncovered a handkerchief, with a yellow stain, embroidered with Clover's initials.

"I am not sure of the cause of death," he said. "Except for her allergies, she was in excellent condition. But, we never know what bodily function will cease when we least expect it. Let's you and me, Mr. Adams, move your wife to her bed until tomorrow, when I can call on assistance."

As we left her suite—with as much courtesy as I

could summon—I asked Mr. Adams if I should inform her friends and family. He yelled "No!" And went on fiercely, "You can serve me best by tending to your own business, and leaving me to mine."

Dr. Hagner, behind Henry's back, shook his head. We left, or rather, were expelled.

"Let me escort you to the White House," Dr. Hagner said gallantly. "I am disturbed," he said. "Heart paralysis is certainly the simplest answer, but I am not sure the right one. You knew her better than I, what do you think?"

"Medicine is not my forte but there *was* an odd odor to her handkerchief and her robe—a faint essence of almonds. Isn't that said to be the scent of potassium cyanide?"

Dr. Hagner nodded, "I'll investigate further tomorrow."

We crossed the square, meeting neighbor Nicholas Anderson. Dr. Hagner told him of Clover's death, and said, "He asked me to tell his neighbors that he is not receiving callers."

Mr. Anderson replied: "I have never quite understood Henry Adams, or indeed his father."

December 7, 1885

Fortunately, we had only a few guests last night. I had to look at my book to remember who was coming. That dreadful afternoon wiped out what's left of my memory. Grover *was* appalled at Clover's death, but wouldn't cancel his invitations. "It's not really a party," he said. "Just a few useful people, her good friends—dreadful if they first learned about her death in the newspapers."

Of course, the evening had a political agenda. I wish I could observe Washington life in its political phase; but I am too near the center for an accurate perspective. Those who live on Mount Athos do not see Mount Athos.

Grover hoped to enlist the guests in the cause of finishing the George Washington monument.

He counted on the George Bancrofts' prestige as historians, and W. W. Corcoran's wealth and eagerness to buy his place back in society.

When the Civil War began, Mr. Corcoran turned his house over to the French embassy, skipped the country, and spent the war in France, selling Confederate bonds.

That doesn't seem to bother his close friend, Susan Decatur, the admiral's widow, also our guest. Mr. Corcoran has an eye for the ladies. He always flirted rather outrageously with Clover—who was charmed by Southern gallantry—and to my amusement, occasionally with me.

I had the meal served in the Red Room, more intimate than either the state or the adjacent "family" dining rooms.

During coffee, appropriately in the Blue Room, I told them about Clover. I went into some detail about finding her, and, being almost thrown out of the house—shown the door—by Henry Adams.

"I feel as though the earth has quit spinning," said Mr. Corcoran. "I cannot imagine Lafayette Square without Clover. Though, the square could do better without Henry—I shouldn't say that."

Mrs. Bancroft shook her head. "It isn't a proper thing to say, Mr. Corcoran. Adams is not the most agreeable man. Clover has—had—a sharp tongue, but she used it as a tool, not a weapon."

"I like Henry, and admire his histories considerably," Dr. Bancroft protested. "He is a witty man. He has a right to be self-absorbed. Heaven knows, Washington has few disinterested observers, fewer have his intellectual powers, or his stamina in research. Clover is—was—charming, a good hostess, and friend. Those are no reasons for putting down Henry."

"The reason to castigate Mr. Adams, if you will excuse me," I replied, "is his chastisement of Clover. Always belittling her intelligence, disputing her views. After she won a photography competition, his jealousy kept her from exhibiting again. Dr. Bancroft, consider the episode when the magazine wanted to publish Clover's splendid photograph of you—and Henry forbade it."

"He did?" said Grover. "I didn't know about that. What reason did he give?"

"None that I know," said Mrs. B. "I seriously considered sending it off anyway, but I was afraid Clover would be blamed and Henry would take it out on her."

"He was a private man. I think he feared the notoriety. I wouldn't wish a wife of mine to show off in public," said Grover. He changed the conversation to how the Washington monument was going to be funded—or if.

The monument looks so forlorn, begun but never completed, like Clover's life.

Dr. Bancroft said firmly, "Of course, it was impossible to finish it during the Civil War. It must be finished, or stand as a monument to our shame."

"Dr. Bancroft, of course, means the War for Southern Independence," said Mr. Corcoran.

"Whatever you choose to call it," retorted historian Bancroft. "In my book—to be published in the spring— it's the Civil War."

"More properly an uncivil war," said Mr. Corcoran.

I stood up, and invited the ladies to leave the men to their controversy, cigars, claret, and chamber pots. We withdrew to the Green Room.

Together, out of earshot of the men, the women were more inclined to condemn Henry. Mrs. Bancroft blamed Henry for spreading the rumor that their childlessness was Clover's fault.

"He told George," she said, "that she was a cold, unfeeling woman. How can I put it delicately? A woman who refused her husband's marital rights."

"Not so," said I, defending her though with some feeling of breaking a confidence. "Clover told me, not able to keep tears from running down her face, how much she yearned for a child.

"She confided that she was still deeply, even romantically in love with her husband, though he disdained her, preferring John Hay and Clarence King. I am sure Mr. Adams was the glacier in the house. The Adams' marriage makes my spinsterhood look golden."

None of the women had ever heard Clover complain of pain or illness that could be considered as a symptom of heart trouble.

"She *did* have terrible hayfever and asthma," I said. "I never understood why, last spring, after her father died, Clover allowed herself to be taken off to Sweet Springs spa. Oak pollen, a powerful cause of asthma, is thick in the Allegheny Mountains, indeed most of West Virginia. Surely Henry knew better."

In what was left of the evening, we praised Clover's wit, taste in art, and research for Henry's histories.

"She introduced Henry to us," said Mrs. Bancroft. "And to a great many others who helped him."

The guests went home later than Washington protocol. I am grateful for their opinions—but glad to have my mind to myself to think over the dreadful day.

So I sit, looking over the murk, and wondering how Clover died, and if there was anything I could have done to keep her alive.

I suddenly remembered seeing two locked suitcases under her bed when I took the cover off. Had she planned to leave her husband? She should have, years ago.

After I finally went to bed, my exhausted brain jumbled specters, seances, secret doors, psychics. Early this morning, I dreamed Clover came toward me through a fog so heavy it seemed more a cloud.

She drifted across Lafayette Square pleading, "Dear Rose, remember All Souls Eve." When I woke, my dream dissipated into wisps of memory.

After such a sleepless night, I hope I can stay awake long enough to record today's events.

Over tea in the Blue Room—Grover having a cabinet meeting in the oval library—Dr. Hagner told me what he'd found at the autopsy.

"I presume you read the *Washington Post* this morning," he said. "The reporter quoted me as saying she died from 'paralysis of the heart.' "

"Isn't that the equivalent of saying her heart stopped beating?" I asked.

"Yes. It is an answer to impertinent questions to which there are no answers," the good doctor agreed. "Because you are Clover's dear friend, and a person I hold in high esteem, I'll tell you, before you read it in the *New York Sun*. Sergeant McCarry asked me, as her physician, to confer with Coroner Patterson about her medicines. No doubt Mrs. Adams's death was due to cyanide—probably from stores in her darkroom.

"I believe she did not swallow, but inhaled it, through her nostrils."

"Could it have been put in her regular nose drops?" I wondered.

"I don't think so. The odor is very noticeable."

"What you say makes sense, Doctor. Though Clover's chronic ailments made her sense of smell less acute."

Dr. Hagner considered that thought over the last dregs of his tea. "In her boudoir, Mr. Adams pointed out a vial near the rug, by its stench, cyanide."

THE NEW YORK SUN   DECEMBER 9, 1885

Although she was still warm, they could not revive her. The fumes of the poison and the empty phial that contained it told plainly enough the cause of her death.

THE WASHINGTON CRITIC   DECEMBER 9, 1885

"Was It a Case of Suicide?"

The certificate of Coroner Patterson and Dr. Hagner in the case of Mrs. Henry Adams, who died suddenly in this city on Sunday last, is to the effect that she came to her death through an overdose of potassium cyanide administered by herself. A *New York Sun* correspondent states further that there is no doubt Mrs. Adams intended to take her own life. She was just recovering from a long illness, and had been suffering from mental depression.

December 9, 1885

"Poppycock!" As I told Grover, when I read the newspapers. "She was no such thing."

"Henry's brother told me she was addled in her brain with grief over her father's death. Otherwise, why did she take poison?"

"She didn't—not on purpose. I know her better than most. She and her sister did everything for her father in his last days. Clover wrote Clara Hay 'of the gaiety with which my father walked to his grave. His humor and courage lasted 'till unconsciousness came . . . he went to sleep like a tired traveller.' "

Death can be an anodyne. "I'm not convinced," said Grover.

This afternoon I paid a call on Mrs. Nicholas Anderson, down the street from the Adamses. "We didn't believe it," she asserted. Nicholas added, "Nothing was more ghastly than that lonely vigil in the house with his dead wife, on the day she died."

I made proper noises and went on with my calls, the next at Adams'.

At the door, the butler told me Mr. Adams was not

receiving. He did say that Adams' brother Charles, Clover's brother Edward Hooper, sister Ellen, called Nella, and her husband Ephraim Whitman Gurney had arrived.

"Please give this card to Mrs. Gurney," I asked him, scribbling on the front *pour condoler*—I trust she knows the French for condolences. The Hooper women are well educated. On the back, I asked her to call on me at the White House for tea. Invitations to the White House, in my brief experience, are rarely turned down.

December 10, 1885

Mrs. Gurney came by herself, as I hoped she would. I had quite enough of Adams' rudeness. The chief usher showed her up to my study.

She was obviously upset. "Henry is very brave," she said. "He refuses to go into mourning. Why last night at dinner, he wore a fire-red tie. He stood on the stairs, tore off the mourning band on his arm and threw it under the table. I must have gasped. He turned and looked at me and ordered—that's the only word—'Never Fear for Me!'"

Sounded like braggadocio to me. Mr. Adams is given to bluster.

Mrs. Gurney twisted her lacy napkin one way and then t'other, until I thought she'd surely turn it into rags.

Realizing what she was doing, she looked at me and said, "I can't imagine why Clover would do such a thing as the newspapers say—the newspapers and

Henry's brother. He was ranting and raving about suicide being inherited in our family. Charles said he warned Henry before they were married that Clover would kill herself. Charles claimed he saw Clover recently on a train, holding her head in despair."

"More likely hayfever. Do you believe she killed herself?"

"Well, Miss Rose, Henry gave me this letter today. I suppose I shouldn't show it to you, but you were her best friend in Washington."

With that, she handed me over an unfinished, unsigned, unaddressed, reckless-looking scrawl. The top part of the paper had been torn off, leaving a ragged edge. What was written on the missing part?

"That was all Henry found," said Mrs. Gurney.

The letter read:

"If I had one single point of character or goodness I would stand on that and grow back to life. Henry is more patient & loving than words can express. God might envy him. He bears & hopes & despairs hour after hour. Henry is beyond all words tenderer and better than all of you even."

While Mrs. Gurney drank her tea, I excused myself and compared Clover's note with an earlier one to me. Certainly differences existed, but I had been a schoolteacher long enough to know that individual handwritings vary greatly, according to the writer's health, haste, pen, and so on. I reserve judgment as to whether Clover wrote it under duress—or wrote it at all. I wish I had a sample of her widower's handwriting.

Naturally, I mentioned none of this to Mrs. Gurney.

Actually, I had little chance to mention anything to the loquacious lady.

"I wanted to call on you today," she said, "because we are leaving tomorrow. We would've left earlier but we had to attend the funeral in their house and the burial in Rock Creek Cemetery."

I am not surprised that Henry Adams did not invite me.

"We are upset because Henry says she will not have an inscribed gravestone, indeed no marker at all. I don't understand my brother-in-law. He has no desire for our help.

"Henry has made all the arrangements himself. He's commissioned Augustus St. Gaudens to create a bronze sculpture for her grave—whatever form he likes. I wouldn't like the idea of tons of bronze in any shape being plunked down on my last resting place. I suppose Henry doubts graves will open to the final trumpet on Judgment Day."

Surely, Henry ordered the statue to keep Clover's spirit in the grave.

I changed the subject with Mrs. Gurney by offering a tour of the State Rooms. She accepted with alacrity.

January 1, 1886

Tonight I can hardly write after shaking hands all day at Grover's first New Year's reception. I endured by conjugating Greek verbs in my mind.

Grover, praise heaven, was amenable to shorten former President Arthur's receiving line which, I have heard, incorporated every respectable lady in town. Instead, we received the cabinet and honored

guests in the upstairs oval library, and descended
with them by the West stairs. The president (without,
I am happy to say, the gloves and buttonhole bou-
quet favored by Arthur) escorted Mrs. Bayard. Secretary of State Bayard offered me his arm. That party
perennial Julia Tyler, the former president's wife,
came down on the arm of her son Dr. Lachlan Tyler.

Then, all Washington crowded in. Guests complimented me on eliminating Arthur's burly guards in
jail-keeper costume. Our handsome young men, taste-
fully dressed in proper frock coats, are more suited
(pun!) to Tiffany's decoration for Charles Arthur. They
do a better watch job by blending into the crowd.

Among the guests were John Hay and his wife, Clara.
She said, "How dreadful about Clover. She seemed a bit
under the weather, but I didn't expect such a sensible,
confident, in control woman to do such a dreadful deed."

Mr. Hay interrupted, changing the subject. "Did
you know we moved into our new house yesterday?
Henry too. It's going to be wonderful to be so close."

I could easily understand why Henry Adams wanted
to move away from the house where Clover's spirit
clung to the walls. What was he doing with her exquisite possessions?

January 5, 1886

W. W. Corcoran called to answer my curiosity
about Clover's treasures. The charmer and cause of
Washington scandals keeps track of all others.

Over tea in the Blue Room, he said, "That rascal—if
you were a man I'd call him worse—gave Clover's Car-
tier diamond necklace to that minx Lizzie Cameron!"

Henry Adams' attentions to Mrs. Cameron had been rumored before the death of his wife. Elizabeth, sold into marriage by her uncle, General Sherman, thought she had every right to flirt with anything in pants. Lizzie is not the brightest—though often said to be the most beautiful—woman in the capital. One recent newspaper report said she was seriously ill. Her mind wasn't functioning as a result from an accident a few years ago. More likely that drunken lout of her husband beat her up because of Adams' gift.

January 6, 1886

The next day, who should call upon me but Mrs. C. herself. I thought she looked rather unkempt, unlike her usual elaborate toilette, very obviously in the family way. I received her in the upstairs West Parlor—she didn't deserve the Blue Room. After the usual formula greetings she began to sniffle.

"Miss Cleveland, I come to you because you are the only one who can stop the slander that's going around the capital.

"Since Mr. Adams gave me his late wife's necklace, I have felt like a leper. My husband has threatened to call him out in a duel. Mrs. Adams' friends have shunned me as though I had committed a crime. A newspaper says I have gone mad. Some have even rumored that my baby is Mr. Adams' child."

I made as many noncommittal noises as I could dredge up. Lizzie Cameron was not ready to stop her complaints.

"It's all upset me so much. The other night, when

I took some medicine to make me sleep, I foolishly forgot to take off Mrs. Adams' necklace. I'd worn it to a ball at Decatur House. In the middle of the night, I woke suddenly. At the foot of my bed stood Clover Adams, staring at me.

" 'Lizzie Cameron,' " she said. " 'What on earth are you doing with my necklace? Give it back.'

" 'Mr. Adams gave it to me,' " I whispered.

" 'And you didn't have the good manners to turn him down. My father bought it for me. My jewelry is not Henry's to give away.

" 'You have no right to my possessions—and certainly no right to Henry—though to have him would be the worst punishment I could wish on you. Give me the necklace, you trollop, or I will return every night of your life.' "

"Mrs. Cameron, for heaven's sake, you can't take nightmares seriously—especially those induced by medicines you shouldn't be taking anyway—surely not in your present delicate condition."

"Not to be rude, Miss Cleveland, but you can't know how real she was."

"When I woke up, the necklace was gone. I stripped the bed, went through every drawer, lifted every rug. Clover took it. She is wearing it in her grave. I know it as well as if I stood over her casket."

Mrs. Cameron fell apart. She and her guilty conscience had to be put in a guest bedroom to dry her tears and pull her few bits and pieces of sense together. Hours later, she knocked—interrupting my reading the *Odyssey*—keeping up my Greek. I sent her home in my carriage, shaking my head. I don't believe in ghosts—except as manifestations of guilt. Clover has better places to go than Mrs. Cameron's bedroom, and others more deserving of haunting than Lizzie Cameron. Though Clover surely would be appalled at Henry's disposal of her necklace.

May 1, 1886

Luncheons, teas, receptions, and dinners, the winter has warmed into spring. Clover's death is replaced by Grover's romance as the *scandale du jour*.

During his presidential campaign, Grover's alleged love affair—the "Buffalo" scandal accusing him of fathering an illegitimate son—brought on a popular doggerel:

> *"Ma, Ma, where's my Pa?"*
> *"Gone to the White House, ha ha, ha!"*

Now, a headline in the *New York Herald* howled *"Washington Gossip—Society Incredulous About the President's Marriage—What If It Prove True?"* They insinuated he was marrying Emma Folsom, widow of his late law partner. Even I became a part of the rumor. Eugene Field wrote a ballad, "Sister Rose's Suspicions." Not suspicions—knowledge.

"Did you read about my pronouncement yesterday?" Grover asked with a certain amount of smugness. "I told that unruly crew of journalists: 'I don't see why the papers keep marrying me to old ladies all the while' . . ."

May 20, 1886

One rare day without an official event. I asked my meals be sent to the small Southwest Study, by my bedroom. Then Grover burst in.

"Frances and Emma will be arriving from Europe May 27. I'm hoping you will be kind enough to whisk the Folsoms away to Gilsey House Hotel.

"I'll send Colonel Lamont with you. But you'll have to handle the reporters' questions. The colonel doesn't have your gift of telling the press less than they want to know—and nothing they shouldn't."

The next day, Grover astounded the nation. Everybody had long suspected the forty-nine-year-old bachelor president was marrying Mrs. Folsom. Instead, he revealed his fiancée was beautiful, twenty-one-year-old Frances, his ward from the death of her father, Grover's law partner.

All the fuss and folderol connected with the June 2 wedding—first of a president actually in the White House itself—leaves me little time to worry about Clover's demise.

Grover invited our sister Mary to "help." I'm sorry to say she'll change my orders and upset our domestic staff. I dread her coming.

June 2, 1886

Grover and Frances sensibly kept the guest list to a manageable number—family friends and vital political supporters, including the cabinet.

A curious crowd completely encircled the house,

listening to the Marine Band's Mendelssohn wedding march, the arsenal's presidential salute, and the church bells' peals.

Down the great staircase came Grover and Frances. She deftly handled her dangerous four-yard white India silk train, which was embellished with orange blossoms. Considering Grover's gifts of diamond necklace and sapphire and diamond engagement ring, it was a good thing we had extra guards.

Staterooms bloomed with scarlet begonias, jacque-minot roses, fireplaces with small pink flowers, mantelpieces with pansies and plaques of appropriate mottoes. The dining room centerpiece reflected a full-rigged ship of pinks, roses, and pansies.

Mary and I collapsed after the newlyweds left on a private railroad car for Deer Park to honeymoon. I am happy to turn over this First Lady occupation to Frances. She is feminine and beautiful—Washington will find her a pleasant change from what they call my masculine manners.

She's young, compared to my forty years, but a woman capable of great development. As I told Mary, I long for my little old house on the Holland Patent—village on the one side and hills on the other.

June 5, 1886

Mr. Corcoran called today at teatime. "Knowing how you appreciate good things, I thought you should know the late Mrs. Adams' effects are being sold by a Georgetown antiques dealer. If you have the time, we could see if there's anything we'd like."

I swallowed my tea in an unladylike gulp, and said "I suppose Mr. Adams couldn't stand looking at Clover's possessions anymore—and couldn't talk Mrs. Cameron into taking them. Let's go now."

Mr. Corcoran smiled. "My carriage awaits at the north entrance."

Along the way down Pennsylvania Avenue I pondered why Henry Adams rid himself of reminders of his late wife. Surely his new house could have accommodated it all. Guilt, no doubt—or greed.

The shop dealer admitted having Clover's most choice chattels, though her paintings were sent to be sold more profitably on the New York art market.

Mr. Corcoran asked for the name of the dealer.

The armoire attracted my attention immediately. But knowing I would shortly leave the White House, it seemed too big to move.

The *escritoire*, where Clover wrote *Democracy* and *Esther*, I would have, even if I had to load it myself.

November 20, 1918
Lucca, Italy

After all these years in Italy, I have decided never to leave. The possessions I stored in Mary's attic have come. Finally I am unpacking. My White House diary turned up today. I might as well use the empty pages to record the years between the White House and Italy.

When the honeymooners returned, I left Washington and went to Chicago to edit a new magazine, *Literary Life*—and to resume mine. As I wrote in my book of essays: "We can do no better or braver thing than to bring our best thoughts to the everyday market; they will yield us usurious interest."

Unfortunately, my magazine did not yield interest—monetary or literary. Fortunately, I had a better offer to teach history in New York, and my novel, *The Long Run*, was published.

A good move it was too, since I met a charming woman, my companion for the rest of my life. My book, *George Eliot's Poetry and Other Studies*, sold 25,000 copies, providing me with enough of my own money to move to Italy with my wealthy friend.

This spring, Mr. Corcoran wrote, telling me Henry Adams died in his sleep March 27. His nieces (trust W.W. to know the young women) found a partly empty bottle of cyanide in his desk.

Though I fear I have caught a bad cold, I will devote today to Clover's desk, the only furniture I asked be sent to Italy.

I unpacked it carefully and polished it up. As I rubbed the middle decorative panel, a drawer unaccountably slid out. The hidey hole held a diary, closed but not locked. Shaking all over, I opened it, afraid I would find the reality of my nightmares.

Clover wrote "To Posterity" in a hasty scrawl, spreading in unruly swoops, ink blots, and tear stains across the page.

The wild writing, she explained, was caused by drugged cocoa provided her without her knowledge by Clarence King, so he and Henry could indulge their sexual proclivities.

No surprise to me, remembering Henry's treatment of Clover, her allusions to unfulfilled marriage, and lack of his own money.

The final horror came at diary's end. She *had* packed to leave. Henry locked her in, refused to allow her to go—no doubt fearing scandal, loss of her money, and his last worshipper.

Now she wrote:

"I will leave—just as soon as I take my nosedrops."

The rest of the page was blank. On the next page, the writing was ground into the paper, summoning all her last energy.

"The bitter burning, unbearable pain sears my head, my brain, my heart. Now I know what was saved from the destruction of my darkroom—the bottle of potassium cyanide. Little time is left to write, though I doubt posterity will read these pages. On the chance, I hide them in my secret drawer.

Henry will claim my books, burn my journal, tear up my letters, sell my paintings, spend my money, obliterate my memory.

I will have my revenge. I will haunt him every day of his life."

And I am sure mine.

SARAH BOOTH CONROY

~~~

SARAH BOOTH CONROY has been a staff writer "for thirty years or so" for *The Washington Post*, and currently writes the "Chronicles" column for that paper. She is writing a novel about Martha Washington. She says that she and her husband Richard Timothy Conroy (also a contributor to this collection) live in a large (but not large enough) bookcase in the capital, and that they have separate but equal studies, computers, dictionaries, telephones, and *Bartlett's Quotations*.

"Grover Cleveland's youngest sister—a historian, lecturer, suffragist, editor, and essayist—was the first intellectual and professional writer to serve as First Lady," the author says. "I met Miss Cleveland when I wrote *Refinements of Love*, a novel about Clover and Henry Adams, to which this short story is a sequel. Rose and Clover were friends, living north and south of Lafayette Square. In "Adams and Evil," newspaper quotations and their dates are as cited. The characters all lived, and actually said or wrote a few words I have attributed to them. Clues—if not my conclusions—

can be verified in the excellent biographies of Henry and Clover Adams. After *Refinements* was published, I learned from Clover's relatives that much in the novel I could not prove has long been rumored in her family. Did Henry Adams murder his wife? Why else would she haunt me?"

A TALE OF TWO SISTERS

RICHARD TIMOTHY CONROY

I'M GOING TO tell you about two sisters. One, pretty as could be, and the other a mite prettier.

The pretty one was Margaret; she was the quiet one, too. And then there was Julia.

They were the Gardiner sisters. And as was proper, they had two older brothers to look out for them. Alex, smart as a whip, and David Lyon—well, David Lyon had a bit of a dark side and one day it would cause trouble. Not much, mind you, not like Dolley Madison's boy. But enough.

These Gardiners, they descended from that old warrior, Lion Gardiner, who was brought over in the early days by the Pilgrims to help them build fortifications for protection from the ungodly Indians they had dispossessed. Lion stayed on in the New World, and for the next two hundred years there were Gardiners on New York's Gardiner's Island, out near East Hampton.

It was from here that Senator David Gardiner, that's Julia's father and a onetime state senator, brought Julia into the city to make her debut in New York society. Julia was fifteen and down in Washington, Andrew Jackson was president.

And wasn't Julia pretty! Delicious, even! Just on the verge of what she would become. The newspapers called her the "Rose of Long Island" and a drawing of a rose became her symbol, her logo, good as a name.

Who could go back and sit still on Gardiner's Island after that? It was a recipe for mischief, and mischief was Julia's nature. And her little sister, Margaret, the quiet one, abetted her every step of the way. The parents stood back in awe and more than a little exasperation at their daughters. But with the senator, who was, after all, a man, it was with much admiration.

That is, until the "astonishingly cheap" episode. That was too much. What happened was the girls, on a visit to the city, allowed an artist to use Julia as the model for a lady on an advertising handbill. The legend on the handbill was: "I'll Purchase at Bogert & Mecamly's No. 86 9th Avenue. Their Goods are Beautiful & Astonishingly Cheap." Julia's rose, below the picture, removed any doubt that the fashionable but cheaply dressed young lady was Julia.

Well! The Gardiners whisked their daughters off for a year in Europe to let the scandal die down. The year was 1840 and Julia was twenty. It was a wonderful tour, doubtless worth the scolding the girls got. The lesson Julia got from it was, she could do what she wanted and shake things up, and something good would come from it in the end.

The girls were presented to Queen Victoria, and Julia was much impressed. The Queen was only a year older than she, and look at her! They saw the Pope in Rome. Just after the start of 1841, the American minister (that was before we had ambassadors) arranged to have the girls presented to King Louis Philippe of France. Margaret, who kept a record of events, great and small, wrote about his Majesty, "The King looks old, is very affable in manners and resembles his paintings except in stature. Auburn wig which half concealed his snow white hair. Principally addressed the married ladies. Asked J and myself if we were sisters and passed on." Julia, for once virtually ignored, was doubtless speechless.

This tale is a complex one, and while the Gardiner's were making the grand tour in Europe, and New York society was recovering from Julia's venture into commerce, things were happening in and about Washington. The Whigs were stirring things up. The Whigs were a comet visiting American politics, crystals of political views clustered around a nucleus of clay. Or to be more specific, around Kentucky's Senator Henry Clay. In a sense, the Whigs were a reaction to Andrew Jackson, and like other things created from repulsion rather than attraction, they were hard to hold together. Indeed, they only held together for twenty years.

True of the Whigs, but not of Henry Clay. Clay was attracted to the idea of being president. But as a pre-Jackson Democrat, the electorate had rejected him, and later, as a Whig, he was unable to get their nomination. So he courted one of his party's factions, the Southern Whigs. Now, for the 1840 elections, while the Gardiners were off in Europe, Clay supported for president an old Indian-fighting general, William Henry Harrison. Clay thought—no he was certain—that with Harrison as president, his hand could govern the country from the Senate. After all, he controlled the Whigs (except with regard to getting himself nominated), and the Whigs controlled both houses of Congress.

But Clay made a mistake. He agreed to accept John Tyler of Virginia as the vice presidential nominee, to assure the support of Virginia Whigs. Tyler, the strict constructionist of the Constitution, a supporter of states' rights, Tyler, the slave owner. All this at a time when the cornerstone of the Whigs was the strengthening of the federal government by holding that the federal government could do whatever was necessary, even if its powers were not spelled out chapter and verse, to accomplish the Constitution's purposes. For instance, founding a national banking system, one way or another. And building a road system, for example. And the Whigs divided, North and South, on slavery.

Nobody asked John Tyler about his contrary views. He said his nomination was neither solicited nor expected, so he had made no promises. Nobody, not even he, gave much thought to vice presidents. Presidents went their own way and vice presidents stayed out of the way.

Well, things were about to change. On the fourth of March, our old inauguration day back in 1841,

General, now President, Harrison told the country he would do nothing to interfere with the work of the Congress. Just what Henry Clay was waiting to hear. And Tyler, too.

Nothing here for me to do, thought Vice President Tyler, and returned to his home in Williamsburg. And there he might have remained had Harrison not caught cold. Harrison was buried an even month after his inauguration. Secretary of State Daniel Webster's son traveled all night to tell Tyler he was needed in Washington after all.

Clay's hand-picked Harrison cabinet told Tyler, when he arrived, that he was still just the vice president and was only acting as president. Tyler quite properly ignored them. It was a momentous step. A president had never died in office before, and Tyler, by insisting that he was now in fact the president, set the precedent for all those succeeding vice presidents who were to be thrust into the highest office by death or dishonor.

In a few months, the Congress, business as usual, set about to establish a district banking system. Tyler demanded certain restrictions on states' rights. Clay stormed. Tyler, his patience at an end, said, "Go you now, then, Mr. Clay, to your end of the avenue, where stands the Capitol, and there perform your duty to the country as you shall think proper. So help me God, I shall do mine at this end of it as I shall think proper."

The bank bill eventually came to the president twice, in two different forms and each time he vetoed it. Each time mobs of drunken, armed Whigs came to the White House, called out the president and burned him in effigy. The second time there were threats against the president's life.

Clay lacked the votes to override and was outraged. In early September 1841, Clay orchestrated a walkout of Tyler's cabinet, holdovers from those Clay had selected for Harrison. Only Secretary of State Webster remained, as he would for two more years before quitting over the Mexico question.

Two days later, Clay called the Whig congressmen together before the Capitol building and had them read Tyler out of the party. Soon, Tyler was being called the president without a party, and the accidental president.

All the while, Tyler, calm and collected, did the business of the presidency aided by a few supporters and a large and loyal family.

But within his family, all was not well, either. Letitia Tyler, his wife, was at age fifty-two an invalid, victim of a stroke. Her duties as White House hostess were being attended to by Priscilla Tyler, wife of her son Robert. Letitia rarely left her bedroom after the Tylers moved into the White House. She was dying.

And so Julia Gardiner came to Washington. She was not yet twenty-two. Men turned their heads as she passed. Julia was five foot three, and her waist so small a man might think he could put his two hands around it. Or at any rate, he would like to try. Her bosom was, well—womanly, and her hair raven. Many remarked on her skin, creamy, smooth, and fair. And more than anything else, she sparkled.

Margaret was different. Oh, I know they said they looked like sisters (even the King of France said that) but Margaret was nineteen and of a thoughtful turn of mind. Honest, too. Some said honest to a fault, perhaps too honest ever to endure courtship and arrive at marriage.

The Gardiners arrived in Washington by train from New York in mid-January 1842, and checked into Mrs. Payton's boardinghouse, a hangout for congressmen, four blocks from the Capitol. At a party a few days later, on the eighteenth, Julia met the president's eldest son, Robert. Julia and Robert spent the evening discussing poetry. They found themselves kindred spirits. And Robert invited the Gardiners to a White House reception two days later. Margaret had a cold and did not go.

Later Julia told Margaret about how she was introduced to the president by Congressman Fernando Wood, and how the president showered her with a thousand compliments. (Clever as Julia was, we have to assume her count of compliments was actually only an estimate.) Julia remarked on the silvery sweetness of the president's voice, his incomparable grace of bearing and the elegant ease of his conversation. (All things considered, it is just as well the president's wife was upstairs and didn't witness his first meeting with her successor.)

Six weeks later, the Gardiners returned to East Hampton. They just missed Charles Dickens' historic visit to the Tyler White House. In September, Letitia died and the president went into mourning.

The Gardiners came again to Washington for the winter social season, arriving on December 4, 1842. With the big parties at the White House suspended, the capital was rather subdued. But the president's second son lost little time in presenting his cards on the Gardiners. Attentive John Jr. managed to overlook mentioning his own current married state.

Julia, no fool, still played the field. The Gardiners had to rent an extra parlor at Mrs. Payton's to accommodate Julia's swarm of admirers. But the attention of the Tylers was persuasive. The Gardiners spent Christmas Eve at the White House, and another evening during Christmas week, and then they sat in the president's pew at St. John's for New Year's Day services. And so it went. By the end of January, the Gardiners and the Tylers were intimate, in the old sense of the word.

On February 13, 1843, there were cards in the Red Room. In the course of the evening, the president came into the room and invited Julia to play cards à deux. The game they played, according to Tom Cooper, Priscilla's hard-drinking, gambling, out-of-work actor father, was Old Sledge, a game approximating Seven Up, one still played today. After most of the guests had left, the president invited the Gardiners up to his private apartments to visit. Later, when the Gardiners were leaving, the president kissed Margaret (in some proper way, no details recorded). When he tried to kiss Julia, she ran down the stairs with the president chasing after. Despite their thirty-year age difference, he finally caught her in the Red Room. Oh, my!

At the Washington's birthday ball, the president proposed to Julia. The prescribed year of mourning for Letitia be damned. Julia was wearing a Greek hat, something like a fez, with a tassel attached to the top. At each word of the proposal, she flicked her tassel in the president's face. Was Julia being a coquette or simply rude? Probably both. In March, the president proposed again to Julia, this time in a carriage and in front of Margaret. Perhaps he was trying to get Margaret's support. If Margaret told him she didn't have the right to vote, she left no record of it.

Nevertheless, by the time the Gardiners were ready to leave at the end of the season, Julia and the president had some sort of understanding and Julia had discussed it with her parents. Juliana, Julia's mother, wanted them to wait until Julia was sure she wished to marry Tyler. After all, Tyler was nine years older, even, than Julia's mother. But Julia was not to be held back for long. When someone mentioned in her presence that Tyler was president without a party, she retorted, "If he wants a party, I'll give him a party."

The year 1843 saw much repositioning. In November, at the urging of their children, the Gardiners bought a house in New York City on Lafayette Place. It was only a coincidence that the president lived on Washington's Lafayette Park.

President Tyler, left between the extremes of the Whigs and the Jackson Democrats, sought to "define his presidency" as we would call it today. He chose for this the annexation of Texas. Texas had broken away from Mexico in 1836 and a year later had asked to be annexed by the United States. Nothing was done, however, because of fears of complicating the slavery issue, an explanation of which exceeds the scope of this account.

But in 1843, Texas began flirting with both Mexico

and Britain, and it was clear Washington would have to act. Henry Clay opposed annexation, believing it would lead to war with Mexico and be costly and without public support. Webster split with Tyler over Texas and left the cabinet, the last of the Harrison/Clay men to go.

Tyler appointed the aptly named Virginian, Abel Upshur, as secretary of state, and through his adroit handling of Congress, it appeared by the end of the year that the question of slavery was sidestepped and there were enough votes in the Senate to ratify a Texas treaty. All that remained was to find some way the United States could deploy enough military forces to convince Sam Houston that any Mexican attack could be countered. A fateful delay, as it turned out.

Into this political milieu returned the Gardiners, or at least the senator and his two daughters, on February 24, 1944. Alex, David Lyon, and their mother, Juliana, remained at their new New York City home.

The White House held a grand levee—as a reception was called in those days—on February 27, for Captain Stockton of the Navy frigate *Princeton*. The *Princeton* was the American Navy's most modern ship, driven by propellers instead of the awkward paddle wheels of other steam-powered vessels. In addition, it was armed with the largest naval cannon in the world, a huge gun called the Peacemaker for reasons that are not quite clear. Commodore Kennon, also at the party, was chief of Navy construction, and to some degree responsible for this advanced technology. Kennon was also the great grandson-in-law of Martha Washington, and as such resided at

Tudor Place, the Georgetown mansion built from the George Washington legacy.

Also at the White House was Dolley Madison, at seventy-five, the grand old lady of Washington, living link with our first ten presidents (with another to go). And there was Payne Todd, Dolley's son by her brief first marriage. A wastrel son, an alcoholic, a reckless, compulsive and unlucky gambler. And the fifty-two-year-old apple of his mother's eye.

But Dolley, a charming, cheerful, and intelligent woman, had a great weakness. She believed, despite all evidence to the contrary, that Payne could be redeemed. This was to the despair of the late President Madison. He had settled, with Dolley's knowledge, $20,000 in Payne's gambling IOUs and another $20,000, which he kept from Dolley to spare her peace of mind. He instructed his executor to show Dolley, after his death, this second batch of IOUs. Dolley spent herself into poverty picking up Payne's later debts, and when the Congress bought the first batch of Madison papers for $30,000, Payne went through that, too. At the time of our story, Dolley was trying to sell Madison's remaining papers. Eventually, she would get another $25,000 for those, but Congress would pay her only $5,000 cash and use the remainder to set up a trust fund. So much for worthless Payne, who was off, secretly selling Dolley's silver spoons and furniture from Montpelier.

But back to the party. Captain Stockton invited the guests at the White House to join him and the president for an excursion the next day down the Potomac. At one in the afternoon, on a cold but sunny

February 28, 150 ladies and 200 gentlemen boarded the *Princeton*.

A small Marine band was playing on deck under the direction of Italian immigrant bandmaster and clarinetist Franco Maria Scala. Below deck, a large salon, or lounge, was stocked with champagne and other refreshments, and crowded with those guests who preferred shelter to the open deck. There were also those who did not wish to be near the Peacemaker when it was fired, twice, on the voyage down river.

The president, members of his cabinet, Senator Gardiner, and Julia of course, were on deck watching the action. Below in the Salon, Margaret sat with Dolley Madison. It was the best seat in the lounge; Margaret could see and hear all the ladies and gentlemen as they paid their respects to Dolley and were, thus, being amusing and being amused.

At about three, the president came below to drink toasts and to open the luncheon. Julia had not followed him, so he sent a steward back for her. She came down with her father. Others drifted down from the deck. More toasts were drunk and people began to sing.

Later, word was passed that the ship was turning around and as it passed Mount Vernon, the Peacemaker would be fired one more time. Senator Gardiner hurried up to the deck and the president started to follow. But just then his son-in-law, William Waller, began to sing sea chanties. The president stopped to listen.

Dolley began to stir. She adjusted her trademark turban, as much a part of her as her slightly old-fashioned dresses. It was crowded and stuffy in the salon and now, with the singing, maybe she should take a turn on the deck. Payne, unexpectedly solicitous, told her to keep her seat. It was nearly four, he said, and the winter sun was not strong. It would be too cold on deck. Payne was very stern about it.

Margaret, the thoughtful one, sat looking on and wondered.

Waller, with what he fancied was a seamanlike baritone, sang, "eight hundred men lay slain" when there was a boom like the end of the world. Everybody but Margaret cheered at the timing as the ship rocked with the recoil.

Then, almost as though all breath and motion had stopped, a soot-blackened officer burst into the salon screaming for a surgeon. Smoke poured in after him. There was a scramble for the deck. Margaret, who told of it later, was stunned but remembered Julia crying out for her father and running for the stairs. Afterward, it was reported in the newspapers that somebody, unidentified, had said, "My dear child, you can do no good, your father is in heaven."

Julia swooned. There is no other word for it. Later, after another vessel came to the rescue of the passengers, the president picked up Julia in his arms and was carrying her across to the other ship when she regained consciousness and struggled to go to her father. "I almost knocked us both off the gangplank. I did not know at the time . . . that it was the president whose life I almost consigned to the water," she said later.

Most of the passengers left the *Princeton*. Seventy-five-year-old Dolley Madison remained behind to help tend to the injured.

That night, Margaret and Julia stayed at the White House. It was unthinkable that they should return to their empty rooms at Mrs. Payton's boardinghouse. Margaret, to pass the time, told Julia about Payne Todd's odd insistence and how it perhaps spared them both.

Seven men had died and eleven were injured. Caskets were set up in the White House East Room for Secretary of State Upshur, Navy Secretary Gilmer (both Virginians), former diplomat Virgil Maxcy, Commodore Kennon, and Senator Gardiner.

On March 1, Alex and David arrived in Washington and a few days later escorted their sisters back to New York. The senator was returned to East Hampton and buried there on March 26.

The political life of the president went on. Within days, Tyler was maneuvered into appointing John C. Calhoun as secretary of state. This was a disaster, the dimensions of which are even now difficult to measure. Virginia Representative Henry Wise, one of Tyler's few remaining political supporters, made the offer to Calhoun without Tyler's authorization. Tyler, to avoid losing Wise, decided to put up with Calhoun. The immediate consequence was to sink any immediate possibility of congressional approval of Texas annexation. The problem, of course, was Calhoun's commitment to redressing the balance between slave and free states, thus injecting the slavery question into Texas annexation.

Tyler set about repairing this in an ingenious way.

He formed a third party with the intention of using it as a bargaining chip.

In April, Tyler wrote to Juliana Gardiner asking for Julia's hand in marriage.

In May, the three political parties met in Baltimore to choose their candidates. Clay was nominated by the Whigs. At the Democratic convention, Van Buren, trying again for the presidency, was unable to get enough votes and the party settled on dark horse James K. Polk, a Jackson protégé. Tyler carried his new Democrat-Republican party, of course.

In June, the Texas annexation treaty was defeated in the Senate thirty-five to sixteen.

And on June 25, President Tyler and his son, John Jr., traveled by train to New York, arriving at 10:20 P.M. They stayed overnight at Howard's Hotel. Tyler persuaded the hotel keeper to lock up the servants for the night to keep his presence secret. At 2:00 P.M the next day, he and Julia were married at the Church of the Ascension. Then, bride and groom, accompanied by Margaret, crossed over the Hudson to Jersey City. On the way, they were saluted by the guns of the fort on Governor's Island, and guns on the *USS North Carolina* and, surprisingly enough, the frigate *Princeton*. Taking the train from there, they arrived in Washington on June 27.

On June 28, the couple held a reception in the East Room of the White House. The room was filled with flowers. Dolley Madison attended without Payne.

Julia, tired from yesterday's journey and the crowd of well-wishers, stood, almost dazed, as more and more champagne toasts were drunk to her and the president, often with some humorous little speech, but in retrospect sounding all alike. She found herself staring at the north end of the room, at the raised area where the coffins had rested, and where, now, the Marine band was resting so as not to drown out the speeches.

Something seemed oddly familiar. It was not the irony of festive occasion replacing the funeral scene she had last seen in this room. No, it was not that; the crowds of friends, and even political enemies on their good behavior, had purged that for the moment, at least. It might return when the room was again empty, but not now.

No, it was the band. She remembered where she had last seen it; it had been on the deck of the *Princeton*, not far from the Peacemaker. Just then, the president commanded her attention but she paid attention to the band as the reception continued. She must speak to the bandmaster before he left.

Later, "You were there, weren't you? And you survived," she said almost accusingly.

"When they fire the Cannone, we move to other side of ship. Loud noise not good for musician." The bandmaster's English betrayed his recent arrival from where? Probably Italy. He paused, "Sorry, Madam, about father."

"If you left, then you didn't see it."

"No, only after. It is terrible—the blood—"

Julia's normally pale skin took on a waxen appearance. She looked away. The bandmaster stood, silent.

Suddenly, Julia turned back to him. "You were there except during the firing."

"Before last time, yes. Last time it get too cold for

play. Is also time we must eat; we go below to Mess. Only just there when cannone fire. Pieces come through deck on table. We run upstairs. Dead everywhere." Once again he looked mortified.

"But you saw them load the cannon?"

"Yes, Madam."

"The last time, too?"

He nodded.

"Was it the same each time?"

"Yes, same."

"Oh."

"Except for man."

"You mean a different man loaded it?"

"Always sailor. All look same."

"Then what was different?"

"Sailor loads cannone. Then man comes by; he also puts bag in cannone."

Julia stared at the musician, her eyes widening. "What did he look like?"

"Just man, not so young. Have coat and hat. A passenger."

"I need to know who he was! Is he here?"

The musician looked around. "Not see him today." Then his eyes fixed on someone. He groped for the right words, then twirled his finger around his head.

"You mean a crazy person?"

"No. He come to ship with that lady." He pointed.

Julia looked across the room; it was suddenly obvious. He meant Dolley Madison, with her turban wrapped around her head.

Many years later bandmaster Franco Maria Scala told about enlisting as a musician when the U.S.

Cruiser *Brandywine* visited Naples in 1841. At the time he spoke no English. A few months after reaching America he was made leader of the Marine Band. As an old man, he described playing at a big White House reception where President Tyler had Julia sit on his lap. There was much laughter, he said.

On July 3, 1844, the president and his new wife left for a honeymoon at Fort Monroe, on what was then called Old Point Comfort, where today's Newport News is located. It would be six weeks long, and during that time, much would happen. Visits were made to Sherwood Forest on the James River, where Tyler was refurbishing an estate he had bought for his retirement.

But more important, things were set in motion to save Texas for the United States. Robert Tyler was working hard in Philadelphia to field a full slate of Democrat-Republicans (Tyler's third party) in Pennsylvania. In New York, Alex Gardiner was persuading Tammany Hall to support Tyler. In the meantime, Tyler was in touch with Polk's Democrats, trying to bargain his third party support for two things: support for immediate action on the Texas Treaty, and inclusion of Tyler supporters in the Democratic Party. This latter ploy was a move to protect his people in their patronage jobs.

It is also apparent that Julia told her husband what she had learned about the mysterious man who must have been Payne Todd. She did not have enough information to know why Todd had wanted to kill the president, but she felt that her father's death must have been an accident, an assassination plot gone awry.

"No, it was probably Clay," said the president with less certainty than he felt. "Clay does not forgive easily and I have stood in the way of his plans too long. Mr. Upshur, too," he mused. "He needed only kill one of us to be able to keep Texas out of the Union. But he may have miscalculated."

"Why Dolley's son?" asked his bride. "Imagine how the truth will hurt Dolley."

"Many reasons, my dear. If discovered, many might believe Payne is solely responsible. I refused him a diplomatic post, you know. He would have been disastrous. Some might think that reason enough. Not so, of course; Dolley wanted it for him more than he.

"But the unfortunate Mr. Todd is a poor, weak man. He would do it for money. Money for drink; money for the gaming tables. He is selling his mother's possessions from Montpelier, you know."

"Does Dolley know?"

"She knows no more than she wants to know."

Julia thought about Payne Todd and how his weakness had brought such misery upon his mother, and upon herself, too. She felt a certain kinship with Dolley. And anger. "Was it really so simple? Making the cannon explode?"

"There was a naval inquiry. Nothing definite was concluded. An overcharging of powder was a possibility, a casting flaw, another. If Mr. Todd dropped a bag of powder into the gun, it probably would have been enough—it probably would have been too much."

"Will Mr. Clay try again?"

"Possibly. But if I am to die, it will be with the

happiness you have brought me. Nevertheless, the stakes are changing. A second attempt would greatly increase the possibility of exposure; and if all goes well, the Texas Treaty will soon be assured."

"But shouldn't he be exposed, now?"

"I think not. It would not be good for our country to see a respected politician trying to undo an election by violence."

Within days, former president Jackson, speaking for the Democrats, published a letter, seemingly welcoming Tyler's supporters and their political goals, which could only mean Texas. On August 20, Tyler withdrew his candidacy.

Julia, as First Lady, opened the social season on Saturday, November 23. She outfitted her coachmen in black with buckles on their hats. An Italian greyhound was ordered from the American consul in Naples. Despite brother David Lyon's comment that the polka was half Indian dance and half waltz, she introduced it to Washington.

She also introduced the playing of "Hail to the Chief" for presidential appearances, and received visitors, seated, while surrounded by a dozen virgins dressed in white, including Margaret, her cousins Mary and Phoebe, the president's youngest daughter, Alice, and other dragooned young society ladies. For herself, she usually dressed in white satin covered over in black lace, often with black and silver trim and sparkling with diamonds, and at times she wore a cape. She also had headdresses with as many as three plumes of ostrich or heron.

To keep her image in order, she hired a reporter

with the New York *Herald*, the first First Lady's press secretary, with sister Margaret acting as social secretary.

During the frantic eight months of her reign as First Lady, Julia seized every opportunity to promote the annexation of Texas. When a Supreme Court justice started to raise a toast at one of her parties, she slipped a note into his hand, "Tyler and Texas." And so it went through the season.

Julia gave her final ball on February 18, 1845. Margaret wrote the invitations, Julia's penmanship being hopeless. The president had tried to improve it by buying her a copybook, but to no avail. The Polks declined the invitation. But there were enough who did come. Two thousand were invited and three thousand came. The president was heard to say, "They cannot say now that I am a president without a party."

In his last annual message to Congress December 3, 1844, Tyler suggested that Texas be annexed through a joint resolution of Congress, rather than by treaty. This was a brilliant move, reducing the vote required in the Senate, where Clay was strongest, from two-thirds to a simple majority. The measure passed in the House without difficulty.

On February 27, the Texas resolution was passed by the Senate with a majority of a single vote, and signed into law by Tyler on March 1. Later, the hostile opposition press would give Julia, in a backhanded way, much of the credit. She "lobbied for Texas in the boudoirs of Washington," they said.

On March 4, the Tylers planned to miss the inauguration and to take the 9:00 A.M. mail boat south to

Sherwood Forest. They arrived at the wharf a bit late and missed the boat. They returned to Fuller's Hotel to await the night boat. At 3:00 A.M. on the night of the 5, they caught the night boat, their way lighted by the burning of Washington's National Theater and adjacent buildings. There was no connection.

Polk reneged his promise not to purge Tyler men from patronage positions and they were fired wholesale. And gloom descended upon the White House where the Polks allowed no dancing or drinking.

For nearly a year after leaving Washington, Tyler continued to get letters from prohibitionist Protestant churchmen, about the flow of spirits, the evil dancing, and the fact Julia had not observed a full year of mourning for her father before marrying. No mention, however, of the murders aboard the *Princeton*. Tyler wrote notes to them all telling them to go to the devil.

Margaret married a poor man for love in 1848. Leaving her with a new baby the next year, her husband went to California to find his fortune. He found only death in a shooting accident. Margaret, herself, died in 1857, age thirty-five. She was writing to the end. Four days before her death, she wrote that her doctor "said I have sneaking chills with torpor of the liver and deranged digestion—all of which I believe to be true."

Julia presented her elderly husband with seven children. Before he died in early 1862, he served as president of a commission trying to avert the Civil War. Admitting defeat, he joined the government of the Confederacy as a senator.

Julia survived the war, spending much of it in New York with her children. She died, however, an unreconstructed Rebel at Sherwood Forest in 1889.

Alex Gardiner, the dependable one of Julia and Margaret's brothers, died dismayingly young, at thirty-two, from appendicitis. Their other brother, David Lyon, lived to sue Julia over their mother's estate, invading with an armed policeman the Gardiner house in New York, looking for evidence his sister had exerted undue influence on mother Juliana. (Not unlikely.)

And Payne Todd? Well, Dolley died in 1849, unaware of her son's perfidy, and Payne followed her three years later.

It tempts fancy to imagine what might have been.

If Clay had succeeded in doing away with Tyler, Texas might either have rejoined Mexico or reached some independent status under British protection. Both options were being toyed with in 1844. The same might have been accomplished by Secretary of State Upshur's death had not Tyler been able to tip the scales with his third party. Or perhaps if Clay had been elected in 1844.

If Texas had not been annexed, the Mexican war might never have happened, and California, Arizona, and New Mexico might have remained Mexican. *Olé!*

Without the opportunity for American expansion to the Pacific through what are now these southwestern states, our domestic political pressure for expanding northward into what was then the Oregon Territory might have proved irresistible. One need only recall those who were prepared for "54.40 or fight." Such a move might well have brought about hostilities with Britain and Canada.

And what might have happened to the seemingly relentless move toward civil war had these factors been altered?

Ironically, the final Whig presidency, that of Zachary Taylor, came about because of the old general's successes in the Mexican War that Clay tried so hard to avoid. It is interesting to note that Taylor said, when he was inaugurated in 1849, that California was too far away to become a state and might better become an independent nation. Spoken, as you might expect, by an old general who had ridden much too far on horseback.

RICHARD TIMOTHY CONROY

———

RICHARD TIMOTHY CONROY has done everything from hunting down bootleggers and drug smugglers to making, though never using, hydrogen bombs. His Foreign Service memoir, *Our Man in Belize*, was published in 1997, and he is also the author of three murder mysteries, including *Mr. Smithson's Bones*. He is the other half of the only husband and wife writing duo in this collection.

"Julia Gardiner Tyler was fascinating but manipulative," Richard says. "Her younger sister, Margaret Gardiner, was at once charming and guileless, and President John Tyler was a quirky, but inspired political tactician. He played the violin and he played the swain to his thirty-years-younger bride. But above all, Tyler and Henry Clay played out a deadly game that cost the lives of the secretaries of state and navy, for which the prize was Texas and more, and a tragic high-born wastrel was the pawn. Nowhere in the history of the American presidency is there better material for murder."

THE SECOND LADY

~~~~

PETER CROWTHER

For Sarah and Richard Conroy

Time is not measured by weeks,
or months, or years, but by deep
human experiences.
—WOODROW WILSON,
from the president's proposal of marriage
to Edith Galt. May 4, 1915

IT WAS THE first week of October 1919 . . . the fall, that calm and magical time of the year when everything seems to be slowing down and preparing for a rest which was both well-earned and deeply needed.

In Washington this reflective mood was perhaps at its strongest, as though—while not widely known—the bedridden president's slow and languorous breathing had drifted out over the capital and on across the entire country, his stroke halting the nation's movement in much the same way as it had paralyzed his own left side. Now, the city once noted for its "magnificent distances" seemed to have adopted more of Charles Dickens' caustic summation—delivered more than seventy years earlier, in 1842—of "spacious avenues that begin in nothing and lead nowhere." Indeed, everywhere carried a sense of waiting, of a time between times.

For Edith Wilson, forty-seven within the month, this was truly a time of holding breath and waiting and hoping, though she wondered whether the hoping was perhaps unrealistically optimistic. For this reason alone—the possibly imminent death of the husband she adored—an increased involvement in matters of state had provided an occasional welcome release. It was something to think about other than the gloomy thoughts that came to her at night, when even the White House had grown silent. Thoughts of life without Woodrow.

Of course, her involvement in the complex business of running the country did not include the actual making of important decisions but rather of deciding what matters should be referred to her husband and, more importantly, when they should be referred.

She had asked Dr. Dercum, one of the medical experts brought in by Dr. Grayson, if it would not be better that Woodrow resign and leave the country in the hands of Vice President Marshall, but the doctor would not hear of such a thing. Both he and Dr. Grayson felt that a resignation at this time—with the war still an angry wound in the collective mind of the people and the troubled League of Nations becoming more complex by the day—would be bad for the country. But even worse, as far as Edith was concerned at any rate, Dr. Dercum felt that standing down from presidential duties might well rob the president of the will to get better.

During these times, Edith had taken more and more to strolling the spacious gardens of the White House, particularly on the east side of the house where she could be easily and speedily reached if necessary. In order to maintain absolute quiet, the gardens had been closed to the public.

On these occasions, her head bowed and her hands clasped firmly behind her back, Edith walked across the soft and springy turf lost in thought and desperately trying to build her resolve for whatever needed to be mentioned to the president that day.

Although she was not as dedicated a gardener as her predecessor, Ellen Wilson, Edith nevertheless enjoyed the openness of the gardens and the feeling of freedom they seemed to bestow. But while she favored the faintly Victorian layout introduced to the East Garden by Beatrix Farrand—who, it was now rumored, was in discussions to work on renovating the gardens at Dumbarton Oaks—Edith felt most at home to the south of the House, wandering alongside boxwood hedges and the beautiful fall arrays of chrysanthemums and blue-violet salvia nestled amid crab apple trees waving in the afternoon breeze.

Edith knew that her increased profile had not been to everyone's liking, particularly as it had led to her decision to disallow casual access to the president. Thus Joseph Tumulty, who until now had been the president's secretary and chief assistant, was adding his own voice to that of Henry Cabot Lodge and other senators and officials who were asking repeatedly just who was running the country. There was no love lost between Edith and most of these people, and the President's wife—now referred to as the

Presidentress and the Iron Queen in some quarters—
tried to ignore their veiled and not-so-veiled criti-
cisms of her attention to her husband's welfare.
Though that is not to say that such remarks did not
hurt. They did.

But the peace and tranquility of the White House
gardens, with their rolling lawns and verdant clusters
of trees and bushes, provided the stability and the
strength that Edith needed.

Thus it was that, on one exceptionally beautiful
but breezy afternoon following a particularly trying
exchange with Henry Cabot Lodge, Edith found herself in the South Pasture, away from the windows of
the Lincoln Wing and the responsibilities which she
had assumed. The air was thick with the mingled
scents of juniper and woodsmoke, at first breath a
faintly cloying aroma which, as Edith became accus-
tomed, quickly gave way to a sense of calm.

It could have been for but a second or two—
though, in truth, it seemed far longer, for such is the
way the mind pulls at sensations and memories and
strings them out like taffy or fun-fair cotton candy—
Edith imagined she was back on her father's Virginia
plantation, back in Wytheville in the early 1880s. The
image was further solidified by a quartet of gardeners lost in their work and the sight of them was
strangely reminiscent of the stories Edith's father
used to recount to her, in the sleepy evenings, about
what it had been like before the war, when slaves
had been in abundance.

The sensation moved away, shuffling itself into the
back of her mind to be pulled on again another day.
One of the three men waved to her, a casual move-

ment of the arm which could just have easily been
a motion to dissuade a troublesome insect from its
unwelcome attentions. But Edith recognized it for
what it was, a passing of the time of day and a warm
but respectful acknowledgment of her presence. She
waved back and now all four had stopped and all
returned her wave. There was old William, and . . .
was it Richard? Yes, Edith thought she knew that
hand-on-hip mannerism too well for it to be anyone
else. And there was Charles Edward, leaning on the
hoe. And, of course, Ruthie. Ruthie was easy. After
all, she was the only woman on the gardening staff,
since Eloise had left to have her child.

A flash of white in the trees just to the right of the
group caught Edith's attention and she jerked her
head to the side. Suddenly, from the protection of a
large laurel bush, a woman appeared briefly, bent
double, as though attempting to conceal herself, despite the fact that her shelter had been momentarily
left behind. The woman stopped and looked across
the grass at Edith.

Edith had heard of the phenomenon of eyes meeting across a floor—particularly in the idle chatter of
the young women around town—and she had heard
tell of men's eyes meeting across a battlefield just as
she had heard of rabbits and deer being frozen for
the briefest seconds, caught in the cross-hairs of the
huntsman's rifle. And this was exactly that.

Edith frowned and looked across at the other
workers. They had returned to their duties and were
now in complete ignorance of either herself or the
woman. She looked back and the woman was nowhere to be seen.

Raising her hand to shield her eyes, though there was no strong sunlight of which to speak, Edith scanned the grove of trees from behind which the woman had first appeared. The trees betrayed no sense of movement. She looked back across the lawns, across a wide expanse of open ground, and saw no hint of the white dress the woman had worn. So she could have gone no other way but backwards, away from the grove but keeping the grove between herself and Edith.

Edith turned and glanced back at the path that ran alongside the south quadrant. Randolph was there, his jaws silently chewing, kicking the pebbles in the dirt, hands in his pockets. "Randolph," she shouted.

The man looked up quickly and started to run toward her.

Edith waved her hand. "I'm fine, Randolph," she said, "but perhaps you could answer me a question."

Randolph Burgin slowed down, his eyes scanning the lawns for any signs of threat to the First Lady. Satisfied that all seemed in order, the Secret Service man came to a halt, having covered the seventy or eighty yards from the path in but a few seconds. "Yes, Ma'am," he said, in a voice that betrayed no sign of exertion.

"Do you see the garden workers?"

Randolph glanced up and then back at Edith. "Yes, Ma'am."

She looked around and craned her neck. "Did you, by any chance, see another one just a few minutes ago?"

"Ma'am?"

"Another gardener, another . . ." Edith stopped.

She had been about to say "lady" instead of "woman." She frowned. The figure's deportment had definitely not been one that suggested service: rather it suggested Society. The woman could not have been one of the gardening staff for she did not wear the characteristic green and brown, either waistcoat and trousers or dress and pinafore. Indeed, she had sported a bright white dress, boldly cut away above the bodice, a dress that looked more appropriate for a ball or some other official function than for gardening work.

"Is everything all right, Ma'am?"

"Do you know if the restrictions have been relaxed for some reason, Randolph?"

"To allow visitors, you mean?"

Edith nodded.

"Not to my knowledge, Ma'am. Do you want me to talk to the gardeners?" Randolph was clearly troubled. He did not look at Edith but rather fixed his stare on the workers, one or two of whom had ceased their work and were staring at the two of them.

Edith shook her head. "No, there's no need. Perhaps I'm overtired." She breathed in deeply, savoring the autumnal air. "I think I'll return to the house."

Randolph nodded. As Edith turned, she saw that he had pulled aside his jacket to expose an ornate holster around his right shoulder. She could see the rounded lump of pistol handle jutting from the leather. She shuddered. "I think it's turning a little cold, anyway," she said.

"Will you be all right heading back alone?" Randolph asked. He had turned back to face the gardens, his head turning first one way and then the other, scanning for any signs of movement. "I thought I'd just take a look around."

"I'll be fine, Randolph. Thank you."

The Secret Service man walked off across the grass, breaking into a trot after a few yards. Edith watched until he reached the trees and saw him turn around to face her. Even from this distance she could see him shrug. Then he turned back, walked forward past the trees, and disappeared from sight.

Back inside the house, Edith went straight to the Blue Room where she spent the following three hours poring over letters and memoranda on a range of issues, deciding which needed to be relayed to her husband at their evening meeting. It was almost 5.30 when she emerged. Walking along the corridor she came across Gerald Merriam, similarly bedecked with a sheaf of papers clutched tightly to his chest.

"Ma'am," Merriam said, bowing slightly. "How is the president feeling today?"

"He is coming along well, thank you, Gerald," Edith said. "In fact, I'm now on my way to sit with him for a while." She patted the papers almost affectionately. "I am delighted to discover that there seems to be less requiring his urgent attention than I feared a few hours ago."

"I'm pleased to hear that, Ma'am," Merriam said with another nod.

Edith stood for a moment without speaking.

"Was there something else, Ma'am?"

She shook her head and tutted at herself. "Probably nothing," she began, "but do you know if we have set on a new gardener?"

"A new gardener, Ma'am?"

"Yes, I thought I saw one in the gardens earlier this afternoon. A . . . *woman* gardener." Again, Edith had to stop herself from using the word "lady."

Merriam frowned. "There's only Ruthie Collier, Ma'am, at least that I'm aware of."

"No, I saw Ruthie. This was a *second* woman."

Merriam shook his head emphatically. "To my knowledge, there has not been anyone newly appointed to garden duty, Ma'am. But I could check for you if you wish."

Edith was about to say that that would not be necessary but then she decided against it. After all, if this woman were not on the White House payroll, there were serious implications for the president's security. And what on earth was she doing there, and dressed so finely?

"Yes, Gerald, I would like you to do that."

"Very well, Ma'am," Merriam said, removing a worn leather notebook from the pile clasped by his arm. He scribbled a note on a page somewhere near the middle of the book. "I'll speak to Mister Mortimer immediately."

"Mister Mortimer?"

"Chester Mortimer is in charge of grounds staff, Ma'am. If anyone will be able to answer your question, it is undoubtedly him."

Edith thanked Merriam for his efforts on her behalf, going to considerable measure to ensure that she downplayed the importance of the task. But though she did recognize that she was probably trying to make something out of nothing, Edith could not shake the nagging concern that something was not as it should be. The discovery that the unctuous Chester Mortimer—who insisted on referring to her as his "dear woman" and who displayed all the characteristics of Uriah Heep—was involved, no matter how trivial that involvement, did little to allay her fears. Indeed, if anything, it only served to heighten them.

Her concerns were immediately forgotten, however, when Edith discovered that the president had taken a serious turn for the worse.

That evening, after several unsuccessful attempts to relieve her husband's suffering, Edith was taken to one side by Dr. Grayson, who advised an operation as the only hope for the president's survival. But, he went on to say, he felt that an operation could itself mean the end of him. The decision, he said, was hers.

Without so much as a second's hesitation, Edith replied that there would be no operation. He should go down and tell the other specialists that nature should be relied upon to take care of things. She then retired to her rooms to pray that she had made the correct decision.

Later that night, one of the White House staff informed Edith that Mr. Mortimer had called to see her.

"Now?" said Edith, aghast both at the lateness of the hour for visitors and at the man's insensitivity. She was about to snap, uncharacteristically, when she realized that perhaps Mortimer had not heard of the president's deterioration. She would give him the benefit of the doubt. And, anyway, she was curious about what he had to say.

Mortimer entered Edith's reception room with a flourish of coattails and a brow whose furrowed indentations were so deep that she imagined the poor man might have spent the past few hours chiseling them into place.

"My dear woman," he began, bowing and taking Edith's hand in his own clammy grasp. "How is the president?"

Edith nodded curtly and retrieved her hand, sweeping it behind her back to dry it on her dress. "Not so good, I'm afraid. The next few hours are crucial." She turned around and walked to the fireplace, staring into the flickering flames. "But surely you did not visit at so late an hour to inquire of my husband's health. Are there problems, Mr. Mortimer?"

"Problems?" Mortimer said. "None of which I am aware." He laughed dismissively, but there was a definite trace of something amiss and, despite her concerns for her husband, Edith was quick to notice it. She turned around and caught the man's eyes in her own. It was then that she noticed the sticking plaster fixed to his left jawbone and extending down to cover his neck and then disappear beneath his shirt collar. Mortimer saw her eyes and raised a hand to the plaster. "Women should give thanks on a daily basis that they are spared the gruesome act of shaving of a morning," he said with a forced smile. "It's a wonder that I'm here to tell the tale."

And a great shame, Edith thought, immediately regretting such an uncharitable wish.

"Rather I thought that it was you yourself who

had a problem," Mortimer continued, raising his eyebrows at the seat beside the fire.

"Of course," Edith said, "please do excuse my rudeness. Other things on my mind. Please sit down for a moment, although I feel it may be no longer as I must get some rest and — "

"I understand," Mortimer said, his face creasing into folds of concern. "You want to spend time with the president."

Woodrow Wilson is first my husband and then he is the president, Edith wanted to say. *And I am his dear woman and not yours*, she thought. But she held her piece and sat in the chair opposite Mortimer.

"Yes," she began. "I would not say that it was a problem, Mister Mortimer . . . rather a mystery."

"A mystery?" Mortimer fidgeted with his cuffs and smiled. There was a slight tic in the left corner of his mouth, close to the sticking plaster.

"This afternoon I was walking in the grounds and I saw a group of gardeners about their business. Stopping to wave to them, as I often do, I noticed a woman wearing a white dress. She seemed to be hiding in a group of trees. She noticed me almost as soon as I had noticed her . . . and then she disappeared."

"Disappeared, Ma'am?"

"I turned my attention away from her for a moment and when I looked back she had gone. She did not appear to be one of the gardening staff."

"Oh?" said Mortimer.

"No." Edith shook her head gently. "As I said, she wore a white dress for one thing."

"And for another?"

Edith shrugged and gave a querulous smile. "Just a feeling," she said.

Mortimer frowned, and Edith thought she saw a hint of a smile in return to her own, as though the man felt he were involved in some elaborate game. "You say she went, Ma'am. Do you have any idea where to?"

"I do not," Edith said. "But I would very much like to know why she was here at all. Perhaps you would look into it for me?" Edith rose and held out her hand. "And now, if you'll excuse me?"

Mortimer got to his feet and nodded. "Of course," he said, "on both counts."

She avoided his hand and took hold of his arm, leading him to the door. "I'll be sure to pass on your kind wishes to my husband," she said, ushering him out into the hallway. Mortimer gave her a puzzled glance and then smiled graciously.

"Please do," he said.

"Do give my regards to your wife," she called after him. "And offer my apologies for detaining you so late."

Closing the door behind her, Edith wondered if Mortimer had really crouched his shoulders at her last remark, as though avoiding a thrown missile, or whether she had simply imagined it. Later that night, she wondered if perhaps she had imagined the second *lady* as well.

The following morning, the patient had made considerable improvement—so much so that both he and Edith were able to make tentative arrangements to receive the King and Queen of Belgium, who had already been ocean-bound when the president became ill.

It was not until early that same afternoon, following a pleasantly informal luncheon of open sandwiches with Dr. Hugh Young of Johns Hopkins, that Edith's mind once again returned to the events of the previous afternoon. She apprised the doctor of what had happened.

"And you have no idea as to whom this woman might be?" he asked.

"None at all," Edith moved a piece of lettuce around her plate and at last set down her fork, leaving it untouched. "She is clearly not one of the gardening staff, of that I am sure. Nevertheless, I have asked Chester Mortimer to look into it, though I doubt there will be much to report. I think that gentleman marches to the beat of an entirely different drum—and to a rhythm of his own making, I might add," Edith said, one eyebrow raised. "I fear there is little love lost between the two of us. Or between him and the president for that matter."

Dr. Young raised his own eyebrows at Edith's comment. "Really? Well, you do surprise me."

"I do?"

"I've known Mortimer for some time now—five or six years I should think—and I have always found him to be fairly dependable. And certainly he has never made any adverse comments about either yourself or the president, at least none that has been reported to me." He wiped his mouth with his napkin and then carefully folded it again before laying it on the edge of his plate. "He's an enigmatic fellow at the best of times and, of course, we all recognize

that he takes subservience to undreamed of levels—
or depths."

Edith smiled and nodded her head slowly.

"Nevertheless, he has not been himself of late. I
do accept though, of course, his present manner
could be a result of . . ." Dr. Young's voice trailed
off. "Well, he and his wife are experiencing some
difficulties," the doctor added in a hushed tone.

Edith leaned forward. "I didn't know of this," she
said. "What form do these 'difficulties' take?"

Dr. Young sat back on his chair and waved a hand
dismissively. "I really couldn't say, Ma'am," he said.
"Let us say that I've simply heard that things are not
all they might be."

Edith decided that it would not be proper to seek
any further information and the doctor was clearly
relieved at her decision.

Though she did not feel as anxious, the First
Lady's earlier concerns over the mysterious
woman—though without real cause—seemed to have
gathered more substance since her conversation with
Dr. Young. Added to this, Edith had had a troubled
night, having spent a considerable amount of it at
her husband's bedside. Thus she decided that, whilst
there was a formidable pile of papers—not least several documents relating to the troubled treaty—
awaiting the president's attention and therefore her
own, a walk in the gardens would offer rejuvenation
or, at least, a pleasant distraction.

With Randolph Burgin once again following, albeit
at a respectful and unobtrusive distance, Edith
walked along the path she had traveled the previous

day and then broke off across the lawns to the grove of trees from behind which the woman had appeared.

Today there were no gardeners at work or, if there were, then they were in another part of the grounds. The sun was watery but bright and even the strong westerly wind could not diminish its heat.

Reaching the spot where the gardeners had been, Edith smiled as she saw the evidence of their work. Small clusters of young chrysanthemums had been freshly planted in two crescent-shaped beds and the lawn-edges had been finely trimmed.

She moved across to the right and saw immediately that, from their position, the gardeners could not have seen the woman, which would explain their ignorance of her. She reached the trees and moved alongside a boxwood hedge which gave way into a clearing which fell down gradually to an ornamental pond and series of wooden huts in which various tools and other implements were stored. She was debating whether to return to the house or to continue her exploration when a sudden breeze took her breath for a moment.

As the breeze subsided, Edith was aware of a single blossom on the magnolia grandiflora a little way in front of her and to her right. Moving a few more steps forward, so that she had almost passed free of the boxwood hedge, she saw that it was not a blossom but a piece of cloth. She looked around to make sure that Randolph was still with her—which he was, some thirty or forty yards behind her—and then moved to the bush and removed the cloth.

It was a piece of the finest silk overlaid and stitched in place with embroidered lace. Edith turned it over and over in her hand, frowning. She looked up and stared down at the pond. This was undoubtedly a piece of the woman's dress only it was now clear that it was not a dress that she had been wearing. It was undoubtedly from an undergarment of some kind. But why on earth would anyone wander around the White House gardens on a fall afternoon wearing only their underclothes? The answer to this question seemed to be powerfully more important than the simple identification of the cause of a lapse in security arrangements.

As she pondered the answer to this conundrum, Edith's attention drifted to the line of wooden huts.

"Is everything all right, Ma'am?" Randolph Burgin shouted.

Edith waved. "Everything's fine," she shouted back.

There were six huts about 100 or 150 yards distant. From where she stood, Edith estimated the size of each hut to be about nine or ten feet across and some six yards in length. There were no windows in either the left side or front elevations and Edith assumed the same would be true for the right sides and the ends.

She turned around the saw Randolph Burgin nervously surveying the gardens. She felt an immediate pang of regret for putting the poor man to such pains. The unwritten law was that she should always remain in sight of the house and, she now saw, having moved some way over the small rise, that was nowhere to be seen. "I'm absolutely fine, Randolph," she shouted.

Randolph's head snapped back to face her.

"I'm going down to . . ." She hesitated from mentioning the huts and, as an afterthought, thrust the piece of material into her pocket. "I'm going down to the pond." She frowned. Why had she phrased it that way?

"I really don't think you should do that, Ma'am," Randolph said, now walking slowly toward her. "If that woman you saw is—"

"Oh, Randolph, I don't think I have anything to fear from her," Edith said, smiling. "And anyway, I have you with me, do I not?"

Randolph sighed deeply. "You do indeed, Ma'am," he said.

Edith turned back to face the pond and the huts. "Very well, then," she said, more to herself than to anyone else, and she started down the slope.

She had not been aware of the general sounds of activity until they stopped altogether. The daily comings and goings at the house, and the sound of traffic on Pennsylvania Avenue clearly filled the air with a sense of movement which, here, partway down the slope and out of sight of the White House, had vanished completely. Now, only the sound of birdsong and the wind could be heard. Edith found the effect quite enchanting . . . as though she had been spirited away into a fairytale world.

She reached the pond and stopped to stare into the water. Gentle ripples could be seen, chasing and stumbling across each other with each fresh gust of wind. Standing up, she saw that Randolph Burgin had almost reached her. He stood a little way back, at the rim of the concrete apron surrounding the pond. Clearly, he had gone to some considerable effort,

Edith thought, because she herself had now dawdled, letting the downhill gradient carry her along.

She glanced from Randolph toward the huts. She had been right, she now saw: The huts had no windows in the right-hand sides either.

Clasping her hands behind her back, Edith started to walk to the first of the huts some ten yards away.

"Shouldn't we be heading back, Ma'am?" Randolph inquired.

"In a moment," Edith said. "I just want to take a look at these huts."

"It's getting late, Ma'am," Randolph's voice had taken on a whining quality.

"I am well aware of the time," Edith said with a gentle chuckle. The poor man was really taking her safety very seriously indeed.

When Randolph Burgin spoke again, there was a harder edge to his voice and one which both startled and then concerned Edith. "There's really nothing in there of interest," he said. "Just gardening tools," he added, his tone altogether softer now.

Edith turned around. "Have you been down here before, Randolph?"

Randolph shook his head and glanced back up the slope, then to the right and the left. Edith followed his stare on each occasion. What was the matter with him? There was clearly nobody within hundreds of yards, certainly too far a distance for anyone to spring out at her. Their eyes met once more and she saw that Randolph was grimacing.

Edith saw the expression and then turned to look in each direction again. This time, rather than seeing nobody who might threaten her, the First Lady saw that there was nobody who might be able to *help* her.

Help me? she thought. *Why ever would I need help? I have Randolph to protect me from any danger.*

Perhaps, whispered a small but insistent voice in the back of her head, a voice carried to her innermost ear by the fall wind, *it is* he *who represents the danger.*

"Are you . . . are you feeling unwell, Randolph?" Edith said.

"A little warm, Ma'am," Randolph said.

Edith turned and glanced at the huts and then turned back to face the Secret Service man. Before common sense could prevent her from doing so, Edith said, "What is it that you don't want me to see? Is it something in the huts, Randolph?"

The man's shoulders slumped and, in that split second, he seemed to diminish in size. "No, there's nothing in the huts. It's just—"

Edith turned around, her heart beating fit to burst, and strode purposefully along the concrete apron toward the path that led along the front of the huts. Behind her, Randolph Burgin called for her to stop.

By the time she had reached the first of the huts, she could hear his footsteps walking behind her, slowly. "Ma'am?" he was saying. "Can't we just go back up to the house?"

Edith rattled the heavy lock on the first door and, discovering that it was secure, moved on to the second hut.

"I want an answer, Randolph," she said over her shoulder.

At the second hut she rattled the chain. Secure.

Burgin had reached her side. She did not turn to

face him but, out of the corner of her eye, Edith saw that he had withdrawn his pistol. She could see it in his hand, hanging limply at his side.

Staring straight ahead, she began to walk to the third hut.

Burgin walked beside her.

As she neared the third hut, Edith saw that the heavy lock was hanging free on its chain.

"I didn't have the key," Burgin said, his tone almost conspiratorial. "She smashed the lock somehow and got out." She could see his arms waving around in front of him, emphasizing his words. "I didn't have the keys to put her in another."

Edith stopped in front of the third hut. She looked down at the door handle and at the chain lying curled on the concrete.

"She said she was going to tell, Ma'am," Burgin said, his voice now a hoarse whisper.

"Tell what, Randolph?"

"She was going to tell my wife. I asked her not to but she laughed at me. I begged her not to."

"*What* was she going to tell your wife?" Edith held her hands together in front of her, working to keep her voice steady. She had already guessed the answer to her question.

"She was going to tell her that we . . ." His voice trailed off and he hit the side of the hut with his hand. "I had a copy of the keys for the huts," he said, calmer now. "We came here a couple of times. But I didn't have the keys yesterday, so I couldn't put her in one of the other huts."

"Is she inside here, Randolph?"

"I left her in there to teach her a lesson," he said,

the wind catching his hair and lifting it down onto his forehead. He swept it back and added, "I didn't mean for anything to happen."

"You locked her *in*? Here in the hut?"

"She must have got out," Burgin said, turning to scan the gardens. "I don't know why she didn't put her dress back on."

Edith raised a trembling hand to the chain around her neck and held on to it. She did not like the dreamy, matter-of-fact tone that Randolph was using to impart such information.

"She was frightened, Randolph," she said. "She just wanted to get away. She wanted to get away from *you*."

"But I only wanted to teach her a lesson."

"And what about when you found her yesterday?" Edith asked. "You found her after you had left me to look for her, didn't you?"

Burgin nodded and averted his eyes from the First Lady's stare.

"Was that—did you teach her another lesson then?"

"I didn't mean to . . ." His voice trailed off.

Edith turned to face the hut. "What did you do to her?"

"Don't go inside, Ma'am," Burgin said. His face was serious for a moment and then he seemed to be fighting a laugh, though only for a few seconds. Then his face became serious again. "Please don't go inside. We could just go back to the—"

Edith reached forward, took hold of the handle, and pulled the door open.

The creak of the rusty hinges gave way to a buzzing sound.

Edith stared at the figure lying crumpled on a clutter of garden tools.

There seemed to be a lot of flies.

In the shadowed interior of the hut, the white undergarments were now marked with what appeared to be a large black stain in the region of the stomach. The woman's eyes were wide open, staring in astonishment at the First Lady. Edith half expected her to get to her feet and give a small bow.

Edith blinked and held her breath, trying to take in in one glance as much of the scene as she was able.

By the woman's side was a pair of wooden-handled clippers. Beneath the clippers, on the wooden floor, another black stain had spread and dried.

Draped across a box at the rear of the hut was a gown, laid incongruously neatly as compared with the crumpled appearance of the woman herself. In the meager light from the open door, Edith could see that the gown was light green—silk, as far as she could tell from the doorway—and embroidered with seed and bugle beads in a pattern undoubtedly designed to follow the contours of the body. The low square décolletage was filled in with a *modesty* of silk net.

The woman's face looked as surprised and as fearful as when Edith had seen it the previous day—when, of course, the poor woman had been staring not at Edith but at the figure standing behind her. The figure of Randolph Burgin.

There was a click.

Edith braced herself.

"I wish you had just gone back to the house, Ma'am," Burgin said. "I would have moved her. I would have moved her last night but Mr. Mortimer had people walking all over the gardens. It's a miracle that nobody found her."

"We *did* find her," a voice said. It was not Burgin's voice. "Put down the pistol, Randolph."

Edith saw Burgin's shadow spin around on the ground, the pistol shadow elongate itself as if by magic, and then she heard mumbled raised voices—though she could not make out what they were saying—and then there was a single shot, and the sound of something heavy falling to the ground.

When at last she felt able to turn around, Edith saw Chester Mortimer and two other men whose names she did not know. Each man carried a pistol and a pair of binocular glasses.

Mortimer bowed effusively. When he straightened up his face wore a wide smile. "My apologies, Ma'am," he said. "We found the unfortunate woman last night. The difficulty was that we had no idea who might be responsible."

"So you *left* her here?"

"Quite so, Ma'am," Mortimer said. "It was clear that the murderer intended to return to dispose of his work. If we had moved the body and then tried to apprehend anyone who merely opened the door to one of the huts we might not have been able to press the case successfully. Your involvement—if you'll pardon the phrase—was unexpected and, I have to say, extremely traumatic." He shrugged. "But we had made our bed, as they say, and we had to be content to lie in it accordingly. I do apologize for the distress."

"Could you not have apprehended him before we opened the door?"

Mortimer shook his head and seemed genuinely regretful. "Not without running the risk of allowing him to get away with the crime, Ma'am. As I say, a regretful business." He reached out his hand and then pulled it back. He rubbed it down the front of his jacket and held it out again. "You did well, Ma'am."

Edith took it and allowed Mortimer to lead her away from the hut and Burgin's body. As they walked, she could hear the other men puffing with exertion.

"Where were you, may I ask?" she said as they headed back up the slope to the White House.

"Up in the trees, Ma'am. We have been there since six o'clock this morning." He rubbed his shoulder. "I fear that my days of climbing trees are long gone, as is my ability to get out of them again reasonably intact."

"You must be tired and hungry," Edith said.

"Indeed I am," Mortimer said.

"You must stay for supper."

"You're very kind," Mortimer said.

Edith tutted, both to Mortimer and to herself. "I think I still have much to learn," she said.

Back in the White House, after having discovered that Mortimer's facial wound was indeed the result of careless shaving, Edith explained with some embarrassment her earlier fears.

Chester Mortimer folded the sticking plaster and placed it in his jacket pocket, then ran his fingers along the thin scratches extending from his cheek, down across his jawbone, to his neck. He smiled and shook his head, dismissing the First Lady's concerns. "Suspicion can be a dangerous ally," he said, "but, though it may not always be well-founded, it is an ally nonetheless."

During the course of supper, one of the men who had been with Mortimer left a message for him. The woman in the hut, it transpired, was well known for the generosity of her attentions, particularly in those parts of town where one might go to find such services. As the man excused himself, Mortimer shook his head sadly.

"It may well be that we will not find out much more about this sorry affair," he said. "But we can hypothesize."

He walked to the window and stared out into the remains of the daylight.

Edith shifted in her chair and watched him, waiting for him to continue. The late afternoon sky was a dark gray shot with gold and red in the distance, and the First Lady found herself drifting toward that far-off horizon and to thoughts of her husband. When Mortimer at last spoke, his voice startled her.

"The woman thought she was onto a good thing," Mortimer said, his tone rational and considered. "Perhaps she even enjoyed the air of clandestine excitement offered by returning here to the White House grounds for privacy . . . and, of course, for intimacy."

He turned around and leaned on the sill.

"One day, she decided that perhaps there was more money to be had," he said, "much more than she could earn during the course of a single evening." He raised his hands and shrugged. "So, she informed Burgin that she would tell his wife if he did not give her money. She didn't realize, of course, that a Secret Service bodyguard is not a high-paying profession. The truth is, it's probably not as high-paying as her own profession.

"They argued, and he locked her up so that she might reconsider her attitude. The fact is, he couldn't think of what else to do with her."

Mortimer turned back to face the window.

"He simply cannot face the prospect of losing his wife." He looked down at his hands and rested them on the sill. "The rest we know."

Edith noted the change of tense and placed her sandwich plate on the circular table and lifted her cup of tea. Staring into its swirling brown depths, she asked Mortimer if everything was as it should be at home, excusing her forthrightness.

"Ah," he said, turning and beaming, "news may travel quickly in political circles but bad news travels quickest!"

"I do not mean to pry," Edith countered. "I merely wondered if perhaps some time away from your responsibilities might be helpful."

Mortimer walked back to his seat and sat down, a thin but friendly smile playing across his lips. "It might," he said. "It could just be the very thing we need."

That evening, sitting on the edge of the president's bed, Edith held her husband's hand and looked lovingly into his eyes.

These were special moments, times within times when the two of them could be together alone, free from the responsibilities of office . . . when it seemed as though they were simply a man and a woman, the only people in this rambling great house which even now was settling down around them for the night.

"You seem wistful, dearest," he said, "lost in thought."

They had just finished going through papers, with Edith allocating various documents to different piles to denote their importance.

"It *has* been a busy day," she said, smiling, and placed her other hand on top of the president's. She would tell him all about the incident when he was feeling better, which, according to the doctors and to her own eyesight, might be sooner than she had feared only a few days earlier.

Woodrow Wilson tried to lift his left hand to clasp their four hands together but he could not.

Edith shook her head and smiled at him. "There is so very much to do, my dear," she whispered.

The president nodded emphatically, withdrew his hand and patted one of the piles of paper adorning his bedside table. "I know," he said. "I'm sure it won't be long. We'll get things back on track."

But the First Lady wondered whether things would ever—*could* ever—be the same again, either for herself and her husband or for the country as a whole.

Her heart is not only true but wise; her thoughts are not only free but touched with vision; she teaches and guides by being what she is.
> —From President Woodrow Wilson's
> dedication to his wife Edith, written to
> appear in the book he never man-
> aged to begin writing

PETER CROWTHER

ENGLISHMAN PETER CROWTHER has sold more than seventy short stories—primarily in the United States, where most are set—and edited ten anthologies. He is also the author of the chapbooks "Fugue On a G-String" and "Forest Plains" and co-author (with James Lovegrove) of *Escardy Gap*.

He says: "I was as impressed by the fortitude of Edith Wilson as I was fascinated by the then current women's suffrage movement. Ever an advocate of the darker side of crime and mystery fiction, I reckon my hybrid of cozyness and chill was inevitable."

THE FIRST LADIES' SECRET

─∾∾∾─

NANCY PICKARD

HARRY TRUMAN WOKE up alone in his bedroom in the White House, startled awake by three strong knocks on his door. In response, the president hurried himself out from under the bed covers, into his bathrobe, and across the wide carpet, calling, "Who's there?" But upon flinging open the door to find out what emergency of national security was critical enough to roust him at 4 o'clock in the morning, he found: no one.

Dammit!

He knew goddamn well that he'd heard three solid knocks as clear and real as if he'd hit himself three times on his own hard head. The president peered down the long, carpeted hallway in both directions, and saw no one. He went and looked into the rooms of his absent daughter and wife, but they were as empty as they ought to be, with Bess and Margaret back home in Independence.

When he returned to his own room, he left his wife's door open.

After locking his bedroom door, the president went back to bed, only to be roused again by the sound of footsteps in his wife's room. Once more, he rushed out of bed to look for the intruder, but again, he found no one there.

Feeling considerably more unnerved than the commander in chief of the armed forces of the greatest military power in the universe liked to feel, he hurried to check things out with the Secret Service. But the men who were guarding him insisted they had seen nothing, heard nothing, and had admitted no one to the family's private quarters. Of course, they insisted on checking things out. Eventually, they declared the Executive Mansion safe enough for its most important occupant to return to bed.

There he returned, but not to sleep.

First, Harry wrote about the incident in a letter to Bess, telling her this verified what he'd always suspected: There were ghosts in the White House. Mary Todd Lincoln had called it the Whited Sepulcher for good reason. This thirty-third president and his First Lady usually called it the Great White Jail, but tonight it felt like a living grave to him.

He was a man who usually told his wife everything.

But this time he held back from telling the Boss the entire truth: He could tell her there were ghosts, all right, and he could tell her the straight fact of the knocks at the door. But what Harry Truman could never confide, not even to Bess, was that he knew what those three hard blows must signify: *the presence in this house of ancient evil.*

A no less ancient oath bound him to secrecy about it.

Deep in his bones, the president of the United States experienced the summons as an urgent warning meant specifically for him: *If there was, indeed, something old and evil lodged within these two-hundred-year-old walls, it must not under any circumstances be let loose upon the land.* There was enough wickedness already abroad in the world, as he knew better than anyone else alive, and there were troubles aplenty right here at home. President Truman slept restlessly through what remained of the haunted night; but he awoke full of resolve and vinegar, knowing exactly what he must do.

Edith Helm passed a mimeographed copy of the First Lady's weekly schedule to the president of the Women's Press Club. "Mrs. Truman," it said, "will hold a press conference at 3 P.M. tomorrow."

The president of the Women's Press Club read the note, did a double take, read it a second time, and then looked up with an astonished expression on her face. "Mrs. Truman will hold a—what?"

"Press conference," replied the elderly social secretary, as if it were the most common announcement she had ever issued from either Blair House or the White House.

"Are we talking about Mrs. *Harry* Truman, Edith?"

Mrs. Helm's eyes crinkled just a bit at the corners, betraying both her amusement and her understanding of the journalist's incredulity. "The very one," Edith assured her, calmly.

"I wouldn't miss this!"

That, Edith thought, as she smiled graciously, *is exactly how we hoped you'd feel.*

The next afternoon, Bess Truman patted her neat cap of gray curls nervously, and thought to herself, "You'd better appreciate this, Harry." She stared out at the uplifted, avidly curious faces of the very women she had worked so hard to avoid during Harry's first term, and opened her mouth to speak.

Quickly, the female journalists took up pencils and pads which had grown dusty from lack of anything to write about this matronly woman standing in front of them. Several of them were old enough to remember Cal Coolidge, and they sarcastically joked among themselves that Mrs. Truman made "Silent Cal" look verbose. From the point of view of the press women, Bess was an acute disappointment in everything from fashion to social activism; she was so drably different from active, forthcoming, controversial, *talkative* Mrs. Roosevelt.

With faint hope, they poised their pencils.

The only other time Bess Truman had ever issued a public statement was to encourage the American housewife to be thrifty in the aftermath of the war, in order to assist America's humanitarian efforts abroad, and that was hardly a major news scoop.

Pencils ready, they waited, expecting not much.

But the First Lady surprised them.

"I wish to say a few words," she said, meaning that quite literally, "about the renovation of the

White House, As you know, it is literally falling down inside. Why, a leg of Margaret's piano crashed through the floor just the other night! It is unsafe for residence, which is why we have moved across the street to Blair House."

Mrs. Truman paused to draw breath.

"Now, some people want to tear the White House down, and build it up again from scratch. The president is strongly opposed to that idea, and so am I. We must all support the alternative plan, which would hollow out the interior of the building, but keep the original walls intact. I urge every American family to support this plan to keep the White House standing."

Grimly, she surveyed her audience.

"Thank you."

And that was that; no questions allowed. But for the assembled, and news-starved women journalists, it was fairly satisfying. Bess Truman, who never came out in public either for or against anything, had actually taken a controversial stand on an issue of great public interest.

"Everybody knows," a reporter for the *New York Times* whispered to a reporter for the *Daily News*, "that the president's plan will cost twice as much, take twice as long to complete, and be twice as difficult to accomplish."

"Congress will never stand for it," the *Daily News* whispered back.

They grinned at each other.

In the back halls of the Senate Office Building, it appeared to onlookers that three prominent senators had gathered together to share cigars and private jokes. So luminous were the three on the horizon of political power that everyone passing anywhere near them allowed a wide, respectful berth, as if orbiting a constellation of radiant suns: Get too far away from them and you'd find yourself out in the cold, but get too close, and you could burn up in the heat of their ambition.

Their public laughter disguised their private agenda.

"Never underestimate the power of symbolism," said the eldest one, quietly, while the other two feigned an air of jovial listening. "Tear down a potent symbol, and you may tear down with it an entire system of government."

"Joshua fought the battle of Jericho," said the one of the trio with the largest constituency. He smiled, waiting for the third member of their coalition to complete the familiar quotation.

The third man obliged, smiling through his cigar smoke.

"And the walls came a tumblin' down."

They laughed, a rich, chesty sound of merriment that could issue only from behind the well-tailored vests of supremely confident men seated at the heart of power.

Harry had made the issue plain to Bess one night when, as was their custom, they closed themselves together in his study at 9 P.M. There, in privacy at last, he could sip a glass of his favorite bourbon, Old Granddad, and confer with her about the issues of the day, while she edited his speeches.

"Bess, there are sons-a-bitches who want to tear

this country down, and there's hardly ever been a better time for them to do it. Why, we're still recovering from the war, and right on top of that, I don't have to tell you, we had almost two million men out on strike in the mines and the railroads, in the electrical and meat industries, in steel and automobiles. I've got that damned lying Bolshevik son-of-a-bitch blocking all our best efforts to get aid to Eastern Europe, and we've still got people starving in Greece and Turkey, and more trouble brewing over Palestine. I'll tell you, Bess, sometimes I do think we're going to end up going to war in Korea, when all I've ever wanted to be was the president who kept us at peace."

She let him vent it all, not even remonstrating with him over his salty language. Bess, herself, had been known to swear a bit, if a private occasion demanded strong talk.

"And now," he continued, her husband who loved history almost as much as he loved her and Margaret, "this very house we're living in has absolutely got to be rebuilt, and no delay about it. I can see those bastards over on the Hill have their eye on it. They know what it would mean to the American people—to the world—to see this great symbol of democracy flattened to the ground during these dangerous days. We cannot allow that to happen, Bess. George Washington built these walls. He insisted they be constructed of stone, he had a hand in every inch of the planning, and he entrusted it to the rest of us small fellows who would come after him. We can't let the president down, Bess."

For the moment, it seemed as if Harry Truman had

forgotten that he was, himself, "the president." He seemed to be speaking, Bess thought as she gazed at him, as a plain citizen, in defense of the bedrock principles of the country he loved.

"What do you want me to do, Harry?"

"Help me, sweetheart," he pleaded, holding his hands out wide.

"All right," Bess agreed, taking him by surprise with her quick capitulation. For once, she who loved to argue, didn't. "I'll write some letters."

He was grateful, for reasons he couldn't tell her.

She was willing, for motives she couldn't reveal, not even to her husband, the president of the United States of America . . . especially, not to Harry.

Bess Truman knew personally four former First Ladies, and she wrote privately to each of them. Not one of the letters was dictated; she personally penned, signed, sealed, stamped, and mailed them. It was imperative they be seen by no eyes other than those for which she intended them.

"Dear Mrs. Preston," she wrote to the former Frances Cleveland, who was the eldest of the surviving First Ladies. In her letter, Bess appealed strongly to the historic connection between herself and the tall woman who now lived in Princeton. She liked Frances Cleveland Preston, because Frances liked Harry.

"Dear Mrs. Wilson," she penned next, imagining that formidable widow in the stands at a game played by her beloved Boston Red Sox baseball team. Bess felt less sanguine about Mrs. Wilson who did *not* like Harry. Still, the First Lady knew that this time, above all times, she must not allow personal feelings to stand in the way of the right thing to do.

"Dear Mrs. Coolidge . . ."

Bess knew that Grace did not approve of Harry's absolutely *right* decision to drop the bomb and end the war, but surely she would approve of this campaign, even if she was a Republican. There were times when partisanship must be left behind. And, after all, they were "sisters" who had endured (or enjoyed, though Bess found that nearly impossible to believe) the Great White Jail that she and Harry were struggling so hard to save for General Washington and posterity.

"Dear Eleanor," she wrote warmly.

Mrs. Roosevelt might have left the White House family quarters in a mess behind her, but for Bess there was no doubting the sincerity of Eleanor's devotion to good causes, nor her kindnesses to the Trumans. In each of the other three letters, Bess had had to hint, to drop clues, to suggest by careful implication that which she meant them to infer. But to her immediate predecessor she could write easily and bluntly, because it was Eleanor Roosevelt who had passed on to Bess the secret in the first place.

"I hardly know whether to credit this story, or not, Mrs. Truman," the exhausted widow of Franklin Delano Roosevelt had confided over a very private tea one afternoon. "But duty binds me to pass it on to you, as it was passed on to me."

"The First Ladies' secret," she had called it, with an ironic twist to her mouth. Neither she nor Bess had mocked it, however, for it was very old—even if it were false—and they supposed there was always the unlikely chance that it was true.

"But you mustn't tell the president," Mrs. Roosevelt had warned her, before she left that day. Bess noted how courageously the widow pronounced those unlikely and unwelcome words, "the president," in reference to the man from Missouri. How awful it sounds to both of us, Bess thought, feeling compassion for the widow and dread for herself. If there was ever anything Bess Wallace Truman had never wanted to be in her life, it was First Lady of the United States. And now it even meant she must be entrusted with a secret she could not confide to Harry! But Eleanor Roosevelt made clear the reason: "If you tell a man about a mystery, he will feel compelled to solve it," she said, firmly, "even if it means tearing down stone walls to do it. And that is one thing we cannot allow to happen. These old walls and their secrets must stand undisturbed."

With an uncharacteristic gesture, Mrs. Roosevelt had grasped her successor's hand. "None of us have told our husbands, Bess. We have passed this strange secret down through the years, but only among ourselves. Will you keep it, too?"

Reluctantly, feeling resentful and put-upon, Bess agreed to it.

And now here she was, into the second term she had desired even less than Harry's first one, and writing these letters she had never dreamed she would have to write, calling upon esteemed women to assist her in keeping a secret she couldn't even be sure was true!

Shaking her head in exasperation at her own fate,

Bess picked up her pen again. While she was in the mood, she might as well write to her friend, Speaker of the House Sam Rayburn, to solicit his support for the cause. She decided she would write as well to the wives of important senators and representatives. Mrs. Lyndon Johnson, for instance. And she would even write to some of the wives of the rising young men, like that nice young woman who was married to Congressman Gerald R. Ford. Bess paused, trying to remember a name to match the pretty, smiling face at the White House tea for congressional wives. It was always harder to remember the names of Republicans.

"Oh, yes. Betty, that was it."

"*Dear Mrs. Ford . . .*"

The vote within the commission appointed to oversee the renovation of the White House was not even close.

"I don't understand how this could happen!" The eldest of the trio of cigar-smoking senators spoke quietly, furiously, through clenched teeth. His jowly face, familiar to millions from newspaper photographs and movie newsreels, looked thunderous. If the other two had been senatorial pages, they might have feared for their jobs. "One vote! We got only one vote to go our way on that damned commission! That son-of-a-bitch in the White House is going to get his way with that damned shack, and I don't understand how this could happen!"

He glared at them, but they shrugged, licking their lips.

Finally, the one with the vast constituency offered

up an idea. "There was overwhelming public sentiment for retaining the original structure. Mrs. Truman lobbied for it, you know. I hear she got the former First Ladies to talk it up, and she sicced Eleanor on to it."

They snickered at the name of the busybody widow.

"Don't be ridiculous." The third senator spoke smoothly, his agile mind already moving onto his next opportunities for influence. "What possible difference could they make? A coffee-klatch of First Ladies! Preposterous."

Their roar of derisive laughter attracted the admiring—and wary—attention of the secretaries and other senators eddying around them.

In Blair House, Bess Truman penned careful, private notes of appreciation to the four former First Ladies. Only to Eleanor, did she come right out and write the words, "So our secret is safe, at least for the duration of this latest renovation of the building. Rest assured, I will pass it on to the next woman to live here."

It was an eventuality which could not happen too soon, in Bess's view. She longed to return to the other roomy white house, the one in Independence, where there might be secrets, but they did not have to be coddled and kept from Harry. But yes, she would do her duty, and pass on the secret of the First Ladies, even if that meant she had to tell the wife of a Republican.

Bess sat back in her chair and closed her eyes.

When the head usher peeked in a few minutes

later, he assumed she was napping, and quietly tip-toed back out again.

Behind her closed eyelids, Bess was attempting to visualize the secret that Eleanor Roosevelt had whis-pered to her. She wasn't a very imaginative woman, she well knew, and she was finding it difficult to see a scene set so far back in time, with so many veils of mystery shrouding it . . .

There wasn't a decent quarry close at hand and there weren't qualified craftsmen to cut or work the stone, even if it could be easily had, which it couldn't. And still, the general insisted the new residence for the president—the first building to be erected in the new Federal town, as Jefferson called it—be constructed of stone!

Masons from Scotland were imported, six of them from a single lodge, hired to perform the delicate work of carving the stones after the slaves had cut them into blocks. But the Scotsmen loathed slavery, and they had refused to come at all until the Americans agreed to allow them to hire freemen as laborers.

It didn't keep the Americans from using slaves, of course.

And on a late August afternoon, when twilight was just beginning to slip across the long marsh leading from the Potomac to the ridge upon which the resi-dence was being built, three of the Scottish masons stopped their work and watched in horror as a brick-layer whipped his slave.

There was no one else about.

The three Scots had worked late, in order to hurry this job they hated in this land where they felt so foreign. Thinking they were alone on the ridge, they had continued to sculpt delicate garlands and acanthus leaves from the grayish-white stone which would eventually be whitewashed to seal it.

But down by the brick kilns which were kept burning night and day, there had come outraged shouts and then the unmistakable horror of the singing and *thwap* of bullwhip on human flesh. Too often, the Scots had heard it. Sometimes the slaves, male or female, cried under the whip or rod, which only resulted in a harder, longer lashing or beating; the stoic ones bit their dark lips until blood ran down their chins.

Immobilized with shared hatred and helplessness, the Scots watched this slave—a huge black man—raise his hands and grab the thick whip from his master's grip. As quick as one might kill a dog, the slave rose to his feet and wrapped the whip around the white man's neck, squeezing until his master fell limp to the ground.

Astonished, hardly believing what they had just witnessed, the Scotsmen stared, and one of them yelled out, no words, just an inarticulate sound wrested from his gut. The slave, hearing it, looked up and saw them for the first time. Terror replaced the fury on his face, and he started to run away. But then, they saw him fall to his knees, and bow his head down to the ground. He seemed to be simply awaiting his fate, which he assumed they would dispense.

As if they were one man, the three Scottish stonemasons walked quickly toward the gruesome scene where the master lay sprawled and the slave remained sunk upon the ground in an abject posture.

When they reached the dead man, one of the Scotsmen bent down and lifted up a stone from the ground.

He looked at his brethren.

And then he raised the stone and brought it down upon the head of the dead brickmaker.

A second Scotsman picked up another stone, and he followed the first blow with a second.

The third of their band did the same.

Three men. Three blows. Evil for evil.

Astonished, the slave stared at them from his bowed position. They bade him rise, and together, the four men slipped the brickmaker into one of the ever-burning kilns, where he was quickly cremated. Now not knowing what to do with the slave whose life they had saved, the Scottish immigrants let him slip away into the forest.

The Scotsmen never knew what became of him, and they never asked. But at their feet, where the master had died, there lay three stones, splashed now with red. Each stone bore a "mason's mark," the unique symbols by which stone craftsmen were identified and paid. The men inserted the bloody stones into the rising walls, in such a manner that no one would likely ever see the stains.

The next day, ashy new bricks were laid against the stones, hiding and insulating the interior walls with their telltale marks.

It was the slave who told Mrs. Washington. He had come, in later years, into the relative safety and anonymity of her ownership. It was a confession, of sorts, on his death bed: *"White and black blood got spilled in the president's house, Ma'am. My master, he*

*was murdered, and his body lies hidden in the bricks and
stones. White blood got spilled on the stones and black
blood, too."*

By this time, the president was dead, and so she
could not tell him. But Martha Washington could do
the next best thing: No, she wouldn't tell that awful
crotchety John Adams who had always made life so
difficult for the general, but she could tell intelligent
Abigail the secret that no one must ever know: No
one must ever be allowed to take apart the stones of
the White House walls. Not if the body of a murdered slave master was hidden there. The general
had so firmly believed in the power of symbolism to
help keep their new government standing, and he
had spoken to his wife of the issue of slavery as
being the single issue which, if ignited, could bring
it tumbling down. If their enemies knew that the
symbolic home of democracy was built upon the
blood of slave and master . . .

"My Dear Mrs. Adams . . ."

Mrs. Washington invited Mrs. Adams to tea.

Most Worshipful Harry S Truman, thirty-third degree charter member and first Worshipful Master of
Grandview Lodge No. 618 and former Grand Master
of the Grand Lodge, Ancient Free and Accepted Masons, State of Missouri, stood alone in the gutted
White House, looking up.

His blue eyes were seeing exposed beams, but his
inner eye was looking at images of his Masonic
brothers: George Washington, James Monroe, James
Polk, James Buchanan, Andrew Johnson, James Gar-
field, Theodore Roosevelt, Franklin D. Roosevelt,

Benjamin Taft, Warren G. Harding. They had all lived here, except for Washington. They had represented the best and the worst, as far as presidents went, and those were only the ten, not including himself, who were publicly known to have been Masons. First among them, always and forever, in Harry Truman's view, was the general himself.

Harry Truman knew his Masonic lineage as well as, or better than, he knew his country's history: George Washington had been initiated as an Entered Apprentice in the Lodge at Fredericksburg, Virginia, in 1752, for an entrance fee of two pounds, three shillings. After attaining the rank of Worshipful Master, he was elected to be Grand Master of Masons throughout the United States, although that had never materialized into a real position.

"Well, we did it, Sir," Harry Truman said to the vast, echoing space where a silent bulldozer waited for the construction workers to arrive again in the morning. An idle dump truck towered above the head of the thirty-third president as he spoke over the centuries to the first. "We saved your walls, Mr. President."

He repeated to himself a question which was a part of the Masonic examination ritual:

"What is the best part of a wall?"

To which he gave the ancient answer: *"Union."*

"What is the strength of our Craft?"

He knew that answer by heart, as well: *"That which fire and water cannot destroy."*

President Truman gazed around as if he hoped the ghost of the general would step forth and tell him why these walls were so important, beyond their an-

cient symbolism for democracy. The British had tried
to bring these walls down by fire in 1814, but they
had failed, and the walls stood. There had been other
fires, and onslaughts of water to fight them, but the
walls remained intact. They had been threatened
anew by the renovation now underway. Harry Truman was positive the present work had posed a danger of an even more profound and hidden nature,
although he had not been able to fathom what that
might be.

The warning had come to him with the three
ghostly knocks at his bedroom door. To a member
of the secret brotherhood, three blows could mean
only one thing, as President Truman well knew from
Masonic lore . . .

His name was Hiram.

If the legends were true, he was King Solomon's builder.

*It was his guild of stonecutters who held the secrets of
geometry by which the glorious Temple was constructed.
They were secrets in a deadly serious sense, for men's
livelihood depended on them. Give away the sworn secrets
of your guild, and you gave your brothers' jobs away.
Steal the secrets of another guild and you might steal your
way out of poverty, into affluence and even honor.*

No other guild was as honored as the stonemasons.

*Stonework, the legends said, had passed from Ancient
Turks to Ancient Egyptians and then down through centuries to the craftsmen who followed them.*

*One evening, when Hiram was passing late through the
city gates, three thugs from another guild assaulted him.
When he would not betray his guild's secrets, with three
vicious blows they slew him.*

For Freemasons ever after, three blows would represent ancient evil.

Harry Truman stood alone in the gutted, empty residence of presidents and their First Ladies. With Bess's help, he had answered the urgent summons of the three blows. A man couldn't ask for a finer sweetheart, he thought, than a wife who aided her husband without question. He sensed there was mystery within these walls which he could not penetrate, but he was content to let that be so, so long as these stones might stand.

NANCY PICKARD

———

NANCY PICKARD is the author of the Jenny Cain mystery series, and the editor of several short story anthologies, including this one and *Malice Domestic III*. She has won Anthony, Agatha, Shamus, and Macavity awards, and twice been an Edgar nominee. She is a founding member and former president of Sisters in Crime, and a member of PEN, the Mystery Writers of America, and the International Crime Writers League.

"Bess and Harry Truman were hometown folks for me," she says. "I grew up only a few miles from their home in Independence, Missouri. It was that connection, more than anything else, which inspired me to choose Bess, because I knew I could drive right over to their museum and even take a tour of their home, which I did one day when it happened that no other tourist was there, just the tour guide and me. But I was also drawn by certain apparently disparate facts about the Trumans: One was Bess' famous reticence and the fact that she broke it publicly only twice; and there was Harry's membership in his beloved Freemasons; and there was also his belief, based on his own spooky experiences, that the White House is haunted. All of those separate ingredients swirled together to form my story."

MRS. LINCOLN'S DILEMMA

———≈≈≈———

JANET DAWSON

THE SOFT YELLOW glow of the lamplight turned Mrs. Lincoln's white silk gown to a mellow cream color. The light also hid the shadows and the tiny wrinkles on her face as well. She vowed it took ten years off her age.

Her blue eyes sparkled. Tonight she wore pearls in her ears and at her throat, and several white camellias pinned in her light-brown hair. As she moved among the guests gathered in the East Room of the White House that evening in November of 1861, smiling and nodding, she felt as though she were still the Lexington belle who, with wit and vivacity, charmed her way through Springfield, Illinois, over twenty years ago. Back then she'd caught the eye of many young bachelors, including a tall gangling lawyer named Abraham Lincoln.

Mrs. Lincoln swept regally past a cluster of cabinet

wives. All of them, to her critical eyes, looked drab and dowdy. The Washington wags criticized her constantly, on everything from her involvement in politics to her extravagance and her manner of dressing. How dare a woman of Mrs. Lincoln's age bare her shoulders and décolletage, they clucked like a chicken house full of old hens. How dare she wear white, which was considered suitable only for a young woman.

She'd been told they called her "The Illinois Reine" because of her fashionable and lavish dress. Well, let them talk. The First Lady of the United States should look as elegant as General McClellan over there, resplendent as a peacock in his dress uniform.

She knew the gossip about her extravagance stemmed from her efforts to redecorate the White House. It was true she'd gone through the allowance set aside for refurbishing the residence. Unfortunately, the expenditures had come at a time when everyone was insisting that every last penny go into the war effort.

But the White House had been downright dilapidated when she, Mr. Lincoln, and their boys had moved in. She'd been appalled at the sight of peeling wallpaper and broken furniture in every room. And the state dining room in the west wing had more broken china than whole. Why, the place had looked like a tawdry boardinghouse. She'd soon remedied that, at the cost of a good deal of money, and even more talk.

Mr. Lincoln is president, she told herself. He must have a suitable place to live. How much nicer the East Room looked with the new damask curtains and the fine carpet that replaced the threadbare rag damaged by the Frontier Guard, who would practice presenting arms right here.

As for politics, she was a politician's wife, and had been for nineteen years. She'd been interested in politics since those early years in Springfield, even before she'd married Mr. Lincoln and began keeping house and raising children. Her husband had asked her counsel many times throughout their marriage, and she'd readily given it. Why should she stop now, just to suit a bunch of pinched-nose critics?

She paused to speak with Secretary of the Treasury Salmon Chase and his red-headed daughter Kate, then moved on to a group of stiff-backed army officers and their ladies. She felt a hint of coolness as they greeted her, and she knew why.

Her half-brothers, Sam, David, and Aleck, had joined the Confederate Army after Fort Sumter. Her half-sister Emilie's husband was Confederate General Benjamin Hardin Helm. These younger siblings were Kentuckians, and their Southern sympathies were to be expected. Despite the pain their allegiances caused her, Mrs. Lincoln felt a good deal of affection for the children born of Robert Todd's second marriage. Her stepmother was another matter. Mrs. Lincoln had left Lexington for Springfield just to get away from the hated Betsey Humphreys Todd.

She pushed away the image of her divided family, an echo of the now-divided nation. Her eyes searched for someone she had invited to the White House soiree, an old friend from Springfield who was in Washington on family business. On the other side of the room she spied Ada Belford, in a brown watered-silk dress decorated with jet beads. Her gloved hand rested on the arm of a slender young man whose straight brown hair tumbled onto his forehead. When Mrs. Belford caught the First Lady's eye, she waved.

Mrs. Lincoln sidestepped a cavalry officer with a dangling sword and headed toward her friend. She passed just behind two men, civilians both, one tall and dark, with a hawklike profile. The other was short and broad, with a head of ginger hair that went with his florid complexion. Their heads were bent together and they talked in low tones, as though they did not wish to be overheard. It was reasonable to assume they would not be, given the crowded hubbub of the room. But Mrs. Lincoln heard a few words anyway.

"Shortage of woolens, as you well know," the tall man said. His voice was deep and flavored with a New England accent. ". . . Play our cards right . . . could all be rich."

His companion nodded in agreement as he spoke, his voice a harsh whisper. "Depends . . . make it worth my while."

Mrs. Lincoln's route carried her away from their muted words. Her lips thinned with disapproval as she drew her own conclusions about what she'd just heard. Speculators, out to make a quick killing in business while others were killed on the battlefields. They talked of getting rich, as though the war was nothing but a business opportunity.

She knew of the shortage of woolens for military uniforms. Mr. Lincoln had mentioned it over breakfast a few days ago. Only yesterday she'd heard with her own ears evidence of such a scarcity. As was her custom, she'd spent some time at one of the many military hospitals in the capital, talking with a young Union soldier who seemed barely older than her own dear Willie. The soldier's leg had been amputated. Now that autumn was giving way to winter, he said, it was cold out on the battlefields and in the camps. The boy told her he and his companions often shivered for lack of adequate clothing.

The government, according to Mr. Lincoln, planned to remedy that problem by purchasing cloth from abroad. However, he added, such a move was sure to raise the ire of American manufacturers.

Her mouth curved back into a smile as she greeted Ada Belford with an embrace. "Ada, my dear. I'm so glad to see you."

Mrs. Belford took the First Lady's hand and squeezed it. "Mary . . . Oh, should I call you Mrs. Lincoln?"

"You've called me Mary for years. I see no reason to change now."

"Back in Springfield you weren't the president's wife," Mrs. Belford said. "It's good to see you again. Thank you so much for inviting us to your soiree."

"When I received your letter advising me that you were in Washington, I said to Mr. Lincoln that of course you must come. You and Edward both."

Edward Belford was a good-looking lad, if somewhat solemn and studious, who had just turned eighteen. He resembled his late father, who had served in the Illinois legislature with Mr. Lincoln. And there was something, not just the name, but in the shape of his face and his eyes, that reminded Mrs. Lincoln of her own son Eddie, who had died eleven years earlier.

"Ada, your note said you are in town for your niece's wedding. A happy occasion."

Mrs. Belford nodded. "Happy, yet somewhat tempered by the course of this wretched war. Rachel is the daughter of my eldest sister, Olivia Hopkins. Her husband, Colonel Hopkins, was killed this past summer at Bull Run."

"A terrible tragedy," Mrs. Lincoln murmured. The war. It permeated everything. She'd never met Olivia Hopkins but she could imagine the horrible loss of a husband. Hadn't she herself experienced the loss of a child?

"Rachel's beau is an army officer," Mrs. Belford continued. "He's posted here in Washington, but she fears he'll be sent elsewhere after the new year. If it weren't wartime perhaps the girl could be persuaded to wait until spring for her wedding. But she's quite insistent on getting married as soon as possible. Young people these days . . ."

Difficult days, the First Lady thought. She and Mr. Lincoln had courted for nearly four years before their marriage, but these were different times. She understood the young woman's haste. A father already killed by this war, the unspoken fear that her sweetheart might meet the same fate.

Edward stood quietly as his mother regaled her friend with news of people back in Springfield. Then Ada Belford stopped and glanced over Mrs. Lincoln's shoulder.

"I hope you don't think I presumed on your invitation, Mary, but I brought my sister Ella and her husband, who are also here for the wedding. Allow me to present them. Mr. and Mrs. John Grayson of Fall River, Massachusetts."

Mrs. Lincoln turned to her right and inclined her head to Ella Grayson, a pretty blond in a stylish blue dress. She was some years younger than her sister, and gave the impression of being quite giddy. Then Mrs. Lincoln glanced up, startled to find herself face to face with the tall hawk-faced man she'd overheard earlier, discussing the economic opportunities afforded by the shortage of woolens. She masked her surprise as Mrs. Belford continued her introduction. "Mr. Grayson owns a factory in Fall River."

"Indeed," Mrs. Lincoln said, turning on him her most dazzling smile. "And what do you manufacture, Mr. Grayson?"

"Woolen cloth, Ma'am," he told her. "To be made into uniforms for the army."

"You have a government contract, then." In the next few moments Mrs. Lincoln endeavored to find out more about Grayson's enterprise. But he was now quite close with his tongue, closer than he had been earlier with the red-haired man. He took his wife's arm and bowed to the First Lady, then to his sister-in-law. "Will you excuse us? There is someone I wish Ella to meet."

When the Graysons had moved away, Ada Belford sent Edward to fetch her a cup of punch. Then she leaned close to Mary Lincoln. "Have you had a chance to consider the matter I proposed in my letter?"

Mrs. Lincoln nodded. Ada Belford had an older daughter, married and living in Ohio. Edward was her only son, and since her husband's death two years earlier she'd been reluctant to let the boy out of her sight. He wanted to join the army, had ever since Fort Sumter. It wasn't unusual. In fact, boys far younger than Edward were with the troops on both sides of the fight.

But Ada couldn't bear the thought of losing him. So she'd written to her old friend Mary, to ask a favor. Surely Mrs. Lincoln could arrange for a government job, any government job. Surely he could contribute to the war effort that way, and avoid any criticism for not being in the army.

Mrs. Lincoln was certainly sympathetic to her friend's feelings. Her own son Robert, the eldest of the three surviving Lincoln boys, wasn't in the army either, and the old hens were clucking about that, too.

Mary Lincoln was certainly no stranger to patronage. Ever since Mr. Lincoln had become active in politics, people frequently asked the politician's wife for favors. She was shrewd about how she granted them.

And how she went about obtaining them. She had examined the guest list for this evening's reception and noted that the secretary of war's party included Major Charles Markham, whom she'd met before, at a reception given by the Chases. The major worked in the War Department, procuring supplies, he said, as he complained of a shortage of clerks. Surely he could use the talents of an intelligent young man like Edward Belford.

When Secretary of War Edwin Stanton had arrived, Mrs. Lincoln sent Henry Wilder in search of Major

Markham. Henry was a clerk on the White House staff, and since he was from Illinois, Mrs. Lincoln had made him her unofficial assistant. She frequently relied on his discretion and efficiency.

Once summoned by Henry, Major Markham readily agreed to interview young Mr. Belford. "How can I refuse the First Lady?" he told her with a charming smile, as he bent low over her hand. "I'm sure I can find some employment for the young man."

Now Mrs. Lincoln lowered her voice and moved closer to Ada Belford. "I've already acted on your request. Edward has an appointment tomorrow with Major Markham, with whom I spoke earlier this evening."

She glanced about the room, seeking the major. Her eyes rested for a moment on the secretary of war, but she didn't see Markham. Ah, there he was. Now, that was interesting. The major was talking with the red-haired man she'd seen earlier with John Grayson.

By now Edward had returned with a cup of punch, which he handed to his mother. He listened politely as Mrs. Belford told him excitely of his appointment with Major Markham.

"That tall officer there," Mrs. Lincoln said. "The one with yellow hair. He'll expect you at noon, at the War Department. Now, I want you to report back to me about your interview with the major. I'll be visiting one of the military hospitals tomorrow afternoon, the one near Union Station."

Mrs. Lincoln left the Belfords and moved around the East Room, pausing several times to speak with guests. Finally she joined her husband. At six feet four inches, to her own five feet two, he towered over her. Abraham Lincoln, the sixteenth president of the United States, looked down at his wife, in her billowing white silk, and smiled fondly. Then he leaned over and whispered in her ear. "You're as pretty as the day I met you."

Later, as the guests were leaving, Mrs. Lincoln caught Henry Wilder's eye. She pointed out the red-haired man, who trailed behind Secretary Chase's party. "Find out who he is," she directed the young man. Henry nodded and moved away. After all the guests had departed, Henry returned and made his report.

"The gentleman is named Simon Chester," he told her. "He's a businessman from New York. He was here as a guest of the senator from that state."

Mrs. Lincoln thanked him. She thought no more about the red-headed man until the next day, when events gave her reason to do so.

Henry and two large troopers of the Frontier Guard escorted her to the hospital that rainy afternoon. She could hear the train whistles from the nearby railroad station as she read to a wounded soldier. When it was time to leave, Henry and the troopers walked with her down a corridor to the hospital's front door. There she saw Edward Belford, who had just entered. He looked so young and slender, in contrast with the bearded, burly soldier who followed a few steps behind him.

Henry and the troopers withdrew a few paces to allow her some privacy during her conversation with Edward. "How did it go, your interview with Major

Markham?" she asked, pulling on her gloves. "Has he a place for you at the War Department?"

Edward Belford looked down at his muddy shoes and the damp cuffs of his trousers which gave evidence of a long walk in rainy weather. His eyes came up, meeting those of the First Lady.

"Mrs. Lincoln," he said slowly, "I kept my appointment with the major, but I told him . . . I mean, I appreciate all the trouble you've gone to but—"

"You're going to join the army anyway," she finished, her voice quiet.

Edward ducked his head in quick assent. "Yes, Ma'am. I want to serve my country and help Mr. Lincoln preserve the union."

"Those are admirable sentiments, Edward. I can't argue with them. Not here, anyway." She looked around her at the bustling hospital, so full of other young men who wanted to help her husband preserve the union. "Your mother will be upset."

"Yes, Ma'am, I know. But I've made up my mind. I thought about waiting until after my cousin's wedding, but . . . well, I've waited long enough. I'll tell Mother this afternoon, as soon as I . . . well, there's somewhere I need to go first, but I'll tell her as soon as I go back to Aunt Olivia's house."

"Good luck," she said, holding out her hand to the boy. "And God be with you."

He hesitated. "Mrs. Lincoln, there's something . . . well, I don't know who to tell. But I saw something that's odd."

"What's that, Edward?"

He lowered his voice. "After I spoke with Major Markham, I got lost in the War Department building.

It's mighty big, and I got turned around. Finally I found my way out of the building. And who should I see outside, but my uncle John, the one that owns the mill in Fall River. I was real surprised to see him there. He was standing to one side as though he didn't want anyone to see him. But I guess he was meeting someone, because of what happened next."

"Someone joined him?" Mrs. Lincoln asked.

"Major Markham. Well, I didn't think that was odd, at least not at first, because Uncle John's got a government contract. He sells all his cloth to the army, for uniforms. Then I got to wondering. If my uncle was there to see the major on business, why didn't they meet in the major's office?"

Why, indeed? the First Lady thought.

"So I followed them," Edward continued. "They went to a tavern, a few streets away. They met a man there, a ginger-haired fellow. He was at your reception last evening. I saw Uncle John talking with him there as well. And the major too."

"You're very observant, Edward. Did you go into the tavern? Could you hear what they were talking about?"

"I went inside, Ma'am. But I couldn't hear what they were talking about. They had a drink together." The boy leaned closer to her. "Then Uncle John pulled out a wad of greenbacks. He gave a fistful to the major, and another to the other fellow."

"Good heavens." Mrs. Lincoln's suspicions were growing, particularly as she recalled that scrap of conversation she'd overheard last night. "They didn't see you?"

"I don't think so, Ma'am. I left that tavern quick,

I can tell you, and walked over here to meet you. I thought about it all the way over here. That's why I was late. Guess I was walking a bit slow." Edward frowned. "I hope I've done the right thing telling you all this. You have enough to worry about, Mother says."

Mrs. Lincoln laid her hand on his shoulder. "Yes, I'm glad you told me, Edward. Now, I'm expected at a meeting. As for the army, you do what you must, and take care of yourself."

She stood and watched as the young man left the hospital, his shoulders back and his stride brisk and almost military. Then her view of Edward Belford was blocked as the burly man she'd seen earlier, an orderly, she guessed, headed quickly out the door.

Once outside in her carriage, Mrs. Lincoln turned to Henry. "I have an errand for you. I need more information on Mr. Chester, the red-haired man from last night. You said he was a businessman from New York City. See if you can find out more about him, especially what business he is engaged in."

She spent the next hour or so meeting with the redoubtable Miss Dorothea Dix, who was superintendent of Union Army nurses, and Miss Clara Barton, a volunteer who was working with the wounded, discussing how to improve hospital conditions. Then Mrs. Lincoln returned to the White House. The president was still at the Capitol. Tad and Willie were being rambunctious, trying their mother's patience. She admonished the boys and went upstairs to take a nap. An hour later Henry Wilder knocked on the door. She admitted him and sent for tea.

"Mr. Chester, it appears, is an agent who represents cloth manufacturers," Henry said.

"Then there's nothing unusual about his speaking with Mr. Grayson," Mrs. Lincoln said in a low voice. "For Mr. Grayson makes cloth. Still . . ." She couldn't forget what young Edward had said about seeing Chester and his uncle with Major Markham in that tavern. Money changing hands, the boy said. Grayson's money. Surely that was not on the up and up.

Her train of thought was derailed by the approach of another member of the White House staff bearing not tea, but a note. "From a Mrs. Hopkins," the man said. "It just arrived, and the messenger who delivered it said it was urgent."

Mrs. Lincoln took the envelope and turned it over in her hands. She recognized neither the handwriting, nor the name. No, wait, Hopkins. Wasn't that Ada Belford's sister, the colonel's widow? She opened the envelope and pulled out a single sheet of paper. As she read the words written on it, her mouth opened in a shocked gasp.

"Mrs. Lincoln?" Henry asked, his own face worried. "What is it?"

"A carriage, Henry," she said in a choked voice. "Call for a carriage, and quickly."

Mrs. Hopkins lived in a modest house on Third Street, near East Capitol Avenue. It seemed to take forever to get there. Olivia Hopkins, a gaunt-faced woman in black, greeted Mrs. Lincoln and Henry Wilder at the door.

"Thank you so much for coming, Mrs. Lincoln. It means so much to Ada. She's simply prostrate with grief, ever since the policeman arrived to tell us the news."

"This is dreadful," the First Lady said. "May I see her now?"

"Of course. She's been asking for you."

The Frontier Guard troopers who had come with Mrs. Lincoln and Henry took up a position in the vestibule, while Henry waited in the parlor. Mrs. Lincoln followed Mrs. Hopkins up the stairs. "Tell me what happened."

"I know little, other than what the policeman told me, when he arrived here late this afternoon." Olivia Hopkins paused at the landing, one knobby hand on the banister. "Edward was found in an alley off Fourteenth Street. He'd been stabbed." Mrs. Hopkins shuddered, then her face hardened as she went on. "Waylaid by some ruffian, the policeman said, and killed for the contents of his pockets."

"I saw him at one of the military hospitals this afternoon," Mrs. Lincoln said. "The one near Union Station. That's just north of here. He was coming back here to your house afterwards, he said." She stopped and shook her head. "No, wait, he said something about having someplace to go. Where on Fourteenth Street was he found?"

"Not far from Pennsylvania," Mrs. Hopkins said, continuing upstairs.

"He was near the White House, then," Mrs. Lincoln said, half to herself. Where had young Edward Belford gone after he left the hospital? It was simply too convenient that he should be dead this rainy evening, a few short hours after he'd told her of what he had seen in that tavern.

When they reached the upper floor, Mrs. Hopkins led the way to a door at the rear of the narrow house, and opened it. She stepped to one side and let Mrs. Lincoln enter, then quietly closed the door, leaving the two women from Springfield alone. Mrs. Lincoln had tried to prepare herself for this moment, on the way here from the White House. Yet it was not enough. Never would she forget the sight of Ada Belford's tear-ravaged face.

Much later she came wearily down the stairs, where Henry and the two troopers waited. In the parlor Olivia Hopkins poured tea. The handsome young woman with her, Mrs. Lincoln had already guessed, was Rachel Hopkins, the one who was to be married.

As Rachel handed tea to Henry and the troopers, Mrs. Hopkins offered a cup and saucer to Mrs. Lincoln. "How is she?"

"Asleep," the First Lady said, taking a seat. "She cried herself to sleep."

"Good. She needs rest." Mrs. Hopkins sighed. "I know. I've been through it. My husband was killed last summer." She stopped and her gaze moved to a portrait of a military officer hanging above the mantel.

"Ada told me of your loss," Mrs. Lincoln said. "I am sorry."

"He was a military man." Mrs. Hopkins's face regained the steely composure she had shown earlier. "A military wife expects casualties, or she has no business marrying into the army. But the loss of a child, no matter his age, is hard."

"I know." As Mrs. Lincoln raised the teacup to her

lips, it was not Edward Belford's face she saw, but Eddie Lincoln's, dead these eleven years.

Rachel joined the two older women. "I'm sorry I wasn't here when the policeman came," she told her mother. Then she glanced at the First Lady, and explained further. "I spent the afternoon with my friend Daisy Markham, shopping for my trousseau."

"Markham?" Mrs. Lincoln, bone tired a moment before, found herself revived, not by the tea, but by the mention of the familiar name.

"My dearest friend from school," Rachel told her. "She's married to an army officer."

"Major Charles Markham of the War Department?" The First Lady carefully set the teacup in its saucer. "He was at a reception Mr. Lincoln and I gave at the White House."

Rachel nodded. "I only know him through Daisy. But I believe he's acquainted with Uncle John."

He is indeed, Mrs. Lincoln thought. Intimately.

"Speaking of your Uncle John and Aunt Ella . . ." Mrs. Hopkins consulted the clock on the mantel and frowned. "I've sent word to them at the same time I sent that note to Mrs. Lincoln. I thought they'd be here by now."

"They're not staying here?" Mrs. Lincoln asked.

"Dear me, no," Olivia Hopkins said, her voice tart. "I haven't the room. Nor is my simple little house enough to satisfy my brother-in-law's pretensions. He's an ambitious man, who thinks himself quite above the rest of us. No, they're staying at Willard's Hotel."

Willard's? Mrs. Lincoln sipped tea, then straightened. Willard's Hotel was located at Fourteenth

Street and Pennsylvania Avenue. Had Edward gone to see his uncle this afternoon, to confront him with what he'd seen earlier?

The doorbell sounded, and Rachel went to answer it. The Graysons had arrived. Mrs. Lincoln greeted them politely, her gaze moving from Mrs. Grayson's round, pretty face and expensive clothing to her husband's shrewd, dark visage. Suddenly she found that she didn't want to be in the same room as the man. She glanced at the clock, then set the cup aside.

"I must be going," she told Mrs. Hopkins. "When Ada wakes up, tell her I'll call again tomorrow."

"Bad news, Mrs. Lincoln," Henry Wilder commented, as the carriage made its way through rainy streets, heading back toward the White House. "Young Mr. Belford's murder."

"Dreadful news," she told him. "Mrs. Belford is overwhelmed with grief. We must do what we can to find out who is responsible for the boy's death."

"You don't believe the murderer was an ordinary footpad?" Henry asked.

The First Lady shook her head. "It's far too convenient that Edward was found dead near Willard's Hotel."

Henry nodded "I see. Mr. Grayson and his wife were staying at Willard's Hotel. I take it you wish me to find out whether Mr. Chester is staying there as well. And whether Major Markham has visited either of them recently."

"All three of them were together, as recently as this afternoon," Mrs. Lincoln said. "At the hospital, Edward told me he'd seen them together, in a tavern near the War Department. Edward saw his uncle handing money to Chester and the major. The three dots are already connected, and to no good end, I'm sure."

"It certainly points to more than a footpad in an alley off Fourteenth." The carriage halted at the White House. Henry stepped down, then helped her from the conveyance.

"Yes, but we must find out why, and how." Mrs. Lincoln bade him goodnight in the downstairs hallway. Mr. Lincoln, it seemed, was still tied up at the Capitol. The boys had eaten their dinner and gone to bed. Mrs. Lincoln asked for a light supper to be sent up to her room on a tray. As she climbed the stairs leading up to the family quarters, she wished she could discuss Edward Belford's murder with her husband, ask him for his advice and counsel. But she had no wish to add yet another burden to his load. He had so many other deaths on his mind.

It was still raining the next morning when the First Lady's seamstress arrived. Elizabeth Keckley was an ex-slave. Mrs. Lincoln, a southerner whose own family was divided on the issue of slavery, would not have thought it possible for two such dissimilar women to become friends. Yet they shared a closeness that Mrs. Lincoln had come to cherish.

Now Mrs. Lincoln needed Lizzie's services for something other than stitching seams. She told Lizzie about Edward's murder. "I can't go out unnoticed, of course. Not without Henry and those troopers. But you can. I've already sent Henry on an errand. But I must know where Edward went after he left the hospital yesterday afternoon. You must be my eyes and ears and feet, Lizzie."

Lizzie Keckley nodded, reaching for her shawl and reticule. That morning Mrs. Lincoln saw to her boys, then she had an appointment with Mr. William Wood, the acting commissioner of public buildings, who was assisting her with the refurbishment of the White House. In the afternoon she took tea with a group of congressmen's wives. By the time the women had left, the seamstress had returned from her mission. In fact, both Lizzie and Henry had information for her.

"I asked people who work in that hospital if they'd seen the young man," Lizzie said. "Couldn't get the time of day from those military people, so I went across the street. Found a grocer's boy who gave Mr. Belford directions to Willard's Hotel."

"So he was going there," Mrs. Lincoln said triumphantly. "To see his uncle, I'll be bound. What else?"

"The grocer's boy saw an enlisted man, a corporal, following Mr. Belford. This corporal was a big fellow with dark hair and a dark beard."

"Was the man a hospital orderly?" Mrs. Lincoln asked. Hadn't she seen a man of that description, about the same time Edward met her at the hospital?

"I don't think so," Lizzie said. "The grocer's boy told me the man's uniform was too clean for him to be an orderly. The orderlies do get a bit worse for wear, working with the wounded."

Mrs. Lincoln turned to Henry Wilder. "Do you remember him, at the hospital?"

"I do," Henry said. "He was in the hallway the same time as Edward. I also assumed he was an orderly."

"This man followed Mr. Belford all the way to Willard's," Lizzie said. "You said the boy was killed near there, so I went to the hotel. A friend of mine works there as a waiter, so I talked with him. Mr. Belford was there, all right, in the lobby. He looked like he was waiting for someone. Don't know if he ever met who he was waiting for, though. My friend didn't see him leave."

"John Grayson," Mrs. Lincoln said. "He went to see his uncle. Did your friend see the corporal who'd been following Edward?"

"Yes, he did. Noticed him, because he doesn't see many enlisted men in the lobby of Willard's. Says he followed the young man right in the door, then made himself scarce."

"Good work, Lizzie." Mrs. Lincoln turned to Henry Wilder. "We must find out who this corporal is," Mrs. Lincoln told Henry. "If I were to make a guess, I'd say he's on speaking terms with Major Markham. Direct your inquiries there."

"I will. As for what I found out this afternoon, Mr. Chester is indeed registered at Willard's Hotel. He has been seen in the bar with Mr. Grayson on several occasions. But not with the major."

"Mr. Grayson's factory in Fall River makes woolen cloth," the First Lady said slowly. "Mr. Chester represents clothmakers. And I'll wager Major Markham's job is to procure cloth for army uniforms."

"You would win that bet, Mrs. Lincoln," Henry said. "The major awards contracts to factories that make the uniforms. As for Mr. Chester, I was wrong to assume that he was an agent representing American woolen manufacturers. His clients are European. Now, I've heard talk during our hospital visits of a shortage of woolens for uniforms. Recently I've also heard there's a plan to purchase woolens from abroad."

"It's more than talk," Mrs. Lincoln told him. "And it's certain to make American woolen manufacturers angry. What if John Grayson found out about the government's plan to buy that cloth from the Europeans? What would he do to prevent that purchase?"

"Murder his own nephew?" Lizzie asked. No one answered her question.

"Go find out about that corporal," Mrs. Lincoln told Henry. "When you return, we'll decide what to do."

The rain had stopped falling later that evening when Mrs. Lincoln, accompanied by Henry Wilder and the Frontier Guard troopers, knocked on Olivia Hopkins's door. The army officer's widow admitted her and told her that Ada Belford was asleep in the upstairs bedroom. "May I offer you some tea?"

"Thank you, yes," Mrs. Lincoln said, removing her gloves. "Make a large pot. There will be some people joining us."

Mrs. Hopkins narrowed her eyes and considered this, then she nodded, and left Mrs. Lincoln and Henry alone in the parlor, with the troopers standing guard in the vestibule. "I hope your scheme works," Mrs. Lincoln said.

"Lizzie and I delivered the messages," Henry told her. "Exactly as you instructed us. Were you able to speak with the president?"

Just as Mrs. Lincoln opened her mouth to answer, someone knocked at the door. One of the troopers made a move as though to answer, but Mrs. Lincoln forestalled him with a wave of her hand. Instead it was Mrs. Hopkins who hurried from her kitchen and opened the door to John Grayson.

"Why, John, I wasn't expecting you. Is Ella with you?"

"You sent me a note," the factory owner said, brows knitted in consternation. "You said it was urgent."

"It is, Mr. Grayson," Mrs. Lincoln said. "It was I who sent for you, not Mrs. Hopkins. Sit down. We're expecting other guests." She beckoned him to join her in the parlor. He, with a glance at the large trooper to his left, reluctantly complied.

"I'll get the tea," Mrs. Hopkins said, frowning as she tried to piece together what was going on. She went back to the kitchen and returned quickly with the tea tray, which Henry took from her.

The door knocker sounded again. Mrs. Hopkins went to answer it. Major Charles Markham strode into the vestibule. He looked at the two troopers, startled, then into the parlor. His eyes widened slightly as he saw Grayson sitting there, with Mrs. Lincoln, Mrs. Hopkins, and Henry Wilder. "What's going on? I got a message that Daisy was here and had been taken ill."

"I'm sorry for the subterfuge," Mrs. Lincoln said, "but it was necessary to get you here. Please join us, Major."

The officer scowled. "I have no time for this nonsense. I must get back to the War Department."

"You'd better sit down and hear me out," Mrs. Lincoln said, her voice cold. "It isn't nonsense. It's far more serious than that, and it concerns you and

Mr. Grayson. And Mr. Chester, who won't be joining us. He's been detained."

When they heard this last name, the major's mouth tightened and Grayson's eyes became hooded. A look passed quickly between the two men. Mrs. Hopkins noticed. Her lips tightened as she looked at the First Lady. "Should I leave?" It was plain that she didn't want to.

Mrs. Lincoln shook her head. "No, I want you here, as a witness to this plot to defraud the government. And murder Edward Belford."

Major Markham swore under his breath, causing the troopers near the door to move toward the parlor. At the same time Grayson rose to his feet, nearly upsetting the tea tray. "What are you talking about?"

Mrs. Lincoln cut both men off, her gesture as sharp as her words. "I overheard you and Mr. Chester at the White House reception, Mr. Grayson. You said there was a shortage of woolens and if the cards were played right, you'd all be rich. Then Mr. Chester said, 'Make it worth my while.' That's what you did, Mr. Grayson. And Edward saw you do it, in a tavern yesterday afternoon. You paid off Major Markham, no doubt for the information about the government's plan to purchase woolen cloth from abroad. As an American manufacturer, you'd prefer that transaction not take place. So you paid off Mr. Chester, the American agent who represents a consortium of European woolen merchants, to call off the deal."

The factory owner's dark face got white around the mouth. Major Markham gave nothing away. "This is absurd," he said. "Nothing of the sort happened."

"You were seen, and you know it," Mrs. Lincoln

said. "Why else would you send Corporal Jackson to kill Edward Belford?"

"Kill Edward?" Grayson shouted. "Edward saw?"

"Yes, he did. And he told me, before he went to Willard's Hotel, to look for you. He was followed by Corporal Jackson. Who, as it happens, works in the procurement office at the War Department."

Grayson turned on Markham in horror. "You only told me we'd been seen. But you didn't say it was my nephew who'd observed us."

"Hold your tongue," the major snarled. "They have no proof for this story."

"All the proof I need is in your faces," Mrs. Hopkins said, revulsion in her eyes as she raked them over the major and her brother-in-law. "Your hands might as well be covered in blood."

"We do have proof," Mrs. Lincoln told them. "When I said Mr. Chester had been detained, I did not mean he was delayed. He's been arrested by the police, on the orders of the president himself. The authorities are on their way here now. Corporal Jackson has also been taken into custody, and I understand he's been quite vocal about it. You see, Major, your clerk has no intention of taking sole blame for this crime."

JANET DAWSON

JANET DAWSON is the author of a series featuring Oakland P.I. Jeri Howard. Her first book, *Kindred Crimes*, won the St. Martin's Press/Private Eye Writers of America contest for best first private-eye novel, as well as garnering Shamus Award, Macavity Award, and Anthony Award nominations. Other Jeri Howard cases include, *Til the Old Men Die, Take a Number, Don't Turn Your Back on the Ocean, Nobody's Child, A Credible Threat, Witness to Evil* and *Where the Bodies Are Buried*.

Janet's comment: "Mary Todd Lincoln is frequently dismissed as the crazy one, the extravagant temperamental shrew who was into spiritualism and who was finally institutionalized by her son. Yet those who dig deeper will find in her a witty, intelligent woman who did not fit neatly into the confines of nineteenth-century society, no matter how she tried. She loved, and was loved by, her husband, one of our greatest presidents. Her life was blighted by her own tragedies. Three of her four sons died before her, and her husband was assassinated as she sat by his side. Her flaws make her all too human."

JULIA GRANT A.K.A. PRIVATE EYE

—◆◆◆—

JAN GRAPE

"**U**LYS, YOU UNDOUBTEDLY will think I am a superstitious person and perhaps you are right but I know what I know and have no better answer," Julia Dent Grant said. Her husband had come into her room when she had called out his name at twelve-thirty in the morning.

Since they had moved into the White House they had been unable to sleep in the same bedroom. Too many nights the president was denied sleep because of matters of state. Julia hated the arrangement but her husband hated it even more and many nights he would cross quietly into the next room and slip into her bed even if only for a few hours.

"Now, my dear, your dreams have proved right too many times for me not to listen." President Ulysses Grant's deep voice belied his short stature and had a way of rumbling authority. His voice inspired trust in everyone who heard him.

386

The whole war-torn nation had believed when the newly elected Grant said, "Now, let us have peace."

The president pulled a cigar from his dressing-gown pocket after crossing to the balcony and opening a French door. He lit the cigar and turned to face his wife. "Tell me about your dream," Ulysses said.

"A young woman came here to our house and she was very lovely with a kind face," Julia said.

"Not too unpleasant so far."

Julia frowned at the interruption but soon continued, "She walked over to you and placed a kiss on your cheek as if she were greeting an old lover. Then while embracing you she slipped a note into your coat pocket, turned, and quickly left."

"Still, this is not exactly anything to disturb you. Was she someone we know?"

"I do not think I have ever met her but I am not sure about you." Julia raised an eyebrow. Not exactly a beauty, Julia nevertheless was rather attractive. Her one flaw was a cocked eye. She had wanted to have her eyes corrected by a new surgical process she had read about. She knew Ulysses's life would continue in public service and wanted to look her best for him. Grant told her that her eyes were lovely, that he fell in love with her eyes and he liked her just the way she was. That ended any talk of surgery.

He smiled at her. "My dearest one, you know there are no old lovers or no young ones for that matter, lovely or not so lovely, in my life." He puffed on his cigar. "You are and have always been the only woman for me, Julia."

She ducked her head and blushed. "And you for me. But I am afraid you might think me mildly crazy.

Or perhaps you will think I am acting like Mary Lincoln did sometimes. You remember when she grew unreasonably jealous of Mr. Lincoln."

In the past when women acted too boldly toward her husband she did become annoyed, but tried not to ever let him see her dismay. Her dream tonight, however, held more sinister connotations than just a flirtatious old flame. She felt sure of that and when she thought of it again, she shivered.

All of her life, Julia Grant had had dreams and feelings which were so strong she felt she must act upon them and did. Her intuition had proved true many times and her husband knew he had best listen to her on those occasions.

The most recent incident of Julia's feeling kept her beloved, "Ulys," as she called him when they were alone, from going to Ford's Theater with President and Mrs. Lincoln. It happened to be the very same night John Wilkes Booth shot Mr. Lincoln. She had urged Ulys not to go and for them to go ahead and leave the city as they had originally planned before the invitation to join the Lincolns had been issued.

General Grant had listened and sent his regrets to President and Mrs. Lincoln saying their plans could not be postponed at this late date.

That evening, as their carriage headed for Philadelphia, a man rode past them and back—on three different occasions—and on the third pass the man leaned toward the general's face and glared darkly.

Julia said he was one of the men she had seen earlier in the day when she and young Jess Grant lunched with Mrs. Rawlins and her little daughter. Later, both women swore one of the men who spent

JULIA GRANT A.K.A. PRIVATE EYE

time at the restaurant listening to their conversation was none other than John Wilkes Booth.

Two days after the assassination a letter came to Grant speaking of how he had been spared. Julia and Ulysses needed no convincing that the letter came from Booth because of her feelings. The newspapers had always reported General Grant would accompany President Lincoln to the theater that evening and it was only Julia's interference which kept her general by her side.

"So what do you make of this dream," asked Ulysses. "Obviously you feel some danger for me from this woman and not in a romantic way."

"No, not romance at all. It is more like a grave danger I feel coming from her presence."

"Then you need not worry. Allan Pinkerton has men on guard duty tonight and for several weeks to come. You know you always feel safer when the Pinkertons are around. And I will be on the lookout for any lovely young women," Ulysses said.

He then began teasing Julia about watching all the young women attending the upcoming receptions and dinners already on schedule.

Since entering the White House Julia had delighted in entertaining. As a military wife she had done her duty without complaint—moving often and never having much to call her own. Now it was time to collect her just rewards. Besides, the country had been deprived of anything remotely like pleasure or fun during the war and she especially wanted to show how the nation would recover with her general in charge of Washington.

It was as if Julia herself had been born to the office.

389

She browbeat Congress to give her money to redecorate the White House, which had understandably been neglected for years. President Johnson's daughter had begun the work and Julia added her own touches.

She soon became famous for the receptions and levees (fashionable afternoon luncheons) she gave, and newspapers gleefully reported the details of the twenty-nine course dinners which were routinely served in the state dining room.

"Okay, Ulys. But I do not know if she is coming tonight and you may tease all you want but I shall keep a special eye on you for the next few days."

"I would expect nothing less, my dear." Ulysses put out his cigar and closed the door. He leaned down to kiss Julia goodnight. Then, almost as a second thought, the president of the United States slid into bed with her.

A week later, Julia Grant was not totally surprised to see the woman from her dreams entering the Blue Drawing Room. She and the president were in the larger oval reception room because they were hosting a dinner for a new diplomat, Lord Schmedley Wentworth-Smythe, from Great Britain.

The woman from Julia's dream looked as if she were with a party of several late-coming English guests and with the slow-moving line it would be a bit of a wait before she would reach their location.

Julia shivered but spied the Pinkerton men nearby.

Whenever possible, Julia shot quick glances back down the line and noted the woman was definitely older than the one in her dream. Her hair was also a darker blond but otherwise she resembled "dream woman" near enough to be a sister.

The stranger, dressed in a dark green brocade with a gauzy white-lace bertha outlining a lower neckline, made a spectacular impression. The revealed tops of her breasts alone were sensational. She carried a small white lace and string handbag and wore elbow-length satin gloves dyed to match her dress. Julia thought her regal bearing alone could make one feel frumpy.

But she thought she looked quite fetching herself in a new red velvet and white satin ball gown ornamented with pearls and diamonds and was determined not to feel intimidated.

She kept a smile on her face, nodding and speaking quietly as each person in the English group was announced. She had a knack for making people feel welcome and they responded to her sincerity.

The woman was still three or four people back in the line as the English group departed, and looked as if she might be alone. Julia could not help being surprised at that. A lady did not attend a formal presentation such as this alone.

However, before Julia could consider the implications, the woman reached the president and stood directly in front of him. She extended her gloved hand and made a motion as if to pull him closer. She tilted her face in his direction and toward him as if to whisper in his ear or kiss his cheek.

Julia tugged against her husband's elbow, gently at first then a bit more forcibly when he was slow to respond. No man could resist looking at the woman's décolletage, Julia thought. Not even her beloved.

The president's head moved closer to the woman's face, then stopped as he turned slightly in Julia's direction.

Grant turned his head a bit more toward his wife. "Mrs. Grant?" he asked under his breath. His voice was barely audible to his wife but she could hear the questioning tone.

The woman in the receiving line suddenly stiffened and Grant turned back in her direction.

"What? . . ." said President Grant.

"Catch her," said Julia. The woman, whose hand the president now held, began slumping, then she went tumbling slowly toward the floor.

A woman standing near the fireplace screamed—a high-pitched shriek, sending renewed shivers down Julia's spine.

The room suddenly became totally silent. The silence stretched as everyone and everything—the people, the tables, the fireplace, the chairs, the chandelier, the food, the drinks, the serving staff—waited, as if each person and item in the room held its collective breath for a giant heartbeat. Then the sudden noise of loud voices and muffled cries split the silent air like a melon being split by an axe.

Julia watched as first a shiny glint and then a dark stain appeared on the green brocade dress below the woman's left breast. She couldn't help the small gasp that escaped her lips when she saw the stain turning crimson red.

Several men pushed forward quickly surrounding the President and one man tried to pull Ulysses free from Julia's grasp. "No," she said, holding tight to her husband's arm. "I will not leave his side."

The man nearest to her said, "Madam, we must protect the president. He is our first priority."

"And my wife is your second priority," said Grant. His voice had that military timbre which meant it was to be obeyed.

Julia seldom ever heard her husband raise his voice since he left the army and she knew he meant business.

"I'm fine," he told her. "And," he looked at the Pinkerton detectives, "you must keep her safe and fine, too." Grant pulled Julia's arm from his. "It will be all right, Mrs. Grant."

Four detective agents quickly surrounded the president and moved him back into the great crosshalls. Two other agents led Julia a few steps behind the others, all were walking in synchronization.

"What happened in there?" she wanted to know.

No one answered.

"Was that woman shot?" Julia asked. "No," she answered her own question. "Surely I would have *heard* a shot. I do remember seeing a shiny looking object like a knife blade. She must have been stabbed, but why?"

The shouts and screams coming from the blue room became muffled as they covered the hallway distance.

One of the men with Julia cleared his throat and said, "We think the woman was trying to get close enough to the president to shoot him or to put a knife into his chest. We think she tried to assassinate him."

Julia shook her head, "No. She did not." They had

reached the great staircase leading up to their private quarters.

The agents looked at each other but did not respond to her objection that the woman had not tried to kill the president.

"Take Mrs. Grant upstairs," said the president. He turned and started for his office.

"Ulys?" Julia said.

Grant stopped and looked back, his face grim. "I'll come and talk to you as soon as I can," he said. He turned to the two men who had accompanied Julia out of the danger zone and gave the order to stay with Mrs. Grant until he could join her.

Both men saluted. "Yes, Sir."

The evening passed interminably slow for Julia. When Ulys didn't come and didn't come she decided to go downstairs. Her agent escorts were visibly upset but she ignored their pleas. Nothing could convince her to stay in her room once her mind was made up and nothing could stop her short of physical restraint.

As Julia reached the bottom of the staircase she met her husband.

"My dear, I was just about to come upstairs," he said and led his wife into the smaller reception room known as the Red Drawing Room. Julia sat in one of the new lyre-back Empire chairs she had recently purchased for the room. The president paced from the Duncan Phyfe sofa to the mahogany table and back again.

Julia soon realized the chair was not very comfortable and moved over to the sofa at right angles to the fireplace. Since the springlike day had by now turned quite cool, she was grateful Mr. Thompson, the head usher, had lit a small fire. "What have you found out about the woman?" Julia asked.

Her husband ceased his pacing and joined her on the sofa. "She was not trying to assassinate me nor was she killed by one of our people. Her death was by someone else's hand," the president said.

"How was that determined?"

"A man was seen throwing a dagger through the open French door, then he was spotted running from the White House."

Julia asked. "Do we even know who she is . . . or was?"

"Papers in the woman's purse say her name is or was Claire Lenander, recently moved here from Minnesota. She's been renting a room across the river, from a Mrs. Jo Ann Johnson," Grant said. "As to why she was at our reception, who knows? But I'm satisfied Robert Pinkerton will find out. He's very thorough."

Briefly forgetting her premonition, Julia's eyes grew moist. "Poor young thing, out for an evening with her friends, a chance to attend dinner at the White House and meet the president and she is killed."

"She can't be too innocent, she *was* killed. When they catch the killer he'll eventually talk."

"Could it have been a mistaken identity? The person who killed her thought Miss Lenander was someone else?"

"Anything is possible," Grant said. "Pinkerton's men are checking every angle."

"Is Allan Pinkerton himself coming to Washington?"

"Probably not yet. His son, Robert, is most capable. He is every bit as good an investigator as his father and I trust him implicitly."

Grant stood and took Julia's hand, helping her up. "Now, Mrs. Grant. Time for you to get some rest. Let me take you back upstairs to your room."

Julia reached up to pat her husband's face. "What about you, my husband? When will you get some rest?"

"In a short while. The British contingent still wants to have a few words with me. While we all regret this young woman's tragic death, the affairs of government must continue."

For the next couple of days Julia kept herself busy planning a birthday dinner for her general on April 27. The menu had been decided finally and Julia double-checked her writing before sending it to be hand printed, one for each of the sixty or so guests who were invited.

She read the list, moving her lips silently: clams followed by crab soup and assorted appetizers. The next course would be river trout with hollandaise sauce, potatoes and cucumbers. Then a fillet of beef, some roast chicken, peas in butter, veal sweetbreads, green beans and asparagus; followed by sherbet to cleanse the palate. Next would be squab and lettuce salad and assorted fruits in compote and plum jelly. Finally, there would be assorted ice creams, fruits, petits fours, and birthday cake and coffee. Each course would be accompanied by the appropriate wines from sauterne and amontillado, to Johannisberger and Ernest Jeroy. The president and his special cronies would retire to the library with brandy, cigars, and more coffee. My friends and I shall have bon bons, chocolates, and champagne, she thought.

Julia still worried about the young woman who had died but her official duties could not be neglected. Fortunately, her military background stood her well when things grew hectic.

Soon, when Julia determined the president had not learned any more about the young woman, she decided to look into matters herself.

She dressed carefully in her light gray cashmere traveling dress so as not to call too much attention to herself as the president's wife and took along a light blue cashmere shawl in case it turned cool. At the last moment she pushed a plain black felt hat on her head. Her maid, Bethany, was happy for the opportunity to get outside the grounds for a short time.

Julia ordered her two-seater carriage brought around to the gate near the south portico. She waited while Mr. Thompson unlocked the gate. It had taken some doing but she'd finally convinced Ulys to lock the gates, giving them a measure of privacy.

It was a lovely day in early spring, the cherry blossoms along the avenue had just burst forth and filled the air with their light scent. The azure sky above was filled with fluffy white cotton clouds reminding Julia of the skies back home in Missouri.

In a few minutes they reached the boardinghouse where young Miss Lenander had lived. Bethany went to the door to speak to the lady of the house. A Mrs. Johnson, thought Julia, if she had remembered correctly. Bethany was to inquire about looking over Miss Lenander's room.

Mrs. Johnson came rushing out, "Oh, Mrs. Grant. Please come in out of the hot sun. And don't pay no never mind to my front parlor. My lady's sewing circle came here yesterday and I just ain't had time to put things back in order." The older lady was slender and fluttered her arms like a hummingbird's wings. Her salt and pepper hair had been neatly pulled back into a braid. She had dark eyes and glasses attached to her gingham dress front. "Oh my, Mrs. Grant. I just can't believe it's really you that's come up here to my house." The woman fluttered her hands now instead of her arms and looked as if she might pass out—although whether from delight or dismay, Julia was not sure.

After going inside, Julia sat and the older lady soon brought a small tray of lemonade and wonderful lemon sugar cookies. When Mrs. Johnson had calmed down a bit, although her face was too chalky white to be normal, they made small talk.

Julia wanted the recipe for the cookies. Mrs. Johnson found a paper and pencil and Julia printed it exactly as Mrs. Johnson recited it to her. Only then did the two women talk about Miss Claire Lenander.

"I thought some of them policemen would come here but not one ever has," said Mrs. Johnson.

"I am most surprised to learn that. No one ever came to examine Claire's things?" asked Julia.

"I guessed it weren't important," said Mrs. Johnson. "But then, I ain't ever knowed a person what got murdered before."

"How long had Miss Lenander lived here?"

"Just a few months. Before Christmas I'd say." Mrs. Johnson scrunched her face and thought a moment. "I remember now it were only a few days after Thanksgiving because she mentioned helping her Ma make pies for their holiday dinner back home."

"Less than six months then, since April is nearly half gone."

"That sounds about right," Mrs. Johnson agreed.

The women walked to the stairs and climbed, continuing then down the long hall to the room where Claire had lived. Mrs. Johnson opened the door and they entered. The late morning sun streaming in the east window made the room cheerful and Julia could see the girl had neat and tidy ways. Everything was in place and not a speck of dust showed anywhere.

"Miss Claire's ma brought her up right, she took care of her things." Mrs. Johnson glanced around the room. "She never hurt none of my things either."

Julia was not sure how to ask the next question but thought it important. "Did she have any gentlemen callers?"

"One special young man. Miss Claire went walking with him but I ain't seen him lately."

"Do you know his name?"

"David . . . Wood I think she told me. He'd been in the army and fought in Tennessee."

"Which side did he fight on?"

Mrs. Johnson shrugged, "Once I heard him say Mr. Lincoln deserved to die for what he did." She whispered the words as if Julia might think they originated from her. "I ain't seen him for about a month or so, though. He must've gone off or something. Miss Claire she moped and cried around here for days, then she got all excited about something a couple of days ago. I never did know what perked her up because I never did see that boy again."

Julia asked to be left alone while she looked around hoping to gain some feel for the dead girl. "I promise I won't mess things up and—"

"Now you go on and do whatever you think is necessary, Mrs. Grant. I'm sure it'll be okay."

The woman hurried back down the hall and down the stairs. Julia sat in the one comfortable-looking chair, an oak rocker. "Claire, Claire? Why would anyone want to kill a lovely young woman like you?" she asked aloud.

In a few moments Julia walked to the tall oak wardrobe and opened the long door on the right side. Two dresses hung there, a plain-looking one made of calico, obviously a day or work dress. The other, a best dress to be worn for Sunday church and socials, was a dark blue taffeta with lighter blue bows and a large white lace collar. A dark gray work shirt and a white broadcloth blouse hung alongside the dresses and two crinoline petticoats.

"Wonder where that beautiful green brocade dress she wore the other night came from," Julia said. "It definitely was new and looked made to order."

Pushing aside the dresses, Julia saw a large carpet bag. Without thinking twice she pulled the bag out and placed it on the bed. When she opened it she saw a pair of leather riding boots laying on top of some newspapers. When she lifted out the boots and raised up the papers, she gasped. Two stacks of greenback paper money sat on the bottom of the bag.

Julia had never seen that much money in one pile in her life. "What? Where?" She took one of the twenties out, looked at it closely. The bill looked strange but she could not explain why she thought so. On impulse she put the greenback into her purse. She quickly replaced the money, papers, and boots and closed the carpet bag, placing it back into the wardrobe.

It felt quite strange taking that twenty dollar bill but she consoled herself that she wasn't stealing. She just wanted to show it to Ulys and try to understand why the money looked strange. Besides, it wasn't as if Miss Lenander had any use of the money now. Julia thanked Mrs. Johnson and left. Bethany headed the horses back up the avenue to the White House.

The Grants always spent thirty minutes to an hour each evening in Julia's bedroom. They had begun the practice when the children were small and it became a special time of day for the whole family to be together and talk over events which had transpired. With the two older boys, Ulysses, Jr., and Frederick, away at school only Nellie and Jesse joined their parents most evenings. Nellie, a young girl at fifteen, about to emerge into womanhood, and Jesse, a gangly twelve year old full of pranks, draped themselves across the foot of Julia's bed while their father sat in a nearby Chippendale padded chair.

The youngsters related the tidbits of the day with Jesse making them all laugh at his recital of how he had led two Philadelphia newspaper reporters on a merry chase around the grounds and back corridors as they tried to get the story on the death of the young woman.

When the children left to dress for dinner, Julia

confessed her transgression of the day to Ulys and handed the twenty dollar greenback to him.

He took the money, looked at and felt it, then suddenly got up and left the room without a word.

"My goodness," Julia said. "'That certainly is not the reaction I expected."

When he didn't return in a few minutes, Julia dressed for dinner. Tonight's dinner guests included her father, Frederick Dent, who was visiting from St. Louis, and a couple of old friends from Philadelphia and their wives.

As Bethany completed buttoning the back of the pink silk dress Julia wore, Ulysses tapped on her door.

"My dear?" he said. "May I come in?"

"Of course, my darling," Julia said, opening the door herself. "Is something wrong?"

Bethany left to attend Nellie.

"That twenty dollar bill you gave me was counterfeit," Grant said. "I called Mr. Wood of the Secret Service over here to take a look at it and he confirmed my suspicions."

"What on earth was that young woman doing with all that counterfeit money?"

"Unfortunately I'm afraid that's what got her killed."

"And she wasn't trying to harm you?" Julia asked.

"No. I don't think so."

"I really never thought so either. In my dream she was trying to warn you of something."

"But in your dream she was an old flame of mine, wasn't she?"

"Yes," Julia smiled. "But that was in my dream

and dreams rarely are totally true. Usually they are only guidelines."

"Of course," said the president. "I'm wondering. If Robert Pinkerton takes the counterfeit money and looks deeply enough, he should find out what Miss Lenander wanted to warn me of."

A few days later Robert Pinkerton made his report to President Grant and the president conveyed the news to Julia that evening after the children were in bed.

"Pinkerton discovered a plot to wreck the economic gains we've made and to discredit my treasury secretary," Ulysses said.

"By dumping huge amounts of counterfeit greenbacks all over Washington?"

"Exactly. Two of the culprits were caught. They had been hired by the Democrats in hopes it would destroy my credibility."

"And what was Miss Lenander's role in all of this?"

"Pinkerton thinks she was in love with one of the counterfeiters. Seems as though he was killed a short time ago by one of his co-conspirators." Grant lit a cigar and opened the doors leading out to the balcony. "They think when Claire got up the nerve to go through her lover's things she found some of the money. She decided to come and speak to me about it."

"She had a good plan," said Julia. "I am sure she took some of the money and bought that lovely dress she wore that night. She had to be able to come here and look as if she belonged."

"I imagine that's so. Pinkerton did find two of the

counterfeit bills in the purse Miss Lenander carried that night. We don't know exactly how, but somehow the other counterfeiters must have discovered her plan and killed her."

"Poor girl. I'm just happy I found out she harbored no malice toward my husband."

"Yes," said Grant. "Your curiosity in going to her home and finding that stack of phony greenbacks led Pinkerton down the right trail."

Grant walked to his wife's bedside and pulled a paper from his inner coat pocket. "In fact, Robert Pinkerton received this telegram just tonight." He handed the paper to Julia.

She read the message aloud. "An excellent investigator. Hire Julie Dent Grant on the spot. Signed Allan Pinkerton."

"Oh, my," Julia blushed.

"I wired back that you had a full-time job here taking care of me," said Grant.

"It's the only job I want, dear," said Julia.

JAN GRAPE

JAN GRAPE is a short story specialist, with eighteen of them appearing in anthologies including *Lethal Ladies I & II* and *Midnight Louie's Pet Detectives*. Her story, "A Front Row Seat," which appeared in the Mickey Spillane/Max Allan Collins collection, *Vengeance Is Hers*, won the Anthony award and was nominated for the Shamus. With Dean James, she is co-editor of the nonfiction book about mystery writers, *Deadly Women*, which was nominated for the Edgar and won the Macavity award. She is a columnist for *Mystery Scene* magazine. Jan and her husband, Elmer, own Mysteries & More bookstore in Austin, Texas.

"I wanted a First Lady with a Southern background to whom I could relate. Lady Bird Johnson is still alive and kicking up her heels in Texas, so I couldn't write about her. While reading short biographies of several of them, in order to make my choice, Julia Dent Grant stood out in my mind. She wasn't Southern—being from Missouri—but many intriguing facts about her began to resonate within me and the next thing I knew, there she was, alive on the page."

BLOOD IN BUZZARD'S BAY; OR, SWEETS TO THE SWEET

---∾∾∾---

P. M. CARLSON

OH, HOW I wept when Baby Ruth died! She was such a dear child, a tomboy, like myself at her age, and hadn't an enemy in the world, or so we believed.

Of course I would never have met her at all, if it hadn't been for the heat, and for the railroad strike that had so cruelly canceled my tour to the Midwestern states as Lady Macbeth. I was stranded in New York City, where the sun, as the Bard says, was a fair hot wench in flame-colored taffeta that whole summer of 1894. Lordy, it was *hot!* I reckon steamed clams were more comfortable than I was that July. My cat Keystone and I were staying in a top-floor room of a tenement in Water Street, for much as I might prefer cooler quarters, the only position I had been able to obtain was as a living statue in Mr. Oscar Hammerstein's tableaux vivants at Koster and Bial's music hall. And Mr. Hammerstein did not pay well.

On Fourteenth Street that afternoon I felt as over-heated as Falstaff, sweating and larding the lean earth as I walked along, although I wore my lightest dotted Swiss shirtwaist, stylish enough for Charles Dana Gibson's art. I paused at a grocer's stand that offered melons and strawberries. Did I dare spend the last of my pennies? There was already a shortage of meat because of the railroad strike, and fruit might become very dear as well. In his wicker basket on my arm, Keystone mewed impatiently.

"I apologize, old fellow, but some of us require more than fishheads and the odd saucer of whiskey to survive," I told him.

A little girl, about six, was looking at me with wide-set sad eyes. "Is it a cat in there, Ma'am?" she asked.

"Yes it is," I said with a smile.

"Oh, Ma'am, please, may I pet him?"

"If your hands are clean, and if you keep him close by," I told her, for Keystone could be mischievous.

She wiped her little hands on her pinafore and held them out to receive my big tabby-striped tom-cat. He apparently decided that it was too hot to go exploring, and when she knelt on the pavement he began to purr at the stroke of her little fingers. She said, "When I grow up I'll have a cat of my own. Won't I, Papa?"

"Of course you will, Lucy," said the grocer, a scrawny fellow in shirtsleeves, apron, and dark hat.

"Bridget! Is it Bridget?" inquired a new voice. I turned to see a sweet bucktoothed smile and curly brown hair.

"Why, Harry Evans! Lordy, it's been a long time!"

"And are you treading the boards, Bridget?"

"Alas, Harry, I was to be in Minneapolis today, playing the wicked Lady Macbeth. But you fellows in the railroad union have stopped the trains, and I am stranded here in New York, reduced to appearing in tableaux vivants."

"Oh, Ma'am, is that true? You are on the stage?" asked Lucy from the pavement, where she still stroked my blissful tomcat.

"I am indeed, Lucy," I acknowledged.

"Oh, that's lovely! No wonder you are such a beautiful lady!" exclaimed the little girl.

Wasn't that a sweet thing to say? I didn't feel beautiful at the moment, red hair frizzed in the heat and damp skin chafed by the weight of my secret pocket containing my Colt and other needful objects. But Harry agreed with little Lucy. "Beautiful indeed!" he enthused. "Bridget, you must join us tomorrow to see the special Independence Day program at Manhattan Beach! But I am sorry that our strike has inconvenienced you. Still, you must admit, great things are happening! The workingman may at last get his due!"

"And what about the working girl?" I asked tartly. "How can I tour the Midwestern states and earn money, and visit my dear niece Juliet in Missouri, if the trains aren't running?"

"They'll run better than ever when we're paid a living wage."

The grocer asked politely, "May I help you, gentlemen?" For the first time I noticed a shy, balding fellow with a dark mustache who had sidled up in my boisterous friend's shadow.

"Not today, thank you," said Harry, and tugged at the bald man's arm. "Bridget, this is Simon Hotchkiss. He used to be a fireman like me on the New York Central, but two years ago he went to work for Pullman. Hotch, Miss Bridget Mooney is an ornament to the stage and the light of my life."

"I'm pleased to meet you, Mr. Hotchkiss." I offered my hand.

Too shy to meet my eyes, he kissed my hand clumsily and murmured, "Likewise," as he blushed the color of beet soup all the way up to his receding hairline. I took pity on him and returned to our subject. "You are both railroad men," I said. "Tell me, is this strike—"

Just then Keystone bounded up onto the piles of fruit and sent a melon rolling down to splatter in the dust. The grocer bellowed "Scat!" in a most unsympathetic tone. I looked around, annoyed that the seemingly reliable little Lucy had let him escape. But my fickle young admirer had disappeared.

I returned Keystone to his wicker basket and attempted to assuage the grocer, but he demanded his money, which Hotchkiss gallantly paid. "Thank you, sir," said the grocer, doffing his hat.

We retired to Danny Doyle's establishment and ordered bottles of Danny's suspiciously pale Guinness. Under the table I slipped a saucer of it to my undeserving but appreciative cat and said, "When do you think I'll be able to travel in the Midwest again?"

"It depends on Mr. Pullman," Harry explained. "He keeps cutting wages and refuses arbitration!"

I sipped daintily at the alleged Guinness. "Why,

Harry, I heard he built a fine town near Chicago for his workers."

Harry snorted, "Tell her, Hotch!"

The bashful Mr. Hotchkiss could not look me in the eye but seemed to draw courage from his Guinness. " 'Tis true, Miss Mooney," he told his bottle. "Mr. Pullman built us a town around his factory. Our houses are company houses, the churches we attend are company churches, the water we drink is company water, even the cemeteries are company cemeteries. Mr. Pullman pays our wages, and we pay him for rent and water and gas. For a while it wasn't so bad."

"Except that Mr. Pullman treated you all like slaves!" growled my fiery Harry.

"Well, yes, that's true," Mr. Hotchkiss admitted, and rubbed his shiny forehead. "There's always been grumbling about that. But things weren't impossible until the wage cuts. I left the New York Central two years ago to join Pullman, and today I'm getting only half what they paid me then."

"Almost everyone has had wage cuts," I pointed out, thinking of the pittance I received from Mr. Hammerstein, and lucky to have that. Thousands were out of work across the nation, even before the strike.

"But Pullman workers have another problem." Mr. Hotchkiss had warmed to his subject, or the Guinness had warmed him. Now he appeared positively indignant. "Pullman wages went down, but Pullman rents didn't go down at all! Some rates even went up! Little children are starving!"

Well, I wasn't very surprised that Mr. Pullman

wanted to get his rents. After all, it takes a considerable amount of money to live a gentleman's life, and gentlemen don't expect to give up their luxuries because of a few difficulties their workmen are having, do they? On the other hand, it seemed rather rude of Mr. Pullman to distribute millions in profits to his stockholders just now, when the workingmen were already restless from earlier cuts, and when Mr. Eugene Debs had just won a victory for his American Railway Union over one of the major railroads.

"Our union is in sympathy with the Pullman workers," Harry said. "We are refusing to run trains unless the Pullman cars are taken off. And I believe that if we stand firm and united now, we'll be treated like men at last."

"He'll never treat us like men," said Mr. Hotchkiss gloomily.

"He will if we stand firm and united!"

"United?" Hotch said. "Do you really think the Knights of Labor will support us, when we didn't support their strike eight years ago?"

"That was different!" Harry yelled.

Well, much as I liked Harry's vision of glorious unity among the splintered unions, he and Hotch were so far from unity now, they were about to come to blows. Hastily I mentioned a common foe. "Aren't you afraid that the government will take action?"

"No, that's the beauty of it!" Harry's enthusiastic bucktoothed grin was back. "The strike is based in Chicago, where people understand the problems. The mayor himself helped organize a clinic and donated 25,000 pounds of flour and meat. And the governor of Illinois is sympathetic to us as well."

"What about Washington?" I asked.

"Well, of course those fellows have been bribed by business interests, but workingmen helped elect President Cleveland. He knows the importance of our vote to his party."

Mr. Hotchkiss nodded solemnly and told his bottle, "The president is a family man. He'll stand by our families. Er, look!" With the briefest glance toward me he opened a little wallet and a few small photographs and a medallion fell out.

"Oh, Mr. Hotchkiss, is this sweet child your daughter?" I asked, picking up a vaguely familiar photograph of a little girl of three years or so with soft curls and pretty wide set eyes.

"No, my niece. But look, this is what I wanted to show you." He nudged the medallion toward me as he returned the photographs to the wallet.

It was a souvenir from the opening of Chicago's Columbian Exposition last year, showing the rotund President Cleveland, his lovely young wife Frances, and their little daughter Ruth, whom the nation had taken to its heart. "Baby Ruth" was written across the medallion in handsome flowing script.

"Yes, I see," I said, thinking longingly of my own little niece, and how much I would like to see her. "Mr. Cleveland surely understands our love for our families, and understands that we must earn enough to keep them healthy and safe."

"Just so!" said Harry stoutly.

Yet that night as I ate the strawberries I'd hooked from Lucy's sour-tempered papa while he was tipping his hat to Hotch, I mused to Keystone that Mr. Cleveland cared for his wife and children by investing in stocks and bonds with his rich friends. What kept the Cleveland family healthy and safe might not be the same as what kept Hotch's little niece healthy and safe.

Independence Day was hot and steamy too. I donned a striped muslin walking dress with sleeves and neckline that were not in the latest fashion but had the advantage of admitting the breezes if breezes happened by. Harry, in shirtsleeves, was already at the appointed corner. He handed me a little American flag. "It will soon be Independence Day indeed for the railway workers!" he cried gaily, waving his own little flag.

I thought it too hot to do anything as strenuous as waving a flag. But Mr. Hotchkiss, when he arrived, looked like a thunderstorm, his bashful air gone. He wasn't waving a flag, he was waving a newspaper.

"Harry, look!" he exclaimed. "The traitor! The idiot! How could Cleveland do such a thing?" He jabbed a finger at the headline, which blared, Troops Sent to Chicago!

"Perhaps it is just to keep order," I said hopefully.

Harry looked stunned as he scanned the article. He shook his head. "No, Bridget. The attorney general says the strike is interfering with the mails. That's not true!"

Hotch nodded vehemently. "Mr. Debs has forbidden us to interfere with the mails or any other federal activity."

Harry said, "Even if it's true that Cleveland sent the troops to maintain order, it's like waving a shirt at a bull. How can the men contain themselves?"

It sounded as though he was having difficulty containing himself too, and there wasn't a troop in sight. Even bashful Hotch had an angry glint in his eye. "Now we're done for!"

"No, we must fight! We must strike at the traitor Cleveland!" Harry declared.

"Oh, now, Harry, it's no use." Hotch seemed uneasy at this unpatriotic suggestion.

"Hotch, be a man! The traitor gets our vote and then lets us workingmen go to the devil! Our babies are starving!"

"But he's the president, with Secret Service men all about him!" Hotch pointed out.

"Hotch is right, Harry," I urged. "Let's go see the show and consider this problem tomorrow."

"How can we enjoy Independence Day if we are being treated like slaves?" Harry demanded, and made as though to throw his little flag to the ground.

Hotch caught his arm just in time. "Don't be rash, Harry!"

"And the problem may be with Mr. Cleveland's advisors," I said. "I found that to be the case when I worked for President Grant. He was badly advised."

Harry's blue eyes and Hotch's brown ones alike snapped toward me. Harry demanded, "You worked for a president, Bridget?"

Too late I realized how foolish my admission had been. "Well, only briefly, and I really worked for Mrs. Grant," I said.

"But you know how things are done at the White House!"

In my head, I could almost see my late sensible Aunt Mollie signaling wildly to avoid any involvement in anti-presidential schemes. I said, "Things have changed too much since Grant's day. Why, the Clevelands themselves closed off the White House grounds because visitors pestered the babies. Besides, isn't revenge for the workingman a workingman's job?"

Harry said, "There are ladies who work at the Pullman Car Works too. And I have heard talk of a union for actors."

"Yes, but—"

There was no stopping his bucktoothed enthusiasm. "And no one will suspect a woman. And an actress could play any sort of a role."

"Harry, I'm sorry, but assassinations are not my line of work!" I said firmly, and—well, yes, you're right, but that was a different situation altogether. Besides, the White House was in Washington, which was probably even hotter than New York.

Harry bubbled on as though I hadn't spoken. "Hotch, don't you think this is a good idea? With Bridget inside we'll know his every move!"

Hotch was still reluctant, and pointed out, "She didn't work for the president; she worked for Mrs. Grant."

"That's why I know this is impossible!" I exclaimed.

"But Bridget, you'll make it possible!"

I tried logic. "No assassinations. After all, would Vice President Stevenson be any better for the workingman?"

"Probably not," said Harry, somewhat subdued. "It would be better to force Cleveland to help us. But how? What weak points does he have?"

Hotch's dark eyes suddenly gleamed bright as his

shiny forehead, and he said, "He's a family man. He loves his wife and children."

"What difference does that make?" Harry asked. "They aren't even in the White House. They're at the summer place at Buzzard's Bay on Cape Cod."

"So much the better!" Hotch exclaimed. "No Secret Service agents there, only the staff! And the Old Colony Railroad stops right on their grounds. We'll kidnap Baby Ruth!"

Well, did you ever hear of such a silly idea?

But Harry stared at meek little Hotch for a moment, dazzled by the simple beauty of his plan, then began to pound his friend on the back in congratulations. "Yes, yes! Cleveland will do anything for that child!"

Hotch said, "We'll make it clear: We won't harm his family if he'll stop harming our families!"

Harry looked at me. "Of course we will back you up, Bridget. And we can get secret money from the union men to pay you, can't we, Hotch?"

In my mind sensible Aunt Mollie shut up suddenly. Money? And after all, this plot would never work. Everyone knew that the president was personally guarded by Secret Service men, and that even Mrs. Cleveland was accompanied by the cautious, watchful White House staff servants who had succeeded in enforcing the brand-new restrictions to keep visitors off the White House grounds. Besides, if these union men insisted on wasting their money on such a plan, who deserved to profit more than a hard-working young lady with no union of her own? After all, as an employer Mr. Oscar Hammerstein wasn't much better than Mr. Pullman, he paid so little for the hours we spent in the hot limelights. Like Hotch, I had a little niece to think of.

Besides, when perspiration trickles down a girl's back, she can't help but think longingly of Cape Cod.

I cleared my throat. "It will take me a few days to obtain a position with Mrs. Cleveland's staff," I said. "And I'll require a hundred dollars in advance."

"Done!" Harry was full of enthusiasm again. "We can ride the Old Colony train from Boston. Bridget will get the baby secretly and hand her over when the train stops at the president's station, and—well, we'll make a plan and all escape easily, before they realize the child is gone!"

His peculiar confidence that the plan would work made me shiver. "Let's not take a child, Harry. Why not kidnap Mrs. Cleveland instead?"

"No, no, it must be Ruth," said Hotch.

"People are quicker to ransom children," Harry explained.

I wasn't sure Cleveland would be so quick. A friend from Buffalo had told me the sad story of Maria Halpin, who had been perhaps too friendly with the young bachelor Grover Cleveland and his married law partner Oscar Folsom, the same Folsom whose daughter was now Mrs. Cleveland. Maria had given birth to a boy whom she named Oscar Folsom Cleveland—isn't that interesting? Cleveland had declined marriage but, as a bachelor, agreed to take responsibility for the boy, whether or not he was the father. He'd paid an orphanage to take the boy—perhaps his son, perhaps his future wife's half-brother—and Cleveland was rid of him. Now I ask you, does that sound like a man who would be quick to ransom his child?

But it made no difference, for the plot would prove impossible. And it was so hot in New York. I beat down my misgivings and agreed.

And so a few days later, a hundred dollars nestling next to my Colt in my secret pocket, I was at Gray Gables dressed in a domestic's black dress, having found a temporary position as assistant children's nurse. The Clevelands' nurse, Gertie, had unexpectedly taken ill and—well, yes, it was quite convenient for us, but it was a mere digestive disturbance; don't we all get them in the summertime? I had made Gertie's acquaintance on her day off, and we had shared a lemonade in the little town of Buzzard's Bay shortly before she was struck by dyspepsia. And— very well, if you must know, it was syrup of ipecac, just enough in her lemonade to make her too queasy to work. And my Aunt Mollie would agree with you, it was not entirely proper, but what do you expect a poor girl to do when she desperately needs to obtain a position very quickly, and the position is already filled?

As I was saying, I had been hired on at Gray Gables. And oh, it was so much more pleasant and cool than the city had been! The air nimbly and sweetly recommended itself unto our gentle senses, as Shakespeare tells us. The house was a perfectly splendid summer place, with a multitude of gray-shingled gables, lots of windows, and a veranda that wrapped around and provided lovely views across the Monument River and the Narrows. Even the cellar was pleasant for those who worked or slept there, because the land dropped down toward the shore, allowing airy windows even in the below-stairs rooms. The house's best feature was possibly its advantageous situation on a promontory where it could catch the refreshing salty sea breeze that blew steadily up Buzzard's Bay.

Or possibly its best feature was its mistress. Frances Folsom Cleveland was a few—well, a dozen—years younger than I, about to turn thirty that very July. She was spirited and genial, with a pretty, animated face and a glowing smile. Her person was tall and well-formed, not at all waiflike, but hearty enough to cope with a two-hundred-fifty pound president. She was kindhearted, and very solicitous of her maid Gertie's health, even visiting her daily in her below-stairs sickroom. "No, no, Gertie! You mustn't strain yourself. Mandy is here to help," she said, indicating me.

I had bleached my red hair, added a Swedish lilt to my voice, and introduced myself as the widowed Mrs. Manderson, for Bridget Mooney was too Irish a name for the elegant Cleveland household. I'd told Gertie that like her I was a child's nurse by trade, but my young charge had been sent off to summer in Europe and I'd taken advantage of my freedom to visit cool Cape Cod.

Mrs. Cleveland continued, "You must rest, Gertie. Besides, we don't want the little ones to catch your dreadful cold!"

"Thank you, Mrs. Cleveland," Gertie gasped feebly, her complexion green about the mouth and eyes.

"Now, just get the rest you need, Gertie, and drink plenty of liquids," I said kindly, replenishing the glass of lemonade at her bedside. Then I returned to the nursery with Mrs. Cleveland, where baby Esther's nurse, Annie, watched both children.

The careful mother was pleased to see that neither of the president's children showed signs of succumbing to Gertie's mysterious ailment. Baby Esther was a fine plump baby whose sweet babbling kept her mother wreathed in smiles. And little Ruth—oh, dear little doomed Ruth!—was a lively child not yet three years old, already showing her mother's ready smile as well as her mother's love for the numerous Cleveland pets. Mrs. Cleveland adored animals and birds, and I believe my striped cat in his wicker basket provided a recommendation as strong as my laudatory though forged letters when she hired me.

Harry and Hotch had asked me to learn the rhythms of life at Gray Gables these first days, and on the third night to meet secretly with them to decide the details of the kidnapping.

The news from Chicago about the strike was dreadful. The Illinois governor objected strenuously to Cleveland's federal troops, claiming that their presence violated states' rights, and that they were making the situation worse. Eugene Debs struggled to keep his American Railway Union men peaceable, and said that any man who committed an act of violence would be expelled from the union. But in addition to his strikers, there were thousands jobless in Chicago, and it's always been my belief that lack of money drives one to actions that may not be considered proper, such as setting fire to the famed Columbian Exposition buildings. Only the year before, the alabaster city on the lake had been the delight of the world with its promise of a bright future; now scores of the buildings were smoldering ruins.

In the East, most trains ran, though the heat wave did not break.

But at Gray Gables the salt breeze blew and we lived in comfort and peace—except for the shouts of Ruth and her little friends, the laughter of Mrs. Cleveland and her visitors, the yapping of dogs and mewing of cats, the chirping of birds, and the retching of poor Gertie in her sickroom below stairs.

My task was to watch little Ruth, which required some vigilance, for she was an inquisitive child, and often chose courses of action that were not suitable for her tender years. She was desirous of climbing an apple tree on the grounds, and if I looked away for a moment I might find her dangling from a lower branch, trying to get her little feet up the trunk. Fortunately, Keystone, as the newest pet, distracted the little girl from more dangerous pursuits. Whenever Mrs. Cleveland's duties permitted, she would join Annie and me near baby Esther's carriage and watch as Ruth ran up to my drowsing cat, calling "Keythtone!" in her pretty lisping voice and then energetically attempting to stroke him. He would suffer her clumsy attentions with forbearance for a time, then rise with a disdainful flick of his tail and whisk up the steps to the high verandah. Her mother would console the little pouting girl by suggesting a game of hide-and-seek.

"I hope my husband can come here soon!" Mrs. Cleveland confided. "He loves his children so."

"I'm sure he does, Madam," I said, hoping she was right for the railway workers' sake. But I couldn't help remembering poor Maria Halpin. When they took her son away, Maria had fought to have him returned to her. Instead, Cleveland's lawyers committed her to an institution for the mentally deranged. Now, I reckon that I or even Mrs. Cleveland beside me might also struggle mightily to regain our children, don't you agree? But of course we're just foolish females, and the gentlemen who supported Mr. Cleveland must have been right, and not at all deranged, no indeed.

Later that day danger struck at me from an unexpected quarter. Mrs. Cleveland made her visits at five-thirty, often accompanied by the children and their nurses. But my eagerness turned to dismay when I learned we were to call on the famed Joe Jefferson and his family at his handsome summer home, Crow's Nest. Although Ruth had great fun with the Jefferson grandchildren, and Mrs. Cleveland thoroughly enjoyed the noted comedian's company, I quaked the whole time, for I had met the illustrious portrayer of Rip Van Winkle backstage on several occasions. Lordy, what a terrifying visit that was for me! I breathed a sigh of relief when we left Crow's Nest, my secret undiscovered.

But it was Mrs. Cleveland herself who made me think our unlikely plot might succeed. The third evening, while Esther's nurse prepared the baby for bed, Mrs. Cleveland decided to indulge little Ruth's wish to say goodnight to the horsies. "Come along, Mandy," she said to me, and the three of us strolled to the stable. Ruth and Mrs. Cleveland chatted happily as she lifted the child to pat the equine noses, but when she put her daughter down the young mother glanced at me and said, in her kind way, "Why, Mandy! You look quite distressed! What is the matter?"

"Nothing, Madam. It is only that I miss my little niece Juliet, who lives far away in Missouri and also loves horses. I would so enjoy seeing her again!"

Of course that was only half the truth, for now I realized that there were gaps in the Gray Gables safety measures, and that Harry and Hotch, inflamed by the army's atrocities in Chicago, would want to go through with the plot. There might be great pain in store for sweet little Ruth and her kind mother. Mrs. Cleveland said sympathetically, "Well, Mandy, you know that we need you here just now, while Gertie is indisposed, but you will soon be able to visit your niece."

"Yes, Madam, if your husband settles the railroad strike."

"Oh, that's true, it's so inconvenient! But my darling husband says it is legal for them to strike, so long as they don't interfere with the mails or with interstate commerce. But if they do interfere, he says that if it takes the entire army of the United States to deliver a postal card in Chicago, that card will be delivered." Her pretty face brightened. "Mandy, you must send a postal card to little Juliet! We'll find one with horses."

"Oh, Madam, that's a lovely thought! Thank you!"

"Yes. You shall come with us in the carriage to the Buzzard's Bay post office tomorrow." Then a worried frown appeared on the young mother's face, and she glanced about.

I pointed to the sole of a small boot pecking out

from a gunnysack that had once held oats. Mrs. Cleveland winked at me and called out in mock distress, "Oh, dear, I can't find Ruth!"

The burlap bag wriggled mightily and the little beaming face popped out, sprinkled with oat bran. Mrs. Cleveland laughed merrily and scooped her up. "Oh, Ruth, you are such a little tomboy! Mandy, tell me, were you a tomboy?"

"Oh, yes indeed, Madam. I enjoyed hide-and-seek, and games of tag, and climbing trees." It seemed best not to mention my other athletic achievements, such as toting heavy trays of drinks in Uncle Mike's saloon or learning to shoot squirrels in the Missouri woods or performing the dances that rich Banker Healey thought it amusing for a little red-headed girl to perform for him, privately. Perhaps the president with his bastard son and long bachelorhood would have understood, but he had made sure that Mrs. Cleveland's upbringing was sheltered from such things, or so I hoped.

She was smiling now at her memories. "Yes, I too loved climbing trees. And leaping into great piles of leaves in the fall!" She nuzzled Ruth, then flicked some bran from the child's hair. "And my mama would scold and brush me clean too!"

Well, who could resist such a pair? Mrs. Cleveland's charm would surely convince the president to bend to the workers' demands. How could he allow this sweet mother and child to be rent asunder?

But the newspapers reported that in Chicago, troops had fired into an unarmed crowd of strikers and their families. Men and women were killed, and babies trampled. Cleveland's army was out of control.

Late that night, after telling the watchful chief

steward that I needed a stroll to alleviate an attack of insomnia, I walked quietly from the house. No one challenged me, and the house remained silent. Even poor Gertie's retching had subsided for a time.

I followed the moonlit shore toward the estuary, where, I was told, the president enjoyed fishing. At the appointed place, Harry and Hotch were waiting by their green rowboat. Harry asked eagerly, "What news? Can we do it soon, Bridget?"

"Well, it is difficult," I said. "There are so many servants and gardeners and visitors about." I searched for reasons that the plot would be impossible, for I truly wanted little Ruth and her charming mother to escape the pain.

But Hotch broke in first. "How is little Ruth? Can you bring along her favorite toys?"

Well, that was a kind thought. I said, "I'll try, Hotch, but it will complicate things further."

"No, no, keep it simple, for we must act soon!" Harry told us. "This is the ideal moment. Our foes have shown themselves for the evil men they are."

"You mean because the troops fired on the crowd?" I asked.

"That, and much more since!" he exclaimed. "First, Mr. Pullman has rejected all appeals for arbitration, and has lost whatever sympathy he had. Second, Mr. Debs has convinced the Knights of Labor to join us."

"The Knights! That's good," I said.

But Hotch boomed, "Those men won't leave their jobs for us, whatever their leaders say," and I suspected he was right.

Harry ignored his pessimistic friend. "And surely Gompers and the American Federation of Labor will join us soon as well. Mr. Debs has led this fight masterfully. We'll win the day if we stay united! And that's not all."

"There's more?"

"Mr. Pullman's own stockholders are deeply divided because of his stubbornness. Half of them want to vote to force him to arbitration!"

"That is good news indeed!" I exclaimed. Never had the stockholders themselves been reasonable about the workingmen's needs. Could it be possible that Mr. Deb's union would win this fight, and workers' families might have enough to live?

Could it be possible that someday even we actors would convince our producers to pay us adequately? I was dazzled at the prospects of success.

And Harry and Hotch were kind at heart. After all, their plot was for the benefit of the workers' families, so little Ruth would be in the best of hands. Yes indeed.

Harry continued, "But the president has not changed his position. When he does, Bridget, our battle is won!"

Well, he was right, wasn't he? President Cleveland could easily find a political excuse to act in support of the workers. And he would act quickly, not only because it was the best course of action, but also because the charming Mrs. Cleveland would be urging him to do everything possible to get their daughter back. Surely Ruth, unlike Maria Halpin's boy, would not have very many hours away from her mama.

Was ever a loving nursemaid in such a dilemma? On the one hand was Ruth's little bran-flecked face, beaming at her mama; on the other was a hungry worker's family, and a worker's hungry little girl, fired upon by Cleveland's troops. I remembered the photograph Hotch carried in his wallet of the sweet little three-year-old with wideset eyes. Was Hotch's niece any less deserving than Ruth?

How unfair the world could be to little girls!

With sudden understanding of what I must do I said, "Yes, Harry, let's act soon."

So we set the time for two days hence at 10:45 A.M., when the train from Boston stopped at Gray Gables. My task was to bundle up Ruth so as to hide her features, but include a distinctive wrap. Her lace-trimmed summer cape would do well. When the train halted I'd give her to Harry, who would keep the cape as a decoy and hand Ruth to Hotch. Hotch would jump off with her before the train gained speed and hurry to the estuary and a waiting boat. Witnesses, if any, would blame Harry, but the little cape would be empty, and he'd claim he'd found it abandoned in the aisle.

We all promised solemnly not to mention the others if we were interrogated.

I walked back through the hazy moonlight to the silent house and returned to my bed by the nursery. The two babies slept peacefully. I removed Keystone from my pillow and lay down to a restless night, the insomnia I had feigned suddenly all too real.

The next day Mrs. Cleveland and the children and I went through the motions of our idyllic life, but it taxed my acting skills to the utmost, for I kept wanting to burst into tears over the sad fate of little girls. Ruth and her little friends were not sad, of course.

They became quite warm and excited playing tag and hide-and-seek among the roses, and Mrs. Cleveland suggested a visit to the music room. "Wabbit! Wabbit!" squealed Ruth, echoed by her friends. So we all trooped into the cool airy house. Mrs. Cleveland cuddled baby Esther in her lap while Esther's nurse, Annie, played the melodeon for the little girls.

And what a wondrous melodeon it was! The little reed organ was topped by a big glass dome covering a decoration in the form of a large cabbage. As Annie played, a white rabbit with a carrot in its mouth emerged from the cabbage leaves and began waltzing about. The little girls clapped happily, and each time Annie finished a song they demanded a new one.

In the corner, watching, Mrs. Cleveland and I conversed quietly. "I am so sorry the president has been detained in Washington so long," Mrs. Cleveland told me. "He is so fond of Gray Gables. But the tariff controversy, and now this dreadful railroad strike, have quite consumed his time."

"The railroad men seem quite determined," I ventured.

"Oh, they are not bad fellows at heart," she said. "Why, earlier this summer a worker at the Buzzard's Bay station rescued my carriage from a runaway horse. I'm certain that with the arbitration my husband desires, they will behave sensibly in the end."

"Mr. Pullman seems rather bullheaded, though," I said dubiously.

She smiled. "He'll find the president is too! Especially when a settlement of the strike will allow him to join us here at last. Oh, Mandy, he is such a good and loving father!"

"Perhaps he is more appreciative of the little ones because he became a father so late in life. I mean a real father."

She looked at me sharply. "Are you referring to those dreadful stories? Mandy, you must understand that he has always been the soul of kindness!"

"I'm sure he has, Madam. And no one pays very much attention to old stories from Buffalo. The president was your father's law partner and later your guardian, wasn't he?"

"Oh, yes, he helped settle affairs when my father died." What a lot of favors the president had done for his friend Oscar Folsom, I thought. She went on, "I was only twelve. I called him Uncle Cleve. We were always jolly friends, and he saw to it that I went to college, and abroad."

"And then he married you and gave you the White House and Gray Gables," I murmured with a rush of fellow-feeling for her. Rich Banker Healey, who had so admired my youthful dancing, might have bought a Gray Gables for me if he had not been married already. As it was Aunt Mollie, that excellent businesswoman, had at least got him to pay a pretty penny for our silence. Frances Folsom Cleveland had done even better.

Yet the bright and vivid Mrs. Cleveland was still paying the price. I had seen the actress Modjeska in a newfangled play by the peculiar Mr. Ibsen of Norway. It concerned a woman whose husband treated her like a doll in a doll's house, and now it suddenly seemed to me that this rambling gray-shingled seaside house, with its flowers and pets and clever melodeons, was not so different.

That night three men who gave their names as Hazins, Griffin, and Welch appeared at Gray Gables, and though they tried to pass themselves off as mere summer boarders, their watchful eyes and bulky side pockets told me they were Secret Service agents. But I could not warn Hotch and Harry. There was no telephone here yet; although a telegraph was set up in the gun room, I could not send a message from it without alerting the telegrapher; and the mails, of course, were far too slow. No, I would have to deal with the three myself.

I spent another restless night.

The fateful morning dawned warm. Mrs. Cleveland greeted little Ruth and her baby sister as always, and they had their breakfasts. We dressed them in summery frocks and took along little lace- trimmed capes in case they caught a chill outdoors. We played hide-and-seek with a gunnysack, and patted Keystone. I felt a stab of guilt, and reminded myself sternly that Ruth was not the only little girl to consider, there was the photo in Hotch's wallet, and many more. Ruth was an enthusiastic and suggestible child, and after I'd mentioned trains a time or two she ran up the road toward the station, shouting "Twain!" I caught her up in my arms, the darling little creature, and told her we'd ask her mama. Mrs. Cleveland consented readily, especially when Ruth lisped, "Pleathe, Mama!"

"Yes, darling, it is almost time for the train. We'll all go meet it. They tell me we will be receiving a package from Papa today." We all strolled slowly toward the railway, alternating games of tag and hide-and-seek. Ruth chased Keystone or grabbed the gunnysack I was carrying and crawled inside, reappearing only when her mother said, "Oh, dear, where can Ruth be?"

The Gray Gables station was small and square and pretty, with fishscale shingling between the long windows that faced onto the track. Mrs. Cleveland greeted Hazins, Griffin, and Welch, the supposed boarders, who happened to be waiting in the shade of the roof overhang, something bulky still in their pockets. I found myself swallowing nervously. So much could go wrong!

Ruth said, "Where twain?" and ran toward the tracks to look.

"No, no, honey!" I exclaimed, snatching her away. "Here, let's play hide-and-seek. The train will come in a minute."

She pouted for a moment, then happily began to play with the gunnysack.

From the town of Buzzard's Bay drifted the sound of the whistle as the train from Boston headed toward us.

Mrs. Cleveland, accompanied by Hazins or Griffin, or possibly Welch, stepped back toward the rear of the station.

I pounced, picked up the gunnysack, and trotted toward the place the locomotive would stop. "We can see the engine better from here!" I chirped to the sack.

A plume of smoke, blowing in the bay breeze, appeared over the trees. I waited till Hazins and Welch and Griffin on the platform were all looking at the smoke, then stepped nimbly across the tracks to the far side. A moment later one of them saw me and took a step toward me, but by then the train was upon us, all steam and cinders and screeching brakes. I could no longer hear Ruth's excited squeals. I wrapped her little lacy cape around the gunnysack.

Through the hiss of steam I could hear the calls of the trainmen on the other side as they handed out the packages. Then, farther down the train, I saw a window being flung down, and behind it Harry's bucktoothed and nervous grin.

It took me a moment to make my way through the rough grass with the weight in my arms, and the train had already given a puff or two and was beginning to roll slowly when I felt the wriggling gunnysack lifted from me.

The whistle filled the throbbing air.

The dreadful deed was done. I hitched up my skirts and hightailed it for the woods by the shore. From the shelter of the first bushes, I peeked back.

Griffin or Welch or possibly Hazins must have seen something through the train window on the far side, because one of them was on the back platform already, his hands outstretched to help the other two board the slowly accelerating train.

Could Hotch escape? I held my breath. Sure enough, he appeared between cars holding the gunnysack. The engine started around the curve. He paused an instant to get his bearings, then jumped from my side of the train. He landed firmly and ran for the waiting green rowboat. The gunnysack twitched in his arms but the train was still too noisy for me to hear anything.

I bundled my skirts tight about me and it was only my sleeves, puffy even in a maid's sober dress, that snagged in the branches as I worked my way down toward a rocky point. In a moment I saw Hotch, keeping near the shore in the shelter of rocks and trees, rowing furiously down Buzzard's Bay. When he had gained enough distance he would set off across the bay like countless other fishermen, land at Marion, and catch the train to New York City.

I ran out to the tip of the point. He was already passing, and I saw the gunnysack at his feet give a mighty wriggle. A face peeked forth.

Not little Ruth's cherubic face, but the angry, snarling tabby-striped face of Keystone.

Hotch had time to gape only an instant before the furious tomcat was upon him, scratching and hissing. Hotch half rose, dropping an oar as he raised his forearm to protect his face. He struck at my cat with the other oar. What a cruel cad! Poor Keystone dropped into the water. Cursing, Hotch shook his fist in anger for a moment and made himself a very easy target. I hit him right in the heart with my first shot.

A look of surprise crossed his face, and he fell backward into the salty waves. A red stain trailed the empty rowboat.

I know, I know, thwarting the kidnapping plan was very unkind to dear wet Keystone, and to poor Harry, who had a dreadful time of it on the train with the three Secret Service agents, and to the railroad workers' families I had hoped to help.

But I'd remembered the photograph that Hotch carried, the little three-year-old girl of the wideset eyes, and had realized belatedly why she was so hauntingly familiar. It was a picture of Lucy, the grocer's daughter, now six. Now why would a grown man carry a picture of a stranger's little girl for three years, and claim she was his niece? And why would Lucy drop Keystone so suddenly and disappear when Hotch came on the scene? It chilled me to think of Hotch carrying little Ruth's likeness too, and of his insistence on kidnapping the girl and not her mother. He didn't care much about the union, as Harry did; he wanted only to seize Ruth. Now, gentlemen will doubtless think me wooly headed and sentimental, but I had resolved that Hotch would never go off with Ruth or Lucy or any other little girl.

I wish that someone of similar resolve had tended to Banker Healey before I met him.

I cleaned my Colt, returned it to its pocket, and waded out to help Keystone ashore. He was extremely miffed and marched, dripping, toward higher ground without so much as a glance at me. We were almost up to the tracks, where little Ruth and her unsuspecting mother waited, before he allowed me to pick him up.

On the walk back Mrs. Cleveland said, "Mandy, Mr. Hazins tells me that we must be cautious, because a plot against the children was overheard in the town of Buzzard's Bay. The White House sent the men here."

Well, I knew all that, for I myself had sent an unsigned warning to the White House along with the postal card to Juliet. I said, "I'm certain there will be no problems, Madam."

But there are always problems, aren't there? The railroad workers were left worse off than ever, for President Cleveland stood firm, Gompers's American Federation of Labor didn't support the strikers, and the strike failed. For years afterward the participants had difficulty finding work. But that's what happens when villains like Hotch try to use a union for their own ends.

Poor Harry, despite his protestations, was incarcerated for stealing the little lacy cape.

Regretfully, Mrs. Cleveland soon let me go, for Gertie experienced a miraculous recovery and resumed her duties as Ruth's nurse. Mrs. Cleveland wrote me a lovely letter of recommendation, but I didn't want to continue working in someone's beautiful home, because living in a doll house doesn't really suit me, except occasionally during heat waves.

The Clevelands lived on happily, much of the time at Gray Gables, until tragedy struck; for at the age of twelve darling Ruth caught diphtheria and died. The entire nation wept for her, and so did I, remembering those hours playing hide-and-seek in the sea breeze or watching the rabbit waltz. The ex-president and his charming wife were plunged into deepest grief and soon sold Gray Gables with its powerful memories. A Chicago confectioner invented a new chocolate candy bar and named it "Baby Ruth" after her, and to me that seemed a good memorial for a jolly little girl. As Shakespeare wrote of another funeral, sweets to the sweet.

But this world is mean as an old yellow dog, and little girls are soon forgotten. Nowadays most folks think the candy was named after a baseball player. I reckon there's nothing can be done about forgetfulness, and console myself that I kept her short happy life free of misery and cruelty, even if I can't keep her memory bright.

P. M. CARLSON

---~v~---

P. M. CARLSON'S mystery novels have been nominated for numerous awards, including an Edgar, a Macavity, and two Anthony Awards. Her short stories about "nineteenth-century guttersnipe and actress" Bridget Mooney have twice been nominated for the Agatha Christie Award for best short story. Fans of Bridget will be delighted with a new collection of her exploits: *Renowned be Thy Grave; or, the Murderous Miss Mooney.*

"Not far from my home in upstate New York, beautiful Wells College sits beside the lake," P. M. Carlson says. "It takes pride in many alumnae, including Frances Folsom, the ward—and later the wife—of Grover Cleveland. She was tall and charming, with Gibson-girl good looks, but closer reading shows a darker side to her Cinderella life. The Clevelands were plagued by journalists who spied on their honeymoon cottage at Deer Park, and by tourists who insisted on snatching up their babies to kiss, so that the White House grounds had to be closed to all. And there were tragic deaths in the family, too . . ."